Shedwyn went to the hearth and reached into a small wooden bowl resting on the mantel. Every Oran home had a seed bowl to bring luck and prosperity to the household. As Shedwyn dipped her hand into the bowl, she remembered the blue crockery, with its delicate white flowers painted on the sides of the bowl, in her parents' house. She withdrew a handful of seeds, a small mixture of barley, wheat, and oats.

Shedwyn spat into one hand and placed the seeds in the hollow of her wet palm. Closing her fist tightly, she concentrated on the image of fields, ripened wheat waving a dull gold in the wind, the gray green of oats and the shaggy heads of barley bent beneath the weight of their beards. She took a breath, the scent of anise from the Mother's Tears still pungent on her lips. Then she exhaled and smiled down at her fist.

"See, goodman," she whispered. "The promise of the seed bowl," Shedwyn opened her hand and heard his wife's astonished gasp. The seeds had sprouted, and where there had been tiny brown kernels of grain, there were now slender green stalks with spreading roots as fine as a spiderweb. "Help me now, and I will promise you land that is rich and fertile."

"An old trick," said the farmer, disbelieving.

"An old power," said Shedwyn. "Oran power. And like   one day it will belong to us again."

SADAR'S KEEP
Midori Snyder

A TOM DOHERTY ASSOCIATES BOOK
NEW YORK

SADAR'S KEEP

A Tor Book
Published by Tom Doherty Associates, Inc.
49 West 24th Street
New York, NY 10010

Cover art by Dennis Nolan

ISBN: 0-812-50912-9

First edition: March 1991

Printed in the United States of America

0 9 8 7 6 5 4 3 2 1

With love for my son, Carl, and my daughter, Taiko

"They made of it a wasteland and called it peace."

Tacitus

Prologue

Zein was hunched between two outcroppings of pink and gray granite, staring down over the craggy face of the Avadares mountains. He leaned his back against the sun-warmed stone and stared up into the sky. High above, the cloudless blue sky promised a clear, dry afternoon. Too dry for the season, Zein thought with a worried sigh. Behind him a gnarled pine tree, bent by the wind, rustled dryly and he smelled its faint, dusty fragrance.

Zein lifted his head, catching sight of a child scrambling up the mountainside. His dark eyes narrowed, trying to identify whose child it was, climbing without caution along the loose scree and rock. Zein shrugged knowingly, recognizing the stubborn expression of Gerad, Farnon's son. Like most laborers' children, Gerad was thin, his gray eyes large over hollow cheeks. But now his cheeks were red with the effort of climbing, and his arms reached eagerly as he pulled himself up the rugged terrain. Behind him, moving more slowly, crossing back and forth over a narrow trail, came Treys, his large form balanced by a staff as he leaned into the steep incline. Gerad looked up and, seeing Zein, waved a letter in the air.

"From the city! News from Beldan!" he shouted.

Zein stood abruptly, gripped with excitement. He had been waiting for this letter. Waiting for the news.

Zein was a small compact man, his movements strong and fluid, as he clambered over the sides of the lookout post and made his way down to meet Gerad and Treys. Small stones scattered before his feet as he hurried.

"Give it here, boy," he commanded.

Gerad handed the letter to Zein who ripped it open, little flakes of sealing wax crumbling to the stones. Zein's dark eyes chased the words across the pages of the letter. He pushed back the black hair from his forehead, and the faint tattoos whorled on his face shone in the morning light.

Zein saw the silent question in the tense face of the boy, the shoulders lifted in anxiety. "Your father lives," Zein said softly.

Gerad heaved a sigh of relief, one hand tightening into a triumphant fist. "I knew he'd be all right."

"And the rest," Treys asked, wiping his sweating brow with the back of his sleeve. "What about the rest?" The twin furrows on the sides of his broad face deepened as he frowned, waiting for Zein's reply. On his prominent forehead, long oval tattoos clustered like thunder clouds over his heavy eyebrows.

Zein glanced up from the letter, his expression guarded. "We must call a meeting. The contents of this letter need to be shared among everyone."

"But is the news good?" Treys asked, his voice more firm.

"It has begun. Not as we wished it, and not without cost. But it has begun," was all Zein would answer. He folded the letter carefully and tucked it into his vest.

They sat gathered around the fires and waited for Zein to read the letter. Closest to him were the oldest members of the New Moon Army, their faces etched with whorls of faint blue and brown lines. They had been in Sadar since the Last Battle, and by the power of the old Queen Huld, they had passed two hundred years of waiting as Avadares pines. Though they were human once more, their skin still carried the markings of the trees they once were. They dressed in the old style, their loose clothing in muted earth colors, rust and brown. Many of the women wore their hair cropped short, or back in a single braid. There were also newer members of this group, culled from those men and women who chose the life of mendicants, carrying to all who would still listen the old stories and beliefs of the Oran world before the Sileans. By the Sileans they were called vaggers, vagrant trash to be imprisoned and starved, if they could be caught. In communion with the ancient army at Avadares, the vaggers had their own faces marked with tattoos. All carried weapons, laying them like faithful servants close to their hands. Pipes were produced, and long stems of dry grass were used to light the bowls of tobacco.

On the other side of the fires were the newer arrivals, men and women recently fled from the Silean landowners, the whips of the overseers and the constant demands of conscription and taxation. These were Oran farmers and laborers, and though they weren't marked with the tattoos of the vaggers, their faces were etched by poverty and hunger. Without the land on which to make their living, they had come to Avadares with nothing more than their children and their fear. The men stood in small clusters, their common anger binding them like sheaves of wheat. The women sat, their bare feet tucked under the thick folds of their skirts, sheltering within their black shawls their babies and smaller children. The older children, like Gerad and his younger brother Naill squatted on their haunches, small sticks in their hand nervously drawing patterns in the dry soil as they waited to hear the news of Beldan.

And sitting by themselves apart, as witnesses to the proceedings, were the three Ghazali travelers that had brought the letter out of Beldan. As Peacekeepers, they would not take up arms; but neither would they renounce the old life of Oran and so they served as messengers for the New Moon. The old woman Fairuz sat on her knees, her hands resting on her lap. Her dress and headscarf were black, absorbing the shadows of firelight. But the gold bangles that proclaimed her wealth sparkled like wreathes of flames on her small wrists. Behind her stood her two sons, their arms loosely crossed over their chests. At their heels two black dogs waited obediently, though one dog began to whimper, sensing the worried tension. Dinar, the younger son, glanced down at the dog and whispered a quiet command. The dog gave a throaty sigh, and settled its body against the earth, its snout resting between its front paws. Dinar looked up again to Zein, who was standing near the fire.

Zein moved closer to the fire, retrieving the letter from his pocket. At one time, he too had been Ghazali. Unlike the broadchested Oran peasants, he was slight of build, his arms wiry. His skin was the smooth brown of oak, and his teeth were white when he smiled. Once he had known the restraint of a Peace-keeper, but that resolve was gone—destroyed by the horror of the Last Battle and the two hundred years that followed. Thinking on the tragedy of that time, his eyes burned with the fire of a man who has resolved to fight, to seek violence as a means to restore the harmony that has been lost. The hands that once wrapped elegantly around the shaft of a flute became accustomed to the curved edges of the Oran longbow. And the music that once filled the air with joy was silenced by the hard twang of arrows.

"We have received the news from Beldan," Zein announced. "Not all of it is good, but there is hope."

Inclining his head to the paper dyed gold in the light of the fire, Zein read in a clear and steady voice.

" 'From Beldan, I salute you in Avadares. The Queens' quarter knot is infinite, and the power of the Oran people, without end.' "

"So it is!" someone shouted. "And will be again!" another added defiantly. Zein was quiet as a murmur of agreement ran through the listeners.

Zein continued. " 'I write to you of Firecircle. Of what has been lost and what has been won in that battle. There was no way that any of us could have foreseen the events as they occurred. No matter that we had planned, and planned well, happenchance is the arrow that wounds us as easily as the enemy. So, we have learned in a harsh fashion to be more cunning, to plan even as we flee the horseman, his sword hovering over our heads.

" 'On the night before Firefaire, our leaders were arrested. Master Donal of Crier's Forge, his son Wyer, and Pedar the Weaver. Pedar's wife was murdered as she tried to prevent the capture of their son, Soltar. Also taken was Alwir Re Aston, well known to you as the Reader who has renounced his Guild and family and joined the New Moon. The laborer Farnon managed his escape and was able to inform us, that we could continue with our plans. We waited until morning, our fury rising with the sun as we saw the gallows hastily constructed at the site of the Great Bonfire.

" 'I waited on the roofs, watching as the Fire Queen Zorah and her Silean butcherboys took their place before the Great Bonfire. Across the plaza the people of Beldan had gathered. From above, I was awed by their numbers: the Guildsmen and their apprentices, the journeymen with their colored scarves, farmers, laborers from the Hiring Fields, even Beldan's street children thronged together. It was as if all of Oran waited in that place, and on their faces I could see the old pride not yet savaged by Silean brutality.

" 'Alwir saw it too, I think, for when the butcherboys brought the prisoners forth to stand at the gallows, he demanded the right of the condemned to speak. The crowd shouted their approval and the Queen was forced to relent. And speak well he did. Perhaps some will say, too well. For the words of an impassioned man staring at his own execution can spark flames that even he cannot control. And from the roof I saw the people of Beldan rise, outrage on every face, demanding the release of Alwir and the others. Even the Queen, as powerful and as terrifying as she is, was stunned into silence.

" 'The rest is hard to write, harder still to remember without grief and rage. For though the Fire Queen was silent, not so the Sileans. I think now they must have prepared for this moment, and even if we had not given them cause, they would have executed this treacherous act all the same. Down every narrow street leading into Fire Circle the Silean cavalry rode, their swords drawn and their mind set on massacre. They slashed and hacked their way through the terrified throng of people as if they were no more than straw. Crammed together on all sides like sheep, there was nowhere to run. The streets were thick with cavalry, and people not slaughtered outright by the Sileans were trampled by the desperate flight of others. So many fell that day, so many were wounded. Old men, women, or even children—to the Sileans it made no difference. All fell beneath the hooves and the sword.

" 'And yet in this time of terror I saw, as if lifted by the hands of fate, the one child we had sought for years in Beldan's streets. The firegirl, unmistakable by the burning crown of red hair. I have learned since that this child was known as a pickpocket named Jobber, and, so well had she disguised herself as a boy, not even Master Donal at whose forge she often stayed knew of the truth. There can be no mistake to her identity. The Fire Queen grabbed her, held her with a look of fury, and I saw on the two of them the same face. I cried out as the Queen drew the girl close, as if to burn her like kindling. But the child did not burn. Her hair gathered the flames and on her terrified face her skin glowed like burnished copper. It was Farnon and his archers who ended it by sending their arrows into the Queen's throat. By the force of the arrows, the Queen fell back, releasing the child. Jobber ran as the Queen fell to the ground, the arrows piercing her neck. I still feel the lingering cold terror on my spine when I recall the sight of the Queen, lying there undead despite the arrows, her eyes like fiery coals as she stared up at the sky.

" 'And then the world heaved and collapsed. Perhaps it was the agony of the Fire Queen herself we were made to feel. The ground shuddered and cracked; boiling steam and flames rose everywhere from the broken earth. Fire spread, blasting buildings to smoky dust and showers of glass. We all fled, even though there was nowhere to go, nowhere that could be safe, between the cutting blades of the cavalry and the fiery destruction of the Queen's city. I spent long hours lost among Beldan's streets, now utterly changed by fire and destruction. Some of us found refuge along the harbors and piers, where the water at least protected us from the flames.

" 'I will write you now of the news that I have learned since Firecircle. The firegirl Jobber has escaped. And along with her I am told went the smith Wyer, Alwir Re Aston and a Ghazali girl. Of the Ghazali girl I know little, but those who saw her say she has the white eyes of the blind, and yet moves as one who is sighted. I tell you this in the hopes that she is known to you.' "

Zein stopped reading and looked up at Treys. "Lirrel. It must be Lirrel." Treys nodded. The others waited as Zein's stern face clouded unexpectedly with pain. He exhaled sharply and took up the letter again.

"It is Lirrel," said Fairuz softly, her old voice like the husky crackling of the fire. "She had met someone the day before in Market Square, a girl with red hair, fleeing the Silean Guards. The tent agreed to hide her on the stage at the Breaking Fish. We put the black garments of a Ghazali dancer over her, though it seemed impossible to hide the fierceness of her face." Fairuz turned her hands palms up. "*Baraki*, we had thought. Good luck in the red hair." Fairuz sighed deeply. "Lirrel left to wander with this child. We thought no harm in it. Then I saw Lirrel the next day." She glanced up at Zein, her eyes deepset in their folds. "She was changed. No longer ours. She has chosen the firegirl, and will follow that road no matter how difficult."

"Do you think she will remain a Peacekeeper?" Zein asked suddenly, his face strained.

Fairuz shrugged. "Lirrel is strong in her belief. You can hear it in the music she plays. She is a child of the air, and hears what lies below the surface of every heart." Fairuz nodded and settled her palms face down again on her lap. "*Ahal*, I believe she will remain true to the Ghazali ways. We shall need that, or this child of fire will destroy us all with her fury."

"Is there more to the letter?" Treys asked.

Zein turned from Fairuz, his distracted expression shifting as he realized he still held the letter. "Yes, there is more." He continued again to read:

" 'Strange too is the news that they fled by ship, captained by Faul Verran, herself once the Firstwatch of Beldan. Why this woman should take on the cause of the New Moon, I don't know. She is skilled with the sword and killed at least five Guards. I saw her name among the list of those whose heads now carry a bounty. Yet, if she comes to you have a care, for her loyalties to the Fire Queen Zorah may still be strong.' "

"What do you make of that?" a voice called out. Zein looked up from the paper at the speaker. It was Veira Rune, as always her hands busy with the fletching of new arrows. A frown settled on her smooth forehead. "Beldan's Firstwatch coming over to our side? Can you trust her?"

Zein shook his head. "I won't know until I see her. But if it is true that she has come to our side, her skill will be more than welcomed."

"How do we know they will come here?" a farmer called across the fire.

"They are with Alwir. He will lead them North. It is the only safe place for them now."

"Huld's peace," a woman muttered softly. "There is still a long journey before them."

"There is more to this letter," Zein said and returned to the pages.

" 'In the days that have followed we have counted our losses. Master Donal is dead, Pedar is dead, the woman Zeenia is also dead and the teahouse, The Grinning Bird, has fallen into another's hands. I have been there once, puzzled by the new owner, a young woman more suited to the streets than to the life of a shopkeeper. The rumors are that Zeenia herself willed the shop to this woman but until I know for certain we are shy of the place. There is not a Guildhouse nor a family in Beldan that did not lose someone to the massacre. We live surrounded by the thick smoke of Scroggles daily burning huge pyres of the dead. Countless others have disappeared without a trace from the city and it is not known whether they fell beneath its crumbling walls or fled. There is a terrible shortage of water and food, and there is a fear that as the summer approaches we will face the threat of disease from the unfound bodies festering in the ruins of the city.

" 'To this the Sileans have salted our wounds with ash. Oran men are rounded up daily to rebuild the harbor so that the Silean trade will not be slowed. We can hardly find shelter for ourselves and yet we must labor on the harbor walls for the Sileans' pleasure. Food is scarce, yet Oran men continue to load sacks of grain on ships bound for Silea. The gallows too have been rebuilt in Firecircle. And daily there are hangings of men and women with no greater crime than their poverty. All this is done to beat us down, to numb us with hunger and terror. But it will no longer suffice and the Sileans by their brutal actions have done much to add to the growing list of New Moon sympathizers. There are few who, imagining that they too may be swinging from the noose, will not at least die having done something. And so out of this crucible of blood and fire, the Queen and the Sileans have molded the army Beldan will need when the time comes.

" 'There is one thing more. The Readers once content to do their scourging at the yearly Naming ceremonies only, now hunt for children of the old power whenever it suits their pleasure. There is a bounty on the children, though I believe it is not the money that attracts them to this work, but the sport of murder. I have seen the Silean Guards, dragging behind them a street child clapped in chains that outweigh the child's miserably frail body. And the Reader casting the cold eye to Read the aura of magic. If the child is lucky and none is seen, they are sent to rebuild the harbor walls. But I have also seen the head of the child gifted—and cursed—with magic, sheared from its neck by a Silean sword, following the Reader's nod. It is a nightmare and I can only free myself from despair when I think of those children that have been rescued. To that end many of the children that Alwir discovered at the Hiring Fields in the days before Firecircle should be coming to you. I pray that they may find a safe refuge among you in the mountains.

" 'And so to now. We continue to build our resistance. The lines of battle are clearer now than ever. Though Beldan resembles nothing so much as a broken city, out of the shards we will piece together a new strength. The Sileans are more afraid of us now than ever and we know that their brutality can only increase with their fear. We will not back away but press our advantage.

" 'I look only to the promise of the future, when the Oran people will be free from the oppression of the Silean armies, when the tyranny of the Fire Queen will be removed and the old magic can flourish in our people and in a new Queens' quarter knot.

" 'Until that day, I will remain in the struggle.'

"The letter was signed, 'Feran Saulter, Guildmaster'."

There was a long silence when Zein had finished reading the letter. The dry wood in the fires cracked, casting showers of sparks into the night sky.

The vagger Go Shing stood slowly, leaning his shoulder into his staff. His face, wizened as a dried apple, was expressionless. "So," he said loudly. "Even so. We must send out riders to find the children fleeing from Beldan. We must find them and bring them here."

"Aye," replied Treys. Treys looked up at Zein, his brows pulled together in concern. "Two have each other," he said. "What about the other two: the child of the earth and the child of water. They will be in danger now, will they not? Having seen the firegirl, surely the Queen must suspect."

"They have always been in danger, just as any child in Oran born with magic. But," Zein added, "they are stronger in their magic, and what is more I believe they will seek each other. They are the new Queens' quarter knot and they will be drawn to each other, compelled like all forces in nature to unite into a single whole. That will give them a greater strength."

"Only if they learn that in time," Veira replied, gathering together the newly fletched arrows before standing.

"They will come to us. I know it as clearly as I know your faces. And we shall be ready for them when they arrive," Zein said firmly. He smiled suddenly, his face lighting up with determination. "We have waited a long time for this, Veira. For nearly two hundred years we have dreamed and planned for this moment. And now, the dreaming is over. The time at last has come to greet us." Zein clapped his hands together loudly, and a baby, startled by the sharp sound, began to cry.

Chapter One

Shedwyn sat with her back resting against the rough bark of a scrub-oak tree and looked out over the fields of red plowed soil. She had been awake since before dawn and had seen the sunlight glisten in the faint traces of morning dew. But it was midday now, and all that was left of the moisture was the sweat that stained her forehead and plastered her dress to her back. The air was dry and dusty, swirls of ruddy-colored soil blowing across the fields with the wind.

Shedwyn looked down again at her lap, her eyes following the line of her thigh, to the outstretched legs, shins powdered with the red soil. She stopped, frowning as she gazed at her bare callused feet. Big, ugly feet, she snorted. Too big, she thought woefully. Same as the rest of me. She tossed the single braid of dark brown hair over her shoulder and self-consciously folded her arms across her waist, trying to narrow the wide reach of her shoulders. Her breasts pressed together and she smelled the damp soil on her skin.

"Damn the drought," muttered old Torin, seated on the ground next to her. "We'll see now't o' rain again, I can tell." The old woman bent her head and Shedwyn saw the yellow streaks that lined the roots of her silvery hair. The skin of Torin's scalp and face was as brown as old boot leather. Next to Torin sat Finnia and Dawer, still wearing their sun caps with the bleached brims that hid the better part of their weathered faces.

Finnia looked up and sighed. "Gets in the nose it does," and she sniffed, wiping a hand across her face to remove the thin film of dust that clung to her cheeks.

"I 'member when it rained in the spring and the sun come on gentle like. Not this blazing heat so early," Dawer replied, tucking her faded skirts tightly around her thighs as she sat in the small patch of shade. She pulled off her cap and Shedwyn saw where the black hair was turning gray at the temples. Her brown eyes were swollen to a squint from the dust.

" 'Member the haymaking?" Finnia said to Dawer, an impish smile softening the features of her gaunt face. Dawer smiled in response, resting her cheek in the hollow of her palm.

"Cut hay in the spring, you did?" Shedwyn asked in surprise. For the last few years the weather had been too dry, and the hay, when it finally came on, had been late in the year.

"Oh, aye, spring and fall then," Finnia said, nodding to Shedwyn, folding back the brim of her sunbonnet. Red dust creased the lines of her high forehead. "The hay came on quick 'cause of the early rain. It was a grand time then. All day you'd work, back bent to the hay, sun heating you up. And just in front of you, a man to cut the hay. And if you was lucky"—she laughed—"maybe the very same man you'd been thinking on. There he'd be swinging his scythe through the new hay, the sound of the cutting feathery soft. Oh, blessed Huld," she exclaimed, sucking in her lower lip over her few remaining teeth. "The sight of his strong legs and back, the sharp smell of him working, and the sweet perfume of the hay." She gave a shriek of pleasure, joined by Dawer. "And every now and then, see," she added as they all leaned in closer, caught by the unexpected gaiety of her mood, "well, he'd turn his head, just so, to look behind. And there'd you be, bodice half-open, sweat shining your skin, and you'd see that smile he'd give you, and your heart would near burst. Nothing else to be done but throw yourselves down and go to. Right there, in the new hay," she finished triumphantly, slapping one palm against the other.

Shedwyn smiled and shook her head in disbelief as the older women continued laughing and talking all at once, comparing gossip years old. They were always telling stories of how it used to be, she thought, always painting the past with fond words.

"It's true, it's true," Torin cackled, catching Shedwyn's skep-

tical expression. "Got on with my first child in the hay, I did.
My old man, well, he couldn't never wait. And in those days I
was a good-looking girl, strong and ready as him any day." She
lifted a scrawny arm and tightened her hand into a fist. Then
she plucked at her skirts, giving the worn fabric a little shake.
"Though Huld knows, all sorts of other nonsense used to run
up yer shift. Mice and crickets. We'd have to stamp our feet
afterward just to knock them all out." She laughed hard, a small
tear leaking from the corner of one eye. Then gradually she grew
silent and thoughtful.

"Ain't that way no more," Finnia said at last, and swallowed
hard. "Sileans don't hold with such."

"And there ain't much hay to speak of," Dawer finished.
"Dry and miserable it is. Frigging drought. Knackers everything." She drew up her knees, folded her arms over her legs,
and stared glumly at the ground.

"On up, here comes Overseer," Finnia warned, protectively
pulling down the brim of her sunbonnet.

Shedwyn stood quickly, seeing the tall man approach them
from the fields. He was, as always, dressed in black, against
which his sallow skin resembled old parchment. His thin lips
were pressed together in anger. Just beyond him she could see
two mounted riders and recognized the Master Re Ameas, and
next to him, on a big bay horse, his son Eneas. Shedwyn stared
at Eneas's blond hair and the darker fringe of a new beard that
covered his chin. She imagined him smiling at her, the glow
from his blue eyes like the summer sky. A sharp poke in the ribs
from Torin reminded her to get moving.

She took a hurried sip of water from a skin and washed her
face with the dampened hem of her skirt.

"Cock's bones," muttered Dawer as she tucked her hair under
her sun cap, "he's looking evil, ain't he?"

"Well, look there and you'll see reason for it," Torin said
with a quick jerk of her thumb. "Master's making the rounds,
ain't he?"

"His young pup too," Dawer said. She set her hands on her
hips, head tilted to one side. "The pup's all right for the eyes,
ain't he?"

"I'd say so," Shedwyn answered without thinking, and instantly wished she hadn't. Her pulse quickened and she felt the
flush on her cheeks as Dawer and Finnia smiled knowingly at

her. Shedwyn swore as Torin gazed at her with sharp black eyes.

"Don't even dream on it, girl. That's nobut trouble."

"I ain't stupid," Shedwyn answered curtly. Oh, but you are, she told herself. Cow-stupid where Eneas was concerned.

"Whist up," Dawer scolded Torin. "Leave the poor girl alone. Who would you have her dream on? There ain't any men here worth thinking about no more. Gone to Avadares or dead they are."

"I'm just warning her, that's all," Torin grumbled back, slapping the dust from her skirts.

Overseer Neverin approached them, his lean face paler than usual from the effort of climbing the small rise to their resting place. His black hair had been slicked back and gathered into a small tail at the nape of his neck. The oiled surface was powdered with dust and the tail curled stiffly to one side. "Rest is over," he barked at them. "There's two fields left to be planted and Re Ameas wants it done today. I've hired on hands for the day, so get a move on." Neverin tapped his thigh with a small riding crop for emphasis, and Dawer, passing him, flinched at the motion.

Shedwyn hurried down the hill, her feet scuffling through the dry soil and kicking up a fine cloud of red dust. At the bottom of the hill she stopped short, looking up at Eneas where he waited, still mounted on his horse. He cast a quick sidelong glance at his father, and noting that his father's back was turned, he gave Shedwyn a warm smile and made a small signal with his fingers. Shedwyn's heart beat faster as she smiled back and nodded. Later, she thought happily, she would see him later.

"Nobut trouble," repeated Torin softly, catching a glimpse of the hand signal.

Shedwyn paid her no notice but went to the fields, letting the promise of pleasure carry her along.

"How many more rows to go do you expect?" asked a weak voice behind Shedwyn.

Without straightening from her task, Shedwyn answered, "Maybe two, or three." She made a hole in the dry soil and tucked the small tobacco seedling into it, tamping the soil with a firm but gentle hand.

The woman groaned wearily and this time Shedwyn did stop and glance over her shoulder. The woman wore a heavy blue skirt, the fabric torn and patched with clumsy stitches. Above the skirt she still wore a bodice, with faded ribbons of pale green. Her face was red from bending over to plant the seedlings. She put a hand to her forehead and Shedwyn saw her sway unsteadily.

A hireling, she thought with sympathy. Here for a day or two and then gone tomorrow. Must be a city woman, dressed the way she was and not used to field labor. Shedwyn left off her planting and came to her. "Go then," she said, giving the woman a little push toward the end of the row. "Take a rest over there. I'll finish your row."

"No," the woman insisted. "I can do it. I won't get paid if the Overseer catches me. A whole day's work, and if he sees me standing idle just once, old bugger will keep my coppers for himself." As if renewed by panic, the woman bent her back to the task once more.

Shedwyn shrugged, returned to her own row, and continued planting the withered-looking seedlings. "Lazy, shiftless bastards," Overseer called the hirelings, repeating the insults he had learned from his Silean masters. But Shedwyn knew differently. A year ago a pregnant woman had hired on for the day to help with the harvesting of tobacco. She was alone, her man having gone on ahead to find work at another farm. Harvesting tobacco was hard and demanding work. They had labored humpbacked as they bent to cut and stack the leaves in neat piles. Shedwyn saw the woman suddenly straighten, her back arched as a bow, and she cried out with short, painful gasps. Shedwyn ran to her, catching the woman as she started to fall, her arms clutched around her swollen belly.

She begged Shedwyn to help her deliver her child, begged her not to leave her alone. Shedwyn supported the woman, half carrying her to a field shack used for curing. As she lay on a pallet of old straw, the woman's face was as brown and withered as the leaves that hung above her. When Shedwyn pulled back the coarse dress to feel for the child in the womb, she was startled by the white oval of the woman's belly.

Nothing she did could have made a difference. She knew that even then. The woman was weak from constant work and constant hunger. Shedwyn remembered with a jab of pity the child's perfect face, the white features as if cut from translucent stone. Though steam rose from his body as he left the warmth of his mother's womb, his limbs looked chilled as ice.

"Let me hold him," the woman whispered weakly, and Shed-wyn handed her the stillborn infant. "Mine own, mine own," the woman wept as she clasped the tiny figure to her breast. She moaned then as blood rushed in a crimson stream from between her thighs, spreading on the dirty floor and staining the edges of Shedwyn's skirt bright red. The woman whispered a name into the child's ear and then turned her face away and died.

Shedwyn buried them behind the curing shack, first covering their faces with a tattered bit of cloth. Her man returned, but it was too late to do anything but show him the bare ground. Shed-wyn remembered how he stood silently by the grave. There had been an early frost the night before and the crumbly brown soil was coated with a thin layer of rime. It glittered like a sprinkling of tiny blue gems among the coarse soil. It seemed to her that the man shrank in size even as she watched him. His head drooped, his shoulders folded over his chest like the wings of a dying bird. And then abruptly he cried out and began to run across the stubbled fields. She continued to stare after him, marking his frantic flight, until he was no more than a moving dot in the shadows of the distant mountains.

Her hands pressing into the soil around a withered seedling, Shedwyn shook her head. No, not lazy and shiftless. Most hire-lings were like herself: Oran farmers lost without their land. Hadn't her own mother been a hireling once after the farm was sold to pay the death tax on her father? And hadn't her mother worked herself to death just to make the necessary money to pay for Shedwyn's five-year contract so that she'd not have to be on the road all year? Shedwyn sighed, feeling the sudden tightness in her chest at the thought of her mother. She could almost imagine the feel of her mother's hands cupped around her face, her breath smelling of apples as she bent to kiss Shedwyn on the forehead.

That's over and done with, Shedwyn girl, she told herself an-grily, shaking the memories away. You've yourself to think on now. And as she worked, surrendering her body to the rhythm of the planting, she let her thoughts piece together her future. After next year her contract would be finished. She'd a little money saved, tied in a kerchief and hidden beneath the boards of the milking house. She'd be off then, heading north to the Avadares Mountain to escape the Readers. She counted herself lucky that Overseer Neverin was too cheap to pay the Readers' fee yearly. Instead, he liked to work the little ones as hard as he

could before he had to see them Named and then given adult
wages. And this way he didn't lose too many younger hands to
the Reader's eye. When they were old enough to be costly and
trouble, then it mattered little to him if they were hanged for
having the old power.

Shedwyn heard the sound of a horse neighing and she picked
up her head, half expecting to see Eneas. Instead she saw Overseer Neverin, standing at the end of her row, his shoulder leaning
into his horse as he watched her work. The riding crop tapped
against his thigh. She quickly lowered her eyes to her work,
taking the seedling from the sackcloth apron tied at her waist.
She frowned at the soil, not liking the look she had seen in the
man's eyes. She half listened as she worked, hoping he would
leave. But as she neared the end of her row she heard the clink-
ing of the horse's bridle, and she could smell the oiled leather
of the saddle. And she was certain she could feel Neverin's gaze,
still on her, burning a scar into her back.

At the end of the row, she had no choice but to stand up and
face him. Her throat tightened as she met his eyes and saw the
look of hunger. She averted her eyes and prepared to leave, but
he called her to wait.

She felt the soft brush of the riding crop beneath her chin as
Neverin forced her to look up. Disgust churned in her stomach
as she met his glance. His eyes were cold and humorless, the
thrust of his jaw aggressive.

"Readers have come, Shedwyn lass," he said in a husky voice.
"All those to be Named must be in courtyard first thing in the
morning."

Shedwyn froze with sudden terror. "But—but I thought it was
done for the season." Her tongue stumbled over the words.

He smiled at her, misunderstanding the reason for her fear.
"After you're Named, lass," he said, "I'll see to it you work
the big house, if you thank me right."

No! Shedwyn's mind reeled with panic, hardly hearing Neverin's offer. It was too soon to leave. Eneas, she hadn't told him
yet. Her thoughts jumbled together, coming in rushes like blood
rising in her cheeks. She had to get away! Tonight. She suppressed a cry. Eneas, she thought, her hands twisting the folds
of her skirts, she would have to tell Eneas. Neverin moved closer
to her, the rank smell of his sweat nearly choking her.

"A moment of pain is all it will cost you, lass," he whispered. "I'll take you like a knife through butter." The riding

crop traveled lightly down her neck and gently raked across her breasts.

Shedwyn jerked her body away from the touch of the riding crop. Neverin let her go and chuckled deeply in his throat. "A fine girl," he said, a leer stretching the thin lips. "And I'll make you into a fine woman."

"I must get to the milking," Shedwyn said quickly, her voice barely audible.

"So you must," Neverin said, and reached out a hand to grope her behind as she hurried passed him.

Shedwyn fairly ran from the fields, her braid bouncing across her back as she fled. She shuddered, her breath lodged in her throat and her stomach a knot of fear. She ran across the open courtyard, seized by terror, imagining she felt the Readers' gaze already upon her face. They would hang her when they found out she had the old power. And the last she would know of the world would be the black shadows seen through the execution hood they would put over her head.

Gasping, Shedwyn shoved open the doors to the milking barn and leaped inside, shutting the doors and closing off the sunlight behind her. Panting hard, she leaned against the wall and bent her head. The stone walls were smooth and cool, moisture condensing on the rounded surfaces. The barn had the strong odor of manure, mingled with the dusty scents of grain and hay. From small windows ribbons of light crisscrossed the empty stalls. A scrawny gray cat, striped like a mackerel, lifted himself lazily from the straw and came to wait by her ankles. When she didn't move, he tilted his triangular head, and the pale amber eyes regarded her with curiosity.

Suddenly Shedwyn hurtled herself from the wall and ran to the farthest stall in the barn. The gray cat had to leap out of her way, hissing at her as she pushed rudely past him. She knelt on her knees and brushed away the straw. Barely visible around the stones were finger holes that she had patiently carved out of the packed dirt around the flagstones. She tucked her fingers in the holes and gently lifted the stone.

It came away from the ground slowly and heavily, revealing a small white cloth bag buried beneath. As Shedwyn went to take the bag, she heard the sounds of the cows bawling to be milked and the herdboys shouting their curses as they led them into the courtyard, returning from the pastures. She tucked the bag into her pocket and quickly replaced the stone. From up above, perched on a low wall, the cat watched like an accomplice.

The doors of the barn were thrown open, and a golden light streamed over the dark stalls. Shedwyn was blinded for a moment and stepped to the side so as to let the cows enter it.

"You're fair eager, lass," shouted Gremor as he came around, nudging each cow to her own stall. Shedwyn watched the old man as he loped from side to side on his bowlegs. The ancient shoulders sloped down into long arms that were still powerful enough to shove and push each cow into her respective stall. His face was like a withered pumpkin, seamed with wrinkles down the sides of his cheeks and sagging around the mouth where he no longer had teeth. In the last few years he had grown more deaf, shouting whenever he spoke and always leaning one ear out to catch the sounds of others' words.

"I'm in a hurry today," Shedwyn answered loudly, and grabbed the bucket and stool off the wall.

The cow shifted uneasily in her stall, a hoof kicking out at Shedwyn's rushed movements.

"Ah, go slow, go slow, lass. You'll get now't from the old dear that way," Gremor complained. "Don't make no nevermind to her if you got elsewhere to be. She wants her singing to, or she'll withhold from you."

The cow edged away as Shedwyn tried to take ahold of the teats. She kicked out again, her hoof knocking over the pail and her head turning around to give Shedwyn a disapproving stare. "Cock's bones," Shedwyn swore.

"Nae good cursing, neither." Gremor clucked, shaking his head. "You'll get now't in a hurry, lass, and that's the truth."

Shedwyn sighed and closed her eyes. All she could feel was the frightened beating of her heart and the almost overwhelming desire to flee. The cow bawled, shifting nervously. A hand clapped itself on her shoulder and Shedwyn jumped, her hands gripping the pail with white knuckles.

"Easy now, lass," said Gremor, his watery brown eyes gazing more closely at her. He sniffed and then leaned back, a pensive look on his face. "Got the scent of fear on you," he said, in a softer voice. "Trouble, is it?"

Shedwyn nodded slowly.

"Tell old Gremor about it?" he asked.

Shedwyn shook her head.

"Right, then." He shrugged, with a disappointed expression.

"I'll manage, Gremor," Shedwyn said.

"Eh?" he barked, not hearing her.

"I'm all right," she said loudly, realizing how impossible it would have been to confide in him even if she had wanted to. She'd be yelling loud enough for the whole courtyard to hear her.

"Then mind you sing to the dears, or you'll be here all night," he finished before loping out the door.

Shedwyn looked at the cow, her ribs showing through the buttery brown hide. "Blessed Huld," she said softly more in prayer than as a curse. Shedwyn stroked the cow's side to calm her and then began to sing a slow, melancholy song. The plaintive tune echoed lightly off the stone walls, the clear sound lingering in the air. Doves in the rafters overhead flapped their wings and then settled again as the melody was punctuated by the rhythmic pinging of milk being squeezed into the bucket.

Shedwyn looked quickly over her shoulder, seeing through the leaves of the trees the distant lights of the big house. She pulled her shawl tighter over her shoulders, feeling the chill of the spring night, and pushed her way through the trees. She was leaving. She was carrying away nothing with her but the clothes on her back and the small bag of coins in her pocket. She knew there were villages along the way that would welcome her and give her food as she sought the way to Avadares and the ranks of the New Moon. For more than two years, the New Moon had whispered its promise among Oran peasants. "Join us and we will free you from the tyranny of the Sileans and the Fire Queen's Readers. Join us." And so she would. All that remained was to tell Eneas. Shedwyn had argued with herself whether or not she should meet Eneas. You'll make it harder on both of you, she told herself furiously. But as quickly as she had resolved not to see him, she changed her mind and decided she must.

Love had been an unlooked-for pleasure. With both parents dead, Shedwyn had not thought to find again its warmth and comfort. And yet the first time she saw Eneas, she had felt the sudden quickening of her heart, and found herself staring at him openly. He had come to examine the new bull purchased at last year's Firefaire. Frowning in concentration, Shedwyn found his strong profile pleasing, the lean cut of his body attractive. His blond hair caught the random shafts of gold light as he brushed it back off his forehead absently. She drew near him, asking about the new bull, all the while noticing other things about him. He was tall, his torso narrowing into slim hips. The hand that stroked the smooth black hide of the bull was long, the fingers heavily jointed, the nails smooth and squarely cut. He asked her something, and when she looked up at him, she smiled at the bright blue of his eyes. He smiled back and Shedwyn saw that the skin of his neck was flushed. They stayed that way for a while, talking about the bull, until Eneas finally asked her name. When she told him, he nodded, as if tucking the information away. After he had left and Shedwyn was alone in the barn, she chided herself for being a fool. Nothing would come of it, she told herself with disappointed certainty.

And yet something had come of it. Eneas found reasons to see her, excuses that took him to the fields when she was working, or hovered around her at the milking, discussing the care of the livestock as if she didn't already know what to do for them. While she craved his companionship, she did not want to encourage him, afraid of the difference between them. She was an Oran peasant and he was Silean gentry. But more than that, she had the old power and knew she would have to flee before the Readers found her. But Eneas was persistent with his attention until Shedwyn feared the talk that might get them both noticed.

"Go away, Eneas," she had said gently.

"Not unless you agree to meet me, alone, tonight," he answered, coming to stand close to her. She could smell the lavender on his starched linen shirt mingled with his own scent. It reminded her of the fields in late summer, the sharp prickle of the pines in the sun.

"All right," she said at last, her heart happy even as her mind scolded her for the danger. "Where?"

"Re Franca's woods, near the Gripping Stone. Do you know it?"

"Oh, aye," she said lightly. "Only to us it's Huld's Throne and it's in commonwoods."

She had not meant to insult him, only tease him gently so that he would understand that they were different. But he had taken it seriously and the smile from his face vanished.

"I know I am Silean, Shedwyn. My father has told me that often enough. Don't punish me for it, for I would be very lonely indeed without your company."

His expression was so somber that she reached out and touched him reassuringly on the cheek, her fingertips feeling the rough patch of a new beard. "I'll be there," she answered. He leaned his cheek into her palm and kissed it softly.

A twig snapped beneath her foot and Shedwyn jumped, clutching the shawl more tightly around her shoulders. I should not have come, she told herself firmly, even as she searched through the dark web of trees for a sight of Eneas. Between the black trunks she could just make out the huge gray boulder that occupied a small clearing. Huld's Throne they called it, in memory of the Queen long since disappeared from Oran's countryside. By day Shedwyn knew it was streaked with ocher-colored lichens and dappled with patches of bright green moss. But at night in the nearly full moon, the lichen glowed a silvery gray, and shadows caused by the depressions in the boulder's side molded into the likeness of a woman's face. Huld's face, the older peasants said wistfully, recalling when Oran's peasants had a Queen to represent them in the Queens' quarter knot. In those days there was harmony as each Queen threaded the strands of her element into a mutual knot of infinite magic. Earth, water, air and fire were joined in the Queens' quarter knot to rule and sustain the Oran land and its people.

Shedwyn approached slowly and reverently, feeling a kinship with the stone. She could almost sense its mute heart, the little veins of mica that chipped and bled at the surface eroded by the grasping roots of the lichens. Shedwyn breathed in deeply, trying to match her anxious pulse to the calm quiet of the stone. Like the Earth Queen Huld, Shedwyn was also an earth element and she sensed the subtle shifts of rock and soil beneath her feet like the exhalations of a sleeping giant.

Arms reached out and grabbed her, wrapping firmly around her waist. Shedwyn gasped and twisted angrily in the embrace, her hands prepared to strike.

"Shedwyn, it's only me!" Eneas said, releasing her and stepping back to avoid being hit.

"Cock's bones, don't do that," she said sharply. "I didn't know who it was."

"Expecting anyone else?" Eneas teased. He pulled her to him more gently, his arms circling her waist again. His face was shining with moonlight, the new beard forming a crisp outline to the square cut of his chin. His eyes sparkled like the mica in the stone. This time she did not stop him, but lifted her arms around his neck and rested her head on his chest.

"No one else, Eneas," she said softly, closing her eyes and listening to the steady beat of his heart. The blond hair brushing her hands was soft. She raked her fingers through it, enjoying its silky fineness. It was going to be hard to find the words to tell him, she realized with pain. And harder still to leave him.

Eneas bent his head and kissed her, his mouth covering hers. She sighed in her throat as his tongue slipped between her lips. Then abruptly she drew back.

"What's wrong?" Eneas asked, concern drawing his brow together. One of his hands moved up from her waist to cup her breast. His thumb stroked lazily over its fullness, teasing the nipple until it became hard.

"Don't," Shedwyn pleaded, moving his hand away from her breast.

"Shedwyn, what is it?" Eneas asked again, leaning down to stare in her face. He didn't release her, but held her closer to him, the better to see her face in the dark.

"Eneas," she started, and then stopped, not certain how to begin.

"Aye," he murmured, taking advantage of her hesitancy to settle kisses on her neck.

"Eneas," Shedwyn repeated, trying to ignore the little chills that traveled up her spine with his kisses. "I have to leave the farm. I have to leave tonight," she blurted out.

Eneas jerked his head back and Shedwyn felt the cold draft of air on her neck where he had been kissing. "What are you saying?" he asked, confused.

"I'm leaving the farm tonight. Now. I came to say good-bye." Shedwyn said the words carefully, slowly, as if to convince herself as well as Eneas of the truth. Until now, Shedwyn had only imagined her flight from Re Ameas's estate. Before, it had seemed easy, something she would do with no trace of regret. But saying the words now to Eneas made the weight of her decision solid and far more painful than she had thought possible.

Eneas pulled away from her, his arms dangling at his sides. The long hands opened and closed as he stared at her mistrustfully. "Why?" he asked simply.

Shedwyn sighed deeply, hurt by his withdrawal. "Overseer told me today that Readers have come. I am to be Named tomorrow."

A spark of hope lifted in Eneas's face. "If you're worried

about Neverin, don't be. I can see to it that he won't have his way—"

"No." She stopped him with a shake of her head. "No, that isn't it." Shedwyn stared at the ground for a moment. She had never told anyone about herself. Only her parents knew and they were long dead. It wasn't a thing spoken easily of in Oran. Not now in the Fire Queen's reign. Not now when there were Readers ready to hang you for having the old power flow in your veins.

Shedwyn felt Eneas draw near, heard the rustle of leaves beneath his feet. When he touched her, his hands traveling up her arms, she shivered. He lifted her chin to meet his eyes and she saw the stricken expression on his face.

"You've the old power," he said softly. "Oran magic."

She nodded silently. She watched the struggle on his face, anger warring with apprehension. Then she saw stubbornness settle his features as he exhaled resolutely.

"I won't let you go," he said vehemently.

"You must, or I am dead."

"I'll hide you."

"You can't, not forever. Please, Eneas, don't make this harder than it is."

"Cock's shit," Eneas swore, and clutched her tighter in his arms.

Shedwyn smiled as the tears burned her eyes. "Spoken like an Oran peasant, dear heart," she said.

"But how will you manage? Where will you go?" he asked, growing angry.

Shedwyn put a finger to his lips. "I'll be all right. There are those who will help me."

"Who?" Eneas demanded.

Shedwyn shook her head again and looked away. "I can't tell you that," she answered simply.

"Because I'm Silean," Eneas said bitterly. "You dare not trust me because I'm a frigging Silean." He grabbed a thin tree branch and broke it with a loud snap.

"Eneas, please," Shedwyn pleaded, not wanting to hear the hurt in his voice.

"Bastards!" he swore. "Frigging bastards, all of them." He wielded the branch like a sword, slashing the new leaves from the bushes.

Shedwyn clasped his arm, holding it firmly to prevent him from tearing at the bushes. "Stop it, Eneas. Please, stop," she cried. Tears were forming in her eyes, blurring sight of his white moonlit face. "Hold me instead. Hold me one more time before I go."

Eneas dropped the branch and hung his head. His breathing was rough as he fought to contain his anger. Then he gathered her into his arms, crushing her with the strength of his frustration. "It means nothing to me that you are Oran," he whispered fiercely. "And even less that I am Silean. I want only to love you."

Shedwyn tightened her arms around his back, the flat of her hands pressed against his shoulder blades. She opened her mouth to speak, but could find no words to say that would not betray her determination to flee. Instead she held him, his body leaning heavily into hers as if to memorize the feel of its contours.

A loud rustle and the snapping of branches startled them and they parted, caught in the sudden glare of torches. Beneath the orange glow of a torch Shedwyn saw Overseer Neverin, his eyes narrowed and his mouth an ugly leer. Beside him, black eyes bright with anticipation, two Silean Guards waited. Shedwyn had never seen them before and could only guess that they had come with the Reader. One of the Guards licked his lips and started to undo the buttons of his uniform, hastily wrenching the jacket open.

"Get away home, young master," Neverin said in a gravelly voice. "This one ain't for you."

"What's the meaning of this?" Eneas said sharply, drawing Shedwyn behind him. "How dare you."

"Oh no," Neverin answered evenly. "It's you that dares, young master. Your father won't hold with the idea of you wasting Silean seed on an Oran field."

"I order you—"

"No," barked Neverin, "you are ordered to return to the big house." One of the Guards stepped forward, drawing his sword. "Come away, young master. Leave the girl for her own kind."

Eneas didn't move, and behind him Shedwyn clutched his arm fearfully. The Guard stepped forward, jabbing Eneas lightly in the side with the sword. It made a small tear in the fabric and blood appeared. Eneas gasped with the pain. Shedwyn released him then and stepped back, afraid for Eneas as the Silean Guard moved closer still, brandishing the sword.

"Come on, lad, I ain't waiting all day. There's other things waiting for me."

"Go, Eneas," Shedwyn said softly. "Go home," she insisted.

"No," he protested, and this time the Guard raised the sword's point toward Eneas's heart, daring him to protest.

"I should kill you, you little snot-nosed bastard."

"What for?" Eneas hissed.

The Guard shrugged and looked over at Shedwyn. "Consorting with the enemy. Maybe this pretty-pretty knows where to find the New Moon, eh? Maybe we should ask her?"

"Eneas, go," Shedwyn said, cold terror spreading like ice through her limbs.

"Aye, Eneas, run on home," Neverin said thickly. "And leave the girl to us."

"Shedwyn," Eneas whispered, but she shook her head. The Guards would kill him if he protested. He thought they were bluffing. She knew they weren't. And there was still a chance she could save herself, but not if he was there to witness her shame.

"Go," she answered steadily. She bit down hard, her teeth drawing blood from her lower lip as she turned her face so he wouldn't see her anguish. She heard the Guard laugh as he led Eneas away into the dark woods.

"Now then, lass," Neverin said softly, approaching her, "to business."

Shedwyn backed away from Neverin, her shoulders butting against the hard surface of Huld's Throne. Her palms pressed against the stone, her fingers digging into its flank. Shards of mica scraped beneath her nails. Her mouth felt dry as cloth and she tried to lick her lips.

Neverin and the remaining Guard moved closer. The Guard held the torch high in one hand, the other working at the buttons of his trousers. Shedwyn glanced from one to the other, wondering which would be first. She could smell the pungent odor of sweat, knowing it to be her own fear.

Neverin swung his hand and slapped her hard across the face. Shedwyn's head jerked roughly to the side, the sting of his palm burning on her cheek. She started to crouch, but the Guard grabbed her roughly by the shoulder and drew her up again to face Neverin.

"That's for disappointing me," Neverin snapped. He slapped her again and she cried out as new pain exploded on her face and sent her rolling to the other side. ''And that's to teach you I don't like being disappointed.''

Tears streamed from Shedwyn's eyes as her cheeks flamed with Neverin's strikes. His eyes rolled white with rage, flecks of spit at the corners of his mouth as he raised his arm and struck her again. This time the soft flesh of her mouth tore against her teeth. She tasted the warm salt of blood.

''I'll give you what you deserve, bitch!'' Neverin shouted to her. ''And then I'll take what I want.''

Shedwyn flinched, raising her arms protectively over her head. Through her tears she saw the slender black line of the riding crop, waiting high above her head. It hissed in the air before she felt the sharp lash of it cut across her shoulders and neck. Her whole body bucked furiously, trying to escape the stinging lash of the whip.

Shedwyn had no thoughts but to survive the searing pain of the whip. She fought against the Guard's grip, twisting her body this way and that to avoid the constant rise and fall of the whip. She screamed as the whip caught her across the neck, opening a long red welt. In frantic desperation, she wrenched herself away from the Guard and crouched into a huddled ball next to Huld's Throne. Straddled above her, Neverin continued to beat her about the head and shoulders.

Through the blinding daze of pain, Shedwyn reached a hand to the stone's surface and grabbed it, squeezing tightly. For an instant she felt the stone come slowly alive, rumbling with indignation. She clung to the rock more tightly and sensed a mounting tension that pried apart fissures in the stone. Shedwyn sensed the solid hardness of the rock shield her from the violence of Neverin's whip. As he continued to beat her, she concentrated on the stone, letting her fear and pain bleed into its depths. The stone responded, and she heard the grinding howl of its outrage. And as Neverin and the Guard leaned down to force her up, the stone exploded with a roar.

It shattered into hard fragments, the edges serrated and glimmering with mica. Shedwyn buried her face between her hands and a thick coating of gravel covered her back.

In the woods not far from the big house, Eneas heard Shedwyn scream. The Guard at his side chuckled to himself. She screamed again, and this time Eneas felt the sound like a knife drawn down his spine. He clenched his fist as nausea swept over him.

No! he protested, rage welling in his chest. He would not allow them to hurt her. He spun on his heel to face the Guard and grabbed the hilt of his sword.

The Guard swore and fought to reclaim his weapon before it left the scabbard. But determination made Eneas quicker and he slid the sword free. The Guard bellowed curses at him, lunging at Eneas. Eneas aimed the sword into the Guard's belly, crying a warning as he felt the sudden weight of the man falling toward him. The Guard sagged heavily, his body folded around the point of the sword.

Eneas pushed him off, blood flowing on his hands, making them slick. He waited, stunned at the sight of the man dying at his feet. He hadn't meant to kill him, only to hold him off. Another scream from Shedwyn spun him around in the direction of the woods. "Shedwyn," he breathed. And ignoring the slain Guard, he bolted through the woods to the clearing.

He ran, stumbling over the thick underbrush. Low branches caught in his hair and scratched his face. The sword in his hand clattered against the trunks of trees. As he reached the clearing, he saw Shedwyn crouched like a cornered animal beneath Neverin and the Guard. He took a step and then faltered as the huge boulder of Huld's Throne exploded with a loud roar.

He fell to his knees, knocked back by the sound and the flying rock debris. A stone scraped the side of his face, tearing the skin. He heard a stifled scream, and he buried his head deeper beneath the tangle of branches.

And then it was quiet. He lifted his head slowly and saw in the clearing three bodies slumped around the blasted rubble that was all that remained of Huld's Throne. He pushed his way frantically through the underbrush and ran to the clearing.

Neverin lay dead, his skull crushed by a rock. Blood and something thicker spilled out on the ground from a carved hollow in his temple. Eneas gagged and reeled back, nearly tripping over the outstretched legs of the Guard. He was lying facedown, his head and shoulders buried beneath a pile of gray rocks. Only Shedwyn remained still crouched on her knees, her arms folded across her chest, her face turned down. She was sobbing quietly and her shoulders trembled.

Eneas touched her softly and she cried out in pain.

"Shedwyn," he called.

She lifted her face to him and he gasped at the sight of the welts along her neck and shoulders. Then he swallowed hard, refusing to oblige the sudden weakness in his knees and the coldness that seemed to stiffen his hands.

"Come," he repeated firmly. "We must go."

Shedwyn stood, her legs shaking. "No, Eneas—"

"I can't stay," he said harshly. "I've killed a Guard."

Shedwyn moaned, a hand to her face as she looked at the carnage about her. "My fault," she said.

"No," he said, shaking his head. "My decision. I'm coming with you."

He took her hand, grateful when she squeezed it back. He slipped his arm carefully around her waist, giving her support.

"There is only one place of safety," she said weakly.

"Where?"

"North," she answered. "To Avadares and the New Moon army."

Avadares, Eneas thought with a quickened pulse. There were few Sileans indeed who would risk venturing too far into those rocky slopes. Eneas glanced down at Shedwyn's face, her eyes dazed like a wounded bird, the welts bleeding. He would not abandon her, not now. He exhaled hard, to rid himself of all further doubt. He would flee with her, even to Avadares.

"Will you go then?" she asked weakly, uncertain of his silence.

"Yes," he said, and drew her closer to his side.

They walked slowly through the clearing, stepping over the shattered remains of Huld's Throne. Then, with Shedwyn leading the way, they fled, scurrying like nocturnal animals into the night-darkened woods.

Chapter Two

Jobber stared out over the railings of the Marigold, *relieved at* last to see the port of Remmerton. It wasn't much of a port, she thought disappointedly. Faul's description had misled her into thinking Remmerton was something grander. A city at least, not this dreary-looking village. The houses were small and drab, bleached of color as they sagged into the wind. There was a small sheltered cove, and rising above it a high bluff of stone, dotted with scrubby trees whose gnarled roots clung to crevices in the stone. From a ribbon of sand on the shore a collection of long rickety piers reached into the water.

Jobber sighed and scratched the dried salt from her cheek. Her red hair billowed about her face, a lock of it catching at the corner of her mouth. She brushed it away, absently. Plain or not, she told herself, Remmerton marked a return to solid land. Five weeks on the water, one of them spent battened down in a narrow cove while they waited out a furious storm, had been enough of the sea for a lifetime. All Jobber wanted now was to stand on the hard earth, see the dust kicking up around her feet, and maybe breathe in the smoky fumes of a neat little tavern somewhere in town. Decent ale wouldn't go amiss, either, she snorted, thinking of the watered brandy that Faul gave them in their rations. Z'blood, Jobber swore, but she was sick of fish, sick of screeching gulls, sick of the ever blue green of the sea, and sick of the constant shifting and rolling of the deck.

"*Aha!*, what a fine sight. Land after so much water," said a low, clear voice near Jobber's elbow.

Jobber turned and cocked a half smile at Lirrel, standing beside her at the railing. Jobber was getting used to Lirrel speaking aloud the thoughts that moments before had been tucked silently away in her head. The black fringe of Lirrel's head scarf snapped gaily in the wind, the little mirrors stitched to the cloth twinkling in the afternoon sunlight. Lirrel faced her and Jobber stared at Lirrel's silvery eyes, their oddity no longer strange to her but as familiar as the moon. Lirrel's oak-colored skin had tanned a deeper brown during the weeks on board ship, unlike Jobber's, which remained as pale as ever despite the hours spent in the *Marigold*'s rigging.

"It don't look too exciting to me," Jobber said, squinting at the light of the setting sun that bounced off the water. A fishing smack coasted into the harbor, its wide rounded hull reminding Jobber of a floating acorn. Only one other packet with a torn mainsail was tied to a spur in the pier. "It sure ain't Beldan," Jobber scoffed, pricked by the sharp pangs of homesickness. There was nowhere as beautiful as Beldan. Or as deadly, she reflected more soberly.

"Jobber," Lirrel teased, "to be a good traveler, one cannot stand in the middle of a new city and complain that it doesn't smell like home. Each place has its own charm. To find it, you must be open to it."

"That's all right if you're Ghazali like you and used to settling for less on the road. But me, I'm Beldan-born, Beldan-bred, and I need a lot more to convince me that there is any other place besides Beldan worth seeing. As it is, nothing out there even looks open, does it?" Jobber eyed Remmerton skeptically.

Lirrel shrugged her thin shoulders. "I, too, had the impression that it would be somewhat busier," she admitted. "Remmerton is a major port of trade for the southern estates. And yet there are few ships here and the docks seem empty."

"Well, busy or not, it's land. And it's where we get off," Jobber finished.

"And then what, Jobber?" Lirrel asked her pointedly. "Have you made a decision as to what you will do next?"

"I suppose you have," Jobber snapped irritably. She had been trying since the day they fled Beldan to avoid this moment. It demanded that she think, plan for the future, something she wasn't accustomed to doing.

"*Ahal*," Lirrel answered in Ghazali, tilting her head to one side, her silvery gaze settling firmly on Jobber's face. One delicate eyebrow was raised in a fine arch. "You know I will go with you. Wherever you decide."

"Frigging shit, Lirrel, don't put it on me," Jobber burst out. Her red-gold hair crackled with her anger. Lirrel stepped back to avoid the small shower of golden sparks. Jobber quickly laid a hand to her scalp, smoothing down the billowing hair. The salty air was suddenly sharp with the scent of copper. "Sorry," Jobber mumbled, embarrassed, and then added, "Don't say it," in warning to Lirrel's look of concern.

Lirrel put a slender finger to her lips as if to seal them. But for once, Jobber could well guess what Lirrel was thinking. Got to get this temper under control before I set everything on fire, she warned herself, not for the first time.

"You must choose a path, Jobber. Or one will be chosen for you. And that you may not like."

"So what's your path then? Following me around?"

"Yes. I choose to follow you," Lirrel replied, refusing to be angered by Jobber's belligerent tone.

"What if I choose to do nothing? That's a path, ain't it?"

Lirrel shook her head, a small smile forming on her lips. "What of Wyer and Alwir's offer," she suggested.

Jobber made a rude noise. They were part of the reason Jobber was now on this stinking boat, on her way to an uncertain exile. Wyer was a smith and a Guildsman and Alwir, an Oran Reader and traitor to his Guild. They had joined the New Moon and, when they were caught, had faced the gallows at Fire Circle. Alwir's call to arms from the scaffolds had ignited the fury of the Firefaire crowds, and in the riot that had followed, the Silean cavalry had found their excuse to massacre the Oran people. How many times on this voyage had Jobber argued with Alwir, cursed him for his stupid idealism and his blind faith in the New Moon. "You know what Alwir's game is, Lirrel. Figures us to be a naffy prize for the New Moon. I don't know about you, but I don't think I'd make much of a Fire Queen."

"Not intending insult, Jobber, but you may be their only choice. There is no one else besides you and the Fire Queen Zorah that carries the fire element. The New Moon would be

more than willing to overlook some of your less than regal habits
if you accepted.''

"And what about you, Lirrel?" Jobber retorted. "You think
you could put aside all your Ghazali noise about peace and join
up with an army of brigands like the New Moon? It's not only
me they'd want, it's you, too. I may be the only fire element left
in this frigging country, but you're probably the only air element
strong enough to handle me." Jobber felt her head grow warm
again, saw the red of her hair lighten with heat. "Are you so
ready to let the New Moon tie you into a new Queens' quarter
knot?"

"Tcha, Jobber, that's nonsense," Lirrel said.

"Is it?" Jobber insisted. Small flames flickered in the green
eyes, and her pale skin pinked. "These are desperate people,
Lirrel. They've taken up arms, they plot to kill people, maybe
even innocent people, something that you as a Ghazali would
never accept. Can you trust them?"

"I've trusted you, Jobber," Lirrel answered steadily, and Jobber saw the delicate features harden. "Their violence dismays
me, but I am not afraid of it. Not anymore. Not since I felt what
you alone are capable of doing."

Jobber blew out a breath of defeat and bowed her head. It
seemed so long ago and yet the memory of Firefaire was still
fresh, like a cut not yet healed that split its scab with a sudden
movement. On the streets there were few that she had counted
as friends. Dogsbody had been one. He was just a boy, Jobber
thought recalling the tangled hedgehog hair and gapped tooth
smile. And yet he had defied his Flock leader Ratcatcher and
had come to warn her when all of Beldan's street snitches were
turned out to hunt for her. There was gold offered for her capture
by the Upright Man, but Dogsbody was loyal to Jobber and not
the Queen's coin.

Jobber saw again the moment of Dogsbody's death. Ratcatcher
and two of his headcrackers had followed Dogsbody to the alley
and trapped them both. Stabbed, Dogsbody swirled and fell to
the cobblestones like a bloody leaf, the hilt of Ratcatcher's knife
buried in his chest. She got even right then. She murdered the
headcracker Skull with his own razor after she shattered the knees
of Nicker, the other boy. And then it was Ratcatcher's turn.
Jobber strangled him, her fingers gripped tightly around his neck
as she burned his flesh with the fierce heat of her fire's magic.
Lirrel had been there, had experienced the raw depths of Job-

ber's rage, and had survived its searing white heat. But despite the violence of Jobber's heart, Lirrel trusted her, and had followed Jobber into exile.

"Frigging shit, Lirrel, I don't know what to do," Jobber muttered.

"There's time yet," Lirrel answered more lightly as the *Marigold* entered the harbor and glided toward the docks. "We'll dock first and maybe once on land, sitting before a tankard, it will be easier to make up your mind."

Jobber smiled, relieved to be postponing her decision. Abruptly she rubbed her chapped hands together. "Oy, Lirrel! You still got that string of coppers on you?"

"What do you have in mind?" Lirrel asked back.

Jobber gave her a look of shocked surprise. "What? You mean you don't know for once? Z'blood, I am disappointed in you."

Lirrel laughed, shrugged her shoulders, feigning ignorance. Then a spark of amusement gleamed in her eyes. "No, wait. I think I know. I will answer you with a riddle," Lirrel said, holding up one finger for emphasis. "Oh, how good it is, and yet it is not eaten!"

Jobber grinned. "The answer is ale, ain't it? You don't eat ale!"

"No, actually," Lirrel replied. "The answer is soap. Tcha, you could use a bath, Jobber," she added, her nose wrinkling in disgust. "I think you're the only one of us, including the entire crew, who hasn't washed."

"You know I don't like water. People piss in it, fish do all kinds of frigging things in it, and you want me to wash with it." Jobber shook her head. "Nah, I told you before, you get sick doing that."

"Oy, you two!" came a loud shout from the wheel. "Get yer arses moving, we're bringing the ship in!" The first mate Harral stood at the wheel, angrily waving his thick arms at them. Jobber noticed Harral had carefully waxed the ends of his long black mustache and they stuck out on either side of his bulbous nose like whiskers on a walrus.

"He's looking flash, ain't he?" Jobber said with a smirk. "Thinking about the dells, no doubt."

"Hmm, could be," Lirrel replied. "What do you think is on Faul's mind?"

Jobber looked back at the wheel deck and saw Faul, the *Marigold*'s captain, staring at the docks with her somber gray eyes.

Her expression was reserved, her lips pursed slightly as if she tasted something sour.

"Probably thinking on the bottle, as always," Jobber answered.

"Not this time," Lirrel said softly, and then left, heading for the galley.

Jobber stared at Faul and growled under her breath. Taking orders from the woman was something she was definitely not going to miss. But, Jobber admitted grudgingly to herself, Faul had been true to her word. She'd given them safe passage out of Beldan and brought them to Remmerton when she could have just as easily tossed the lot of them overboard. Staring at the razor-thin figure of Faul, Jobber remembered their escape from the docks. The streets of Beldan crowded with people fleeing before the Silean cavalry, the air thick with the smoke of exploding fires, and the sounds of screaming mingled with the moans of the dying. Faul had killed six Guards, dispatching them with a fearful, deadly grace. And all because of the red hair, Jobber thought again, tugging at a stiff copper-colored strand. Faul had thought she was protecting the Fire Queen from the Silean Guard, only to discover that Jobber was a Beldan street snitch, but a snitch with a face and hair that matched the Queen's. As she climbed the riggings for a final time, Jobber reflected that she would miss Faul in spite of her nasty humor and the fact that she drank too much. She was still a good blade and that Jobber had to respect.

Faul and the first mate Harral sauntered down the rickety pier toward the shore. Behind them Jobber struggled to follow. Her eager steps down the landing plank and onto the pier resulted in her abruptly losing her balance and tripping sideways into an equally unstable Lirrel.

"Z'blood," she swore, "you've ruined me, Faul! I can't walk no more!"

Faul turned around and scowled. The wind brushed back the short black hair and showed amusement in her gray eyes. "Take it slow. Your legs just aren't used to the land."

Jobber steadied herself and watched the way Faul and the mate walked, their stride rolling from side to side as if to make up for the lack of waves once on land. Jobber tried it and moved with more sureness, though she felt vaguely silly. She turned and grinned at Lirrel, who was walking as she always did, her hips swaying with the grace of a Ghazali dancer. It seemed as if the rolling gait was natural to her. Jobber glanced once over her shoulder, satisfied that Alwir and Wyer were having more trouble than she herself keeping a steady stance. Alwir's long, rangy body wobbled like an uncertain puppet and beside him Wyer stepped with careful plodding steps so as not to upend his wide, solid girth. Both men were so gravely absorbed by their movements that when Jobber laughed at them, they didn't even look up.

"Well then, Captain, shall we take a meal at the Gull? I could use a bit of someone else's cooking for a change!" Harral said, twisting the long ends of his waxy mustache.

"No. The Three Swans, I think," answered Faul.

The mate turned to her, a black eyebrow lifted in surprise. "Expecting trouble?"

"Could be," Faul said. Though her head faced forward, her eyes wandered over the streets and she frowned, not liking what she saw. "Things don't seem right here. Where is everyone? I didn't see the *Black Pearl* in port and yet she was due in same time as us."

"Maybe she missed the storm and has gone on ahead?"

Faul shook her head. "The captain and I had business to discuss. He would have waited."

They continued walking up the shore, Faul studying the thin wisps of smoke that rose from the stithies and stone cottages. The village was strangely subdued, as if someone had come through and swept away its occupants. They saw two sail menders talking quietly in the shadow of a doorway, their knees draped with heavy white canvas. As they neared, the men grew quiet until they had passed, and behind them Faul heard them whisper. In the unsettling quiet a child burst out of a shop door, laughing, and was quickly dragged back in by a scolding parent. On Anchor Street Faul caught sight of a face behind a window peering out at her. As she stared back, the face disappeared quickly.

"Faul?" Alwir called from behind, and Faul turned sharply, hand going for her sword.

Alwir stopped short, seeing the gesture. "Ah," he said, eyeing the sword. "I had wondered if this was usual for Remmerton and I see that it is not." Alwir ran a hand through a sparse brown beard. The sun had browned his skin, but not before burning the skin of his nose. Across the bridge the skin was peeling with pink flakes. "What do you make of it?" he asked softly.

"Don't know," was Faul's curt reply, "but I don't much like it."

"Do you think they've heard about Beldan already?"

"Perhaps," Faul said, tight-lipped.

"It's going to make it difficult to get the horses and supplies we need to go north," Alwir said worriedly.

"We're going to the Three Swans," Faul said carefully, feeling as if every stone-faced shop and curtained window waited hushed to hear her words. "Perhaps we shall be able to find out what's happened here."

Jobber stared out scornfully at the dirty streets of the small port city. "Like the end of the world this place was. Nothing here but a few old buildings, a lot of dried fish and cats," she muttered disgustedly to Lirrel. They watched an orange tomcat stretch his front paws and then settle down again on the stoop, tucking his paws beneath it. "What do you suppose they do for fun?"

"They work," Faul snapped, wishing Jobber would be quiet.

"Z'blood," Jobber grumbled. "This is going to be a banger of place, ain't it?"

At the end of Anchor Street Faul stopped before the doorway of the Three Swans and looked around again suspiciously at the street. She entered quickly, and from behind her, she heard Jobber's squeal of delight.

"Hold on, Jobber," Faul said as Jobber pushed them both through the door.

Once inside, Faul felt more secure surrounded by walls, but no less concerned by the unnatural quiet of the village. The inn was dark but clean, small squares of light falling across the wooden tables from windows on the inn's street face. There were two people drinking by the great hearth, one of them jabbing the fire with an iron poker. They looked up sharply as Wyer entered, his broad chest momentarily hiding Jobber. Jobber's head peered over Wyer's shoulder, and as the drinkers caught sight of the red hair, they stood quickly, abandoning their half-full tankards in their haste to leave. They gave a quick nod to Faul as they brushed past her and out the door. Faul saw the panicked look that crossed their faces.

"Z'blood, you'd think we brought the plague," growled Faul to Harral.

"Ah no, som'at worse," said the innkeeper, who appeared suddenly behind the bar. He brought a taper with him and moved around the inn, lighting the lamps. He'd a sharp profile as if hastily cut from wood, with a large hooked nose and jutting chin.

"What's that then?" Faul asked, threading her way through the clutter of tables and chairs.

"Silean Guards."

"The local militia?"

The innkeeper nodded and turned to gaze at her. From beneath the black eyebrows, gray eyes stared back, startlingly light in a face otherwise darkly hued. "Aye. And another, come straight from Beldan five days ago."

"Alone?"

"At first. Then a full squad arrived two days ago. The local lads were called off the farms and pressed into service, not that they mind the brutal bastards. Remmerton's been turned into fair nest of butcherboys."

"Who gave the order?" Faul asked in a low voice, growing cold with fury.

"The Regent himself, acting in the interest of the Fire Queen."

"What are they after?" asked Faul, hand wrapped tightly around the hilt of her sword.

"Not a what really, a who." The innkeeper leaned forward, his bony face angled like a figurehead on a ship. "Word's out, Faul, that you killed a parcel of butcherboys in Beldan as you were escaping with a cargo hold full of New Moon rebels. There's a price on your head, along with your passengers. An extra sum will be given for the girl with red hair if she's brought alive. No gold if she's dead."

"Frigging whore's shit!" Faul exploded.

"Yeah, well, that ain't all I'm sorry to say," the innkeeper continued. He turned to light another lamp. "They've confiscated your land, Faul, shoved off your laborers, and hauled away your livestock."

"In three days!" Faul shouted angrily.

"Did it in one. That Guard who came from Beldan is keen on seeing you finished off."

"Did you catch his name?"

"Rubio. A big fellow with a punched-in face—"

"I know him."

"Captain," Harral said.

Faul nodded. "Let's get back to the *Marigold*. We've enough supplies to take her farther downcoast and maybe out to one of the islands."

"What about us?" Alwir asked Faul.

Faul frowned. "If it wasn't for you, I'd not be in this mess. From now on you're on your own. I'll just give you this advice. Head off through the marsh. They won't find you there. But keep a sharp eye out for the quicksand and the fog."

"Thanks a frigging lot, Faul," Jobber said angrily. "You know it's me they want as well as you!"

"Look, I didn't want any part of the New Moon or you!" Faul said, pointing her finger at Jobber's scowl.

"Too late, ain't it? You're already a part of it."

"I had no choice in the matter, then."

"Yes, you did!" Jobber shouted back. "You chose to defend me!"

"Because I thought you were the Fire Queen!"

"Who's to say I won't be one day?" Jobber yelled. Faul heard the desperate panic in Jobber's voice. Jobber's red hair crackled with yellow sparks and the room reeked with a metallic odor. From a dark corner Lirrel stared silently at Jobber, the opal-colored eyes gleaming an eerie white in the shadowy room.

"Are you joining us?" Alwir asked in the heavy silence.

Jobber groaned. "I don't know. Don't ask me that now. I just said it. Look, Faul, take us with you," Jobber pleaded. "Z'blood, don't leave us here!"

Faul stared, stone-faced, blood draining from her cheeks at the sight of the crackling red hair and Jobber's bright green eyes. She shook her head stiffly and turned briskly, heading for the door of the inn. Harral hurried after her.

Faul wrenched open the door, leaned out, and then just as quickly jerked back, knocking Harral to the floor behind her. The man fell heavily and the air huffed loudly from his chest. He swore gruffly as Faul slammed the door shut. She spun around, her face livid and her eyes wide with outrage. From the other side of the door came the repeated thud of a dozen or more arrows as they hammered the wooden door of the Three Swans.

Faul cast a furious glare at Jobber. "I should have known better than to waste time arguing with you. You'd make me late for my own funeral!" Pulling the mate up off the floor, she barked out an order: "Through the passage, now. Be quick about it. I'll follow directly."

"Can we fight them?" Wyer asked, pushing a chair out of his way to peer cautiously out one window.

"Not unless you know how to dodge the quarrels of a crossbow. Those aren't city Guards out there. They're local lads and you know nothing about fighting them. Now get out!"

"Don't argue," Harral insisted, grabbing Jobber's arm and pulling. The rest quickly followed the mate behind the bar, Jobber turning back once to see Faul staring out a window. The yellow lamplight drew a hard gleam from Faul's eyes.

"Watch it now," Harral warned as Jobber nearly tumbled down an open hatch door in the floor of the inn.

"Where does it lead?" Jobber asked as she climbed down a narrow wooden ladder and was swallowed by the dark passage.

"Out to the bluffs," he answered gruffly. "Now get a move on."

"Can't see a frigging thing," Jobber complained, her head disappearing from Faul's view as she slid uneasily down the trapdoor.

"This way," Faul heard Lirrel's quiet answer from the tunnel below. "It's a fair passage, Jobber. Tall enough that you won't crack even that thick skull of yours!" Lirrel's voice was light but Faul heard the edge of fear beneath it.

"Feel like a frigging mole."

"Quiet down," ordered the mate. "They'll hear you and then you'll feel like a rat in a cage."

Then it was quiet, except for the soft spluttering of candles in the inn. Faul turned to the innkeeper, who had remained behind, and shook her head.

"I'm sorry, Radigan."

The innkeeper shrugged. "You're family, Faul. We're all that's left of the Verrans. But before you go, just tell me this. Is it true the New Moon tried to kill the Fire Queen? Is it true that Beldan went up in flames because of that girl back there?"

Faul snorted and shook her head. "As near as I have it figured, it was one frigging mistake after another, all of it costing in blood. The New Moon are in on it, all right. Alwir, that tall skinny one, and Wyer, the bigger man, were both on the scaffold, waiting a hanging at the Queen's pleasure. People didn't like it, so the Regent decided to settle the matter by calling out the Silean cavalry."

"Z'blood," Radigan spat, and his face darkened with hate.

"Bad business all around. It was a massacre, from what they tell me. Jobber, the red-haired one, got tangled up with the Queen, trying to free Wyer and the others."

"Is she—"

Faul nodded slowly, her eyes seeing the moment on the docks when Jobber had come running to her, followed by the Guards, her terrified face wreathed in a flame of red hair. "She's a fire element. Same as the Queen. The Queen tried to kill her, but the New Moon distracted her with a handful of arrows."

"And Beldan? Is it still standing?"

Faul shrugged. "Hard to say. All I saw of it as we fled the harbor was smoke."

"Think she did it?" Radigan asked, blowing out the taper he held in his hand and carefully setting it on a table. "Caused Beldan to burn?"

"Who, Jobber?" Faul asked, distracted by the sudden appearance of a familiar face. It was a Silean Guard waiting in the street, flanked by a squad of the local militia. "Don't know. I don't think anyone does. It doesn't matter anymore, now." She jerked the hard point of her chin toward the windows. "But this does."

Faul grabbed an empty tankard from a table and smashed the glass through one of the small windows.

"Rubio," she shouted. The grizzle-faced Guard looked up and smiled maliciously. "Frigging bastard," Faul muttered at the window. More loudly again she called out: "I have to thank you for this welcome you've provided."

A second volley of arrows shot through the air, their heavy points driving like spears into the door.

"No trouble, Faul. Nothing less than you deserve," Rubio shouted back.

She peeked out again at the Guards, guessing on how many more were waiting at the back entrance to the inn. They'd not move until he gave the order. And he was waiting, thinking he had them tied down tight. She knew what Rubio wanted. A chance first to settle an old score.

She gave a humorless smile. "I see you've brought friends to carry home your pieces."

"Yes," Rubio answered harshly. "But it'll be you in pieces, Faul. And it'll be to the beach with them, where we shall toss them to the seabirds."

"How poetic," Faul said, chuckling at the utter certainty in his voice. She looked at Radigan, who watched her, his eyes narrowed and his dark skin blanched gray. "No one here knows you're my brother, do they?" she asked quietly. He shook his head.

Faul turned back to the window. "Rubio, this fight should be done with honor—"

"You don't have any honor, Faul. Not since you changed sides and joined the New Moon."

"I doubt I could convince you otherwise of that, but instead I will ask that the innkeeper be allowed to leave this place unharmed. Let us save this fight for those who have reasons to die."

Faul waited while Rubio considered the request. She was sure he'd agree; after all, he thought he had them where he wanted. Even Jobber. Perhaps he could afford to be generous.

"Send him out," Rubio shouted back.

Faul turned back to Radigan. "Good-bye, brother. Maybe we'll see each other again."

Radigan smiled and hesitated before leaving. "Strange, isn't it? For all our running, Faul, we've come full circle."

Faul laughed dryly. "To have been Firstwatch of Beldan, only to tumble back to my origins as a smuggler's brat. Perhaps I was not meant for the straight-fingered life after all."

"Will you go to Stormfast?" Radigan asked.

"Perhaps." Faul nodded and then quickly turned her head to the window again. "Now you should leave. Patience is far from one of Rubio's talents."

Zorah's blood, how she hated running! Faul swore, the air huffing noisily out of her mouth as she ran through the underground tunnel. Too much like the last time, when she had been a child; running in the dark, the glimmer of torchlight following behind, her mother's voice urging her to make haste for the ship. Someone had betrayed them. The Silean Guards had appeared on the beach instead of the merchants who had bargained for their smuggled goods. In the underground passage Faul shivered, tasting the dank air. She thrust away the image of her parents, the firelight dancing over their dangling legs and their heads twisted at impossible angles from the end of a rope.

Faul gasped, struck by the sudden sharpness of cold air as she burst from the passageway and onto the beach. Rock piles shel-

tered her from the wind and hid the entrance to the passage
carved in the cliff face. She stopped, her head thrown back to
face the open sky and her chest heaving as she sucked in the
crisp sea air. It was nearly dark, the last shreds of sunset a dying
streak of dull orange over the western sky. Evening stars winked
and the wind gusted, blowing fine sand. She listened to the
murmur of the waves pushing upward on the shore and breaking
against the rocks of a jutting headland. Faul shook her head to
clear it of unwanted memories and fears, and then looked around
for the others. A small strip of sand made a narrow path along
the base of the cliff face. She looked down, peering through the
increasing darkness, and made out their footprints heading west,
back to the docks and the ship.

She brushed back clinging strands of hair and followed the
tracks, careful to stay within the shadow of the cliff.

Climbing around the tumbled boulders of a rocky headland,
Faul stopped, seeing the *Marigold* drifting in the harbor. The
ship was engulfed with fire. In the early night the sails flared a
brilliant orange, red, and yellow. Sparks exploded from the mast,
flying into the sky like a flock of angry birds. Faul could hear
the throaty roar of the fire as it gutted the wheel deck. The hull
moaned and cracked, and then the wood split with a thundering
boom that shot forth another shower of sparks across the water.

"Z'blood," Faul cursed, and raised her fists. "My ship!
They've destroyed my ship!" Her voice grew louder with rage.
"I'll get the frigging bastards," she bellowed at the fiery skeleton of the ship. It was drifting in a circle, pieces of the shattered
hull floating away in the water. Steam hissed and spat as the
water received the ragged burning embers.

"Captain! Captain!" Faul tore her gaze away from the ruined
ship and saw the mate running down the narrow beach toward
her. Behind him followed the others, running unevenly, sand
kicking up around their heels. "Captain . . . too late . . ." he
shouted in a rasping voice. "I got there too late. The Guard had
already set her on fire and cut her adrift." He stopped running
and leaned against a boulder, his shoulders lifting with the effort
of his labored breathing. "She's gone, Captain, and the crew
with her," he added bitterly, shaking his head.

"Faul!" Lirrel called out in alarm, pointing to the high cliffs
above them. "Up there on the bluffs."

Faul's head jerked up sharply. Along the dark ridge of the
cliffs she could see the bobbing of torchlights as the Guard made

their way down a zigzag path cut in the stone. Looking back at the docks, she saw more torchlight as the Guard gathered farther down the shore. "They're sending out the search parties for us," and as if to answer in agreement, they heard the faint, shrill caw of the Silean alarm. Faul's muscles snapped taut. "To the marsh," she ordered. "We can lose them in the marsh."

She started running up the strip of sand, hearing the grunts of the others as they struggled to keep up. The waves rushed in, icy water lapping at her boots and cold spray from the rocks stinging her cheeks. She glanced at the sky and saw the half-moon surrounded by a thin web of clouds. Out across the breaking waves and the patches of white foam, the evening mist was rising and forming a blanket of fog. If they reached the marsh soon enough, the fog would close in and hide them. Even the local lads wouldn't venture far into the marsh when the fog was thick. Through the muffled thumps of their footfalls on the sand and their harsh and labored breathing as they ran, Faul continued to hear the shrill caw of the Silean alarm. She leaned her body, urgency filling the long-legged stride. They'd caught her once, long ago. They'd not do it a second time.

They turned sharply from the beach and followed the sluggish tidal pools surrounded by the long-withered seagrass. Faul's feet splashed in the murky water and the sound grew more plodding as around them the vegetation thickened. Trees decorated with clinging vines sprang up around the fringes of the pools. The ground hardened, turning slick with mud along the beaten path. Beside the path, clumps of stout-leaved gacklebushes replaced the spears of seagrass. Faul veered off the path and plunged into the dense underbrush. The mud sucked at her feet, and behind her the others struggled to follow. Faul refused to pay attention to their cries, listening only for the sounds of the Silean alarm.

She ran on, branches snapping back as she passed them with no other thought than to drive herself as deeply into the shelter of the maze as possible. She glanced up once, seeing a scattering of stars between the black branches. And then they were gone, swallowed by the bank of mist that rolled through the marsh. She ducked her head and concentrated on not losing her footing among the black pools of mud.

How long they had been traveling Faul didn't know, or care. But the sound of Harral's voice stopped her in her tracks.

"Captain," Harral called out in the shrouded darkness of the marsh. "Captain," he repeated. "We've got to stop. We're too tired to travel like this."

"Not yet," came Faul's hoarse reply. Her legs were trembling with fatigue but her mind was fixed on the desire for flight. "We must push farther into the marsh."

"But Captain, we've lost them. We've not heard the alarm for a long time now. There are no torches, nothing behind us."

"Don't trust your eyes," she answered harshly. "They're here, the frigging bastards. If we stop, they'll be on us. We have to keep moving."

"Zorah's tits, Faul, all this slogging about in the muck. It's worse than being caught by the Sileans!" Jobber moaned from behind.

"How would you know?" Faul snarled. "Go on then, stop. Sit down. Light a fire, for all I care. And then mark my words, they'll be on you in an instant and tomorrow your heads will be staked outside Remmerton for the gulls to feed on."

"You've gone daft, Faul," Jobber shouted angrily and nervously. The gloomy marsh was frightening enough without hearing the shrill edge in Faul's voice. "We're alone out here. Frigging, stupid alone." Jobber wiped the clinging mist from her face, leaving behind a streak of mud.

Faul grunted and turned away. Jobber could hear the squelching of her boots as she continued tramping over the muddy trail.

"Stop, Faul!" Jobber cried, peering into the thick gray coat of fog. The half-moon, draped by clouds, cast an uneven light over the dark landscape of the marsh. The mist swirled, and for a moment Jobber caught the black form of Faul's back as she trudged through the marsh.

"We're going to lose her," Wyer said wearily, but none of them moved to follow her.

"Come on," growled Harral, "if we don't keep up with her now, we'll never get out of here. Let's move." He pushed his way through the shrubs, the mist closing quickly about him.

Jobber looked over to Lirrel, trying to see her face. She could just make out her black silhouette and saw Lirrel raise a hand to touch her in the dark.

"Come on," mumbled Alwir wearily. "We've got to move."

Before they'd taken a step they heard a strangled shout and a noisy thrashing amidst the soggy brush of the marsh. A branch snapped with an eerie crispness in the damp air, followed by a wet sucking sound.

"Faul?" Jobber called, at once concerned and terrified, remembering Faul's parting words. Had the Sileans been waiting all this time? "Harral?" she cried out louder.

There was an ominous silence, broken suddenly by the sound of more thrashing and a choked cry.

"Quicksand!" Alwir said in alarm. "One of them must have stumbled into quicksand."

"Z'blood, the great frigging—" Jobber swore, and bolted in the direction she had last seen the disappearing figures of Faul and Harral.

"Faul!" she cried out, peering into the gray fog. "Faul! Answer me!"

"I'm here," Faul cried back, and Jobber felt a tremor of relief. "Watch the ground. There is some quicksand."

"Is Harral with you?" Wyer called back.

"No!" Faul answered, and they heard the snapping of branches as Faul shoved her way through the underbrush.

Jobber picked her steps carefully but quickly through the ooze of mud and duckweed. "Faul! We've lost him," she yelled, desperation rising in her voice. She thrust one foot forward and then jerked it back again as she felt the black mud grab. The mud gave a loud sucking protest as it clung to her boot. Z'blood, she thought wildly, the ground was a whirlpool of mud.

Lirrel collided into her from behind, managing to grab Jobber by the shoulders before she pitched into the quicksand. "In there!" she called frantically. "Harral's in there. I'm sure of it," she yelled in Jobber's ear.

Faul appeared suddenly between two gnarled trees, their long spindly branches hung out over the black mud. Jobber gasped, seeing her wade into the mud without hesitation.

"Harral!" Faul shouted as the mud claimed her, rising quickly to her shoulders with a sucking noise. Her head turned this way and that as she tried to penetrate the thick coat of mud. "Where the frigging shit is the man?" she bellowed. "I've got him!" she shouted, and as Jobber leaned forward she saw the mud rise over Faul's chin.

"Let go of him," Jobber screamed. "He's pulling you under!"

Faul thrashed, her neck stretched up, her narrow face seeming to float on the surface of the mud. "I can't . . ." she started to say, and then the mud pulled her under.

"Lirrel, your scarf," Jobber demanded, and even before she

had finished speaking the words, Lirrel handed her a knotted corner of the fringed scarf.

"Let me go," said Alwir.

"Nah," Jobber said over her shoulder. "You and Wyer will have to pull us out again. Hold fast now while I go in." She handed the other end of the long scarf to Alwir and then turned back to face the black pool.

Jobber shuddered as she stepped into the quicksand. Within an instant the wet clay sucked and oozed coldly up around her knees. She tried to walk through it, shoving her weight forward. But there was nothing solid under her feet and she quickly sank thigh-deep. The blackened limb of a broken branch hung over a slowly churning spot in the pool of quicksand. "Don't let go," she cried to Alwir. "Whatever you do, don't let go!"

Jobber clung to the scarf, fighting back the rush of panic as the quicksand reached to her breastbone. The weight of it pressed against her ribs, and in the terrified effort to push it away from her she opened her arms wide. She slid forward a few inches, closer to the broken limb, and swept again with her arms. The mud now rose to her shoulders and she clenched her teeth. Once more she spread her arms and her hand hit something hard. She clutched it and felt it was an arm. Whether it was Faul or Harral, she didn't know.

Jobber pulled harder on the arm and felt the rest of the body move grudgingly closer toward her. It was Faul, she decided, for the arm was thin in her grasp. Jobber held on to both the arm and the scarf while she searched deeper into the mud with her other hand. It contacted the hard lump of Faul's shoulder, moved along her neck, and grabbed her hair. Jobber yanked Faul's head toward the surface. In the ghostly mist Faul's face emerged from the black pool, mud-spattered and lifeless.

"I've got her. Pull us out!" Jobber shrieked, the quicksand closing a cold clammy hand around her throat. "Z'blood, get us out of here!"

Jobber held on to Faul's hair, trying to keep as much of Faul's face out of the mud as she could. "Silly raving bitch," she shouted to the face as if the words could chase away the cold terror of the quicksand and awaken the face.

Arms reached out, a voice grunted hard in her ear as Jobber was pulled from the quicksand, still gripping Faul by the hair. Wyer leaned down and took Faul under the armpits and dragged her out. Jobber turned over and crouched on all fours, breathing hard.

"Is she alive?" Jobber asked. All she could see was Alwir's back, his shoulders hunched as he leaned over the prostrate body. Alwir pushed against the middle of Faul's back.

"Come on, Faul," Alwir was saying, vigorously pushing and kneading Faul's back. "Help me turn her over, quickly!" Alwir commanded, and Lirrel and Wyer leaned down to turn Faul's unresponsive body.

Alwir wiped Faul's face and mouth clear of the mud and tipped her head back. He leaned his own face close and breathed into the open mouth. Twice, three times he tried. Each time he stopped and looked back at Faul, waiting. Still nothing. He leaned again, blowing air into Faul, watching the gentle rise and fall in her chest.

Then Faul spluttered, groaning, and her back arched with a sudden racking cough.

"Quick, turn her over again!" Alwir shouted. They turned her over to her stomach again as Faul began to retch mud and water. Black liquid spewed from her mouth and seeped from her nostrils.

Jobber's forehead sank to the ground between her hands as she sighed, relieved by the awful noise of Faul's retching. At least she was alive, the stupid banger.

Faul moaned, her arms drawn tightly across her chest. Jobber looked up again and saw that Faul was shivering violently, her teeth chattering like a pair of rapping spoons.

"We have to get her warm or she'll die!" Alwir said.

"We can't start a fire here. We've no dry wood, no tinder," Wyer answered.

Lirrel lifted Faul's shoulders from the ground and wrapped her arms around her. "Jobber, come here," Lirrel called. "Help me."

Jobber dragged herself up and moved slowly with apprehension toward Lirrel. She knew what Lirrel was going to ask.

"You can do it," Lirrel was saying, her pale moonlight eyes watching her steadily.

"You don't know that."

"You must try," Lirrel insisted.

Jobber knelt and dragged Faul's shivering body from Lirrel's arms. Jobber held her awkwardly, Faul's head drooping over her shoulder.

"If you don't try, she'll die," Alwir said gruffly.

"Bugger yourself, Alwir. You don't know what she's asking me to do," Jobber snarled back. "I didn't pull Faul from the muck just to peel the skin from her with fire." She paused, turning to Lirrel. "Like I done to Ratcatcher," she added.

"I'll help you," Lirrel said, pulling her flute from her pocket. She sat down beside Jobber on the wet ground. "Concentrate on the music and don't think of the raging fire but of gentle warmth like the sun on your back—"

"Ale in your belly," Jobber said wearily.

Lirrel nodded. "Not all warmth scalds." She lifted the flute to her lips and began playing. Jobber clutched Faul tighter to stop the violent shivering. Faul was wet and cold, and both of them smelled like a damp grave. Jobber's red hair, matted with mud, hung around Faul's face.

The flute breathed, a sweet clear sound. Its voice pierced the gloomy dark of the marsh, cutting through the mist like the first promising rays of sun. Jobber closed her eyes and imagined she held up a glass of Fran's brown ale to the sun, seeing the light sparkle in the amber-colored liquid. She imagined its taste, thick and warm in her throat.

The flute changed its song, the notes deepening as if sun was lifting itself from the edge of the horizon, rays of brilliant gold and red spreading across the water. Jobber sighed at the song and felt a flush rise to her cheeks. A breeze swept across her and she could have sworn the breeze that touched her face was dry. It was strange. Jobber knew that she sat, cold and wet with mud, lost in a marsh that was shrouded in mist. And yet as she imagined it, heard it in the sweet voice of Lirrel's flute, the world became different to her senses. For all of it, she might have been anywhere else, sitting warm and dry. She could see spangles of golden sunlight bouncing off the planks of the *Marigold*, or herself sitting on the stone wall of Market Square, her eyes half-shut as the heat of summer collected around the stalls, wilting newly picked flowers and turning the fresh bread stale.

Jobber became dimly aware that the others now huddled close to her. She could feel the narrow ridge of Lirrel's spine as they rested back to back. Alwir and Wyer crouched on either side of her. Faul's shivering had quieted and she was becoming pliant and relaxed in Jobber's arms. Jobber laughed softly, seeing herself shaped by Lirrel's song into a hearth fire, bringing them warmth out of the cold night.

As it happened at Fire Circle, power bloomed from deep within her like a rose of fire. The petals were opening, a rich burnished red, and the heart of the fire was pure and blazing white. Jobber stopped it, afraid the opening flower would bring too much heat. Lirrel's flute played a gentle encouragement, drawing the warmth out and wreathing the rose of Jobber's power in a fine smoke.

Jobber breathed and the rose flared bright red. Heat glistened on her skin and crackled with sparks through her hair. She concentrated hard to control the ripening fire and temper it to her need. The petals responded, folding inward to become a fiery bud, burning evenly and steadily, its warmth never diminishing. Jobber heard Alwir's long sigh, like a chilled man standing at last before the warmth of a fire. Jobber looked down into Faul's sleeping face, for once peaceful without its stern expression.

"Lirrel," Jobber whispered.

The music stopped, but not the gentle warm wind that had gathered about them.

"Hmm?" Lirrel answered sleepily.

"I can do it," Jobber said with amazement. "I can control it."

"Ahal, Jobber, this time you have."

Jobber frowned suddenly. "Lirrel, what of Harral?"

Jobber felt Lirrel shake her head.

"He's crossed over into the Chaos, Jobber. I can not 'hear' him anymore."

"Shit," Jobber swore. "Do you think—"

"Sleep, Jobber," Lirrel interrupted. "We will all need it if we are to survive tomorrow. There is still a long way to travel."

And before Jobber could protest, Lirrel had begun playing her flute again. Its low voice carried across the marsh, settling on the branches like the soft flutter of wood doves. Alwir curled beside her, his chin tucked in the corner of his arm, and his legs drawn up close. Wyer leaned his broad back against Jobber's shoulder while his head drooped to his chin. Jobber relaxed her hold on Faul as Faul settled herself more comfortably on Jobber's lap, her head turning to find a softer spot on Jobber's thighs. Lirrel's song gradually stretched into longer repetitive passages, the notes rolling over and over each other until at last Jobber was lulled into sleep.

Chapter Three

"*What* do you figure it means?" *Slipper asked, screwing his* face to see if the black wiggles on the page might not make more sense that way.

"Trouble. That's all it is," Kai answered him, and propped her elbows on the table. Her large dark eyes focused on the writing and she frowned.

"What are we going to do on it?" Slipper asked, leaning back in his chair and setting his lighterman's hat on his head. He rubbed his hand over the beginnings of his first beard, his pale blue eyes distracted.

Kai looked sharply at him and he quickly dropped his hand. "Why do I have to have all the answers?" she said crossly. She twisted her black hair into a single knot at the base of her neck, yanking the hair back tightly in her annoyance.

Slipper smiled gingerly, his lips parting to display the crooked teeth that fanned out from either edge of his face. " 'Cause you're Flock leader, Kai, that's why."

"I ain't hardly got a Flock anymore," Kai said testily. "I got this place!" and she threw her arms out, gesturing to the front room of the teahouse. She caught sight of her reflection in one of the huge brass urns and realized what an odd pair the two of them made. They were snitches, better suited to life on the street, but now they held the deed to the Grinning Bird, and suddenly they were part of Beldan's propertied. Kai was a thin woman, still young in years, though made older by the harsh life of the street. Her profile sloped from a high forehead into a pointed nose and then disappeared in a very small chin. Her eyes were large and black beneath two finely arched brows. Her neck was unwashed and skinny, but she carried her shoulders and head erect. Across from her Slipper slouched in his chair, his gangly legs cluttering the space beneath the table and never failing to bump the table, spilling the tea every time he shifted in his seat. He wore a black coat at least one size too large for him that accentuated the pale skin of his cheeks now covered with a light down. The blue eyes studied Kai seriously as one long finger stirred slowly his cup of cooling tea. Behind them, water bubbled quietly in huge brass urns that from time to time emitted small puffs of steam. The glass windows had several large cracks on their surface and the front door now hung at an odd slant, all of which Kai thought was little enough damage considering that most of the city near Fire Circle had been either flattened or burned out during the massacre. The Grinning Bird had done all right, and when she and Slipper had opened the door the first time after the riots, knowing it was their place now, Kai had sighed with relief.

It made a fair change from the old days when she lived with her Flock the Waterlings in the tunnels beneath the streets of Beldan. Kai was the bastard child of a poor Oran housemaid and a Reader father. She had inherited the Reader's sight that let her Read the magic aura crowning the heads of Oran children cursed with the old magic. She had searched and found them among the street poor. Gathering them into a Flock, she sheltered them in the safety of the dark tunnels below. They had survived like bats, venturing at night to pick the pockets of wealthy drunks. That was all changed now. Except for Slipper, her Flock was scattered, having fled with Orian to the Avadares mountains just before the massacre of Fire Circle. There was still comfort in Slipper's companionship and in a bed that no longer smelled like the rotting straw of the tunnels.

But Kai's relief quickly turned to frustration. Zeenia had willed Kai the Grinning Bird as she lay dying in the street. "Keep it open to the vaggers," she had asked, "and help them." Kai shrugged angrily, wrapping Zeenia's old black shawl tighter around her bony shoulders. She had thought it would be easy.

After all Zeenia herself had seemed a crazy enough sort and even she had managed to keep the shop open, the tea always hot and food always available. I'm a smart dell, Kai told herself, I can figure this dig out in no time. But inside of two weeks Kai had learned that smart on the street didn't always count for much in the shop. Twice she and Slipper had been cheated out of money because of not being able to read the bill of goods. The Grinning Bird was running low on everything and everything was scarce now since the massacre—fresh water, bread, blankets, even tea. Kai had tried to understand Zeenia's account book, tried to keep track of what was owed to the Grinning Bird, but she had not been able to manage it. The Silean Guards had come three times, and each time it had cost her money and supplies. They had written a script for what they took, but she had no way of knowing its value or where to use it to replenish her meager supplies.

And then today yet another order had come. All she had understood from what the Guard was saying was that it was different from the orders that had come before. She had accepted the papers from the Guard, afraid to let on that she had no idea what it was asking of her. She merely nodded at him and, with as much bravado as she could muster, told him to come back later after she'd a chance to study it over. The Guard had hesitated, but Kai shooed him away, just as if she were any respectable Beldan shopkeeper. It had worked for the time being, but the Guard would be returning.

"Frigging shit," Kai swore, and slapped a palm over the paper. Slipper jumped at the sharp sound. "I can Read the power in a child, pick them right from under the noses of those high-class Readers, but I can't make sense of the words on a piece of paper. A Reader that can't read and that's gonna land us back in the street."

"The vaggers will help us," Slipper answered confidently. "You'll see."

"In case you haven't seen, there ain't any vaggers in Beldan just now. They all scuttled out of the city after the massacre, and smartly so, I might add. Have you seen the way the butcherboys are going round, gathering up anybody standing idle in the street?"

"Yeah, I seen it," Slipper said glumly. "They picked up Flea yesterday in Market Square."

"That old bugger?" Kai said angrily. "What was he doing?"

"Same as usual, begging with that withered hand of his out. The Knackerman come by, pointed her finger, and whist—" He whistled between his teeth. "The snitch is gone now. Ain't no one heard a word of him, so you know he didn't just get taken off to Pirate House to work. Word on the street is everyone that gets picked up goes under."

"And we'll be joining them soon if I can't figure this frigging bit of paper out." Kai pushed back her chair and walked to the cracked window. She rubbed against the glass, taking care not to cut herself on the uneven surface. Peering out, she saw the other shops of Twopenny Street, many of them boarded over or braced with charred beams of wood. The cobblestone streets were cracked and bumpy and in one place a huge hole had sunk into the ground. Birds fluttered in the exposed beams of a burned-out shop that Kai knew once housed a smokehealer. She grunted at the cold humor of seeing the white and green standard that announced the smokehealer's trade hanging forlornly in front of the blackened building.

The chair behind her scraped as Slipper stood. She heard him stretch and then gritted her teeth as he cracked his knuckles. Getting ready to go out, she knew. That was another thing the Grinning Bird couldn't change. They were used to working the night hours, prowling the streets in search of an easy take. But now someone had to be always in the shop, ready to keep it open for whoever might need a place. And lately it had fallen on Kai's shoulders to remain inside while Slipper took the night air.

"You off then?" Kai asked without turning around.

"For a little bit."

"Keep a sharp eye out, you hear?"

"Always," he said. "And Kai?"

Kai turned from the window to face him where he hesitated at the door. She could see he felt guilty about going out, leaving her. But not guilty enough to stay, she thought, annoyed. "What?" she asked, more sharply than she had intended.

Slipper's face pinked and he ducked his head. "It'll be all right, I tell you. I can feel it. Trust me," and this time he faced her squarely and smiled. He buttoned his coat and cocked the lighterman's hat to one side. "Later, then."

"Yeah, later," Kai answered softly, and returned her face to the window. In the mist condensing on the glass Kai could just make out the shape of her narrow face. Light trapped in the water droplets made a halo of shimmering colors around the darker image of her face. Just like them, Kai thought with a sudden bittersweet longing, like the children with the old power seen through a Reader's eyes. How beautifully the light of their power shone; green for the earth elements, white for air, and blue, like the color of Slipper's eyes, for water. Kai touched a finger to the glass and watched the shimmering light disappear as the mist condensed around her finger to form a tiny rivulet of water.

A Reader who can't read, she thought sourly. She stared a moment longer at the street, hearing again Slipper's confident optimism. Maybe, she thought with a small start of hope, maybe there was something in the power that called one to another, answered the need in another. Slipper was a water element and came by most of his knowledge of the world from the information that fell like unwanted garbage, floating through the meandering waters of the river and tunnels. Perhaps, she sighed with resignation, it made sense that he should wander the night. For if they were to find help, he would know it before her. Kai turned away from the window and settled herself to washing the few dirty cups that had collected from the day.

In the stillness of night, the Fire Queen Zorah dreamed for the first time in two hundred years. As the nightmare gnawed the edges of her usually untroubled sleep, she twisted on the bed.

She saw herself standing in the west gardens of the old Keep. She could feel the sun shining warmly on her back and arms. She could smell the salt sea air and the dry fragrance of cedar trees. Wind lifted her coppery hair and blew it gently across her face. She heard the voices of her sisters, calling to her, and she turned, her hand reaching up to pull away the curtain of hair.

They approached her, climbing the parapet steps of pink and gray stone, smiling and waving. Fenni held up a handful of green rushes gathered from the riverbeds. In her brown face her white teeth were like little cubes of salt when she smiled. At her side Laile shook sand from her wet hair, the blond strands hanging limp and dark like flax. She shouted a greeting to Zorah and Zorah heard herself answer.

And behind them, traveling the stairs alone, was Huld. Her black hair was wreathed with flowers, but her face was somber.

A wintry smile flickered briefly and Zorah sensed its chill in the noon sun.

In the bright light they cast short shadows. Except Huld. Behind her fell a long black stain, spreading down the stairs. Huld raised her hand and Zorah saw the shadow rise like smoke, ominous and frightening. It spread its darkness over her sisters and they turned puzzled faces to the sun. Only Huld walked unafraid with her face of carved stone.

Zorah wanted to go to them but Huld's dark visage rooted her to the spot. She was afraid to approach. Fenni and Laile beckoned with their hands, and all the while as Zorah watched, the dark shadow condensed solid as a shroud around them.

No! Zorah cried out in her sleep. No, she would not go to them. She would not shelter beneath the blackness. She wanted only the light.

They reached out and touched her, pulling softly on her arms. But she panicked as the black shroud seemed to cloak her. Out of her terror the fire erupted, flames flashing wildly from her hands. She fought against the blackness and the world collapsed around her into a caldron of fire and thick black smoke. She heard Fenni scream shrilly, and after her Laile, writhing in agony. On the bed Zorah cried out in horror.

Her sisters were burning, trapped in a wave of fire, the flames transforming their skin brilliant red and then black. Their eyes rolled white and unseeing, their screams lost in the roar of the fire. Their charred bodies grew thin as wraiths, dissolving into twists of smoke. The threads of their released power exploded like thunder, and Zorah bowed under the crushing weight of Chaos. Water, air, and fire floundering in the howling winds of Chaos. In her sleep Zorah frowned. Where was earth? Zorah cried out. Where was Huld?

Zorah continued to spin like a child's top whirling in the flames, catching glimpses of a burning city. Black smoke belched from windows jagged with broken glass. Bodies lay in the roads and heaped in rooms where they had huddled against the dense smoke. Everywhere Zorah looked, death followed her. The skulls lying in fields turned their empty faces upward to mark her passing. But where was Huld?

Zorah searched through the countryside, and as she flew, twisting and turning in a smoldering column of fire, the world beneath her split and tumbled into crevasses.

And then she saw Huld waiting stark as a tower against the

rising mountains. Around her shoulders she wore a cloak of blackness. And on her face, mottled white and gray like granite, Zorah saw her wintry smile.

Huld! Zorah screamed, and black smoke blasted from her mouth. But Huld made no answer to Zorah. Instead the rumbling ground reared back clods of earth, and from rank-smelling gouges in the soil, skeletons pushed themselves free of the clay. They clamored toward Zorah, dancing in a tangle of white and gray limbs through the flames. Skulls with split grins and clacking teeth chattered in her face and bony fingers reached to pluck at her breast and arms. They circled her tighter, and tighter, and just beyond them she could see others climbing up from the ground, ready to join the dance. Zorah grew cold with terror. The column of fire faded, doused by her fear, and left her alone with the skeletons on the charred plains.

In her bed Zorah sat up moaning and held a hand before her face to ward off the hideous images. She pleaded for the skeletons to release her, but they laughed at her, the teeth chattering in mockery. Arms folded over her head, she shrank, crouching to the ground. She felt the earth shift beneath her, the soil yielding to her body, and a hand from beneath the wet clay reached and grabbed her ankle, pulling her down, down, down.

Moaning and shaking violently, Zorah woke to find herself clinging to the bed curtains, fighting to pull herself up on the length of gauze drapery. She whimpered, her breath coming in hard uneven rasps as the terror of her dream lingered. Dimly she realized she could not feel the trembling earth or hear the rattling of bones. The room was quiet and peaceful save for the muffled sounds of her own weeping. Zorah drew a deep, harsh breath and held it. Now she could hear the gentle crackling of wood in the hearth and the soft snoring of her young maid.

She released her breath and, at the same time, unwound her hands from the curtains. She passed a shaking hand over her damp brow, down her cheek, neck, and chest, where she stopped it, feeling the rapid beating of her frightened heart. She reached out, drew back the bed curtains, and stared apprehensively at the room.

Her sleeping chamber was dimly lit by a small fire in the grate, and though the ribbed ceiling was high and shadowy, the room was warm and comforting. Wooden chairs with gaily embroidered cushions rested by the hearth. Above the broad mantel an ancient tapestry showing a harvest dance rippled with life in the flickering firelight. Across the room Zorah saw her maid sleeping on a small wooden bed. The young woman lay on her back, one arm flung carelessly out of the bed and the sheets slipping to one side.

Zorah untangled her nightdress where it had entwined about her legs and stepped out of bed. She shivered when her feet touched the flagstones but more from the residue of fear than from cold. She went to the hearth, plucked a taper from a pewter vase, and then lit it from the hearth fire. She wrapped her fingers around the glowing candle and stared lovingly at the little flame. She turned then and sat at the small dressing table that held a broad mirror and an array of brushes and jeweled combs. She fitted the candle into a sconce and stared at her reflection in the glass.

She stroked her neck and smiled with satisfaction and relief. The arrow wounds had closed, healed without trace. No, she thought, neither age nor death would mar the perfect beauty of her face. She would never grow old. She would never die and lie buried beneath the soil like the skeletons of her nightmare. She still controlled the magic that made her eternal youth possible. She paused, thinking, as if listening to music played at a great distance. There was still something that disturbed the flow of magic. She could sense it in the odd shifting of power, hear it in the soft murmur of its motion.

"Madam?" came a soft voice from behind. "How may I serve you?"

Zorah glanced at the face of her waking maid reflected in the mirror. Not pretty, she thought, appraising the drowsy face. But in the maid's imperfect features, Zorah saw the true bloom of youth. There was no coldness or guile in the half-lidded eyes; her skin was soft and supple, innocent of experience. A dart of jealousy silenced the Fire Queen. Zorah picked up a brush with an ornate silver handle and gave it to the maid.

The maid curtsied and laid the bristles against the falling sweep of fire hair. The hair shimmered and crackled in the light, but the maid's gentle stroking calmed it. Zorah closed her eyes and tried to relax.

But she could not undo the terror of the dream. It haunted her, the images suddenly vivid behind her closed lids; the blackened corpses of the burned dead, Laile and Fenni, the mocking skeletons and the hand that tried to pull her down beneath the wet clay. Panic rose in her breast. The muscles of her neck and shoulders tensed, resisting the soothing rhythm of the brush. Zorah tossed her head and tried to shake the offending images away.

Then her eyes snapped open and she leaned into the mirror, staring keenly at herself. That girl at Fire Circle. Zorah had poured fire into her veins to destroy her but the girl had taken it, welcomed it as water to a parched man. But there were no fire elements left in Oran, Zorah insisted, even knowing the truth. That girl should not have existed and never with such power. Then Zorah shook her head slowly and sat back as unwelcome thoughts formed in her mind. It couldn't be, she whispered to herself. Yet it had to be. There was no one else besides Huld who could torment her with nightmares, no one else besides Huld who could create the destruction that this year's Firefaire had become. With evil deceit Huld had led her once again to the edge of Chaos. And she had sent the fire-haired girl as a warning, a message of her return. Zorah's body contracted, feeling again the icy hand that closed on her ankle. Huld was still alive, still working magic somewhere in Oran. There was no other explanation.

Hands braced on the dressing table, Zorah struggled to compose herself, to shove back the unwanted terror that skittered on her spine. She would turn the fear to hate, turn Huld's knife back on her. She would use the strands of the knot to find where Huld was hiding and destroy her.

At the mirror, Zorah hesitated, afraid after so many years to touch Huld's mind, to feel its sharp pull against hers. She became agitated and her hair began to heat, filling the chamber with a sharp, metallic smell. The maid dropped the brush as its handle, grown hot from the firehair, seared her palm. The maid stepped back, afraid of the angry swirling hair that snapped with blue electric sparks.

She must use the Queens' quarter knot. She must know if the old threads still held life! Zorah closed her eyes and concentrated. She let her mind wander in darkness, searching for the fragments of the shattered knot that had once bound them together as Oran's Queens. As she drifted, she sensed the deep wound of her loneliness, the long years of isolation. She saw the strands floating in the distance and in her mind she moved toward them.

Interwoven were two broken strands, their ends frayed and ragged. Fenni and Laile. Zorah's own remained taut and firm, stretching like a thin cord into the infinite darkness. And twisted loosely around it was Huld's strand, slack and lifeless.

Zorah frowned at it and reached to pluck it away from her own strand. As she touched it, it hummed with life and the coil of thread tightened like a noose. It burst into life, throwing off showers of verdant green sparks. Zorah gasped as its fierce strength sucked her beneath the undertow of a vast whirlpool. She felt herself tumbling and turning over and over as she was dragged by Huld's brightly colored strand.

"Come, little sister," a ghostly voice whispered. "Release us!"

Zorah writhed and fought against the driving current. She clung to her own strand as a lifeline, reaching hand over hand to pull herself free of the undertow.

"NEVER, HULD!" she screamed in answer. "Why didn't you die with the rest of them?" Zorah summoned her rage and sent it hurtling along the twinning thread of Huld's strand. "I shall destroy you, Huld!" she bellowed to the ghostly voice. The firehair lashed out in fury. The air around Zorah exploded with fire, heaving the maid against the wall and engulfing her in a hot static charge of blue flame. Dimly Zorah heard the maid scream as if from a far distance.

"Huld!" Zorah cried along the strand. "You will not win! I shall! I shall remain, forever."

Abruptly the pulling stopped and Zorah, startled by the release, felt herself tossed backward. Her mind wavered, lost in vertigo. She clutched her own strand, held it as it steadied her. She shook her head, the confusion lifting, and saw that her strand lay still entwined by Huld's. It no longer dragged her, but she could feel within it the steady pulse of life. Wary and tense, Zorah waited for Huld to answer her challenge. But there were no more words spoken and Zorah could hear only a dry sound like the rustle of leaves in the autumn wind. And then she saw the other strands, as finespun as gossamer. The threads of a new Queens' quarter knot, pulled like spider's silk from the immense Chaos, not yet formed, not yet twined, but there nonetheless. So that was the game, Zorah thought, seeing the frail threads. Huld no doubt had not expected Zorah to see this. Well, just so, Huld, Zorah spat; two can play with pawns.

Wearily, Zorah released herself from the knot. She floated once more in the blackness, surfacing slowly to an outward consciousness. She stared, confused and dazed, when she saw the

ugly black streaks of charred and smoking wood on the surface
of her dressing table. The linen nightdress had disintegrated into
a fine ash that dusted her shoulders and knees. She could smell
the stinging odor of burning wood and something more.

She turned stiffly and saw the body of her maid where it lay
slumped against the stone wall. The youthful face was scorched
black, exposing stumps of gray bone.

"Death will not have me," Zorah murmured, shock and fear
making her numb to the horror of the corpse. She turned away
from the sight to look at the mirror. Smoke had left a smear of
greasy soot on the glass. She wiped it clean with her hand and
stared at herself. "I am Zorah, the Fire Queen. I am immortal.
And even the new Queens will not change that. I will use them
and they will be mine forever."

Oblivious to the destruction, the face stared back, white and
beautiful, surrounded by shimmering copper hair. Zorah spoke
again as if to give a promise to the youthful face. "I will fight
you, Huld, and I shall win, once and for all!"

In a small stateroom filled with heavy wooden furniture, the
Silean Regent to the Fire Queen, Silwa Re Familia made notes
to himself on thick white paper and sketched out a series of
battle plans. With sharp strokes of the pen, troops traveled along
dotted lines and arrows through Oran villages and, with heavy
black marks, slashed across the fortifications of Sadar. The massacre at Firefaire had given Silwa the opportunity he wanted. He
was no longer the obedient hound waiting to do the Queen's
bidding. No. Now things were as they should be; as military
regent, he was in command. And with the Queen grown more
withdrawn since the attack, he had done as he pleased, without
her interference.

He turned from the maps of Sadar and contemplated the re-
ports coming in on the state of Beldan. In the aftermath of Firefaire, the city was in complete disarray. The earthquake and
fires had done considerable damage to much of the city. People
petitioned the Keep daily for more supplies, food, and Guards
to protect the remaining portions of the city that had not suc-
cumbed to the destruction. Fire had gutted whole sections of the
city, mostly the poorer areas and the crowded Guild streets.
Ramshackle tents and shelters sprang up everywhere in the
streets, constructed out of whatever trash and remnants were to
be found. At the moment, however, the plight of Beldan's or-

dinary didn't concern him in the least. The miserable bastards who lived there should take it as a warning, a punishment for their actions at Firefaire, he thought coldly. He was more interested in seeing that the docks were repaired as soon as possible so as not to interrupt trade. He signed an order that allowed the building masters to conscript any able-bodied on the streets into service, laboring on the crumbling seawall and rebuilding the docks.

Fresh water was scarce, though it still found its way in abundant supply to the Silean neighborhoods and to the Keep. Food and water would have to be rationed among the poor, he thought quickly, as would building materials for new shelters.

But that would have to wait. Silwa rubbed away the light sheen of sweat on his forehead and tugged at his black beard. Other things lay pressing on his mind. There was military business to attend to even before Beldan was restored to a semblance of order. He intended to organize the local Silean militias throughout Oran. He wanted them to begin preparations for the attack on Sadar he was planning for late summer. They'd be furious with him, he knew that. For despite their Silean heritage, they had become farmers and would not take kindly to being forced into the military before harvest. Ah, but he had a proposition, he thought, smiling at his desk, a proposition they'd not be able to resist. He would allow them to wreak whatever havoc they wanted on Oran farms. By his orders they could confiscate Oran lands and Oran livestock and burn Oran fields. In so doing, Silwa could be guaranteed of their support, and he would isolate the New Moon, cut them adrift from the peasants. They would have to fight without supplies, without food. That would keep the New Moon hungry and weak. Then a quick campaign at Sadar and the task would be done.

He riffled through the piles of papers and found a copy of a letter he had written requesting more troops and arms from Silea. This was his second concern. If they arrived in the next two months, he would have troops ready for the attack on Sadar. Silwa frowned. The letter had not been easy to compose. He knew it had to strike just the right note or the Silean parliament would refuse the request. They were tight with the purse strings and Oran was a small consideration in their grander schemes. He needed to convince them of the importance of protecting their trading interests and their continued access to the western farmlands of Oran. The loss of profit would be damaging to the Silean coffers.

He pursed his lips angrily. They were bureaucrats, titled gentry, and moneymen who knew little of soldiering. The seeds of Oran rebellion would never bear fruit, he told them, if they acted quickly to destroy the New Moon. Despite his arguments he knew they would send him half what he asked for and expect twice as much in return.

It didn't matter, though, he thought. There would be enough for a campaign. At his desk he smiled and rubbed his cold hands. Out of habit he blew a warm breath on them to keep them supple and ready to draw the sword.

Old bones but he was finished, Shefek thought wearily as he circled Beldan's sky, his wide outstretched wings fanning over the dark alleys. He flew silently, the flapping noticeable only in the quiet gusting of wind. He glanced down, golden eyes catching the rare glow of torchlight.

It was worse than he had thought, looking into the rubble-strewn streets, his sensitive nostrils picking up the stench of decay. A dog howled at his passing, and Shefek resisted the urge to swoop on him and silence him with his talons. Hunger gnawed his belly. But not for that kind of meat. He lifted his body higher in the air, banked in the night's breeze, and headed for the Keep. He had to find Faul. He hoped he was not too late.

He moved swiftly in the air, his large body and massive wings blotting out the stars as he passed. He saw the parapets ahead and shuddered with relief. His limbs ached with fatigue. He needed to rest and eat. And then maybe find a new weapon. He wondered briefly if Faul would still be angry at him for that night. He chuckled to himself, the noise like the coughing of an owl. He'd robbed her of her gold, but not before he'd given her something else he considered more precious: his respect. But would she see it that way? he asked himself. Humans were always so unpredictable. Not like himself.

Shefek saw the crenellated wall of the Keep loom closer. His eyes widened, spying a small figure leaning against an opening in one of the gaps. He circled closer, recognizing the slender frame of a woman's body. He could just make out the short black hair that reached to the chin, brushed back by the breeze. Ah Faul, he thought growing warm, so you have waited for me after all.

He lifted his wings high into the air to break his speed, his neck arched as he reached forward with his taloned feet, seeking purchase on the rough stones. The shock of hard stone jarred his footing and set him flapping his wings wildly to remain upright. He felt embarrassed by so clumsy a landing, but there was nothing else to be done. His large body, at once elegant and graceful in the air, was awkward and top-heavy on land. He tottered from side to side, his beak snapping open and shut with annoyance, until at last he could stand reasonably straight. Folding his wings over his back, he raised his head in a dignified manner.

The woman at the wall hadn't moved. She merely stared back at him from the shadows.

Well, Shefek grumbled to himself, he hadn't expected her to approach him with loving arms, but she could have at least greeted him. Unless of course she was still mad. He shrugged his heavy wings; mad or not, this was important. He needed her help. Better get on with it.

Shefek closed his golden eyes and concentrated. He felt the slight wind that circled him, signaling his transformation. The wings shortened into arms, pinions into fingers. The head that crouched in the valley of his wings lifted, resting squarely on his neck and shoulders. His legs stretched and lengthened, the talons into feet. Shefek shivered again with the chilly wind and let his feathers grow together into the likeness of a cloth that covered his portly figure. The large vulturelike bird was gone, and there remained in its place a man dressed in the simple garb of a vagger. Shefek lifted a hand, touching experimentally the round knob of his nose, and then lowered his hand to smooth the wide ruff of a beard that covered his chin. Pleased with the changes, he straightened the robes over his stout middle and stepped down off the parapet wall to join the woman on the walkway.

"Ah Faul," Shefek said, moving slowly, not yet accustomed to traveling by foot. "Have you no words for me?"

The woman shook her head slowly, but made no other reply.

"My dear Faul, it can't be that you are angry?"

Still no reply. Shefek wondered if he had made a mistake to come here. But then he shook the thought away. She was the only one who could help him find the firehaired girl in this mess of a city. And it was essential that he find her soon, before things got worse. He had made the long journey from the north, counting on that, and he couldn't let her bad temper thwart him in his goal now. And besides all that, he was hungry and in desperate need of a meal.

He tried again. Opening his arms wide, he approached her. "Faul, my owlet, let us work out these differences and I promise not to take advantage of your womanly nature again."

It was only because the woman hesitated before she struck that Shefek was able to leap back out of the way of her slashing sword. All the same, the blade caught him across the upper arm, tearing through the fabric of his vagger's cloak and slicing open a gash. She stepped forward, terror evident on her young face, and Shefek, in one gasp of pain and fury, realized that the woman was not Faul, but another wearing the same black uniform of the Firstwatch, her hair cut in the same fashion. Shefek screeched angrily, a chilling cry that echoed off the stone walls. The woman crouched warily, and Shefek, wounded, took advantage of her confusion to scramble back onto the parapet. His wounded arm hung limp, throbbing with pain, but he could not wait. Already he sensed the woman gathering her courage to strike again. She raised her sword and he sprang into the open air, his injured arm dangling, his other arm outstretched, the fingers splayed as if to stop the onrushing wind.

His body changed as he fell, tumbling heavily into the wind. One powerful wing flapped and slowed the downward progress of his diving form. He skimmed across the tops of the buildings, teetering in the air and shrieking to the night wind. He glanced quickly beneath him, his eyes dazzled by the glittering sparks of torchlight reflected on Hamader River. He tried to control the mad veering of his body but instead slammed against the side of a balcony that appeared suddenly in the dark. With a final screech of pain, Shefek rolled in the sky and fell headlong into the Hamader River.

Water closed around his head, ice-cold fingers reaching under his feathers. He floundered, one feathered arm splashing wildly on the surface of the water. His wounded arm dragged him under, his beak barely able to stay above the waterline. And beneath him, he felt the strong pull of the current sucking him down. He tried one last desperate attempt to transform to a man, and cursed himself for his stupidity as the heavy weight of his vagger's cloak dragged him further under the cold, black water.

* * *

Slipper heard a splash. Not the small splash that comes from a stone tossed into the water, but the huge splash that comes from a man taking a dive into the river. Slipper knew that sound well. Listened for it, as did all the Waterlings. A man in the water was either out to kill himself or dead drunk. Either way, the Waterlings were quick to take advantage of the situation and relieve the hapless fool of whatever valuables he had on his person before his corpse made its way down to the Ribbons and the open sea beyond.

Slipper ran alongside the river, darting up a rickety bridge that spanned the river between Barley Row and Teegs Street. He peered down into the water, his eyes trained on the ripples. He listened for the noise of thrashing, and for the whispered messages that the river would send.

He saw the wing, flapping on the water, and the sharp point of a beak cutting the surface of the water. He straightened up, pushing back the lighterman's hat to stare in amazement. What bird was there that was so large as to have a span such as that? he asked himself. Something in the water spoke of urgency, hastened him in the rippling song of the splashes to help the struggling figure. Slipper hesitated, fearful of the long beak and the huge drenched wing. He sucked in his lower lip as he saw the figure slowly twirling in the water beneath the bridge. It had changed, and the wing had become a man's arm, the fingers reaching out to grab at something. Again the water urged him to help and this time Slipper didn't wait.

He ran alongside the river, trying to reach a boatman's landing before the drowning man. He saw it, a few yards in front of him. He sprinted down a flight of crumbling stone stairs until he was at the river's edge. A barge pole rested in its stocks along the wall and he grabbed it, grunting at its weight. He reached out with it into the water, praying that it was long enough to hook the man as he drifted by in the current. He felt it bump into the sagging figure and knock it away. Slipper cursed and tried again, reaching farther out so as to catch it and draw it closer. This time he was lucky and he felt the sudden drag on the end of the pole as it tangled into the folds of the drowner's cloak. The water continued to plead with Slipper, pushing against the drowner as if desiring not to be the cause of his death.

Slipper managed at last to bring the body alongside. He reached down and turned it over. It was a man, all right, and he was still breathing. Slipper dragged him up by the fabric of his cloak, pulling him slowly onto the hard stone of the landing.

When he was done, Slipper sat down heavily and, breathing hard, eyed his catch.

The near drowner was an elderly man with a thick fringe of gray beard. He'd long hair as well, black with the damp and lying in snarls around the broad face. Where was the bird? Slipper asked himself as he looked over the man. He was certain he had seen a bird. Like a giant hawk. Slipper glanced back into the water, wondering if the bird had come with the man and now was drowned. But the water was quiet, breathing soft sighs of relief as it murmured to itself in the current. There was nothing else there. Only this one.

The man groaned and reached a hand to his arm. Slipper looked and realized the man was injured. Through a tear in the fabric, he saw the gash, blood pooling with water beneath the man's shoulder.

"Come on, old duff," he said huskily to the man. "Got to get you to Kai. See if she can fix you up."

"Wait," the man replied, and Slipper was surprised by the deep timbre of his voice, sounding stronger than the elderly body suggested. "The Bird," the man said.

Slipper shook his head apologetically. "Sorry, duff. I saw your bird go down, but couldn't find it nowhere in the water." He bent down to help the man up.

"No," the man said, shaking his head slowly. "Take me to the Grinning Bird."

Slipper smiled widely. "That's it, old duff. That's where we're off to." He ducked under the man's good arm, bracing him under the shoulders. The man's feet dragged behind, moving with unsteady steps, but Slipper carried him aloft and set a determined march for the Grinning Bird.

"Kai!" Slipper shouted. "Kai, open up, damn it!"

"Wretch," Kai swore at the dishes. Her arms were elbow-deep in soapy water. "I ain't a servant. Open it yerself, I'm busy."

"Z'blood, Kai, open the frigging door!" Slipper's voice sounded urgent. Kai turned sharply, wiping her hands quickly on her apron. She glanced out the window and could just make Slipper out through the thick glass, his shoulders bowed beneath the weight of another man he was dragging.

"Z'blood," she swore, and yanked the door open. The pair staggered into the room and Kai barely had enough time to catch the old man before he slid off Slipper's shoulder and onto the floor. "Here now," she barked, her arms suddenly straining with the unexpected weight of the sagging man. "Here now, help me get him to the back room. Come on then," she shouted at Slipper. Slipper's face was white, showing the strain of carrying the man home. He was breathing hard, gasping like a fish. Still he managed to take ahold of the man's cloak, and between them, they dragged the man into the back room and rolled him into Kai's bed.

Water and blood instantly soaked the sheets. Kai looked him over quickly and then glanced over her shoulder at Slipper. He was wavering on his feet, his clothes wet. "Go on," she ordered, "get out of those wet things there and wrap up in a blanket. Get some hot tea into you. I'll call you if I need anything."

Slipper nodded dully and stumbled out of the room.

Kai turned her attention back to the man lying in a bedraggled heap on the bed. "A vagger," she said out loud, noting the brown robes. "Come on then," she said softly to the man, "let's fix that gash."

Kai started to undress the man, and then stopped when he groaned and his uninjured arm thrashed out, as if he thought he was still in the water.

"Easy now, easy now," Kai murmured, and tried again to remove the wet robe. "You're safe enough." She managed to get the uninjured arm out of the sleeve and frowned, not a little surprised at the pronounced musculature of the bare arm. You don't get arms like that begging, she thought to herself. And then she started to remove the sleeve from the other arm as carefully as possible so as not to cause further pain.

She tugged at the sleeve and the man on the bed groaned. Kai bit her lower lip and pulled again. The robe fell free from the shoulder and Kai saw the white skin streaked by the bloody gash. She had the robe nearly off when the man began to thrash on the bed, crying out in a hoarse voice. Kai went to lay a hand to his shoulder to quiet him. His eyes snapped open and she gasped, startled to see the pupils shining like flat golden disks. He screeched at her, his neck straining forward, and the lips of his mouth closing into a long sharp beak.

"Z'blood!" Kai screamed, and jerked backward as his arm sprouted long gray and brown feathers, speckled with blood. "Z'blood! What is it?" Kai screamed.

Half man, half bird, and driven with pain, the creature on the bed thrashed frantically. "Slipper! Slipper!" Kai called as the huge wing batted her. With both arms over her head she shielded herself, terrified of the screeching and the golden eyes.

"Frigging all," Slipper said as he stood in the doorway, his mouth agape at the scene. He had a blanket draped around his shoulders.

"Do something, for shit's sake. You brought it home!" Kai shouted at him.

Slipper frowned and then snatched the blanket from his shoulders and held it before his face. He walked into the room, using the blanket like a shield, and when he came close to the bed, he dropped the blanket, falling with his weight to pin the bird-man down. Slipper swallowed hard, his Adam's apple bobbing as the face shifted back and forth between the likeness of a predatory bird and the old man.

"Oy," Slipper said, feeling the terrified struggling of the injured wing. "Oy, you're at the Grinning Bird, man. Let us help you, for pity's sake."

Beneath the blanket, the creature stopped struggling. The old man's face appeared again. His skin was haggard and as gray as his beard. But the eyes were a clear amber, and he blinked slowly before speaking. Slipper felt the man relax.

"Shefek," the man said weakly.

Warily Kai came closer. "Your name?" she asked.

The man closed his eyes again and Kai tensed, waiting for the violent metamorphosis to begin again. But he merely nodded in agreement.

"Zeenia?" He opened his eyes asking the question.

"Dead," was Kai's flat reply.

"And you?"

"Kai, new owner of the Grinning Bird."

"Look here," Slipper said earnestly. "You're among friends. We want to help you."

The old man sighed and cast a half-lidded glance at his injured shoulder. "Stupid. Getting old," he muttered to himself. Then he sighed deeply. "Let me rest—"

"But that gash. It'll need stitching," Kai protested. "And dry clothing."

Shefek shook his head. "Rest only. And food. A lot of food."

Kai rocked back on her heels. "One thing we ain't got much of. Suppose it's particular?" she whispered to Slipper; there was always the odd bit of horse meat to be stolen from the knackerhouse. Slipper shrugged.

"One more thing," Shefek said weakly.

"What?"

"Brandy. As many bottles as you can get."

"Z'blood," scoffed Kai. "Now I've heard it all. Next you'll be wanting gold coins to suck on."

"Later," Shefek said, opening one eye. His lips twitched with a smile. "Later." He closed his eyes again and seemed to slip into a deep sleep, his chest rising and falling evenly as a scratchy snore issued from his throat.

Kai twisted her long hair into a tight knot and then shook her head in irritation. "What have you brought home, Slipper?" she asked.

Slipper grinned and scratched his cheek. "Just what we needed, Kai," Slipper reached across and picked up one long tapered feather from the bed. In the lamplight the feather's shaft glowed a creamy white. "Oh, yeah"—he nodded to her—"just what we needed, I'll wager."

"I hope you're right," Kai said, and went into the main room to make herself a bracing cup of strong sweet tea.

Chapter Four

Shedwyn was dreaming of barn cats at the farm. They were lying nestled close to her, their fur warm, the low rumbling of their purring vibrating in her ear. Then suddenly they scattered and she felt a cold draft snake across her arms and back. She frowned in her sleep and drew her arms tighter over her chest, trying to hug the fleeing warmth.

She heard a noise like a hard stream of water splattering against the leaves. Her eyes opened and she saw the thick reddish leaves of a gacklebush growing near a clump of pale green maiden's woe. The splashing noise stopped and was followed by a soft rustling.

Someone nudged her. "Shedwyn." She didn't move, needing time yet to collect her waking thoughts. The voice belonged to Eneas; the warmth she had dreamed of was not cats, but the closeness of his body next to hers, and it had been the sound of him urinating that woke her. She blushed, embarrassed.

"Shedwyn," Eneas repeated, gently nudging her. "Are you awake?"

Shedwyn rolled over carefully and squinted up into Eneas's face. He looked different to her: the usual confident smile was gone, his yellow hair was tangled in knots, and mud streaked his forehead. Even his blue eyes were a bleak gray in the dawn's

light. He was tired and his expression uncertain. Shedwyn felt
a pang of sadness mingled with guilt. She gave him a smile and
reached a hand to his cheek. Pain stopped her and she grimaced
at the tearing sensation in her neck. With her movement, the
blood that had clotted along the welts tore open.

Then Shedwyn remembered the beating, Neverin's face white
with rage as he drove the riding crop over her prone body; the
Silean Guard unbuttoning his trousers in anticipation. And then
Huld's Throne exploding in a shower of jagged rock.

"Here," Eneas said, and with an arm beneath her shoulders
helped Shedwyn to rise. She moved her body slowly, fearing
every motion. She clung to his arm as she stood, her aching
joints stiff. Her back and shoulders burned, her neck afire with
new pain. The muscles of her legs ached and she shivered in the
cold morning mist. The ground undulated beneath her feet and
she groaned, light-headed with the rush of pain.

"Shedwyn, what can I do?" Eneas asked, brushing away a
leaf that had caught in her hair. He took off his jacket and
wrapped it carefully around her shoulders. It smelled like damp
leather and reminded her of the cows.

Shedwyn looked around, feeling bent and crippled. "Where
are we?" she asked softly. Her lips were swollen, her tongue
thick.

"Don't you know?" Eneas said, concern tightening his voice.
"You led us here last night. We're somewhere in Soring Marsh."
He looked around anxiously. "Somewhere. But that's all I
know."

Shedwyn nodded, her thoughts consolidating as he spoke.
"Oh, aye," she answered, "Soring Marsh. It travels the length
of the river in a wide band. It's the safest place to travel for now,
until I get farther north. It'll be hard for them to track me in
here."

"Us," Eneas corrected.

"What?"

"Hard to track us," he repeated. "I'm coming with you."

Shedwyn looked at him and felt the tears brimming in the
corners of her eyes. "Eneas, I'm sorry, I never meant for you—"

"Of course you didn't." He gave a dry laugh. "Neither did
I. But when I saw you, when I saw them hurt you—" He paused,
his lips pursed tightly. He shook his head and smiled grimly. "I
don't regret what I did." The smile froze and his expression

shifted, becoming taut. "Unless, that is, you don't want me here."

Shedwyn put her fingers to his lips. "I am glad of your company. Very glad, indeed," she answered honestly. He breathed a small sigh and she felt the warm air on her fingers. "But," she added, and saw him stiffen, "but it will not be easy."

He shrugged it away. "I can't return to the farm. I killed a Guard."

"Yes, you can," Shedwyn insisted. "You're a Silean. The law is more lenient for you. The punishment won't be harsh, and most likely Re Ameas will protect you."

"No," Eneas said angrily. "I will go with you."

"Eneas, if you go, it must be for other reasons than me," Shedwyn said firmly.

"Isn't love a good enough reason?"

"For me, yes. But not the New Moon. I don't think they will be so trusting. You may have to fight people you know, maybe your own brothers. Can you do that out of love for me alone?" Shedwyn stared at him earnestly. "You may come to hate me when you learn how much you have lost from your world by joining mine."

Eneas was silent as he considered her words. He stared tiredly out at the mist that veiled the craggy trees of the marsh. Shedwyn watched him, not wanting him to go and yet not wanting to be the reason he stayed. When his eyes returned to meet hers, they were a solid blue. A new crease etched his smooth forehead. "I'm coming with you," was all he said.

Shedwyn sighed quietly and nodded. "Then there is no time to waste. They will have the dogs out by now and I wasn't very careful last night about covering our tracks." Shedwyn began searching the ground, taking a few tentative steps away from Eneas.

"What are you doing?" Eneas asked.

"I need a certain kind of moss, sunwort. It's dark green, flat stems, and with little yellow fruits. It usually grows near maiden's woe. That plant there, the one with all the tiny leaves."

"Maiden's woe?" Eneas asked as he bent to look at the base of another clump of the growing plant.

"Hmm," Shedwyn replied, distracted. "A tea of the leaves will separate a maiden from her shame."

"What sort of shame?"

Shedwyn leaned back on her heels to regard him for a moment. "A baby."

"That's awful," Eneas said, frowning.

"Oran women don't use it much. Most babies are welcomed, even those born on the wrong side of the bed. It's Silean women ask for it. Many have come down from the big house to the shacks just to get this tea from Old Torin. She always told 'em it weren't right, but they always took it anyways."

"Who?" Eneas demanded, suddenly curious. "Which women?"

"None of your business," Shedwyn said tartly. "I figure if you Silean men got your women confused into believing it's a shame to have babies, then you don't deserve to know."

"It's not a shame so much as it's impractical. How's the land to be divided when you got bastards running about everywhere? It's for their own protection, you know. A man will protect his own in the bonds of marriage, but he's got to know for sure it is his own."

"Spoken like a true Silean lord!" Shedwyn scoffed angrily.

"And I thought I was learning how to talk like a peasant," Eneas snapped in reply.

"You'll have to do more than learn the talk. You'll have to learn the life. Orans don't hold the land in so tight a grasp as do Sileans. And neither are women and children servants to the men who own it."

"Because Oran men are nowhere to be seen. They're off in Beldan fending for themselves, or drunk on Mother's Tears in some hidden dale. They leave their women and children behind to hire on the farms. Cock's bones, Shedwyn," Eneas swore, kicking a gacklebush, "look to yourself. Where was your old man that your mother and you had to come begging at the farm? I'd never let that happen to you."

"You wouldn't have much choice if you were dead," Shedwyn answered flatly, facing him squarely, fists resting on her hips. "My father was killed by a Silean that said he'd stolen fallen wood from the master's land. It was Oran land, commonwoods, used by Oran farmers for hundreds of years. Then one day it wasn't Oran anymore, but Silean, and my father was hanged, right there in the yard, from a tree I used to climb."

"I'm sorry," Eneas mumbled.

Shedwyn continued talking, her eyes glistening black. "They wouldn't let us take down the body. He stayed there for a week, maybe a tenday. My mother sat in the house by the window and keened. But *I*," she whispered fiercely, a hand tapping against her chest,"I had to go out to milk the cows, and every day I passed him hanging like some rotting fruit from the tree. Then one day I walked out and he wasn't there. When I looked about, I found my mother in the back of the house, covered with mud and stinking like a corpse. She'd done it, all right." Shedwyn stared deeply at Eneas, the welts a vivid red along the brown skin of her neck. "She'd cut him down herself and buried him. And for that, they took our farm and sent us out on the road."

Eneas closed his eyes and his head drooped, his chin grazing his chest. He rubbed his hands slowly on the length of his thigh as if to rub away a stain. "I didn't know," he said.

"It's what I'm telling you, Eneas. You don't know. It's not only the Readers I run from, it's the Sileans as well. Your own people. And if you listen well, you'll hear my story over and over again from a hundred other Oran mouths. Eneas," Shedwyn said urgently, "I'll ask you again: are you sure you want to come with me?"

Eneas bent, his knees giving a little crack. He carefully removed a small pillow of green moss from beneath the delicate fronds of maiden's woe. He stood up slowly, picking off the bits of dried leaves from the moss. Then he handed it to Shedwyn and she saw the stubborn set of his jaw, the steady blue gaze of his eyes. "Is this it?" he asked.

"Aye," she answered, and took the moss from him. He remained standing, watching her, his arms dangling at his sides. Shedwyn scooped up a handful of water from a puddle and began to crush the moss. When it was like a muddied paste, she gingerly pressed it to the welts on her neck. She winced with the pain, her shoulders raised. Eneas came closer to help her.

"Let me do that," he said. With gentle fingers he patted the moss along her neck. She watched him, his face concentrating on his task. She gasped sharply at a dig of pain and then smelled the fading scent of lavender on his shirt and the peppery odor of his sweat. "Shedwyn," he said as she closed her eyes. She opened them, and stared back into the resolute blue eyes. "I may have been born to the Silean manor, but I live here in Oran. My life, my future is here, not in Silea, a country I'll never see. I must learn what it is to be Oran. But," he said, the steady gaze never leaving her, "will you stand by me? Can you in your Oran heart and with your fierce Oran pride defend me, a Silean-born, to the New Moon?'' His eyes raked her face, as if fearing signs of hesitation.

Shedwyn shivered, realizing what Eneas asked. It was not only Eneas who faced the challenge of loving her, it was she, too, who had to share in the consequences of his decision. Defend him to the New Moon, protect him from those whose hatreds ran deep against any Silean. The words echoed in her head and she wondered if, when it came time to do that, she would be able to speak with a clear mind. And if still they didn't accept him, what then? Shedwyn's stomach contracted uneasily, her heart beating more rapidly. She reached up and brushed away the strands of blond hair that stuck to his cheek. The feel of his hair, even wet and bedraggled with mud, was soft and silken. Then she smiled at him, feeling the warmth of his love, his need for her as great as her need of him. That mutual need would be enough to see them through it all. ''I will,'' she answered simply.

He bent his head to her, kissing her on the mouth, lightly at first and then more deeply as she folded into his arms. And as she heard the steady beating of Eneas's heart against her chest, Shedwyn answered him again, this time with the conviction of her embrace.

Jobber gasped, waking with a start as her body was seized by a violent twitch. ''Z'blood,'' she swore, shaking her head, quickly trying to make sense of her surroundings. It was always like that. Sleeping just deeply enough to let the body rest, but never so deeply as to trust the oblivion of sleep. She always came awake as if stabbed, fists clenched, waiting for the first assault of pain. Sometimes it was from the swift jab of a Silean Guard kicking her out of the trash she'd nestled in. Sometimes it was another snitch, angered to find her in his territory. And sometimes, if she was lucky, it was the ringing pain of a hangover. A few seconds was all she had to gauge her surroundings and raise her defenses.

But as Jobber stared out at the unfamiliar scene, she frowned. Gray mist drifted through the trees, and try as she might, the shadowy trunks and looming branches refused to merge into the likeness of any Beldan street she knew. It was quiet, the rustling of small animals strangely muffled in the dampness.

''Frigging shit,'' Jobber whispered as she then recalled how far from Beldan she was. ''What a soggy mess this is,'' she said to the dreary marsh, eyeing with disgust the pools of muddied water, brightened only by the light green of duckweed. A pain in her belly made Jobber realize that her bladder was uncomfortably full. She looked around uneasily and recognized the sleeping figures of Alwir and Wyer. Alwir's head rested on one arm, the other arm folded over his face to keep out the light. Wyer had curled his body into a solid shape, the flat black of his cloak making him seem like a boulder rising from the mud. Jobber turned her head and saw Faul and Lirrel lying side by side, like two spoons nestled together with Lirrel at Faul's back. Lirrel had one arm thrown over Faul's side as if to protect her. Faul was covered with dried mud, and only her face had been wiped free of the ocher-colored mud.

"Strange lot we are," Jobber mumbled, and stood uncertainly in the marsh. She turned around slowly, not wanting to wake anyone but not wanting to move from where she stood. The need to urinate became stronger, but she held back, not knowing which way was safe to walk. Supposing she found another puddle of quicksand. She shivered thinking of the cold mud and of Harral, drifting somewhere beneath its thickened surface. She took a step toward a stand of sturdy-looking plants.

"Jobber, wait," someone whispered, and Jobber's shoulders hunched at the sound.

She turned and saw Lirrel's face peering at her from over Faul's back. "I'll come with you."

"Nah, I'd go alone."

"Why must you be so shy?" Lirrel answered testily, standing up. Her brown face was sallow with fatigue and her eyelids swollen. In the early dawn her silvery eyes shone with a dull pewter light. "You can be so vulgar when it suits you, and yet a turtle in its shell about simple things."

"What's wrong with doing certain things alone, eh? You Ghazali are always doing things in herds."

"I've a riddle for you."

"Ah, come on, Lirrel, a bit early for it, ain't it?" Jobber said crossly.

"I won't let you go alone unless you answer it."

"Z'blood," Jobber grumbled. She didn't want anybody else waking up and deciding to join her. "You're a pain, you know."

Lirrel smiled smugly.

"All right then, let's have it. But be quick about it." Jobber could see Alwir stirring and Wyer had already straightened his legs, preparatory to waking fully.

"She drinks but never pisses," Lirrel said, and waited, head cocked to one side. The silver earrings shaped like crescent moons dangled lopsidedly in her black hair.

Jobber tried to think of an answer but the pain of her bladder made her impatient. "I don't know. What, what?" she asked angrily.

"A hen," Lirrel replied.

"A hen," Jobber repeated with irritation.

"You never see them piss," Lirrel said, laughing lightly. "Just like you."

"That's right!" Jobber snorted loudly. "I got better sense—"

"Ah, frigging shut up," Faul said in a cracked voice, "or I'll piss on the both of you." She groaned, a hand raised to her face. "I've a blasting headache and my mouth tastes like something died in it."

"Yeah, you did!" Jobber snapped angrily, and then stalked noisily through the bushes, her footsteps squelching in the soft mud.

Faul got up slowly, moving like an ancient crone. Dried mud cracked and peeled from her clothes. Her hair was matted with little clods of mud, hanging like beads. "Zorah's tits," she said softly, staring down, amazed at herself. "Last thing I remember is feeling the quicksand over my head." She looked up at the others, scanning them with a confused expression that rapidly grew more alarmed. "Where's Harral?"

Alwir sat upright and began slapping the mud from his trousers. "We lost him."

Instinctively Lirrel reached out and touched Faul's arm, but Faul jerked away and swore savagely.

"You tried, Faul," Wyer said, pushing back the matted tangle of his hair with his thick fingers. "You tried to get him out and that's how you wound up in there as well."

"Who pulled me out?" Faul asked sourly.

"Jobber," Wyer replied. "Went in after you and grabbed you out by the hair."

"Jobber," Faul repeated, shaking her head. "She hates the wet."

At the loud snapping of a branch, they looked up, faces tense and alert. Jobber reappeared, trudging through a gacklebush and swearing at the mist. She saw their sober faces staring back at her and her expression darkened angrily.

"Can't I take a piss without everyone knowing about it?"

Wyer and Alwir looked away embarrassed and Lirrel bent her head to hide the shadow of a smile. She made a pretense of being occupied by undoing her braids and combing her fingers through the snarled hair. Only Faul continued to watch Jobber's approach, the gray eyes mournful, her cheeks hollow in the dawn's light.

"Thank you," Faul said to Jobber, her voice gruff. "Thank you for pulling me out."

Jobber shrugged. "I owed you one. That settles the score at the docks. Sorry about Harral, though. Couldn't find him." Jobber raked out the last bits of dried mud from her hair. She caught sight of Faul's haggard but still-animated face. "Z'blood, Faul, you looked like a frigging corpse last night."

Faul was silent, but across her face the emotions flickered unevenly. Jobber saw the little twitch that rippled the smooth surface of her cheek. Faul exhaled and with an effort straightened her shoulders. "I owe you all an apology. I should have been more careful in leading you through the marsh. It's dangerous enough even for one who knows it as well as I. I chose haste rather than care."

"You were frigging daft!" Jobber shouted at her, angry at the sudden contrite expression on Faul's face. "You were running scared and blind like the rest of us. We might have all followed you into that shitting quicksand."

Beneath the streaks of mud Faul blanched white. Her hands closed in fists and Jobber saw her struggle not to strike out at her. Good, Jobber thought, be angry, Faul, you think better that way. Then Jobber frowned, disappointed as Faul lowered her head in resignation.

"You're right, Jobber," she said.

Jobber growled. "What a prime tweak you're being, Faul. Where's that Knackerman pride of yours? We're here ain't we? Most of us anyway. Gave those butcherboys the slip. It was you brought us here, even if you did go crazy. Harral, well, I ain't happy the mate's scaffered either, but he took his chances with the rest of us and you're only spitting on his corpse by turning into a sniveling wretch." Jobber felt her face grow pink with heat, the deep green eyes brightening with yellow flames. Faul saw it, too, and Jobber watched her spine grow rigid, her lips tighten into a surly frown. That's it, Jobber thought to herself as she saw the tension gather in Faul's angular frame. "Be your nasty self, Faul. You're more use that way."

Faul stepped closer to Jobber, driving the hard point of her chin toward Jobber's face. "You little bastard!" she whispered. Jobber saw the slate gray of Faul's eyes and felt the fury coiled in the woman's shoulders. Just beyond, Jobber could see Wyer and Alwir exchange worried glances.

"Maybe," Jobber answered slowly, her own gaze locked firmly on Faul's face. "But I know you, Faul. And your misery ain't worth half as much to me as your anger. You're a raver not a teary dell. Don't bend over for me."

Faul's lips parted as if to speak and then closed again. Jobber saw the edges of her mouth twist up in a dry little smile. She looked into Faul's eyes and saw that the hard gleam had softened. But the tension in her body remained, like a spring ready to snap. Faul gave a small nod of acknowledgment and then spun furiously on her heel.

"Let's get out of here," she barked, and choosing a path amidst the clumps of gacklebush, bramble, and green pools of duckweed, she started walking.

Alwir glanced thoughtfully at Jobber before turning and falling into step behind Faul. Lirrel brushed past Jobber, as always one hand squeezing her lightly on the shoulder. Wyer, still slapping the dried mud from his trousers, waited for Jobber.

"That's a fair thing you did," he said softly, falling into step beside her.

"Eh?" Jobber said absently.

"Rip out her pride with one hand and give it back with the other."

Jobber shrugged and smiled. "I know all about losing control. But it don't help to sit down and cry about it. And besides, she's our only way out of this slog."

Wyer laughed and clapped Jobber on the shoulder. His hand stayed a moment, feeling heavy and warm on her skin. Jobber stared up at him, puzzled by it. Wyer was looking at her, his square face pensive. Then he smiled, embarrassed, and removing his hand from her shoulder, studied the path before them.

Jobber sighed and looked down at the muddy footprints she was following. She wanted nothing more in the world than a beer, except perhaps two beers.

Chapter Five

Kai moved slowly between the tables, balancing in her arms a tray laden with food. She checked it over with a quick eye and grumbled to herself. It seemed like such a luxury for one person. There was a whole roasted chicken, which she'd managed to cook without burning, two loaves of black bread that Slipper had snitched off a cart, a thick wedge of hard cheese with only a little blue mold speckling its rind, and four apples, bruised, but otherwise good. All this for one creature, she sighed, thinking how at another time it might have fed all the Waterlings for a few days. Her hip bumped against a chair and the tray wobbled dangerously.

"Frigging shit," she hissed between her teeth as she watched an apple roll off the tray and go bouncing on the floor.

"Oy Kai," Slipper called, "have a wink!"

Kai ventured a quick glance over her shoulder and saw Slipper standing half in and half out of the front door, in his hands two black bottles of Oran brandy.

"Get in with that," she ordered, suddenly nervous. "Don't be seen waving it about, you fool."

The smile on his face faltered and he bolted inside, shutting the door with a kick of his heel. "It's all right," he answered crossly. "I bought it with sillers. All legal like."

"Where'd you get sillers?" she asked archly, turning her attention back to the tray. A second apple was rolling on the tray, threatening to join the other one somewhere under the tables.

"Off a drunk, where else?" he replied.

"Gonna get nabbed."

"Bah," he scoffed. "You're turning straight-fingered, Kai. Not me, though," Slipper said proudly. "I know what I am, and that won't change."

"Maybe you're right." Kai sighed, looking at the tray. "Too much work to being straight up and all. Wouldn't mind a bit of the tear right now. Up the river, just pole our luck, eh?" She smiled at him, her black eyes twinkling with merriment. Then a cough from the bedroom sobered her expression. "Come on," she said irritably. "Your guest is waiting."

As Kai entered the bedroom her nose wrinkled back at the sour odor. "Z'blood," she snorted as she put the tray down on a small table. "What's that stink, then?"

"Me, I'm afraid," Shefek replied, sitting up in the bed. "Part of the healing."

Kai frowned as she moved cautiously toward the bed. "Worse than the tunnels." She came beside the bed to inspect the wound on Shefek's shoulder. The old man was propped up, his long gray-black hair hanging in dirty matted clumps to his shoulders. In contrast his beard was a silvery color, the hair long and straight as it fanned thickly around his chin. His skin was pulled tight around the eyes, which were now brown, with only small flecks of ocher to suggest the golden eyes she had seen the night before. His nose seemed too large for his face, and though the rest of his complexion was a biscuit color, his nose remained ruddy. Too much drink, that, Kai told herself. "Let's have a look at your arm," she said, pulling back the covers.

Kai swore as she saw the wound, red and festering with quantities of light green pus oozing in the gash. Around it the flesh was discolored and swollen with vivid blotches of violet and blue. Red streaks reached across the lean chest and down the curve of his arms. The wound smelled strongly of rotting fruit.

"How'd this happen so fast?" she asked, holding a hand over her mouth to mask the worst of the smell.

Shefek gave a low sigh. "Not as quick at healing as in the old days. Takes a bit more power and there's precious little left of it."

"You should have let me clean it out for you last night," Kai said angrily. "You're gonna lose that arm. And if you're lucky, that's all you'll lose."

Shefek pulled the tattered ends of torn cloak over his arm. Stray feathers disengaged themselves from the folds of the tattered garment and one white feather floated lazily in the room. "I think not," he said confidently. "I shall be fine again. That is, if you brought me food."

"At least let me wash it," Kai insisted.

Shefek shook his head. "It takes care of itself. But I need food. And drink," he said, catching sight of the bottles in Slipper's hand. "Ah, good lad, bring those here to me."

Slipper brought the bottles over to Shefek, setting them on the bed.

"Do us a good turn, my lad, and open one of these beauties," Shefek said pleasantly, holding up his one arm while the other lay motionless, the slate-gray fingers resting on the covers. "Yes, yes," he murmured, "lovely."

Slipper's face pinked with embarrassment as he hastily opened a bottle and handed it to Shefek.

"Glass?" Kai asked.

Shefek shook his head, the yellow flecks in his eyes gleaming brighter as he lifted the bottle to his lips.

Kai and Slipper stared at one another in astonishment as the amber liquid poured in one continuous stream down Shefek's throat. It seemed he needed no air, no time to swallow as the contents of the bottle transferred into his open mouth. Only the soft gulping sounds and the slight rise and fall of his beard indicated that Shefek drank. Kai held her breath, letting it out with a loud exhale when Shefek finally released the bottle and set it down on the bed.

"It's empty," Slipper said in a shocked whisper. "Drained the whole frigging thing, he did."

Shefek gave a contented belch. "Good lad," he murmured. "Now for the other one."

"Ah, no, you don't," Kai snapped. "Not till you've answered a few questions. I'll not have you getting piss drunk and then just dying without so much as a thank you."

Shefek looked at her, his eyes hooded. "Ah, my raven," he said, "could I at least eat the meal you've worked so hard to prepare?"

"Yeah, well, that too," Kai replied gruffly. "Be nice, you know, on account I went to so much trouble."

She brought the tray of food over and set it on the bed. Shefek grunted and sat up straighter. The pallor of his skin was changing, becoming flushed, and his nose was now blooming like a rose. Whatever else he is, he's a frigging sod, too, Kai grumbled to herself.

Between thick fingers Shefek picked up the chicken by one leg and dug his teeth into the thigh. His lips smacked noisily as he ate, his tongue licking at the grease that accumulated on his lips. He cracked open the bigger bones, sucking out the marrow before crunching them delicately between his teeth. Kai felt her stomach churn and she sat down, repulsed and captivated by the thoroughness with which Shefek consumed the chicken. Nothing remained of the bird, not even the fatty triangular bit of its tail. Shefek sucked his teeth, teasing out the small fragments of chicken stuck between his teeth and making contented rumbling noises in his throat. When he was done, he licked his fingers and dried them off by stroking them through his beard.

"Tell me about Zeenia," Shefek said as he reached for one of the loaves of bread.

Kai shook herself, realizing that she had been staring with her mouth open. At the mention of Zeenia's name she felt a rush of sorrow. "She was killed like so many others at Fire Circle."

"Stabbed," Slipper added, "as she tried to free some of the New Moon from the noddynoose."

"What happened?"

Kai shrugged. "The same story, only bigger. The Queen made a bad guess of the crowd's mood. And the Sileans decided to call in the cavalry. Afore it was over, half of Beldan was on fire or falling down into the streets. And the Silean Guard was killing anything and anyone that was moving. Slipper and me found Zeenia dying not too far from here. She give us the deed to the Bird and told us to keep it open for vaggers."

"And why would she trust you to do that?" Shefek asked, staring hard at Kai.

Kai was silent, her expression turning dark. She twisted her black hair into a knot at the nape of her neck.

" 'Cause we're Waterlings," Slipper said boldly. He met Kai's angry stare. "I say we trust him, Kai."

"Good lad," murmured Shefek, looking pointedly at the other bottle of brandy. Slipper handed it to him and this time Shefek uncorked it himself with his teeth. "Well, my raven?" he said to Kai, waiting before he drank from the bottle. "Will you talk?"

"Will you?"

"When it's my turn."

"How 'bout you go first."

"Will 'it make you happy?"

"Probably not," Kai said irritably. "Inwit tells me that you're trouble from the beginning."

Shefek chuckled. "I'm nothing more than a challenge." He stared up at her again with his strange golden-flecked eyes. "Will you take that challenge?"

"I ain't never backed down from a thing in my life," she answered sharply.

"Good," he said, and took a long swallow from the bottle. "Good enough. What do you want to know?"

"What are you?" Kai asked, her hands curling in the folds of her skirt.

Shefek looked to the ceiling and closed his eyes. He opened them slowly, the lids pulled back completely to reveal twin golden disks like bright suns. "A Kirian," he said. "Only two of us remain, myself and my daughter."

Kai frowned and looked at Slipper. He sat next to the bed, his shoulders gathered up, his face intense with excitement as he listened to Shefek.

"I ain't never heard of that," Kai answered.

"We are Oran's oldest race, born in the time of Oran's childhood. Oran himself fashioned us out of the Chaos."

"You mean, Oran the God?" Slipper asked in a hushed voice.

"Yes. Oran created us long before your kind were born. We are fragments of the first clay, our bodies still transmutable. Once shaped with wings, we soared in the driving winds of the Chaos, perched on the very edges of Oran's cradle, and looked upon the face of the Mother, Amatersoran."

Shefek paused, his eyes blank.

"Z'blood," Slipper exhaled softly.

"Vagger blow," said Kai disgustedly, shaking herself from the spell of Shefek's words. Shefek's eyes snagged her in their hard gleam. Kai lifted her chin to them. "I've heard like tales a hundred times from you brown coats." She turned away from the bed. "When you got something serious to say to me, and not some bit of poetry sipped from a bottle, call out. I got a shop to run."

"Wait," Shefek's voice called to her. Kai stopped, one hand

on the doorknob, but refused to turn around. "Look at me," his voice commanded, and reluctantly she turned.

Shefek was standing beside the bed, his injured arm hanging limply to one side. "The Kirian are a proud race, my little raven. And I would have you know of them before you so easily dismiss me." He closed his eyes and bowed his head. The ruff of his beard rested above his chin.

Kai gasped as she watched him change, his portly body growing bigger and wider as the bones of his shoulders erupted from the small frame, huge and white, reaching in a wide graceful arch into the air. Along the length of the curved bone, brown and gray feathers stitched together, lapped over each other in rows. Slipper shouted in alarm and scrambled away from the bed. Shefek's head rolled upward to the ceiling as his neck stretched impossibly long, bent like a snake. The elderly face cracked open, the blooming red nose drawing to a hard sharp beak the color of burned amber. Fierce golden eyes stared unblinkingly at her from either side of a nearly bald round head. Taloned claws scrabbled at the ground, as he lurched forward. The bedroom had grown small, unable to contain the full measure of the massive bird approaching her. His wing feathers were bent, crushed beneath the confines of the ceiling. He reared back his head on its long neck and launched his beak toward her.

Kai flung herself against the door, her back pressed into the wood as the point of his beak touched her chest. It was like a polished brass dagger digging into her breastbone and holding her prisoner against the door. Wings enclosed her in a feathery tent. Then abruptly Shefek released her and, pulling back his head, opened his beak and screeched.

The noise was deafening and the stench of carrion overwhelming. Kai grew faint and she might have fallen but for the taloned claws that grasped her around the waist. He held her in his grip like a mouse caught within a hawk's grasp. He clutched her tightly, her body rigid and stiff with terror and then finally limp, as she resigned herself.

As she looked up Kai saw only the gray-brown bands of feathers of his breast and flanks, the cream-colored shafts glowing dully like the rays of moonlight. Then between the rows of feathers rising and falling with his movements she saw cracks, jagged spaces, black as night and sprinkled with stars. Beneath the stiff rustling of his feathers, she heard the sound of a howling wind. She was frightened, her senses confused, as it seemed she was no longer in the narrow confines of her room but lost on the edge of a great cliff, with only this net of feathers to shield her from the driving winds.

Kai opened her mouth to scream, clutching the dull black tarsus of his leg. It was like clinging to cold iron and her fingers slipped along its metal-hard surface. He leaned down to regard her, his head cocked to one side as he gazed at her from the depths of his golden eyes. Kai shut her eyes, feeling tiny and lost.

And in the next moment a furious resentment ignited her anger. So, she admitted, he was powerful enough to destroy her as easily as a pantry mouse. But he had no right to taunt her, force her into this undignified fear. And he wasn't invincible. Someone had already beat her to it and cut him. Kai's eyes snapped open. She knew the truth. Shefek needed them and the Grinning Bird to stay alive. Anger made her struggle and refuse to capitulate entirely to his terrifying presence.

She heard a throaty rumble and, looking up, realized he was laughing. The talons released her and she collapsed against the door. Shefek backed away from her, the massive wings diminishing, his head drooping to rest more squarely on his neck. As Kai watched, Shefek transformed into the figure of an elderly man again. She caught the vague glimpse of his naked human form, his rounded belly protruding over the darker trinity of his genitals, the gray hairs that curled on his sturdy legs. Then the feathers closed over his skin, weaving together into the semblance of cloth. A stray, nearly all-white feather drifted upward in the room.

Shefek sat down heavily on the bed, his head sagging between his shoulders. He was panting, his breath shallow and wheezing. "Getting harder to do," he muttered to himself.

Slipper came out of the closet, his eyes darting back and forth from the hunched figure of Shefek and Kai, who was slowly rising, her face white.

She sat down in a chair, one hand absently twirling her hair into a knot.

"All right, then," she said, trying to mask the trembling in her voice. "You made your point." Kai rubbed the spot where she could still feel the steel edge of his beak. Her arms felt bruised, the skin nearly crushed by his embrace.

"As I said, the Kirian are a proud race," then he smiled

knowingly at her. "But you, my raven, have a spirit of your own. I salute you."

On Kai's wan face a small, grudging smile appeared. Then she grew serious again. "How come someone as powerful as you got sliced?"

"Ah," said Shefek, shaking his head. He reached for the cheese and broke off a corner of the slab. He put it in his mouth and chewed thoughtfully. "Even the Kirian have their weakness. Mine was a woman."

"Nah," blurted out Slipper, who reverently handed Shefek the bottle.

Shefek regarded him a moment, one eyebrow cocked. "Don't tell me lad, you've never done a foolish thing for the sake of a woman." His eyes strayed to Kai.

"It wasn't foolish what I done," Slipper said in his own defense. "Kai knows that. Don't you?" Slipper asked Kai, who now rolled her eyes.

"Oy, who's telling their bit now, you or Shefek?"

Shefek shrugged. "It wasn't all for sport. I came looking for the Firstwatch, Faul Verran."

"You've been gone awhile," Kai answered. "She ain't Firstwatch no more."

"So I learned. The hard way," Shefek said ruefully, holding up the injured arm. "I was in the north and had lost track of the days. When I felt the changes in the flow of magic, I knew I was late. I only hoped not too late."

"Too late for what?" asked Slipper. He had taken off his lighterman's hat and was punching a crease in its crown.

Shefek sighed. "As you may guess, the Kirians are air elements. Besides this changeable form, we have also a unique sense of time. We see time, experience it as a whole, from the beginning to the end."

"Must get confusing, don't it? Not knowing whether you've done a thing or are going to do it?" Slipper asked.

Shefek chuckled. "I've often anticipated myself coming just as I was going. It is one of the reasons I'm late arriving from the north."

"How come you didn't see your attacker then?" Kai asked impatiently. "What good is knowing the future and past if you suffer in the present?"

"Ah, good point. But the experience of time we have is not exact. We experience only possibilities. There is always then

room for change, and even surprise.'' Shefek's expression grew
serious and his voice became husky. ''There is a Kirian proph-
ecy that the Oran world will end, and with it, the Kirian.''

''Go on, you're raving,'' Slipper said uneasily.

''You said possibilities. The possibility but not the certainty
of the end,'' Kai argued.

''Correct. I came to Beldan to find someone. Someone who
may tip the possibilities in another direction.''

''The Firstwatch?'' Kai asked with a puzzled frown.

''No. A girl with red hair. A fire element. I had hoped that
Faul would help me find her.''

Kai and Slipper looked at each other as the same thought
flashed in their heads. ''Jobber,'' Kai answered. ''That's who
you want. But you missed her, too. She's gone from Beldan.
Fled during the massacre of Fire Circle.''

''Where?'' Shefek asked sharply.

Kai shook her head. ''Dunno. Everyone scattered during the
massacre. It was all I could do to keep my own head on in one
piece.''

Shefek swore silently and passed his hand over his eyes.

''What do you want with Jobber?'' Slipper asked, sitting on
a chair and leaning his chin in the palm of his hand.

''The Fire Queen Zorah steals time. That is the secret of her
immortality. She uses Oran power to capture time in the blade
of a Fire Sword. As long as the sword remains intact, time and
all of Oran's magic will bleed into it.'' Shefek looked up at
Slipper and his face had become haggard again, the eyes weary.
''Even the Kirian die slowly as the Queen's Fire Sword drains
us of our strength. Only another Fire Sword can destroy Zorah's
sword, and it must be another girl blessed with the fire element
in her veins to wield the sword.''

''Jobber, against the Queen?'' Kai asked in a hushed voice.

''I had come to Beldan to find her. Teach her how to use the
sword and most of all how to control the fire. Without that, she
will be as deadly as the Queen.''

''Why don't you do the job?'' Kai asked. ''If you know how
to use the sword?''

''I know how to use *a* sword,'' Shefek corrected, one finger
raised in the air. ''But I can not use a Fire Sword. I am an air
element, and for me, the sword will not come to life. But I have
come too late, it seems, to do any good.''

''Maybe not,'' Slipper broke in. ''I'm willing to lay a wager that Jobber got away. I heard about it down at the docks. Red-haired girl took off on a ship headed up the coast. Left behind a stack of cut-up Guards.''

"Jobber doesn't use a blade,'' Kai said, shaking her head. "She follows the old style and relies on her fists and feet.''

"Maybe she had help,'' Slipper said excitedly. "Someone who knew how to swing a blade.''

"Like Orian or the New Moon?'' Kai suggested, remembering the night the vagger woman had come and taken her Waterlings out of the city.

Shefek roused himself. "Orian? You've seen her?''

"Yeah,'' Slipper said. "She took some of our Waterlings up north. You know her?''

"Intimately. She's my daughter.''

"The other Kirian?'' Kai asked quickly, recalling, too, Orian's large brown eyes, the stare open and intense.

"Indeed. If your Waterlings left with her, they were in good hands. Orian is skilled, even if she does get a bit sentimental about human affairs.''

"What's that supposed to mean, then?'' Kai snipped.

"The Kirian do not often become involved in the ways of humans. It leads to weakness. As you can see, my own involvement with a human woman has brought me to this state.'' Shefek leaned back heavily on the pillows and sighed tiredly. "But I need to find the fire girl. For all my disdain of mortal ways, I need to find her and teach her what sadly enough no Kirian can do. And so I am obliged to serve humans.'' Shefek yawned loudly, his mouth stretched wide, his eyes heavily lidded.

"From where I stand,'' Kai said angrily, "it's me serving you.''

"Ssh, Kai, he's knackered. Let him sleep awhile,'' Slipper said in a hushed voice. "Come on. I'll get us a bit of tea.''

He ducked out the door, leaving Kai to stare down at Shefek's sleeping form. He was snoring slightly and Kai heard the echo of the rushing wind as it howled beneath the Kirian's feathers. In the long shadows of his face she saw the black night and the stars like scattered bits of mica. For a moment it seemed to Kai that she waited at a strange crossroad where all manner of power and magic flowed, brushing past her on its way elsewhere. Even her own Reader's curse seemed to loosen from her flesh, eager to join in the rising current that would sweep them all away. Kai felt a sudden chill in the room, and before she left, she covered Shefek with a warm quilt.

The Fire Queen Zorah stared out a high window, her eyes following the movements of two Guards sparring on the training ground in the yard below. They were clumsy fighters and she watched with a sour expression. The Regent Silwa was talking to her, occasionally asking her permission to carry out specific plans relating to the restoration of Beldan. She said yes without interest, knowing that Silwa himself asked her only out of formality and not because he had any desire to have her approval. Since the massacre—and it was a massacre, she told herself—he had assumed more control, more power of the city. And she had let him.

It had been difficult to argue with him that the peasants, her own people, had defied tradition, even the sacred trust with which she was held, and had tried to do the unthinkable. Murder her on the scaffolds. Zorah raised a hand to her neck, remembering the stinging shafts of arrows piercing her flesh. And then the crashing of magic, like a hurricane pounding the streets of Beldan, toppling buildings as it rushed to preserve her life. Unable to die, she had waited until the turmoil subsided and then had risen from the collapsing scaffold, mounted her horse, and ridden away from Fire Circle.

Zorah watched the man below swing at the padded arm of his opponent. His opponent cursed loudly as the practice sword landed savagely on his forearm. On Zorah's smooth cheek a muscle tightened, seeing suddenly the hacked limbs of the dead in Fire Circle. Always death would follow her, she thought morosely, but never would it claim her.

"Madam? Madam?" a voice said insistently.

Zorah turned from the window and saw the Regent Silwa staring at her, his black brows knitted in an angry frown over his blue eyes. His beard was neatly trimmed over his jaw, giving him a crisp appearance. But in the morning light, Zorah noticed, too, the strands of gray hair that were beginning to lighten his temple. She would dismiss him soon, unable to tolerate any signs of aging. She almost laughed to herself. He's been so excited by all the havoc he's created that he has forgotten to dye his hair. But maybe not, Zorah reflected again, maybe he knows this is his last hour and wants to make the most of it. Face it head-on like the Silean soldier that he is.

"What is it, Silwa?" Zorah asked, and saw him stiffen at the familiar use of his name. Oh, she thought with a small smile, he definitely imagines himself to be in camp. Perhaps I should begin addressing him as Captain.

"Madam, there is still the problem of the dead."

"What do you mean?" Zorah asked, the smile stiff on her lips. Images of her nightmare, the burned body of her maid, flared vividly behind her eyes.

"We need more wood to burn the dead still trapped under the rubble in certain parts of the city. It is coming into summer, and if we have not finished the job, the heat will spread the pestilence that is sure to follow. I must have your permission for the conscription of wood from all available farms and the labor to bring it to the city."

"Yes, of course you have it," she answered, letting the terrifying images slip away. She turned back to the window again. Two new Guards were practicing, though from her vantage point Zorah thought them as badly poised as the other two.

A knock at the door turned her head and she saw the Firstwatch Gonmer, waiting to enter. At Gonmer's side was her new page, Lais. Zorah studied the page for a moment and thought she looked vaguely familiar. But then, she shrugged, after so many years, to her all the Firstwatches had come to resemble each other. Gonmer had been different in that she had refused to cut her hair short and wore it in a long black braid that she draped like a necklace around her neck to keep it out of the way when she worked. But the page standing before her was like a stamped coin bearing the face of a similar woman, maybe the nose a bit shorter, or the forehead a bit higher where the minter's hand had slipped.

"Madam," Gonmer was saying, "my page Lais has brought some important news."

Zorah pulled herself out of her reverie, smoothing the wrinkles out of her yellow silk dress. She stared at the page and noticed now that the girl was pale, her eyes large and frightened. Of me, Zorah wondered, or of what she had seen? At her side, though she tried to hide it, the page's hand trembled.

"Yes?" Zorah asked.

"Madam—" Gonmer started primly, but Zorah interrupted her with a wave of her hand.

"I'll hear the news from your page," Zorah said. The page's

eyes darted back and forth between the Firstwatch and the Fire Queen as she hesitated.

"Come on, girl," Silwa broke in impatiently. "Give the Queen your report."

Zorah watched the page's face darken at Silwa's use of the word "girl." The page bristled with annoyance and, lifting her chin proudly, addressed the Fire Queen.

"Last night on the western parapet I was attacked by a creature," Lais began, her voice growing more confident as she spoke.

"Damn those peasants. How are they getting in?" Silwa fumed.

"Not peasants," Zorah said without taking her eyes from Lais. "You said a 'creature.' What sort of creature?"

"He was first a bird. I saw him flying toward the Keep from a long way off. I'd never seen anything like it. Taloned and beaked like a hawk but much much larger, with a wingspan almost as wide as the stateroom—"

"Nonsense," growled Silwa. "There are no birds in Oran with such dimensions."

"Not birds as you know them," Zorah added softly. "Go on," she urged Lais, drawing closer to the page.

"Well," the young woman continued nervously. "Well, I watched it land, and then, of a sudden, it changed from a bird into a man. It came closer, talking like it knew me. And then it attacked me."

Zorah frowned. "Attacked you?" she asked sharply. "Why would it attack you?"

Lais raked her lower lip with her teeth and Zorah knew the page was lying. "Well, it seemed that way," Lais continued.

"What weapon did it have?"

"I don't remember."

"You don't remember?" Zorah said in a cold voice. "You remember that it attacked you but not with what?"

"Well, I'd seen its talons. I figured it meant to harm me."

"But it came to you as a man."

"Yes," Lais said softly to the floor.

"Unarmed, I would guess, if it had been flying?"

"Yes," Lais mumbled, and glanced up at the Fire Queen, her face, if anything, paler than before. At her side the Firstwatch Gonmer clutched her sword with repressed fury. Oh yes, thought

Zorah, your page probably told you a pretty tale. But Zorah knew the truth already.

"You panicked," Zorah said archly, and watched the page hang her head. "When it got close enough, you panicked and attacked it first."

"I swung at it with my sword and wounded it," Lais answered glumly.

Zorah grabbed Lais tightly around the wrist, jerking the page closer. Fire flashed in Zorah's green eyes and the red-gold hair reeked of copper. "You didn't kill it, did you? Too quick for you, wasn't it? Even unarmed, you are no match for it," she snarled as the page continued to shake her head.

"I'm sure it's dead. I watched it fall over the parapets, half man, half bird." Lais was talking quickly. "It crashed straight down, I tell you. I didn't know what it was. I didn't know."

Zorah released the page and turned to Gonmer. "Did you recover a body?"

"No, madam."

Zorah swore angrily, aware now that Silwa had left his place by the table and come to stand next to her.

"What is it?" he asked harshly. "What manner of creature is it?"

"A Kirian, my regent," answered another voice from the door.

Zorah spun on her heel and saw Antoni Re Desturo, Advisor to the Regent, enter the room. He was wearing his black cloak, the hem spattered with mud as if he had only now entered from the streets of Beldan. He unwound a black silk scarf from his neck, the skin of his throat white above the collar of his cloak. Zorah felt the hairs of her neck lift as she watched him and she turned away uneasily, not wishing to meet his piercing gaze.

"For a change you know your history, Advisor Antoni," Zorah said, facing the window.

"Thank you, madam. That is indeed a compliment from you, considering how much of Oran history it is not permissible to know."

"That means you only need to learn half again as much."

"Not now," Silwa interrupted angrily. "If you wish to argue the fine points of Oran political history, do it later. This is a military matter and I want information."

"As you wish, Regent Silwa," Antoni said with a touch of iron in his voice. "The Kirian are part of an indigenous Oran race. Air elements, capable of transforming into big, vulturelike birds. There are, in fact, some very fine paintings of them on the frescoes in the halls of the old Keep.''

''I don't give a shit about paintings,'' Silwa growled. ''How dangerous are they and what are they doing here?''

Antoni moved to the table, the leather of his black boots creaking softly. He's been out, Zorah thought; his boots are still damp and mud-covered. She watched him from the corner of her eye as he lifted a small flagon of wine and poured himself a glass. His hands were long and slender, the fingers ending in tapered nails that were polished a milky white. It seemed to Zorah there was a tension surrounding him like an irritating noise, heard but not understood. He's too clever, too ambitious, she thought. He tilted his head at a slight angle, his profile a jagged edge, and Zorah saw in turn that he studied her. She lowered her eyes to gaze out the window again, disturbed by the brittle black gleam of Antoni's stare.

''It was believed that all the Kirian died at the time of the Burning,'' Antoni was saying.

''They fought for Huld,'' Zorah said, ''and when she died, they were swept again into the Chaos.''

''But one at least has survived,'' Silwa argued. ''Perhaps there are others.''

''Hmm, interesting that,'' Antoni said, a finger tapping against a tooth. ''They are of course dangerous. Like predatory birds they are cunning, and their ability to change from human form to bird makes them more difficult to catch. But it is for their martial skill that they are most notable. Are you not Kirian-trained, madam?'' Antoni asked, drawing the glass close to his lips to sip the wine.

''Yes,'' Zorah answered, not turning from the window. ''All those who used the Fire Sword were once trained by the Kirian. For them the sword was a path to knowledge of the self. In training with the sword one learned to close the gap between thought and action. Complete control in the unity of mind and sword. In the handling of the Fire Sword that is important, as the sword responds, awakens to the emotions of the holder. Self-control becomes essential. Only the Kirian, so removed from the emotional trivialities of humans, could teach that kind of control.''

The flat tone of Zorah's voice as she spoke did not convey the sudden turmoil she experienced beneath the surface of her words.

Memories erupted through the hard carapace of denial, showing her the past. She saw again the slanted wagon and, beneath its broken wheel, a woman whose face she knew well. A woman she had loved. The copper-colored hair was clotted with the black spring mud as the wheel turned, planting her body deeper into the soil. The redness of blood, vivid against the stark white of the woman's skin. Zorah remembered the way it flowed in two small rivers beneath the eggshell-white nostrils. Zorah's eyelids fluttered, hearing again the shrill screams, some of them her own. Then had come Huld's wintry face, solid and gray like the boulders of the north, her hands of stone weights bearing down her shoulders. Black hair shrouded her wide cheeks. "An accident. It happens," Huld offered as explanation in a voice that grated in Zorah's ears like the millstones grinding seed. The words rested like the rocks over the cairns, covering the deadly wounds but never healing them. Only the Kirians had brought a measure of peace to Zorah's troubled heart. They had given her command over death. Zorah inhaled sharply, the muscles of her neck tightening, blood pounding. She stared at her hands, small and white, the nails a rosy pink. She closed them in a fist, feeling the throbbing power of the Fire Sword as all her sorrow and all her terror had exploded it into life. At the Burning, the Kirians had been among the first to die.

"What do you expect it was doing here?" Silwa was asking Antoni.

"Madam?" Antoni said, deferring to the Queen.

Zorah was silent, struggling to free herself from the sudden onslaught of the past. "Why don't we find it and ask?" she replied in a tight voice. "I suggest, Firstwatch, that you take your page and begin searching the usual haunts of the vaggers. It is most likely that the Kirian would find a welcome there. Especially one that is wounded. Take a Reader with you. As the Kirian can assume different shapes, it may be difficult to find it."

Gonmer hesitated before leaving. "Yes?" Zorah snapped.

"Then you wish the Kirian brought in alive?"

"I don't care," Zorah answered shortly.

"Excuse me, madam," Antoni interrupted. "Perhaps it would be wiser to bring the Kirian in alive. So that we may question it."

Zorah gave a grim smile. Easy for them to think they could,

she mused. How little they know of the Kirian and how much they assume of their own power.

"Try," Zorah said to Gonmer. "But if it comes to a choice, kill it," she added with finality.

Gonmer nodded her head in salute and left, the heels of her boots clicking angrily against the stone. Behind her Lais followed, her shoulders hunched.

"I don't like the idea of this creature mixing with the rabble," Silwa said, his expression clouded with annoyance. "We have enough problems with the New Moon stirring up trouble without these Kirian."

"The Kirian came for its own reasons," Zorah said lightly, running her fingers through her hair. The red strands crackled. "It isn't likely to be interested in the affairs of ordinary humans."

"Do you know why it is here then?" Antoni asked, taking another sip of the wine. The eyes watched her closely over the rim of his glass. The color of the wine seemed to reflect pinpoints of red in the black pupils.

Zorah flashed him a cold smile but didn't answer. "I shall be in my chambers if you need me, Silwa," Zorah said, and gathering her skirts swept past the table, toward the door.

Once in the corridor, Zorah inhaled and then exhaled slowly, calming the racing of her heart. Oh, yes, she thought to herself as she walked, the skirts rustling softly as they brushed the polished floor, I can guess the Kirian's reasons for being here. Ever since last night, since she had touched Huld's mind again, felt the life that pulsed in Huld's thread, Zorah's perceptions had sharpened. Oran power drifted unclaimed in the air, cutting across the current of her storm. First there had been the flute she had heard the night before Fire Circle, and later, after she had embraced the girl with red hair, she could sense the faint but familiar hum of the girl's power; one fire element attracted to the other. The girl was still alive, of that Zorah was certain. And if she listened closely, Zorah could hear the flute, and knew it to be the sounds of an air element like a single strand of melody lifted out of the cacophony of the storm.

In the corridor Zorah stopped walking, her head raised in expectation. Guards stationed along the corridor glanced uneasily at each other. But Zorah ignored them as she concentrated on the feel of Oran magic. There was yet another presence to be sensed. It lay buried just beneath the surface of Huld's thread.

It settled on her tongue like the rank taste of mushrooms still speckled with the forest dirt. Zorah licked her lips, discovering them parched. So, she thought, an earth element. She smiled knowingly, a finger drawn to her pursed lips. That was it, then. She knew what Huld intended. Huld was not strong enough to challenge her openly. She was gathering the elements together, sending a new Queens' quarter knot against Zorah. And the Kirian had come to find the girl with red hair, to train her in the use of the Fire Sword.

Zorah's hands strayed from her lips to her cheek and then dug into the thick strands of coppery hair as she saw the possibilities leap before her eyes. A game of strategy, Huld, a game of warriors and pawns. She had not known at first the game was there. But now she saw it.

"Two can move the pieces," she said aloud to the corridor, and the Guard closest to her stiffened to attention, his face puzzled. Zorah continued on her way, her stride growing longer and more eager. If she and Huld could not fight directly, they would use their little pawns to do the trick for them. Let Huld pull the Queens together. It was to Zorah's advantage now. And when the moment came, as she was certain it would, Zorah would be ready to use the fire girl as a sword against Huld. All that remained to do was to find the Kirian and keep it here in Beldan.

Chapter Six

*S*hedwyn let out a long weary breath and wiped her hand across her forehead. It left a black muddy smear on her brown skin. She had a headache and a dull buzzing in her ears. Her neck was sore, the welts, despite the poultice of moss, stiff and painful. She looked back and saw Eneas struggling to free his booted foot from the mud. He was swearing at it, giving his leg a savage wrench. Shedwyn glanced down at her own bare feet covered with the black mud of the marsh and decorated with clinging green stems of maiden's woe. Looking out at the trail before them, she sighed, seeing only the thick bushes and straggly trees that crowded the marsh. Mist gathered in the low spots, and though the patches of yellow marshmallows glittered like gold coins scattered through the gray, the marsh retained it dreary appearance. Even the birds were quiet, and Shedwyn heard only the constant drone of insects excited by their warm-blooded presence.

Earlier, the morning had seemed to hold the promise of a clear day, but by afternoon it had become overcast with a thick blanket of clouds. Shedwyn glanced up at them worriedly. Normally she would have welcomed rain to the parched farmlands. But not now. They would need to find shelter and, she thought, her stomach rumbling softly, something to eat.

Eneas touched her shoulder and Shedwyn turned to give him a small encouraging smile.

"Don't say it," he muttered, and his blue eyes looked sunken and tired.

"Say what?" she asked.

"That we've made great strides and that any moment we will be sitting down before a warm country fire and drying ourselves."

Shedwyn chuckled. "Ah no, I wouldn't be so bold as to give you that lie. It's a good ways yet we have to travel."

"At least we've not been followed," Eneas answered wearily.

"Don't be too sure. They'll take their time because they know they have the advantage to us."

"Maybe, but we may have just lost them traveling the marsh."

His wishful ignorance annoyed her. Shedwyn rested her fists on her hips. "Eneas," she said sternly, "Re Ameas is not likely to let his son—"

"His youngest and least regarded son," Eneas interrupted irritably.

"—his youngest son run off with an Oran hireling. You know how it goes," she said plainly. "You've seen it. They'll gather themselves for it like a hunt. First they'll drink, then they'll loose the hounds. And then they'll follow on horseback, wild and driven with the thrill of it. No," she said sadly, "we've only bought a little time."

"It's the spring planting. My father would sooner see me gone than waste the man-hours hunting me. Especially since I've disgraced the family and murdered a Guard. He'll be glad to be rid of me, no doubt figuring if I don't finish the job on myself in the marsh, then the New Moon will."

"Makes no difference," Shedwyn argued. "The Guard will demand satisfaction because you are a Silean traitor." She watched his face cloud over as the words sank in. Didn't Eneas understand anything? she thought angrily, and then she sighed, sad and confused. How did it happen that she had become entangled this way? With a man not of her own people? Eneas had grown pale, his blond hair lank with the mud, his shoulders sagging forward. And she knew from his stubborn expression that though he was unwilling to argue with her, he was just as unwilling to accept her point of view. A mistake to let him come, Shedwyn thought heavily. She could feel already the resentment between them.

"Come on, then," Eneas said, looking out at the marsh. "Let's go."

He put his hand around her arm and his fingers were cold and damp on her skin.

Sorrow and disappointment formed a lump in Shedwyn's throat. She wanted to feel the familiar pleasure at Eneas's touch, smell the lavender of his shirts. To laugh with him and talk of nothing more important than the fields in summer and the health of the livestock. But all that belonged to another place and another time. The moment they had left the estates, they had begun to change, or perhaps, she thought sadly, to discover how little of each other they really knew. Miserable and weary, Shedwyn wanted to cry.

The shrill baying of the hounds made her stop in her tracks.

"Huld's peace, they've scented our trail," she cried to Eneas.

"Come on," he urged, and began running, dragging her through the thickets by the arm.

She stumbled, unable to keep up with his furious pace. He stopped long enough to lift her to her feet again before continuing to run.

Mud splattered on their legs as they ran, barely skirting the edges of murky pools covered with fine duckweed. Behind them the baying grew louder and more pronounced. Now Shedwyn could hear the shouting of men, urging their mounts, and the cracking of branches as the horses followed the hounds through the underbrush.

Shedwyn gasped in startled terror as before her, Eneas tumbled into a pool of thick black mud. It oozed rapidly over his waist with an eager sucking sound as he floundered. With a cry he released his hold on her hand, freeing her where she teetered along the slippery edge.

"Go on," he shouted, wallowing clumsily in the mud. "Keep going." The black mud was reaching up with long fingers, pulling him deeper into its murky breast. His arms splashed on its surface, setting up small waves that undulated beneath the carpet of duckweed.

Shedwyn glanced quickly over her shoulder, hearing the shouts close by. A hound snuffled and growled. She held her breath and then plunged into the black pool. It was cold and viscous as it swallowed her. She moved her arms, spreading them wide to push herself closer to Eneas.

"Why did you do that?" he shouted at her. His face was stark white against the mud, fear drawing his features to sharp points.

"Take my hand, Eneas, and swim with me to the edges of the bushes over there."

"I can't swim," he spluttered.

"Move your arms. Kick your legs," she insisted. "That's it," she said as he struggled to move through the mud, spitting out a mouthful of duckweed.

She motioned with her chin to a stand of gacklebushes, the long woolly leaves drooping over the boundaries of the pool. "Quickly," she hissed.

She grabbed his shirt at the shoulder, half dragging him through the muddy pool. Together they kicked their legs, moving with glacial slowness to the other side. Behind them, the duck-weed closed over their path, re-forming its carpet of light green. At the edge of the pool, Shedwyn ducked her head under the mud, trying not to gag at the cold thickness. She pushed to the surface and lifted her face out of the murk again, her head now the same blackened shade of the mud. Eneas followed her ex-ample, and in a moment the two of them waited, hands clinging to the roots of the gacklebushes, while their muddied and cam-ouflaged faces floated almost unseen on the surface of the pond. Duckweed floated around her cheeks and she inhaled slowly and carefully through her mouth so as not swallow any more of the mud and slime.

Shedwyn stared up at the underside of the overhanging leaves and, through eyelashes clotted with mud, saw the fine web of a marsh spider clinging with white threads between the leaves. A brown snail left behind a silvery trail on the purple leaves. She gave a sidelong glance to Eneas, his profile barely visible on the surface of the mud. Only the slow blinking of his blackened eyelids indicated he was alive.

"Oy,! They must have come this way!" someone shouted at the far shore of the pool.

"Damn the frigging bastards," came a slurred reply. "We'll gut them when we find them."

"Frigging marsh, it's like wading through shit."

"Do that often, do you?" came a terse reply. Shedwyn rec-ognized the voice of Re Ameas.

"Oy, stubble your insults. It's your cock of a boy that has us out here. One of my men is dead and I mean to find that little shithead."

"And the girl," said another voice. "Don't forget, I want to see the girl." Beneath the muddied water of the pool, Shedwyn's body contracted. Not a Guard that one, but a Reader. She could hear it in the lilt of his accent. Oran to be sure, but cultured and not country sounding at all.

"Well, you're not about to see anybody now," grumbled the first man. "They've been here but this is as far as the hounds can follow the trail." Shedwyn heard the loud rustling of bushes as the Guard searched around the edges of the pool. In a moment she was certain he would discover their hiding place. Something had to be done to distract them, but not, she thought, anything that might attract the Reader's attention. Something small and subtle. Almost natural.

Shedwyn closed her eyes and concentrated. She suppressed the urge to cough the muddy water that clogged her throat and instead opened her mind to the weight of the earth around her. The pool was deeper than she had thought, veins of water traveling up from deep-set springs. But the solid ground where Re Ameas and the other Guards waited on horseback was not as solid as it appeared. Shedwyn reached her mind to the earth beneath the horses' hooves. She pressed against the fine etching of cracks in its dense structure. The mud gave beneath her pushes, sliding apart gently as water spurted into the newly formed gaps. Shedwyn kept pushing, sensing the mud soften and the hard hooves of the horses sinking deeper into the growing mire. The horses shifted nervously, lifting their legs. But as they set them down again in a jittery prance, they sank deeper still.

"Mount up, Alvas," shouted the Reader to the Guard still searching the perimeter of the pool for signs of the fugitives. "We're sinking into this muck. Let's move on. Maybe we can pick their trail up again farther west."

But Alvas was reluctant to give up his search and he slashed angrily at the shrubs with his sword. Shedwyn continued to force the mud apart, freeing more water into its tiny crevices. Water began to pool on the surface around the horses' hooves.

"Come on, damn it, or we'll be drinking the shit."

"Z'blood," the Guard swore, and gave up the search. Shedwyn could feel his footsteps through the vibrations of the ground close to where they hid. Had he but looked down and peered beneath the leaves of the gacklebush, he would have seen two strange faces staring back at him.

"Send the dogs forward, Gregio," commanded Re Ameas.

"Maybe Eneas thought to reach the outlying farms of the Orans. We can still catch them if that's the case."

"You give him too much credit for thinking, Father. It's more likely he chased after the Oran bitch and got himself drowned," Gregio answered.

"More likely the bitch drowned him," a Guard countered, and then laughed harshly. "Let's get out of here."

Shedwyn and Eneas waited in the muddied pool, clinging to the roots until it seemed that the marsh had again settled into its muffled quiet. Slowly Eneas dragged himself from the pool, the black marsh slime coating his body. The light green of duckweed dappled his shoulders and hair. He coughed, a loud hacking noise, and blew his nose to clear it of the muck. At his side Shedwyn struggled to drag herself out, her skirts heavy with the mud.

Eneas clasped her under the armpits and dragged her onto the bank. She lay next to him, one arm around his mud-covered waist. The slight breeze settled on her skin and she shivered with cold. Neither of them spoke.

Then Shedwyn felt a burning itch along her ankles. Roused by curiosity, she peered down and saw the long flattened ribbons of black attached to her ankles.

"Leeches," she rasped. She reached down to pluck them off, but Eneas stopped her.

"No, you'll make it worse. Leave them till we get to a fire."

"Huld's peace, I can't bear them," she cried in a tight small voice. She started to shake with fatigue and cold.

Eneas held her protectively in his arms and whispered soothing words to her. "Come," he said, trying to brush away the muddied hair from her face. "Come, we must get to a fire. I'll burn them off then. Don't worry. Don't worry," he murmured over and over again. "Imagine the fire," he said to encourage her. "We are walking to where there will be a fire and warmth and dry clothes and food. . . ." His voice trailed on, soft and comforting.

They stood at last, helping each other upright. And leaning heavily on Eneas's shoulder, Shedwyn led the way again.

"We'll go deeper into the marsh," she said, pointing through a dense portion of shrubs and low-growing trees. "It'll take longer, for it's a wider circle we're making, through Soring Basin. But I think it the only way to avoid the hounds and the Guards coming back."

"All right," Eneas agreed, an arm clutched around her more tightly. "We'll go that way."

Overhead, thunder sounded, and along the gray expanse of sky, lightning flitted in bright flashes.

"Huld's peace. Anything for a fire," Shedwyn murmured. She kept her eyes trained forward at the dense trees to avoid thinking about the leeches clinging with sharp teeth into her ankle.

"Go on, Faul, admit it. We're lost!" Jobber said angrily. "You ain't got a clue where in Zorah's tits we are." Jobber threw herself down on the muddied ground. She drew her knees up and wearily hung her head between her hands.

Faul glanced at her and then back out at the marsh. She frowned and tapped one hand against her thigh in annoyance. Beside her Alwir, looking gaunt as a bedraggled scarecrow, scratched his beard. He turned in a slow circle as if hoping to catch sight of some well-marked trail.

"Z'blood, it feels as if we've done nothing but gone round in circles in his frigging muck," Jobber kicked a tussock of marsh grass. "I'd bet Queens I was here earlier."

"Shut up," Faul snapped irritably, but said nothing further. She took a few steps forward and then veered to the left, brushing aside the leaves to peer at the ground. Then she swore loudly.

"What is it?" Wyer asked, coming to stand beside her.

"Footprints," Faul answered dourly.

"What'd I tell you!" Jobber said, throwing her hands up in disgust. "We've trampled around in a circle." Overhead the sky rumbled and the air was filled with the pungent scent of approaching rain. "Frigging shit, I hate the wet," she growled. Lirrel came and sat down beside her. She drew her knees up and rested her forehead on them. The little mirrors of her head scarf were splattered with mud.

"Are you sure those are our footprints?" Alwir asked Faul, a hand tugging nervously at his sparse beard. He freed tiny bits of duckweed trapped in the curly hairs.

"Ours or the Guards'," Faul answered glumly. "Either way it's not good." She straightened her back, pushing aside the strands of graying hair that stuck wetly to her cheeks. Her eyes were as cold and gray as the lowering sky.

Lirrel pulled out a flute and began to play softly, her silvery eyes closed. Jobber watched her, lulled momentarily by the low voice of the flute. The music seemed to filter like sunlight through the thick, moist air of the marsh, pushing back the heavy clouds and discouraged mood. Then abruptly Lirrel stopped playing and her eyes snapped open, surprised. Though her brow wrinkled in puzzlement, she smiled.

"Faul," she called, standing quickly. "We go this way." Lirrel pointed through a narrow gap between a stand of trees leaning drunkenly into each other, the lower branches tangled together.

"How do you know?" Faul asked.

"I just do," Lirrel replied with a light shrug of her shoulders.

"You know that's the way out of the marsh," Faul repeated flatly, unconvinced.

"No, I didn't say that," Lirrel corrected her with a smile. "I said it's the way we should go."

"What's that supposed to mean?"

"Just what she said," Jobber snapped. She stood, giving her shoulders a shake. The red hair bristled. "I'm going that way, and if the rest of you are smart, you'll follow."

Lirrel turned to Jobber and touched her on the arm. "You feel it, too, don't you?"

"Feel what?" Jobber asked warily. She didn't look directly at Lirrel, but pretended to stare distractedly out at the leaning trees. Lirrel wasn't fooled, for she recognized the tension in Jobber's shoulders, the sharp scent of copper from her hair, and above all the noisy crackle of Jobber's thoughts.

"All day," Lirrel explained to Faul, "I have sensed another's presence, here in the marsh. At first I thought I was mistaken, hearing the echo of something from the past, or not yet done. But I wasn't mistaken," she said, firmly clasping her flute in one hand and holding it up. "There is someone else here. Someone I must find." She glanced over at Jobber, who was digging a toe into the soft mud and scowling. "And you feel it, too, Jobber, don't deny it to me," Lirrel finished quickly.

Jobber opened her mouth to protest and then shut it again. She shrugged and nodded her head. "All right, I won't deny it. But look here, Lirrel, I ain't as good as you at this." Her face screwed up, worried. "I don't get feelings like this, that's your lay, not mine. I've been feeling it, like a snitch tugging at my pocket ever since we started out today. I keep thinking all I've got to do is turn and I'll see whoever it is." Jobber pushed back the red hair from her face, her green eyes bright as the leaves of maiden's woe. "But something else holds me back and I can't tell whether it's someone I want to see or to run away from. Know what I'm saying? I ain't got a good feeling about it, but I can't leave off neither."

"Oh, frigging shit," Faul exhaled noisily. "Can't either of you make sense?"

"There is no doubt in my mind, Faul," Lirrel said with steady calm. "We must go this way," and again she pointed to the gap between the trees.

Faul looked at Wyer and Alwir, as if hoping for their support. But Alwir's eyes were staring thoughtfully where Lirrel pointed, and Wyer had already come to stand beside Jobber. Faul yanked the edges of her leather vest closer together in an angry gesture. "All right then, we'll go that way," she replied.

Lirrel led the way, stepping gracefully even over the rough and slick trails of the marsh. She stared ahead eagerly, her moonlight eyes seeing something not yet visible to the rest. Behind her, Jobber followed, one foot dragging even as the other hurried forward. Of two minds; Lirrel could sense it in the busy chatter of Jobber's thoughts. But growing more clear to her, Lirrel could hear the thoughts of the other presence, troubled but determined and just as loud as the first time Lirrel had heard Jobber's in the crowded city streets of Beldan. She caught the peppery scent of tobacco and the dry dusty taste of the red farmland soil. Her hands reached to push aside the bushes and she urged her feet to travel faster. She was close. Very close.

"Wait," Lirrel called to the trees. No one was there, and only a thrush startled from its nest cried in answer as it lifted through the dense tangle of branches. "Wait," she called again, growing breathless as she ran. "I know you're there. Please, we mean no harm." She edged her way through the soggy bushes, the hem of her dress catching on a bramble and ripping noisily. Behind her, the others followed more cautiously, eyes searching everywhere through the trees.

Lirrel stopped running and stood, her slim hands folded together in front. Jobber slowed her steps, hesitating, as Lirrel turned in a low circle, her eyes casting a net. And except for the soft panting breaths of the others, the marsh was quiet.

Lirrel spoke to the trees. "We are like you, fugitives traveling north. We are chased by the same hounds." There was light rustling in the shrubs behind a tree. A tall man, not much older than herself, stepped out into a small clearing. He was not what she had expected at all. She stared at the dirty blond hair and the coating of black slime and weed that covered his clothing. Lirrel frowned, not smelling the tobacco and the earth of the fields but lavender and the papery odor of fine linen. It wasn't him she waited for, though she sensed he belonged here, too.

"Who are you?" the man asked, not moving from the tree. Lirrel tried to peer around his shoulder.

"We are from Beldan," Alwir answered. "And we are escaping from the Silean Guards."

"Your name?"

Alwir paused, looking uncertainly at the others. Faul shook her head, her expression tight and disapproving. "Go ahead," Wyer said in a low voice, shrugging his broad shoulders. "I trust Lirrel's inwit."

Alwir turned back to the man, waiting in the distance. "I am Alwir."

"Alwir Re Aston?" the man replied in a shocked voice.

"Am I known to you?" Alwir asked nervously.

"I am Eneas Re Ameas. I met you at the trading fairs in Remmerton two seasons ago. Do you remember?"

"You bought the bull with the black hide?"

"Frigging shit, talking like a bunch of farmers at Firefaire," Jobber grumbled to Wyer.

Alwir approached closer and the two men stared uneasily at each other across a divide of gacklebushes. "What is a Silean nobleman doing here, without horses or dogs, or even a sword?" Alwir asked.

"And what is a Reader doing here as well, in the company of fugitives?"

"These are times of change, Eneas."

"So it would seem." Eneas paused, as if wanting to say more. He glanced uncertainly at Faul and Wyer, his eyes trailing over Jobber's fiery red hair and coming to rest on Lirrel, the bright silver eyes gleaming. "Odd company you keep, Alwir."

"No stranger than your own traveling companion," Lirrel replied.

"I am alone," Eneas said stiffly.

"You are not," Lirrel insisted. She turned to the trees and spoke again. "Please, come out."

"I told you—" Eneas started to insist, but stopped when the bushes rustled again and Shedwyn stepped out from behind the tree to stand at his side.

"*Aha!*." Lirrel nodded. She had been right. Everything about the woman called to her with as clear a purpose as Jobber's mind had captured her at Firefaire. Lirrel smiled with pleasure. She could hear the solid, careful thoughts of the woman before her. An earth element, she told herself, and it showed in every movement of the woman's body; broad-shouldered, wide-hipped, and the long sturdy legs. Like Eneas, she was covered with the black mud, but it only served to make it appear as if she had risen from the earth, created out of its substance. The woman's face was like wood, sculpted with quick strokes to reveal the long planes of an oval face. Beneath a generous forehead almond eyes stared back above high-jutting cheekbones. Two heavy braids lay draped over generous breasts. When she stepped through the bushes, Lirrel smelled the faint odor of Oran soil.

"I am Shedwyn," she said to Lirrel. "But it seems you know me?" she asked.

Lirrel shook her head. "I do in here," she answered, two fingers lightly touching her chest. "And here." She pointed to her temple. "I have 'heard' your passing all day."

"An air element?" Shedwyn asked, drawing nearer, her eyes still fixed on Lirrel's face, studying it intently.

"Aha!," Lirrel answered, and impulsively held out a hand to Shedwyn, to touch her on the hand. The woman was warm and Lirrel sensed generosity and compassion as well as a vein of stubbornness in her touch. "I am Lirrel mir Amer, a Ghazali. And this—" she reached out with her other hand to pull Jobber closer. Her hand closed around Jobber's arm, and she gasped, startled as she was scalded by the heat of an unexpected rage. She turned to Jobber, confused by the intense hatred and the sword sharpness of Jobber's anger.

"I'm Jobber," Jobber answered in a tightly controlled voice. The red-gold hair reeked of copper, and around her temples it began to glimmer and shine an iridescent blue. Her skin was white, the green eyes illuminated with flames. Lirrel felt as if her fingers were singed where she continued to cling to Jobber's arm, wanting desperately to understand the sudden outburst of fury.

And then, as if in reply, Lirrel sensed a hard coldness that numbed the fingers of her other hand. She turned her head and stared into Shedwyn's face. Shedwyn smiled at Jobber, but it was a wintry smile, without warmth, and beneath its iron surface Lirrel sensed envy. It was a leaden emotion, burying all other emotions in an avalanche of frustrated jealousy. The warmth and generosity of Shedwyn's hand was gone, her skin transformed to the unyielding texture of granite.

Lirrel let go of both of them and drew her arms protectively across her chest. She squeezed her eyes tightly shut and tried to "see" beyond the unexplained turbulence. It was like music played in different keys, clashing with harsh and strident notes. She listened, able to hear the separate melodies as if forced through a single instrument. She pounced on one note, followed it with the trained ear of the musician as she tried to separate one thread of music from the other. But it was impossible as the melodies twisted and turned, wrapped like competing vines in a trellis.

Lirrel hummed her own tune; a small trickling of notes designed to restore peace. They began softly, insinuating the gentle tune between the discordant notes. She could feel the tension loosen, the notes curving more gracefully into the semblance of music. The sharp, clear brass of Jobber's thoughts sparkled against the soft mellow tones of Shedwyn's voice. And between them, Lirrel heard her own song, like the breath of air blown through the flute's throat, soft and rhythmic.

"Z'blood—Huld's peace," Jobber and Shedwyn said at the same time, shaking themselves free from the spell of music. Jobber looked down at the ground, unwilling to meet Shedwyn's face.

"What's going on?" Eneas asked brusquely. "What is it?"

"I don't know," Shedwyn said, turning to face him.

Faul grabbed Lirrel by the arm and swung her around. "What happened, Lirrel?"

Lirrel took a deep breath. She exhaled slowly, taking the time to steady herself before she spoke. "It's a riddle, to which I have not the answer, Faul."

"Straight talk," Faul snapped. "Not Ghazali poetry."

"Tcha." Lirrel shrugged angrily, freeing herself from Faul's grasp. "It is like explaining music to a deaf mute."

"Are we in danger from these two?" Faul tried again.

"No," Lirrel answered, knowing that she was in part lying. The man, Eneas, meant no harm, she could sense that. His concern was for Shedwyn's safety. And even Shedwyn, Lirrel thought, meant no harm. But there was danger in knowing her. That much Jobber had been right about. But it wasn't clear. None of it was clear to her.

"Are you sure?" Faul was studying Lirrel's face closely.

Lirrel shook her head. "There are times when the past or the future becomes tangled in my thoughts. Then there are visions, moments when emotions are so powerful that they exist even beyond our time." She looked first at Jobber and then at Shedwyn, her hands spread wide in apology. "It is that, perhaps, that you felt, that I experienced. Not something of your own feelings, but a moment from another time attracted to us."

"But why us?" Shedwyn asked.

Lirrel gave a smile, the delicate features lifting. "All incidents of great power, whether past or present, retain life beyond the boundaries of time. And like floating dreams they are attracted, or perhaps called forth, by a like power. That is why the Kirians could see time past and future like islands risen suddenly in a stream. I am only a musician, and though I can hear the patterning of a melody, I must hear it note by note, and only when I reach the end, can I understand the beginning."

"What we felt," Jobber said slowly, "was it the past or the future?"

"What did you feel?" Faul asked sharply.

"Misery."

"I don't know, Jobber," Lirrel said quickly. "I only know what my inwit tells me at the moment."

"And what's that?" Jobber said.

Lirrel looked at Shedwyn and Eneas, her expression hopeful. "Let us travel with you. We need you to get out of the marsh."

Shedwyn hesitated. Lirrel could feel her slow measured thoughts, appraising each one of them. The man at her side was already one problem; could she suffer to make it worse? And in the back corner of her thoughts she mistrusted herself, for envy that had once been unknown to her before was now etched like an acid burn in her mind. Lirrel hummed to herself, a noise barely more audible than a sigh. She knew it wasn't fair to influence the woman so, but they needed Shedwyn. She smiled as she saw Shedwyn's expression soften.

"Aye, I'll take us all through the marsh. And," Shedwyn added, the deep brown eyes gazing steadily at Lirrel, "don't think I can be won over by a bit of a tune. Takes more than a song to move stones."

Lirrel laughed out loud, embarrassed at having been caught and pleased at knowing it wasn't the reason Shedwyn had made up her mind to help them. "So what then has moved you, Shedwyn?"

Shedwyn spread wide her fingers and shrugged her shoulders, her breasts jiggling lightly with the movement. The fabric gapped at the front buttons, straining where she had long since outgrown the dress. The nipples had hardened in the chilly air of the marsh and were raised beneath the thin fabric. Lirrel could almost hear the catch in Eneas's throat at the sight, joined by Alwir and Wyer. It wasn't lust, she thought curiously, so much as admiration. How strange that she thinks herself ugly, Lirrel mused to herself in surprise.

"It's not in my nature to abandon people in need of help. I'll guide you to the edge of the marsh. And from there we'll see how our paths go," Shedwyn said. "Is that agreeable with you?"

"Yes," Lirrel said quickly before Faul could object. "Yes, thank you."

"What's that there?" Jobber asked, pointing to Shedwyn's ankles.

Shedwyn refused to look down.

"Leeches," Eneas answered for her. "I'll get them off when we find a fire."

"Can't you just yank 'em off?" Jobber asked, bending down closer to see the parasites. They had swollen, their bodies like fat tubes. Blood trickled down Shedwyn's foot. Shedwyn moved her foot away impatiently. The leeches wriggled with the sudden movement.

"Don't touch them," Eneas warned more sharply. "They must be burned off with a brand or the heads will remain buried in the flesh to fester."

"Hold still, I'll burn them off," Jobber said, and grabbed Shedwyn's calf. Her long fingers closed tightly around the muscled calf, preventing Shedwyn from moving away. "I'm a fire element. But you know that already, don't you?" She glanced up at Shedwyn. Shedwyn nodded silently and held her leg still.

The reek of copper joined the moist rotting odor of the marsh as Jobber concentrated on pulling fire into her hands and along the reach of her nimble fingers. Lirrel could sense the effort it took Shedwyn not to tear her leg away from Jobber's grasp. There it was again, that bitter envy that jarred her common sense and turned her cold and hard. Lirrel looked at Jobber's face and saw the eyes shining a brilliant emerald, lit from within by golden flames. She reached out with white-hot fingers. Her hand trem-

bled and Lirrel panicked, thinking that Jobber could not control
the fiery hand. It seemed as if Jobber meant to clasp Shedwyn's
leg, scald her with the white-hot fingers. But at the last moment
she touched a leach and the air was filled with the greasy smoke.
The leech released its grip on Shedwyn's leg and fell to the
ground, writhing. Jobber nodded to herself, as if pleased that
she had won control over her emotions. She touched the remaining two and they fell to the soft mud to join the first one.
On Shedwyn's ankles three angry red marks remained.

Jobber stood stiffly and moved away from Shedwyn. Her red
hair was a bright orange flame, casting yellow sparks that glim-
mered and then dissolved into wisps of powdery ash. Her face
was white and smooth, the mud having dried and fallen away.
She exhaled, and the cheeks of skin flushed pink as she cooled.

"How's that?" she asked with a half grin.

"Fairly done," Shedwyn replied.

"Let's go then."

"This way. Through that stand of trees."

"How far is it?" Faul asked as they started to walk. Lirrel
trailed behind her, trying not to think of how cold and tired she
already felt.

"At least another half day," Shedwyn called back. Thunder
rumbled more loudly overhead and another flash of lightning
filtered across the belly of the sky. "Maybe longer," she added
glumly, glancing quickly at the sky.

"Shit," Faul swore, staring angrily at her feet. A sharp crack
of thunder and the sizzle of lightning answered her. The rain
began to drizzle. "Frigging whore's shit," Faul cursed again as
the rain quickly and quietly drenched them.

"It will at least keep the Guards off our trail," Eneas shouted
back.

"What good is that if we die anyway of the frigging wet and
cold," Jobber snarled like an angry cat.

"There are things far worse than the wet, Jobber," Alwir
answered.

"Not for me," Jobber said, her teeth starting to chatter. "Not
for me."

Lirrel's foot caught on an unseen root and she started to stumble. Wyer grabbed her, lifting her up lightly to her feet again.
"Thank you," she said, and then looked up at him, puzzled, as
his hand remained around her arm.

He was holding her back, waiting until the others had gone

farther ahead. The he leaned down to her, his voice a quiet murmur. "What do you really make of this?" he asked with a worried frown. "A Silean nobleman and this other woman?"

Lirrel gave a small smile. Her eyes followed Wyer's troubled gaze. Alwir and Eneas walked nervously side by side, each mistrusting the other. Sileans and Readers were allies, it was true, but never on this side of the struggle. Jobber and Shedwyn cast each other furtive looks, afraid and attracted to each other at the same time. And following behind these two couples, Faul Verran, former Firstwatch of Beldan, cursing at the mud and slime of the marsh and looking lost without her sword.

"As Alwir said, these are odd times," Lirrel replied. "The whole world seems to be changing for us."

"Or because of us," Wyer replied pointedly, and released her.

"*Ahal*," Lirrel said, "perhaps you are right," and she began picking her way through the wet bushes again.

Chapter Seven

As they stumbled through the reeds, the rain buffeted them, snatching at Shedwyn's hair, reaching underneath Eneas's thin shirt, and dripping steadily off the point of Jobber's nose. Faul blinked and wiped her eyes, trying to see through the sheet of falling rain. Her bones ached, every joint feeling inflamed and stiff. The cold numbed her hands and she hardly noticed when the sharp edges of the cattail stalks sliced thin cuts in her palms as she pushed them aside.

"How much farther do you make it?" Faul called. "We've been near the river for a long time now."

"A little ways more," Shedwyn answered with far more confidence than she felt. Where were they? Where were the boats? she worried. The old laborer that had come through last year had told her that if she should make it to the edge of Soring Basin and the marsh, she would find boats hidden along the banks of the river to ferry her to the other side. She looked up, searching for willow trees marked by a carved new moon notched in the side. Beneath the crook of one of those trees would be the boats they needed. Shedwyn searched the willow trees lining the bank, each one of them draping its long branches over the river, thin stems of leaves like fingers trailing in the rushing water. Then she smiled, seeing the sudden curve of the moon, a white scar in the rough bark. There! She spotted the tree at last. It hadn't yet leafed out and it looked skeletal, the long drought robbing it of yellow spring leaves.

Lightning crackled and sizzled in the sky, and by its momentary blue light Shedwyn saw the prow of a boat, half-buried by reeds. "This way, toward the old tree," she called above the noise of thunder and the growing sound of rushing water. She plunged through the reeds and gasped with shock as the cold water of the river splashed around her legs.

The water was high, churning an angry brown in the fast current.

"Come on," she shouted. "Give a hand with these."

"We'll be going the wrong way, downriver again to Remmerton," Faul said angrily.

"No, up here the river forks west, traveling the far side of Soring Basin. We need to follow it down a little ways and to the other side of the marsh. From the west bank we should be able to find a welcome of sorts among the Oran farms."

"A roundabout way north, if you ask me."

"But safer. There are no Silean estates on the western marsh."

"Are you so sure that Oran farmers will be glad to see us?" Faul asked skeptically. "I doubt that we will be a welcome sight to them."

"Find your own way then. I have no fear of my countrymen," Shedwyn said sharply, "nor doubts that they will help me."

"I don't fear them either. Only question their noble purpose. If the Sileans have been before us, there will be silver, or perhaps even gold offered for us. Do you really think you can trust them?"

Shedwyn bit down hard on her lower lip and refused to answer. Instead she jerked the first boat free of weeds, standing thigh-deep in the fast current. Her teeth chattered as she undid the ropes that bound the small boat to the old willow. "Take the other one," she shouted to Alwir, pointing to the second boat, hidden deeper within the reeds.

Alwir and Wyer wrenched the boat out as Faul worked at the ropes. The boats were narrow and long, the wood musty from its damp hiding place.

"Are you sure these things'll float? They look pretty snarky to me," Jobber yelled out.

"They'll make it," Shedwyn replied. "Just get it out to the

middle of the river and let the current do its work. Keep its prow forward and watch for rocks."

"Watch for rocks?" Jobber shrieked in dismay as she hoisted herself into the boat. It tipped dangerously to the side, dipping low enough to allow water to splash over the sides.

"Be careful," Shedwyn said. "You're filling the boat with water."

"You try it then," Jobber snapped back, sitting uncomfortably on a wooden seat, hands clutching the sides.

Shedwyn lunged over the edge quickly, but the boat dipped again and more water filled its bottom.

"Ain't so easy, is it farmer girl?" Jobber said, and reached over to give Lirrel a hand.

Lirrel's feet kicked out behind her as Shedwyn and Jobber pulled her into the boat. Eneas was the last in, and when he released his hold on the ropes, the boat spun and bounced with the current.

The boat floated dangerously low and the rushing water breached the sides, splashing in.

"Here," said Lirrel, finding two wooden scoops beneath her feet and handing one to Jobber. Together they tried bailing out the water, though it splashed in as quickly with every bump and dip of the roiling current.

Eneas had his hands tight on the long oars, trying to keep the boat steady in the center of the river. Ahead he could see Wyer, the oars moving smoothly over the water, guiding the boat. Eneas tried copying his gestures, pulling the oars out over the water in long flat strokes, adjusting the direction with an extra paddle on one side and then the other. He followed as best he could, trying to ignore the wrenching pain in his shoulders as the boat bucked in the water. But his hands were cold and soon gripped the oars clumsily. His arms began to tire from handling the oars in the fast-moving water. He missed a stroke and the oar slapped against the water, drenching them.

"Zorah's tits!" shouted Jobber, who took the worst of the splashing. "Watch yourself!"

"I'm no oarsman," Eneas snarled back. "You do it if you think you're better!"

Jobber didn't answer him, just gritted her teeth against the cold wetness of the water and the queasy feeling in her stomach from the rocking of the boat.

"Here, let me," said Shedwyn, sliding herself alongside to

relieve Eneas of the oars. He didn't want her to take them. He felt it should be his responsibility, and yet he was tired. Too tired to argue. She took the oars from him, and as he let go of them his shoulders sagged, freed from the wrenching pull of the water. In the driving rain he stared at his hands, now curled like a crone's. Though occasional farm work had toughened his soft palms, they burned with newly formed blisters. The boat rocked and lurched to the side. He grabbed the seat to steady himself, stifling a cry at the searing pain in his hands.

Lirrel leaned closer and wrapped an arm around his waist. "I'll hold you," she said, one hand firmly gripping his shirt at the waist, the other holding tight to the sides of the boat. Eneas leaned against her, at once embarrassed to accept the support of so slight a woman and yet relieved to have it.

They continued downriver, the furious rushing of the river spilling out over its banks and sucking branches and mud to join in its turmoil. The driving rain gusted in fits and starts as the clouds scudded overhead. But within a short time, as twilight approached, the rain abated, becoming a gentle evening mist. The dark gray sky of the storm lightened to a dirty yellow, and there appeared faint patches of blue sky. The sun made a final appearance, thin shafts of gold light piercing the straggling clouds that remained. For a brief instant the riverbank was dusted with light, the overhanging willows shimmering gold against the brown water that clawed angrily at the banks. Then the light faded, leaving the sky a muted gray.

"Oy, look ahead," Jobber called out to Shedwyn, pointing to the far bank. "They're turning into those weeds over there."

Shedwyn nodded and began stroking the water with one oar, carefully angling the boat toward the shore. The boat glided with a whisper into a bed of reeds. Wyer waded toward them, holding the boat steady while they scrambled out into the cold water again. Together, they hauled it deeper into the reeds, until the boat rested firmly on the muddy bank alongside its mate.

Lirrel and Jobber helped to cover the boat with the reeds until they were hidden from sight.

On the riverbank they joined Faul and Alwir. Faul was standing hunch-shouldered as she tried not to shiver. She turned as they approached and Jobber was startled by her haggard face.

"I'm getting too old for this," Faul said sourly. "Come on. I saw the lights of a farmhouse ahead. And from the look it, it's got a fire going." She took a step and then stopped, turning to

Shedwyn. ''I'll give you your chance to talk to them, though in my experience no one clings harder to his brass than an Oran farmer. But make no mistake. I will take what I need if they don't give it.''

''With what?'' asked Shedwyn angrily. ''You've no sword.''

Faul bent, pulled a dagger from inside her boot, and held it up.

Shedwyn said nothing, but stared at the blade. Faul returned it and straightened.

''I, too, am dangerous,'' said Shedwyn. Faul gave her a measured stare. There was nowhere on the tattered dress that Faul could see a hidden weapon. And yet something in Shedwyn's voice gave her pause. ''I will not be threatened by the likes of you, nor will I allow you to threaten people whenever it suits your purpose.''

''Spoken bravely,'' answered Faul tensely. ''But save your words for the farmers.'' She started walking up the bank, making her way toward the small stone house nestled between a pair of spindly poplars and a spreading willow.

Eneas came alongside Shedwyn, eyeing her worriedly. ''I'll talk to them if you wish,'' he offered.

She shook her head, still staring after Faul. ''No. You're a Silean. They'd have even less trust of you than of that stick of a woman. Her they'd understand. Acts like an Overseer, she does,'' Shedwyn said. ''Come on. We'd best get to the house before her.'' She hurried herself, ignoring the cold ache in her shoulders and the grumbling of her empty stomach.

She reached the door first and turned to face the others. ''Won't do if we all go in. Let me go on my own and get what's needed. The rest of you wait yonder in the barn.''

''No,'' Faul answered sharply. ''I don't intend to sit on my hands while you arrange my capture.''

''Cock's bones!'' Shedwyn spat.

''Perhaps Jobber and I could join you,'' Lirrel suggested quickly. ''And Eneas remain with the others; that way there could be no reason for mistrust.''

Shedwyn hesitated and then gave Eneas a questioning glance.

''Fair enough.'' He nodded tiredly. ''Anything to get us some dry clothes and something to eat.''

''Will that suit you, Faul?'' Lirrel asked pointedly.

Faul grumbled under her breath but agreed. ''Don't be long,'' she snarled, and followed Alwir, Wyer, and Eneas as they walked slowly toward the ramshackle barn.

"Thank you," Shedwyn said to Lirrel. And then turning to Jobber, she eyed her with misgivings. "Keep quiet and let me talk to them. Your hair is going to be problem enough without them hearing that Beldan accent of yours."

"You don't need to tell me my business, farmer girl," Jobber answered gruffly. "I ain't got nothing to say to a bunch of dirt twirlers anyway. Just get us something to eat."

Shedwyn turned back to the door and knocked hard.

There was no answer and so she knocked again, the wood scraping the skin off her knuckles.

"Who's there?" a man's voice demanded.

"An Oran farmer," Shedwyn answered.

"From where?" asked the voice.

"Re Ameas's estate."

There was a pause as the voice considered this information.

"Friendly buggers, ain't they?" growled Jobber.

"Scared is more like it," said Shedwyn. "Perhaps Faul was right and they've heard the hunting horns." She knocked again and shouted through the door. "We've money to pay for food."

They waited again and Shedwyn felt Jobber growing restless behind her.

"Maybe Faul was right and we'll have to take what we need," Jobber hissed in Shedwyn's ear.

A bolt in the door creaked and a ribbon of amber light limmed the edges of the door, now open a crack. A face eyed them suspiciously, one eye peering into the darkness.

"Let us in, goodman," Shedwyn said softly in Oran. "We are wet, cold, and very hungry."

"You are many," the man said uncertainly, looking them over.

"Yet we mean no harm."

"Who can be certain of that?"

Shedwyn came very close to the door to let him see her clearly in the light. She held her hands in front of her, palms up. "Empty, goodman. We are without weapons."

The man hesitated once more, staring hard into Shedwyn's face, his eyes moving over the high cheekbones and the square set of her jaw. Then he looked to her upturned hands, wide across a palm thickened with calluses. He nodded as if convinced by her hands.

"Come in then," he said, stepping away from the door and opening it wide enough to let them pass through.

They filed in, the warmth of the small cottage settling on their shoulders like a blanket. Steam rose from a black caldron hanging over the hearth. A woman in a brown dress and a little girl waited by the hearth, watching nervously as they entered. Shedwyn smiled at the woman and then at the child, whose face was bright with astonishment.

Last to enter the cottage was Jobber. The child's dark eyes widened to saucers as she stared first at Lirrel's silver eyes and then at Jobber's red-gold hair. As Jobber entered, the farmer mumbled under his breath as he closed the door and firmly replaced the bolt.

Jobber crossed the small cottage quickly to warm her hands over the hearth fire. She turned once to look at the woman and saw the frightened face that stared back. The woman had light brown hair, pulled back in a single, thin braid that coiled in a knot at her neck. A network of tiny wrinkles stretched the corners of her green eyes in a tired droop, and her mouth was small, the lips pressed together. Jobber noticed the woman's hands grip more tightly on the shoulders of the child, as if she would yank her instantly away should Jobber prove dangerous. Jobber smiled at the woman to reassure her. At that the woman shrank back and Jobber had the sudden impression that she must look like a grinning ghoul come out of the night. She turned back to the fire and decided to ignore them.

Lirrel and Shedwyn sat themselves down on the wooden benches that lined the wall of the cottage. Lirrel half closed her eyes and leaned her back against the rough surface of the wall. The child wriggled free of her mother's grip and skipped across the room to stand in front of Lirrel. Though the child's dress had a ragged hem, torn above scraped knees, the bodice had been carefully embroidered with white flowers. The small face was dominated by large, dark, and inquisitive eyes. She gaped at Lirrel. Leaning forward, she boldly rested her hands on Lirrel's knees and stared directly into her eyes.

Lirrel smiled back, not speaking.

"Can you hear me?" the girl asked, and then fell silent. Lirrel frowned a moment, the dark brows pulled over the opal eyes. Then her face brightened with delighted surprise as she heard the tiny whispers of the girl's thoughts. She was singing softly within herself in a feathery voice like the breezes rustling the dry wheat.

"Ahal." Lirrel nodded, smiling at the curious face.

"Are you a ghostie, then?" the girl asked, brushing black bangs from her forehead.

"No. Ghazali," Lirrel answered.

The little girl looked momentarily confused. "My ma says only ghosties can hear me and that it isn't safe to be talking to them or they might take me away and do harm."

"Brea, come tend the fire," her mother said sharply.

"Go on now," Lirrel urged, giving the child a little push, "do as your mother says." She glanced up at the woman and sensed the rush of fear from the angry face. So did Brea, who started crying.

"Come here now," said the woman less harshly. The child crossed the room and the woman scooped her up in her arms protectively. Brea clung to her neck and wrapped her thin brown legs around her mother's waist. Still holding the child, the woman turned her back on them to stir the contents of the caldron.

The farmer stared at them gravely, his gaze moving slowly over them, up and down, and with each person it passed, his expression became more troubled.

Shedwyn took out the small purse of coins in her pocket and placed it on the table. Three silvers and a handful of coppers rolled out on the wooden planks of the table. Without needing to be asked, Lirrel followed suit, reaching into the long pockets of her black dress to bring out a string of Silean silver. Jobber, standing by the fire, growled softly to herself and reluctantly pulled out two gold coins and one silver. She laid them down on the table and quickly turned back to the fire.

The farmer stared, unspeaking, at the money. The coins shimmered in the light. On the face of the silvers the Regent Silwa's profile stared off into the distance, scowling at something unseen. The two gold coins gleamed a buttery yellow. The farmer took down three loaves of round bread that were warming on the mantel of the hearth and a knife. He placed the loaves on the table. Shedwyn took one and held it up.

"Give me the knife, goodman, and I'll cut the bread," she offered.

The farmer hesitated, knife in hand, as if unwilling to trust her with it. Jobber cast a sidelong glance in his direction but Shedwyn continued smiling, denying the tension in the room.

Then suddenly he gave it to her, holding it by the blade, that she might take it safely by its bone handle.

She held the loaf in one hand pressed firmly against her breast. With the knife in the other, she cut the bread in long jagged strokes toward her breast.

He sat down at the head of the table and slid the money aside, laying it to rest on a shelf in the wall behind him. His wife set Brea on a small stool close to the hearth and then turned and ladled out the food into wooden bowls. Shedwyn gave each a thick slab of cut bread.

Exhausted and hungry, they spoke not a word during the meal, each intent on filling the empty places in their stomachs. The broth was thin and the meat scarce, but it was enough to blunt the sharp edge of their hunger. Jobber slurped noisily at the soup and smacked her lips. And even Lirrel turned her bowl upward to catch the last drops of soup clinging to the bottom.

Only Shedwyn ate slowly, as was her habit. "You'll be planting wheat soon," she said.

The farmer grunted and shaved off a slice of dried cheese before passing the slab to her. "Spring has been either too wet or too dry. Each day it seems a marsh grows, taking more of the land into it."

"Aye. That's the way of it now." Shedwyn wiped sweat from her brow, suddenly aware that the room was warm and the steam of soup had gathered on her face. "Time was when a farmer could count on the spring and the land. No more, though, it seems."

"No more," the man agreed, shaking his head. His black hair fell in thick locks, and like Brea he wore bangs, cut straight across a prominent forehead. He was brown already from the sun; Shedwyn guessed he'd been haying at least.

"Hay been good?"

"Bah," he scoffed. "Too dry to grow enough, too wet when it's cut to cure properly. We'll not get a good crop in this year."

"Still, there's a peace of mind that comes with the spring," said Shedwyn, wiping the bottom of her soup bowl with a crust of bread.

"Wouldn't know about that. The Silean Guard came by here this morning, shaking their swords and making threats," said the farmer, staring into his bowl as his wife ladled another helping of broth into it.

"Oh, aye?" said Shedwyn quietly. "Come round often, do they?"

"Only if they want to make trouble. Or if others make it for them."

Shedwyn lifted her gaze to look at him. Was Faul right? she wondered. How much had the Sileans offered for their capture?

"What did they want?" she asked.

"They were hunting."

"And the quarry?"

He shook his head, and Shedwyn noted that he now held the bread knife upraised almost like a dagger. "Lost it, they said. Come by here to see if I'd any news of it. Offered money, they did."

Shedwyn gave a small laugh. "They always offer money when they feel hard-pressed, don't they? Throw a few silvers your way and they think it solves everything. Who knows what precious gifts we've bartered away for a few of those white coins."

"Gold, they offered," the farmer went on. Jobber shifted nervously in her seat. Lirrel set her bowl down quietly.

Shedwyn shook her head. "But still farmers lose. For when they give it to you with one hand, they take it away with the other."

"How so?" asked the farmer suspiciously.

"They'll find a hundred reasons to tax you sore till you're forced to give it in, leaving you with a handful of coppers for your trouble. And then the Overseer will come to demand his share to keep silent about the bit of wood poached from the estate—"

"Used to be commonland," the farmer grumbled loudly. "My father and his father always had the use of it. Now we must pay for every stick."

Shedwyn tched in sympathy. "True wealth is in the land, ain't it? Not in the coin they'd have us love, but in the land. And that they never give away now, do they?"

The man stared a moment longer and then nodded his head slowly in agreement. He turned the knife blade toward his breast and cut into another loaf of bread.

Shedwyn pushed her bowl into the center of the table. "Thank you," she murmured to the woman. "Your food was good, but there's more I'd ask of you," she said softly. "I see you've a jug of Mother's Tears." She pointed to a squat brown jug resting on a sideboard. "We're all in need of a taste."

The woman looked to her husband and he nodded. She crossed behind him and fetched the jug, handing it first to Shedwyn. Shedwyn pulled its cork and sniffed. She looked up at the woman, her eyes suddenly red and tearing. "Strong." Then she put it to her lips and tipped it back. She took only a small sip and shuddered visibly as she swallowed the clear liquid. She handed the jug to Jobber, who took it eagerly.

"Just a small sip," Shedwyn warned. "It's very finely made," she said, complimenting the woman.

Jobber upended the jug, preparing to swallow deeply.

"A sip!" repeated Shedwyn more loudly.

Jobber pulled the jug from her lips and gasped even with the meager swallow she had taken. Her skin turned ruddy, and her eyes leaked tears as she took a deep breath and began coughing.

On her breath she tasted wood and anise. "Z'blood!" she exhaled loudly, and held a hand to her burning throat. "Go blind with this frigging stuff," she exclaimed in a harsh whisper. She passed the bottle to Lirrel, who stared at it, impressed that one swallow had been sufficient to intimidate Jobber.

Lirrel sipped it cautiously, shocked at the sudden fire that scorched her mouth and throat. She closed her eyes, her toes curling as the liquor made its way slowly to her stomach. Sighing deeply, she handed the bottle back to the woman.

"Goodman," Shedwyn said smoothly, "lend us a place to sleep this night, for we are all weary."

The farmer shook his head. "No," he said, "and you know the reason of it already. Fugitives you are, wanted by the Sileans. The butcherboys and even the high-up Re Ameas came here this morning. They'll be back tonight. You mustn't be found here."

"Give us a horse and cart then that we may get away more quickly," Shedwyn asked, leaning forward to meet his eyes.

"No," he said. "We have little enough as it is."

"There's enough money there for a new horse. A cow as well, if you buy wisely," Shedwyn argued.

"They offered more than that for you."

"But they're butcherboys."

The farmer leaned back in his chair and his lips twisted in a bitter smile. He reached into the pocket of his vest and pulled out a pipe, the long clay handle broken off. He tapped out the old ash and began filling it with new tobacco from a small pouch resting on the table. "You were right when you said them butcherboys would take back whatever they gave for the trouble of turning you in. Most likely we'd be no better off then we are now. And though I'd not have the butcherboys profit from such a bargain, still you ask too much of us.''

''Nice to know your frigging conscience wouldn't worry you none for squealing on your own kind,'' Jobber said hotly. Shedwyn glared angrily at her and mouthed, ''Shut up.'' Huffily Jobber turned toward the fire again. Unperturbed, the farmer lit his pipe and sucked hard at the stem.

''I can't give you as much money, goodman,'' Shedwyn said. ''But I can give you a promise worth far more than the hard rattle of coins.''

She went to the hearth and reached into a small wooden bowl resting on the mantel. Every Oran home had a seed bowl to bring luck and prosperity to the household. As Shedwyn dipped her hand into the bowl, she remembered the blue crockery, with its delicate white flowers painted on the sides of the bowl, in her parents' house. She withdrew a handful of seeds, a small mixture of barley, wheat, and oats.

Shedwyn spat into one hand and placed the seeds in the hollow of her wet palm. Closing her fist tightly, she concentrated on the image of fields, ripened wheat waving a dull gold in the wind, the gray green of oats and the shaggy heads of barley bent beneath the weight of their beards. She took a breath, the scent of anise from the Mother's Tears still pungent on her lips. Then she exhaled and smiled down at her fist.

''See, goodman,'' she whispered. ''The promise of the seed bowl.'' Shedwyn opened her hand and heard his wife's astonished gasp. The seeds had sprouted, and where there had been tiny brown kernels of grain, there were now slender green stalks with spreading roots as fine as a spiderweb. ''Help me now, and I will promise you land that is rich and fertile.''

''An old trick,'' said the farmer, disbelieving.

''An old power,'' said Shedwyn. ''Oran power. And like the land, one day it will belong to us again. What say you now? Will you help us?''

The farmer drew back as if to avoid touching her. ''I've already given blood to the New Moon. Oh aye,'' he said quickly as Shedwyn tried to speak. ''There's no denying that's who you are.''

''And so I won't,'' she answered.

Lirrel stood suddenly and addressed the woman, huddled near

the hearth clutching at Brea. "A son," she said softly. "You have a son."

"I had a son," the man answered. "But he left two years ago before his Naming. He fled north in the spring, telling no one but his sister."

"Before his Naming?" Lirrel asked him again.

"Aye. The New Moon took him. Lured him away with the same promise of land."

"Or perhaps the promise of life," countered Lirrel. "His own. Surely your son had power? And where else but among the New Moon could he survive?"

"It's a lie," the man snapped.

"It's truth," said Lirrel softly, shaking her head. "He had to flee. And Brea is like gifted. These are your children, goodman. Will you empty the precious contents of your seed bowl into the hands of Sileans and the Readers? Help us now, that we may grant them a future."

The man slumped in his chair and tenderly pulled his daughter onto his lap. The child leaned her head against his shoulder. Brea lifted a hand to her father's rough cheek and stroked the sad face.

"Take the gray, pastured in the field," he said roughly. "There's a cart and harness in the barn."

"Thank you," Shedwyn said, relief evident in her voice.

"Oy—" Jobber started to say, and Shedwyn stopped her, knowing in advance what was on her mind.

"There are others with us," Shedwyn said. "We need some food for them as well."

The farmer rose to protest but his wife stayed him.

"Here"—she spoke quickly—"you'll need some blankets for the journey and a shawl for yourself." Throwing open the lid to a carved wooden clothes chest, she pulled out thick felted blankets, torn and mended along the fringe but still usable. They were dark blue with stripes of dirty white on the border. The woman paused before the open chest and then pulled out two gray wool smocks. She handed them to Shedwyn.

"They were intended for my son's wedding day, but I think now we shall never see that," she said simply. Then she gave her a black shawl and an extra skirt to Lirrel. "And here, take these," she said, stepping into the pantry and returning with an orange globe of dried cheese, a string bag filled with dried apples, and three more loaves of bread. Lastly she handed her the jug of Mother's Tears. "It's not much—"

"It's far more than we hoped for," answered Shedwyn.

"One thing I ask in return," the woman said, staring hard at Shedwyn. "Send me word of my son, whether he is living or no."

Shedwyn nodded. "I'll try. What is his name?"

"Arnard Bestin," she said. "He's black-haired, black-eyed like Reave here, but he's got my face. And a scar," she said hastily, "that runs the length of his forearm, where he caught it on a rake." Her face was pale and green eyes brittle. Around her mouth lines hardened. "I had five children. Arnard and Brea are my last and the only two still surviving. Please find him." Then she turned her face toward the hearth, unwilling to let them see the tears that brimmed in her eyes.

Shedwyn spoke, though her throat felt constricted. "I'll get word to you as soon as I can."

Jobber opened the door and led the way out into the night. As they stood once more together in the dark, Shedwyn huffed a relieved sigh.

"That was done well," said Lirrel.

"We must be quick," Shedwyn answered roughly.

"Don't trust him, do you?" Jobber said knowingly.

"Wish I could."

"Makes you wonder, don't it, why anyone would want to get mixed up in the New Moon. Fighting for a bunch of dirt twirlers that would just as soon sell you when your back was turned."

"And in the streets of Beldan, are they always so honest?" Shedwyn asked angrily. "Does hunger never send one against another? Are you so trusting of your kind?" She stopped walking and turned angrily to Jobber. "Beldan-bred you are and giving the bitch to the rest of Oran life that you know now't about."

Jobber faced Shedwyn squarely and the two women edged closer together, anger bristling between them. Shedwyn planted her feet solidly into the ground, her posture almost daring Jobber to come at her. Jobber's shoulders relaxed as her hands tightened into fists. She poised herself on the balls of her feet, ready to attack.

"Please," Lirrel said, darting quickly between them.

"Get out of the way," Jobber said in a low, menacing voice.

"Please, this is no time for an argument," Lirrel insisted.

"The others are waiting. They are cold and hungry and you are both being foolish. Settle this another time. Not now."

"Huld's peace," Shedwyn breathed heavily. Turning stiffly away from Jobber and Lirrel, she set off for the barn.

"Jobber, tell me," Lirrel demanded, "why must you fight with her?"

"She thinks too much of herself."

"That's not it."

"She's a frigging farmer. I ain't got nothing to say to her."

"Another excuse."

"Then you tell me, Lirrel," Jobber said fiercely. "I see her face, and all I want to do is wipe off that cold, smug look."

"Cold look?" Lirrel repeated softly, puzzling at the strangeness of Jobber's words.

"Leave it," Jobber growled, "just leave it."

"Can you control your temper? At least until we are safely away?" Lirrel asked coolly.

"As long as that farmer girl doesn't push me."

"Try, Jobber. It's important to the rest of us," Lirrel finished pointedly.

"All right," Jobber answered testily. "Now let's go, before they leave us behind for the butcherboys."

Jobber and Lirrel joined the others where they waited by an old fence of stacked stone. Alwir and Eneas had already put on the woolen smocks, and Faul had wrapped a blanket around her shivering shoulders. She was eating a thick slab of bread, scarcely giving herself time to chew before swallowing.

"What's on?" Jobber asked Faul.

"Shedwyn's getting the horse," she answered, her voice thickened by the bread she was chewing.

"Had any of the jug yet?"

She shook her head. "What jug?"

"Ask the farmer girl. Mother's Tears, she called it."

"Z'blood." Faul sighed. "Don't I know it. Go blind if you drink too much, but not half worth the trouble. So who's got the frigging jug then?" she demanded. Wyer turned in the dark and gave it over to Faul's eager hand. Jobber could hear him gasping, sucking air in noisily as the liquor burned his tongue.

Shedwyn had slipped quietly through the gate and was standing in the empty field. The wind rustled through the thin limbs of the poplars, turning the undersides of the new leaves toward the rising moon. She whistled and then clucked her tongue. Jobber peered out across the moonlit field, not seeing anything. Shedwyn whistled again, a single high note from between her teeth.

Then from the far edge of the field, where it dipped down toward the river, a horse whickered in reply. Jobber heard the steady thud of hooves running across the short grassy field. As it lifted from the dark ground like one of the thunderheads, Jobber suddenly saw the horse's head as it appeared over the crest of the bank. It rose higher and higher, the rest of the massive body coming into view as it cantered up the bank and over the field toward the gate.

"Z'blood. Big un, ain't he?" Jobber said.

The horse stopped short, cautiously eyeing Shedwyn, his nostrils catching her unfamiliar scent. Shedwyn walked slowly toward the big draft horse, all the while talking in a low, calm voice. The horse bobbed his blocky head up and down, his shaggy ears pricked forward as he eyed her nervously. But he stood still as Shedwyn reached him and allowed her to stroke his cheek. She ran her hand down along the length of his neck, stopping to scratch in the rough hairs under the shaggy mane. Shedwyn continued to talk to the horse, letting him sniff the sides of her face and take small nibbles of her braid. She laughed softly when he snorted a blast of warm, moist air on her chest and captured his gristled chin in her palm. The horse snuffled her upturned palm.

Shedwyn whispered to him and the gray came willingly to the gate, his big hooves plodding deeply in the mud. As they passed through the gate, Jobber took a step backward, finding the sheer bulk of the horse daunting. Her head was barely level with its croup, and when he twisted his thickset neck, the better to see her, Jobber felt small. He reached out to nip at her hair, jerking back his head and snorting as Jobber yelped in surprise.

"There's a good lad," Shedwyn said, tucking her arm under his jowls and pulling him gently toward the wagon. "Come on lad, don't be cheeky."

Later, under a clear night sky, Jobber lay on her back and stared up at the cold glimmer of stars. On the buckboard of the wagon Shedwyn held the reins, guiding the draft horse down the dirt road while next to her sat Eneas. To any passing them, they appeared a tired Oran farm couple coming home from marketing in Remmerton. In the back of the wagon, concealed for the most part by musty hay, lay the others. Jobber scratched her nose, blowing away a stray stalk that tried to push its way up her nose.

"Faul?" she whispered.

"Hmm?" came a sleepy reply.

"What are you going to do?"

"Sleep."

"Not now. I mean later."

"Drink."

"Z'blood, Faul," Jobber said angrily. "You know what I mean. What are you going to do when the others head north. Are you going with them to join the New Moon?"

Jobber heard a rustling in the hay as Faul shifted in her hiding place. "All my life only one thing has mattered. Me," she said with finality. "At my age I am not about to change that. I'll go to Stormfast."

"What do you mean 'your age'? You ain't so old. It's the Queen turning you out for a few gray hairs that's made you think that way. So now you're running off to some hidey-hole—"

"Stormfast Island isn't a hole!" Faul said smartly.

"Right. It's a piece of rock in the middle of the ocean. What's the difference? You're burying yourself, Faul, tucking up the sod right around your chin."

"So are you joining the New Moon, Jobber?" Faul asked abruptly, turning the subject away from herself.

"Don't know yet," replied Jobber softly. "I used to think like you, Faul, that the only thing that mattered was myself. But it's getting harder to think that way."

"Why?" asked Faul in a muffled voice. Jobber guessed she was nearly asleep again.

"Well, for one thing there's people that have died because for some reason I mattered to them," Jobber said, thinking of Donal and Dogsbody, and even before them, Growler.

"A foolish gesture on their part."

"Or heroic."

"Don't be a hero, Jobber," came Faul's reply. "It doesn't pay well."

Jobber snorted. "Should've left you in the sinkhole, Faul."

"See what I mean?" Faul said dryly. "Already you're complaining that I'm not grateful enough for your one bit of heroism. If you join the New Moon, you'll need a better reason than making yourself a hero."

"And you ought to be able to find a better way to bury yourself than heading of to some piece of rock in the ocean."

"Meaning?"

"Why not die with your sword drawn?"

Faul was quiet a moment and then spoke softly. "Perhaps. Now be quiet and let me sleep."

Jobber was silent, staring moodily at the stars. Questions gnawed unanswered in her head. The world has changed much since Beldan. Had she changed, too? What should she do? What choices did she have? Round and round she went until her head started to ache with the confusion.

"Chose a path," Lirrel whispered sleepily.

"Stop reading my mind," Jobber snapped.

"Stop thinking so loudly."

"Now, how in the frigging fire can I do that?"

"Close your eyes and listen," Lirrel said.

Frowning, Jobber squeezed her eyes shut and listened. The wheels of the cart groaned as they rolled heavily over the road. The leather of the harness creaked with the jostling of the draft horse, and the hooves made a soft thumping on the dirt. Between the noises of their traveling Jobber heard a voice singing. She listened more closely and realized it was Lirrel's voice. Jobber sat up and looked over to where Lirrel lay. She was sleeping on her side, curled like a field mouse in the straw. Her face was still, eyes shut, and her lips unmoving. Yet Jobber continued to hear the music of Lirrel's singing in her mind's ear. Slowly she lay back again in the hay, confusion replaced by a sense of wonder. Lirrel's singing blended with the star-struck night, and in Jobber's head it seemed to sketch a semblance of order to her scattered thoughts.

Chapter Eight

"*How long before we reach the village of Cairns?*" Eneas asked Shedwyn. His back ached from the hard ride of the buckboard and his hands chaffed where they gripped the reins. He squinted, his brow deeply furrowed as he stared straight ahead at the bobbing gap between the gray's pointed ears. The road had become more dangerous in the last day, stretching up away from the plains as they entered the low foothills of Avadares. As the ground grew more barren and rocky there were fewer places to hide, a fact that made Eneas increasingly nervous.

"I don't know for certain," she answered. "I've never been this far north."

"I have," Alwir said from the wagon. "It's not much farther. We should get there today."

"And beyond Cairns?" Shedwyn asked, turning to face Alwir.

"Once we get into Avadares, the New Moon will find us."

"How do you know so much?" Eneas asked sharply.

"I left the Readers Guild a long time ago, Eneas. It was a journey I made on my own," he added pointedly.

Eneas's cheeks flushed red. "What are you saying, Alwir?"

"Nothing, really," Alwir answered, looking down at the plains behind them and then up to the sloping wall of pink and gray stone rising in the near distance about them. Small twisted pines trees speckled the rock face. "Just that I hope you know what you're doing here. Can't say as you will be a welcome sight."

"If they accepted you, a Reader, Alwir, then I, too, may be welcomed," Eneas replied with more confidence than he felt.

Alwir was quiet, tugging thoughtfully at his sparse beard. He looked over at Wyer and gave him a thoughtful shrug. Wyer knew the truth of it. It hadn't been all that easy for Alwir to convince the New Moon he was sincere. Not until he had signed his name to the maps of the Keep, documents that would incriminate him if found by the Sileans. And now, of course, since the massacre at Firefaire, Alwir was a hunted man whose only future lay with the New Moon.

"Ah, a host of traitors and turncoats to their noble origins," Faul said sarcastically. "Now, that's an army to trust in battle."

"You're not one to snicker, Faul," Jobber spoke up. "After all, you're here, too, you know. You've gone from being Beldan's upright Firstwatch to a murderer of Silean Guards. I'd say that since leaving Beldan, you've made quite a reputation for yourself."

"You made my reputation," Faul snapped. "You did that."

"Aw, my arse. It was you that wanted that brangle with the Guards the first time we met at the Anvil, remember," Jobber said, her cheeks pinking with irritation. "You make your own choices. Always have. I just gave you the opportunity."

Faul snorted angrily, refusing to answer Jobber's charge. Instead she turned her attention to her dagger. They had been using it to cut the dried cheese and she cleaned it now vigorously with a piece of fabric torn from the hem of her shirt.

"Do you miss the sea?" Lirrel asked Faul with a consoling smile.

"I'm not opposed to land as long as it's near enough to smell the sea. But out here there's only an ocean of dry land." Faul slapped her thighs and uttered a low "Bah" as little clouds of fine red dust swirled into the air.

"What do you think of it?" Lirrel asked Jobber. They sat on the back end of the cart, their legs dangling over the edge. Lirrel had undone her braids and was shaking out bits of chaff and straw caught in her black hair.

"Think of what?" Jobber asked, still annoyed with Faul.

"The countryside. Oran's broad plains. Aren't they're beautiful?" Lirrel coaxed.

Jobber sighed, her cheeks puffed with air. In one way the western plains were more beautiful than anything she had ever seen before. And in another, more desolate than any back alley and trash-strewn street she'd ever slept in. They had traveled out of the black muck of Soring Basin over the last two days and now cobbled along the edges of the west country. The broad plains unfurled below like an immense blanket of rose-colored wool. Here and there ran stripes of pale green lucerne bordering the empty fields. Small houses of stone squatted at the field's edge, a few bare poplars to give them the promise of shade. Above, the sky was an endless blue expanse; no towers or Keep, no decrepit buildings shouldered together to blot out the wide-open beauty of the sky. And yet it seemed to Jobber that it was a land devoid of life, barren and parched. They had seen few fires in the stone chimneys, even fewer people, and had heard only the distant bleat of thirsty animals and the occasional harsh clank of goat bells. In Beldan in the spring, there was a ripe, earthy smell that rose with the morning mist off the Hiring Fields after the last frost. But here, there was no damp scent of spring and few signs beyond the long red scars in the plowed earth to show that people lived and farmed here.

"I don't know, Lirrel." Jobber shook her head. "It seems sort of dead to me."

"It's early yet, Jobber. Spring comes later to the north," Lirrel answered.

"No," said Shedwyn from her place upfront. "Jobber's right. Years of drought are turning the plains into deserts. Look how the dust clings to us and how we carry away with us on our clothes, our hands, and our faces the last handfuls of fertile soil." She shook her head gravely. "First comes the plowing and then the planting, but without the rain, all hope is blown away. Even the wheat and rye planted last winter can't amount to much, given the lack of rain."

"*Ahal*," Lirrel murmured softly, and shook her hair free in the dry wind. "I had hoped I remembered wrongly since the last time I was here. But you force me to see the truth. The drought has changed everything."

"When were you here last?" Jobber asked curiously.

Lirrel pursed her lips and her eyes turned upward as she counted back the months. "Two years ago. The Ghazali are always on the road. There is no place in Oran that I haven't been," she added proudly. "Even the islands, when the weather permitted.'' Then she smiled at Jobber. "One day I will take you to Myre's Cave high up in Dalarna Mountain."

"Never heard of it," Jobber said, shaking her head.

"Oh, but you must have!" exclaimed Lirrel.

"It's where the first Fire Sword was made," Wyer explained. He took off his boot and emptied it of red gravel. His feet were big, the solid blunt toes now a pale pink from the dust of the road. "I'd like to go there myself." He smiled at her. "To see the forge."

"Yes. The cave holds the remnants of a great forge. It took thirty men to pump the bellows!" Lirrel said with a slight nod of her head. "It's one of the old places of power. Ghazalis used to visit it while on pilgrimage."

Jobber continued to look perplexed. "Fire Sword?"

"Don't you know the story of the first Fire Sword and how the Fire Queen Myre welded flame to steel? And how the Kirian stole it from her out of jealousy?"

Jobber shook her head and straightened her shoulders, interested. "Nah. I don't even know what the Kirian are."

"Tcha, Jobber," Lirrel said, "your old teacher Growler must have told you about the Kirian at least. Surely he did?" Lirrel looked at Jobber hopefully.

Jobber shook her head. "Guess there wasn't time. So you tell me, because I know you will anyway. But look, make it story-like, will you? I hate those lectures."

Lirrel gave a pleasant laugh. "*Ahal*. I will give you the story of Myre and the Fire Sword." She settled her hands in her lap. "It begins like this. . . . " She bent her head, silent for a moment, as if thinking of the right words to start her story.

Jobber glanced out over the reddened plains, waiting for her to begin. A lone cloud drifted across the blue sky and she absently watched its shadow pass over the land.

"Well?" she said. "What happened?" She nudged Lirrel with her elbow. Lirrel's head lifted slowly in mute reply and the delicate features of her face were cinched in an expression of terror. Her eyes stared, huge and white against her brown skin.

"Z'blood," Jobber swore, shocked at the change in Lirrel's features. She grabbed Lirrel roughly by the shoulders and shook her. "Lirrel!" she shouted in alarm. "Lirrel, what is it?" Lirrel's graceful body was rigid and resisted Jobber's grasp. Her arms pressed tightly against her body, and her small, shapely hands curled into claws over her breasts.

But it was Lirrel's eyes that caused Jobber's pulse to hammer fiercely. The silver of Lirrel's eyes changed as colors seeped into them, first pink and then the rose color of Oran's soil, and last the deep rusty red of blood.

Lirrel moaned and her head drooped forward, black hair covering her face.

"Lirrel, what is it?" Jobber pleaded. Lirrel trembled like a trapped sparrow beneath Jobber's hands. She gave no answer but moaned and whimpered, drawing her body into a tighter knot.

"Stop the cart!" Jobber shouted to Eneas. "Stop the frigging cart. Something's wrong."

The cart lurched to a halt, knocking them sideways. Faul swore and clutched the side of the wagon, then hastily returned her knife to her boot. Eneas pulled the brake lever as Shedwyn jumped down from the buckboard. She ran to the back of the cart where Jobber held the coiled Lirrel.

"What's the matter with her?" Faul asked. She leaned over Jobber's shoulder and gently pulled Lirrel's head back again to examine her face. Her black hair parted, revealing her eyes, devoid of pupils and glittering red, as hard as two garnets.

"Huld's peace," Shedwyn gasped.

"What's happened to her eyes?" Faul asked. Lirrel began keening, singing harsh, guttural-sounding words in Ghazali. She scarcely drew breath, choking as if the words were forced through her throat.

"Trance. She's in trance," Jobber answered. "It's happened before, at Firefaire. She saw the massacre—no worse, she experienced it—before it happened."

"Can we help her?" asked Alwir.

Jobber shook her head. "I don't know how."

Jobber dragged Lirrel erect by the shoulders. She forced herself to stare deeply into the red eyes. "Lirrel!" she called. "Lirrel, come back."

"She can't hear you," Shedwyn said.

"Lirrel," Jobber shouted again, more desperately. Lirrel shook her head wildly and fought furiously against Jobber's hold. She started wailing, long piercing cries of despair.

"Use your head, Jobber," Faul said gruffly, tapping the side of her temple. "Lirrel always complains that you think too loud. Call from inside."

Jobber hesitated, afraid. The bloody eyes leaked tears, and as the drops mingled with the red dust on Lirrel's cheeks, they left pink tracks on Lirrel's terrified face.

Jobber screwed her courage tighter and forced herself to concentrate. She closed her eyes so as not to see Lirrel but to imagine her as she always was, calm and resolute. She had no clear notion of how to think her way to Lirrel. Only the idea that if she reached to her own magic source, perhaps that would guide her. She allowed herself to slip inward, moving in her mind toward the center of the fire. But there was no light to be seen, no warmth to be felt. She found herself instead surrounded by darkness. She could hear the baying of a storm and she felt a sudden wind circling her face. It was cold and snatched her breath away.

"Lirrel?" she called apprehensively as the sound of her voice seemed to evaporate in the wind. Jobber tensed, angry at the impenetrable darkness. At once the darkness was broken by the tiny heart of flame that burst into life in the palm of her hand. Jobber recognized it as her own power and was glad that her anger could still summon fire, even here in this dark wasteland. Holding aloft her flaming hand, she called again, more boldly. Around her she saw vague shadows, drifting forms caught in a current of wind. *"Lirrel, I am here. Come to me. Come to the light."*

The flame flickered higher even as a wind blew with its mournful cry. And from the shadows Lirrel appeared, and in her midnight dress, her face and hands seemed to float. She stirred, and like a lunar eclipse, shards of white light were shining on the edges of her body and spiking the darkness. *"Lirrel,"* Jobber said, and Lirrel looked up, her face contorted with weeping.

"Jobber," she said, her voice a reedy flute in the wind. *"Jobber, they've blinded me with their hate."*

"You're safe among us," said another voice. Jobber peered into the shadows and saw a faint green image of Shedwyn, hovering near Lirrel.

"You here, too?" Jobber asked, surprised and strangely relieved to see her.

"Aye, I thought I might be able to help," Shedwyn answered simply. Along Shedwyn's body, tendrils of green light circled, leafing out the length of her arms and fingers.

Jobber stared at her own hand, astonished to see the orange

and yellow fire bursting from her fingertips like lit tapers. *"Where are we?"* Jobber asked, confused.

"At the edge of Chaos," came Lirrel's reply.

"Z'blood," Jobber swore, looking at Shedwyn uncertainly as the ghostly green face wavered in the shadows.

"Now that we have found her, how do we get out of here?" Shedwyn asked Jobber.

"I don't know. I ain't never done this." Jobber imagined shaking her head and was disconcerted by the sensation that her body moved, but at the bidding of the wind rather than by her own will. *"Maybe we just have to think our way out. Same as we got in."*

"Aye, perhaps you're right. But Lirrel's got to join us, or it's no good. She'll be left behind."

Jobber spoke to the weeping figure. Tears of quicksilver flowed down her face. *"Come on, Lirrel, we got to leave this empty place."*

"No!" Lirrel said, and Jobber was brushed by a gust of rank-smelling wind. Jobber knew well the odor and recognized the taint of Lirrel's fear in the air. It made her grind her teeth and she had to force herself to speak again.

"This ain't no place to hide, Lirrel," Jobber urged, trying to stave off the contagion of Lirrel's terror.

"Come, Lirrel." Shedwyn spoke calmly. *"Think of the light, Lirrel, and we will go there together. Whatever it is, you will not face it alone."*

Lirrel silenced her weeping. Her form wavered and to Jobber she appeared vaporous, as fragile as the mist. The wind keened fitfully, and Jobber willed the fire nestled in her palm to bloom brighter.

Lirrel saw it and she clung to Jobber. She sighed a chord of sadness. As Jobber watched, Lirrel's form began to shine more brightly, until Jobber was blinded by its brilliance. Jobber closed her eyes and concentrated on recalling herself to the hardness of the wagon, the warmth of sunlight on her back and the powdery itch of soil on her skin. The keening howl of the wind faded and she breathed easily hearing the solid crack of Faul's loud swearing.

Slowly Jobber opened her eyes, blinking at the brightness of sunlight reflected in the pink granite rocks of Avadares. Lirrel sagged in her arms, her head falling forward to rest on Jobber's shoulder. She shuddered once and then drew in a deep breath.

"Is she . . . ?" Alwir asked.

"Aye," Shedwyn answered, leaning her head against the slats of the wagon's side. "She is back."

"But where was she?" Faul asked.

"I don't know."

Lirrel picked up her head and Jobber saw her eyes had become silvery again. But her face was lined with misery. The opal sheen of her eyes was a tarnished silver. Too much, thought Jobber, she had seen too much.

"Z'blood," Jobber said, still holding Lirrel firmly by the shoulders. "What did you see? Was it like Firefaire?"

Lirrel nodded stiffly and rubbed her arms as if they ached from cold. "A vision."

"The future?"

"Yes and no."

"What's that supposed to mean?" Faul said angrily. She tugged at her vest with agitation. Her slate-gray eyes darted over the hillsides as if expecting an onslaught of Guards at any moment. She wanted an enemy she could see, could fight.

Lirrel's head drooped with fatigue and she sagged. Jobber drew her arm over Lirrel's thin shoulders and pulled her close. Pain flared in her chest, and she swallowed hard at the dryness in her mouth. Lirrel was here, she told herself, safe from the nightmare of the trance. And yet she was no longer the Lirrel that Jobber knew, that she loved. Before Lirrel had looked upon misery, she had believed as a Ghazali that only peace and compassion could conquer the destruction caused by hatred and violence. Jobber had rarely agreed with her, and yet she had come to rely upon Lirrel's insistence of peace as a shelter and a hope that life could be lived without its usual horrors. And now Lirrel had seen something terrible, so terrible that her spirit had withered. She was made old by a vision of terror, and an unknown despair had hollowed the youthful curve of her cheek.

"Let's go," Jobber said gruffly. "Let's get the frigging shit out of here," and she clutched Lirrel protectively.

Shedwyn climbed into the back of the cart and sat next to Lirrel. She took her hand and held it gently between her own. Eneas silently returned to the buckboard. He pulled the brake lever and the cart slipped backward until the gray found his footing again on the gravelly road. The big horse grunted, heaving his weight forward. The wheels groaned as the cart started up the path through the foothills again.

For a long time no one spoke. Eneas kept his eyes to the road, cursing every rut and stone that jostled the cart and slowed their progress. Wyer sat staring out at the fields, the muscles of his forearms bunching reflexively as he thought of Crier's Forge and the solid feel of a hammer. Faul returned to cleaning her dagger until there was not a speck of dirt on the handle or blade. And still she cleaned it, not wanting to look up and see Lirrel's slumped back.

Alwir tugged his beard and chewed the already ragged ends of his mustache. Then he drew up his knees and rested his forehead against the hard bone of his kneecaps. While Shedwyn and Jobber had searched for Lirrel, he had Read them. Jobber first, her whole body seeming to burst into fire like the Great Bonfire of Firefaire. Then Shedwyn joined her and the green aura had merged with the orange flames. Colors twisted together like a newly strung warp of light. And when they had found her, Lirrel's white aura wove its thread through the warp, with a shuttle of moonlight. Alwir was convinced that the three of them had enough power, together and apart, to be what the New Moon and the vaggers had been searching Oran to find. A new Queens' quarter knot, a knot to challenge the blasting power of the Fire Queen. Alwir leaned his head to one side and glanced at Lirrel's back, his face troubled. But what then had she seen? A vision of death? Her own perhaps? What else could be so frightening and bloody as to turn the silver of her eyes so red a color?

Lirrel's head lifted and angled to the side. He saw the fine line of her profile, the dark tangled hair blown back by a gust of wind. "Much worse, Alwir," she said softly, and he knew with a sudden shock that she had heard his thoughts. "Much, much worse," she repeated, and turned away again.

"There it is," Alwir said, pointing to the black streams of smoke curling up into the cloudless sky. "Cairns is just over that ridge where the smoke rises."

"Z'blood, at last," said Faul, stowing her dagger in her boot. She sat up straight and stretched her back. Then she looked up at the tall columns of smoke and frowned. "For a village with not much wood they keep a lot of fires."

"It might be spring chores they're doing," Shedwyn said, watching the smoke. "Shearing's done, perhaps they're scouring wool or slaughtering pigs. If the village does it together, it means using less wood."

A breeze gusted down the side of the hills and blew more fine particles of red dust in their faces. Jobber wrinkled her nose at an unpleasant smell that was carried by the wind. "Stinks like the crematorium Scroggles back home in Beldan," she said uneasily to Shedwyn.

The cart reached the top of the ridge and the village of Cairns came into view. It was a small village, nestled in the rock face of the mountains. Great heaps of pink and gray stone collected at its back, threatening to roll into the village square. And yet around the heaped boulders, houses perched, clinging like the yellow-green lichens to the stones.

"Look!" shouted Wyer, pointing out to the village. "There's a house afire!"

"And another one over there!" added Alwir. Thick black smoke lifted from the burning thatch of a stone cottage.

"Z'blood! the whole village is burning," said Faul. "Everyone out of the cart!" she ordered.

They scrambled out of the cart, Jobber helping Lirrel down. Faul stood on the ridge, staring down at the village. There was no movement, no sign that anyone moved to put out the fires. "It's too damn quiet," she said softly, and Jobber felt a chill creep along her spine. "Where is everyone?"

"Hiding," ventured Alwir. "Many villages in Avadares have hiding places higher up in the mountains, as protection against the Sileans, especially at tax time. Maybe they've fled, waiting until it's safe to return."

"Yeah, but what happened? Who did this? And are they still about?" Jobber insisted.

Lirrel came to stand next to Faul. She gazed at the village, her hands clenched in tight fists at her sides. "I will riddle it to you," she said in a rasping voice. "I have neither village, nor home, nor hands, nor feet, yet I wander everywhere."

Faul's face grew ashen at the words. She spoke softly, completing the riddle: "I have neither mouth, nor teeth, nor bowels, yet I eat food steadily." She finished reciting the riddle and saw that Lirrel's expression had softened, the harshness chased by sorrow. "Your vision," Faul asked Lirrel, "their past but our future?" Lirrel nodded. Faul exhaled with an angry hiss and turned away, shaking her head slowly. "They're not in hiding, Alwir," she said flatly. "They're dead. Death has been here and claimed this village. Come. This will be hard business. Better to get it over with."

She started down the other side of the ridge, heading for the village. Behind her the others hesitated, afraid to follow. Faul didn't blame them. She had looked often enough on the face of death and never found it agreeable. And yet most of those deaths had come about in fighting against an opponent ready and willing to do battle. The battle had shaped the deaths, giving them purpose and at least a skewed sense of honor. But she knew with cold certainty as she put her foot on the wooden bridge that served as an entrance to the village that there would be no honor in the death found here.

She walked across the bridge and up the main street of the village. Smoke swirled from the first house. The door had been ripped from its hinges and hung forlornly to the side. Blood-stained linens lay piled on the threshold and crockery was smashed in the street. Beside the whitewashed wall of the cottage a dog lay in a stiffened curl. Flies buzzed angrily about the bloodied muzzle.

Faul turned away and started up the street, the feeling of dread slowing her steps. The stench grew stronger, stinging her eyes till they teared. She gagged, choking on the smell. She wiped her eyes clear and saw them lying scattered like tossed debris along the streets. Corpses everywhere, still and silent except for the crackling of the dying fires and the faint seething of flies. She couldn't move, but stood staring, not wanting to believe she saw them.

"Z'blood," whispered a horrified Jobber. Faul's shoulders gave a sharp twitch at the sudden sound of a human voice amidst so much carnage. "Z'blood what have they done?" Jobber asked again.

Shedwyn passed them, both hands pressed against her cheeks. She walked up to each slowly, staring with numbed horror at their rigid forms. One woman lay on the remnants of a small garden, her legs splayed at obtuse angles. Her skirts were thrown over her head, exposing her naked body. Her torso and thighs were covered with scratches and small cuts. Shedwyn leaned down beside the corpse and straightened the woman's legs, drawing them together. She then reached up, pulled the skirts down from over the woman's head, and covered the body again. Tears spilled from Shedwyn's eyes as she stared into the face of the corpse. A woman, not much older than herself. Her face was mercifully serene except for the coarse gash that opened the side of her head, the black of her hair turned brown as old iron from the blood.

Shedwyn drew away from the corpse and continued with the others, blinded by the tears that refused to stop and shaken by sobs of grief. They shuffled through the streets of Cairns, witnesses to the final hours of the village's existence.

Alwir found a group of men and boys collected behind the stone wall of the inn. They had been bound and then shot with arrows in a mass execution. Layered as they fell, one row atop another, they formed a wall of corpses, sealed together by a mortar of blood. Some were naked, some still wore their night smocks, and Alwir guessed that the attack had come at night, catching the village unawares. He saw an arrow lying near his boot and bent to pick it up. The head gleamed malevolently in the sun. It was heavy and the fletch of gray and black matched the colors of the Silean Guard. He threw the arrow down and took one last hard look at the jumble of bodies. His eyes could not contain the whole of them, the men and boys whose lifeless forms lay tumbled together in an obscene harvest. Eyes like milky glass stared back, mouths opened as if to speak remained eloquent in their silence. Alwir bent his head and left them, capable only of recalling the strange blending of their faces until they became in his mind like a fresco of ghostly figures carved on the rock face.

Eneas and Wyer met him in the street. Wyer gripped Alwir hard about the arm. Wyer's eyes were heavy-lidded, refusing to meet Alwir's gaze, and his cheeks appeared deeply seamed with anguish. "I can look no more."

"There's no one left alive," Eneas whispered. "No one." Beneath the dirt of travel, his skin was bleached and the blue eyes seemed faded.

"Silean butcherboys did this," Alwir spat, barking the words. "Your people."

"No!" Eneas shouted hoarsely, and a flush of red colored his neck and cheeks. "No, not my people." His eyelids shut tightly and then fluttered as he forced the lids open. They were red-rimmed as tears of rage brimmed along the lashes. "Not my people anymore," he repeated softly.

"Where are the others?" Alwir asked, his voice sounding strange and thick to him.

Wyer shook his head.

"Let's find them."

They walked together, seeking the others and averting their eyes to the scenes of violence scattered everywhere. They found Jobber bent double as she retched beside a cottage wall. Not far from her a child lay partially hidden by burning staves. Alwir saw only its small outstretched hand, thin lines of dried blood etched in the palm.

Alwir pulled Jobber upright and supported her while she fought to gain her breath. She lifted her face skyward, and tears streamed down the sides of her face. Her red-gold hair clung to her back like tangled threads of weathered copper, the shine subdued by dull verdigris.

"Come away," Alwir urged in a quiet voice. Jobber followed him, stumbling over the cobblestone streets.

Faul stood in the middle of the dark cottage, her eyes frantically searching every dark corner. Light from the burned-out roof fell in straight shafts through the room below. Dust and ash swirled in the ribbons of gold light. She picked up fallen chairs and kicked aside the broken dishes and smashed possessions. She was searching for something. Something in particular. She had gone through five cottages and still she had not found it. Z'blood, she swore savagely, they must have had at least one sword. One sword that might have been raised against the Sileans. They could not have gone so horribly, so defenseless without struggle to their deaths.

Furiously she threw open the splintered lid of a chest and rummaged through the collection of linens and woven blankets. There beneath the carefully washed and folded fabrics of a woman's dowry chest, Faul found what she was looking for. Groaning, she reached down and pulled it out. She pressed it gratefully against her cheek and then held it out to examine it. It was an old sword. Very old and of Oran make. Its scabbard a plain black, the handle long and slim, the grip wrapped in fine leather. She freed the blade and gazed with awe at the flash of metal. The steel was good, the edge still keen and free of nicks. Along the blade's edge was a pattern of red and silver steel, undulating like the flowing movement of waves. Faul returned the blade and heard the quiet click as the guard locked in place. She gave a dry humorless smile and silenced the old nervous tic that rustled the side of her otherwise calm cheek. Just the feel of a sword in her hand steadied her, brought back the tuned instincts of the fighter. With sword in hand, she was in command. And in command again, death no longer posed a tragedy, but was an accepted reality of her life. She held the sword tightly, as if the shining white steel inside its dull black scabbard could shield her from the numbing horror of death's touch.

She left the cottage, sword in hand, and fury boiled white hot in her breast. They had never used the sword. Perhaps they hadn't known how. But by Zorah's blood, she, Faul Verran, was no stranger to the sword and she would use it, too. Every Silean she met would fall beneath it, their bodies severed by the sword and her own stinging hate.

Silent but for the soft scuffle of the stones under her feet, Lirrel walked around the village square. The hem of her dress brushed against the dead lying scattered on the ground and blood soaked the soles of her shoes as she made no effort to avoid the drying streams and puddles. Flies buzzed angrily at her passing before settling again. The vivid memory of the trance shone in her eyes, and pain echoed in her chest and limbs. She touched her throat absently as if to find her own faint pulse. Her skin felt dry and leathery beneath her fingertips. Had she died when they died? Was she now a ghost, wandering restlessly among its dead companions? And if she came at last upon her body, lying commingled with the others, would she cry out or simply lie down and accept it? Lirrel continued walking, dazed, as she searched for herself in the battle-torn faces of Cairns's dead.

At the outskirts of the village she stopped suddenly and wheeled around. She listened and heard the sound of scraping rock and soil, punctuated by the bleating of goats and the discordant clang of the goat bell.

She stepped slowly toward the sound and Lirrel saw a boy, coming around the last cottage before the north gate of the village spade in hand, digging in the hard, dry soil. To one side lay several mounds of freshly risen soil. One corpse remained, a child from the small size of it, respectfully laid out, a tattered cloth covering the face. A braid escaped from underneath one corner of the cloth and Lirrel saw the fluttering of blue tassels. In a small pen farther off, moving restlessly and bleating anxiously, was a herd of piebald goats.

Lirrel approached quietly until she stood close to one side of the boy. He didn't notice her, for he was intent on his task, his eyes concerned only with the spadefuls of dirt that lifted from the ground. Lirrel studied him as he worked. In profile his face

was sharp, the features precisely drawn, from the point of his
nose to his small square chin. He'd a prominent forehead, un-
covered as his short black hair stood up, stiffened with clods
of red dirt and sweat. A drop of sweat trickled down the side
of his temple and left a dark track on his dusted skin. Short of
stature and wiry, he was nevertheless strong enough to hoist
spadeful after spadeful from the hard-compacted soil.

Lirrel drew a deep breath, her chest filling with air. Her senses
felt slowly replenished as the numbing emptiness dissipated in
the music of the boy's labor. In a place so discordant with violence, he seemed to her strangely gentle. There was no malice
in his movements, no ragged fitful gestures of vengeance, just
an even steady rhythm, dipping and swaying as he dug, accompanied by his quiet grunts as he flung the dirt on a pile. Lirrel
understood intuitively that it was the constant movement of the
spade, digging into the compacted soil, that held his grief at
bay. Focused on this one task alone, the boy pushed back the
nightmare of the village.

"Do you mean to bury them all?" she asked quietly.

"Aye," he answered, and then spun around, startled. She
heard the sharp intake of his breath.

"I didn't mean to frighten you," she apologized.

Dark eyes ringed with violent shadows stared disbelievingly
at her. "I thought it was the dead that had begun to speak," he
said.

"Is there no one else alive in Cairns?" Lirrel asked.

The boy turned to the small body waiting burial and shook
his head. "No one. No one but me . . . and the goats." He
exhaled hard as if to cast out the strangling sorrow. He wiped
his dust-streaked face, running his fingers through his cropped
hair. His hand closed convulsively into a fist around his hair and
he tugged at the roots. He stopped and Lirrel watched him struggle to open his hand and return it to the spade handle. With
renewed determination, he continued digging.

"Wait," she said, stepping closer.

"Can't," he said furiously.

"Wait," Lirrel repeated softly, and touched his arm.

At her touch he ceased digging. She turned him slowly to meet
the dark tormented eyes. Lirrel cried out as the jagged edge of
his anguish tore at her heart. She held him tightly as the fierce
clash of his emotions cast aside the vestiges of her ghostly perceptions of the village. In her trance she had seen them die,

ceptions of the village. In her trance she had seen them die, brutally and violently. Their agony had exploded before her eyes in a curtain of blood and cracked bones. Their screams had deafened her until her own music had been lost in the shrill cacophony of their dying. She had fled into darkness, lost without the music that might recall some semblance of peace and harmony. Despairing, she could not even imagine the first compassionate note that would begin the road to healing. Jobber's voice had found her, staggering, mute and blind, toward the brink of Oran's Chaos.

But standing here, awash with the palpable grief of this survivor, Lirrel understood why she had lost her voice, her music. Though she had accompanied the villagers in their death, experienced their final moments of torment, she had not known them when they were alive. They held for her no other image, no substance beyond the thin fabric of her vision woven with the horror of their death. But the boy knew them in his bone and blood. They were his people, his family and friends. Only now in the presence of his turbulence, studded with memories of faces and voices, did Lirrel sense the once-living flesh of the villagers. Their presence seemed to seethe around him, rising into the air and spreading out like thick hammerheaded clouds.

Lirrel embraced him, circling her arms around his narrow waist and drawing him close to her body. She sensed him resist, afraid of sorrow that would drown him if he allowed even this weakness. But Lirrel clutched him firmly, feeling his anguish in the taut muscles of his shoulders, in the wooden mask of his face, and in the tension of his throat where strangled sobs burned. She shared his sorrow, tasted its bitterness, and heard the long silent cry of his heart.

"Lirrel?" Jobber called softly.

Lirrel released him, but stayed holding his hand, and turned to the others. Jobber's face was chalk white, her lips a near bloodless line sketched on her face. Near her, Shedwyn wore a face of stone, her brown skin dusted with ash and turned gray as gravel. Alwir's eyes that once shone a glittering blue, bright with the passion of his cause, gazed cataracted and dulled. Along the broad sweep of Wyer's shoulders and arms, the muscles bunched and twitched, and his craggy head drooped on his chest. At his side Eneas's cheeks were red, scoured with fury and shame. Lastly Lirrel looked at Faul, and when she saw the hard set of her angular jaw and flat gray eyes, she shivered. Faul carried a sword, the handle tilted upward. Lirrel thought how like the sword Faul was, a blade not content to rest in the scabbard until it had reaped its share of vengeance and death. The icy, calculated precision of Faul's warrior art filled her with dread.

"Who are you, boy?" Faul demanded.

"Dagar Zegat," he answered.

"And those?" Faul asked, pointing to the graves.

"My father, my grandfather, my two older brothers. Over there is my mother, and this," he said, pointing to the small body, "my younger sister."

"How is it that you are alive?"

"I was in the hills, with the herd," he answered. "I should have returned last night but I lost a goat amidst the rocks. By the time I had found her it was too dark to travel. I stayed in the hills and waited for morning."

"And came back to this?' Alwir asked. The boy nodded silently. Alwir shouted as if his whole body were seized by fury. "Why? Why have the Sileans done this?"

"To start a war with the New Moon," Faul answered sharply.

Alwir ran his hands through his hair. "But why massacre everyone?" He looked up at Faul with a stricken face. "Even the children?"

"This is the hard truth of your rebellion, Alwir," Faul said. "Look well on it. It is no longer a matter of argument, of polite dissension in the high courts of Beldan. The Sileans will never release their hold on the land. They would sooner see you all dead and the land all theirs. The New Moon has given them good cause to kill and the butcherboys will do so without mercy." Faul looked around, eyes narrowed at the sight of the graves. "We must leave here now."

"Not until the dead have been buried," said Lirrel, feeling Dagar's hand tighten in hers.

"Impossible," replied Faul with a slash of her hand. "There are too many and it's too dangerous. It will be night soon and the wolves will come, attracted by the scent of flesh."

"I can do something about it," Jobber snarled, abruptly facing Faul. Faul stepped back, intimidated by the flames that leaped into the jade-green eyes. The dull copper of her firehair crackled with new heat and blazed around her head like a crown of molten copper.

Jobber confronted the village. She reached for her power, feel-

ing the rose of fire expand and blossom within her, answering
to her rage. The petals opened, revealing the core of blue surrounded by yellow, orange, and red fire. Heat rippled in waves
about her as tiny flames erupted in the dust at her feet. Her
cheeks flushed crimson and a thin blue smoke trailed away from
her shoulders and legs. The wind roared in her ears like the
hoarse breathing of a giant bellows. Jobber thrust her hands
forward as if to clasp the village between her palms and released
the store of gathered power.

At first there was complete stillness; a silence as if air was
sucked into a void as the world held its breath. And then the
whoosh as Cairns exploded and filled the air with the sounds of
shattering glass and the blasting of timber and rock from their
foundations. The ransacked village churned with fire glowing
fiercely like the coal bed of a massive forge. From every stone
cottage, flames and smoke belched. Still smaller explosions
tossed clods of dirt and flaming brands into the air where the
wind swirled and thickened with black ash.

Jobber swayed weakly. She licked her dry lips and with both
hands smoothed her flaming hair flat against her skull. Sparks
scattered on the ground. Shedwyn came to stand beside her,
untroubled by the heat radiating form Jobber's body as she stared
out at the remains of the village.

There was little left but smoldering piles, blackened stones,
and the blasted well of the square. Shedwyn looked to the heaps
of mountain boulders that had rested like the folded knuckles of
a giant fist around the village. She opened her senses to the earth
and stones. She saw amidst the piled boulders the fault lines
running like fine veins, separating the boulders and the small
pebbles sandwiched between them. She pushed the little stones,
shoving them out of their compressed cracks. Gravel scraped
noisily and as it loosened, the scree began rolling down the
mountainside. Shedwyn encouraged it, pulling out more and
more stones from under the boulders until at last even the massive stones were obliged to rumble down the mountainside with
a roar of protest.

Pink and gray dust rose in the air like sea spray as the rocks
careened down the mountainside, covering the village in wave
after wave of rock and soil. The ground beneath Shedwyn's feet
vibrated with the furious tumbling of the mountain. She turned
her head away, coughing as the rising cloud of dust choked her.

And then the roaring stopped and Shedwyn looked back at the

village with grim satisfaction. As the dust of the rockslide subsided, the stones settled into repose over the remains of the
village. There was nothing left to mark the village except a hump
of broken rock. And where they had been pulled away from the
mountainside there remained a fresh scar of moist red soil.

Eneas took the spade from Dagar's limp hand and finished
digging the last grave with a few vigorous strokes of the spade.
Wyer handed the small body of Dagar's sister to him, and Eneas
laid her in the grave. He climbed out of the grave and, sweating
heavily, quickly shoveled the soil over her.

But when it was done, no one moved to leave. As if compelled
by the unspeaking voices of the dead, they could not find the
will to depart. Faul was restless, but each time she tried to set
out, she stopped, her gaze drawn back to the village. Something
yet remained undone.

Lirrel knew what was needed and she clasped Dagar's cold,
shaking hands.

"Remember for us," she said softly. "Remember for them,"
she said, looking at the neat row of graves.

She felt the murmur of a song vibrate in her throat. The silvery
glimmer of her eyes searched Dagar's heart. The song issued
from her lips and the white gleam of her power covered them
all like gauze. She smiled, sensing their surprise as within the
net of light, she shaped a vision of the village called forth from
Dagar's mind. Even Faul loosened her grip on the sword to allow
the images to penetrate her wall of vengeance.

The women of Cairns gathered at the well, skirts tucked up
and water sluicing down their bare legs as they hauled the water
jugs. Their voices rose, raucous and laughing as they gossiped
and complained to each other. A baby slept, cheek damp where
he lay tied to his mother's back, lulled by the pounding rhythm
of the butter churn; men sat in the square at twilight, arguing
and gambling, small glasses of Mother's Tears in their hands,
dogs resting at their feet; around the doorways children fought
mock wars or shaped animals from the red clay. Herdboys tick-
led the sows with long switches, driving them into pens. A pair
of lovers quarreled, the woman's angry face contorted with tears.

In the net of light, the village of Cairns drew breath again,
smelled of human sweat and manure, rattled with the sound of
the goat bell, the laughter of the village fool, and the shrill
crying of a colicky infant. It shimmered with the pettiness as
well as the wealth of village life. Lirrel showed the man who

beat his wife, and the woman whose stinginess deprived her of
a loving husband. She showed also the shepherd who cast longing glances at a girl by the well who wore red tassels in her
braids and traced her upper teeth with the tip of her tongue when
she smiled. There was the barren wife and a fertile widow, who
after five years alone still bore babies that toddled fat-cheeked
around the door, having no father willing to confess to his obligations. There were sheep and goats rambling the streets and
kicking up the dust, a dog baying at a scent carried down from
the mountains. And last there were quiet moments by the fire,
fingers always busy at knitting or the carving of spoons as stories
were told or the old songs were sung in hushed voices. An old
man snored openmouthed and toothless as his wife frowned and
squirreled deeper under the covers.

Lirrel harvested Dagar's memories like a sheaf of ripe wheat,
binding them together with the rope of shimmering light. And
when she could hold no more, she faced the devastated village
and, opening her arms, released the stalks of memory into the
sky above. Dagar looked up and gasped as he saw the butterflies,
their salt-white wings beating against the blue sky. Lirrel, encased in a cloud of fluttering wings, smiled at his wonderment.
Butterflies rested in her hair and on her shoulders, their wings
pulsing delicately. They hovered around her eyes and fragile
stems of antennae brushed against her lips as she continued to
sing. Lirrel lifted her hands and they flew up, catching the breeze
and scattering into the sky.

They circled overhead and then fluttered across the fallen rock
and stones of the village. They rested briefly, giving the impression of a field of white blossoms. The wind gusted lightly down
the mountain. They opened their wings to it and were carried
aloft by the breeze.

In Lirrel's heart there came a measure of peace. She finished
her song and a sigh escaped her lips.

"Come with us," she said to Dagar.

"Yes," he answered, "anywhere."

"To Avadares and the New Moon," Jobber said, her voice
cracking.

Faul kicked a stone and sent it rolling. "I'll come as well.
I'm sure the New Moon would have use for another blade?" she
said to Alwir.

"The more there are, the quicker our victory," Alwir answered.

"Don't be too sure on that. Though I have little love for your political speeches, Alwir, I can't let those Silean bastards get away with this."

"Shedwyn." Eneas called to her where she stood, watching the last of the butterflies flitting across the rubble.

"Aye," she replied without turning around.

"What happened here—" he stopped unable to complete his thought.

Shedwyn's head jerked around, her expression thoughtful. "Eneas," she said, and reached to take his hand. "I see now how fragile our love is. I would not let anyone's hate destroy it. Not the butcherboys' or the New Moon's."

She squeezed his hand tightly.

"All right, then," Faul said, brushing the dust from her vest with one hand while she held the sword clutched tightly in the other. "Let's be off," she ordered. "Alwir, you know the way."

"The horse and wagon?" Shedwyn asked.

"Leave them. They will be of no use to us in the mountains," Alwir replied.

Alwir led the way up the dirt trail that traveled north. Dagar had freed his goats and they followed close behind, the clanking goat bell of the leader and the bleating of the others marking their passage. As they rounded the top of a ridge Alwir glanced back. On the field of fallen rocks and boulders a few of Lirrel's butterflies lingered, their wings shimmering with the golden light of the afternoon sun.

Chapter Nine

With the sun at her back, the Fire Queen Zorah sat, shoulders hunched forward as she gambled knucklebones with her maid. She was winning as usual and laughing at her maid's increasing frustration. She could just hear the curses muttered under the maid's breath as each unlucky toss of the bones cost her another copper. Zorah cast a sidelong glance to the window where the Regent Silwa sat studying recent dispatches. She knew that Silwa disapproved of women gambling, so she had taught her maid and then never missed the opportunity to gamble in his presence. Usually he scowled, ground his teeth in frank annoyance, and— Zorah's favorite—paced with his military walk, hands clasped firmly behind his back like an angry cock.

But not today. As they waited in the stateroom for the arrival of Antoni Re Desturo, Silwa kept his head bowed to the sheaf of papers he carried, more intrigued by the dispatches than irritated with Zorah's noisy gambling. Zorah frowned, a crease wrinkling the smooth white forehead. What was in them? she wondered. They had come early this morning by courier ship from Silea. He had waved away her inquiry, saying they were nothing more than matters of the Silean parliament that would not interest her.

The maid shrieked with unconcealed delight, having thrown

a winning toss at last. Zorah pounded her palm flat on the table and uttered a loud vulgar oath. Once more she cast a sidelong glance but he paid scant attention to her, only raising his eyes briefly to her, and then, sensing all was well, returned to his dispatches. Zorah let the maid roll again, deciding to finish the game quickly and discover what in those dispatches held Silwa's attention captive. But as she prepared to dismiss the maid, Antoni entered the stateroom and quickly crossed to Silwa's side. He inclined his head to Zorah in a cursory gesture of respect.

She watched him without responding, her hand clicking the knucklebones over and over in her palm. Since Fire Circle an aura of coldness had grown around him and Zorah felt uncomfortable in his company. She couldn't put her finger on the source of her unease, but she felt more wary of him than before, and it bothered her. He was politically corrupt. That much she knew and accepted. After all, who among the Sileans in power wasn't? They all considered themselves cunning and sly, able to exploit the riches of her country beneath her nose. Or so they thought. She found them greedy, stupid, and entirely predictable, like grat carrion birds shrieking and striking at each other for more. For reasons of statehood she let it all pass by her like so much detritus flowing in an otherwise clear stream. They maintained in Oran a semblance of peace, and after two centuries of eternal youth, Zorah found it increasingly difficult to be interested in the everyday affairs of governing Oran. She had turned over the responsibility to an army of bastards and bureaucrats, gentry thieves that hoarded land and merchants who skimmed away the last of the wealth. Together they kept Oran going. And if the way was brutal, it mattered little at the present to Zorah. Another generation of destroying children of power would leave her free from the tyranny of the past. Then would she purge Oran of the Silean lice and in the eyes of her people she would be forever beautiful and loved.

Zorah ground her teeth as she stared at Antoni's profile. He wasn't like the others she had known. He was a dangerous crow, secretive and intelligent. She imagined that he carried his black wings tightly folded to hide the razor talons. His eyes seemed to glitter with their own private malice for Oran and Sileans alike. There were times when he approached her that Zorah thought she felt the faint vibration of power, cloaked and hidden like a bubble beneath a rushing stream. Through a dim watery haze she could almost see it glimmer at the edges of his form.

Zorah cast the knucklebones roughly and they clattered across the table. No, she argued with herself, that was stupid and illogical. Antoni was a Silean, he had no power beyond the ordinary ambitions of most men. But ambition alone in a man like Antoni Re Desturo was enough to make Zorah consider the wisdom of a quiet assassination. Later, she thought as she watched the bones come to rest on the gaming table, later, she would speak to the Firstwatch Gonmer.

Zorah lost the cast, the knucklebones turning against her. She swore in disgust and picked them up to try again. The fading sunlight from the western window had crept across the floor and laid a long amber finger on the gaming table. Zorah shook the bones in her hands, blew on them for luck, and tossed them out on the table.

Zorah didn't hear the maid's happy cry as she lost the cast again. All she heard was the deep-throated rumbling of earth and the harsh scraping of gravel. The table erupted before her eyes in a fierce bloom of fire, shards of splintered wood flying like red daggers in her face. She reared back, hovering unsteadily while the ground bucked and swayed beneath her feet. She opened her mouth to scream a warning but the only sound she produced was an inward gasp. An intense pressure pushed against her chest and spine as if she were being crushed between two clashing walls of stone. Blood clamored in her ears as she arched her long white neck, and her lips parted like a dying fish seeking air at the surface of a clogged pond. She stared terrified at the ceiling, pinpoints of yellow sparks scattered overhead as the wooden beams and vaults spun deliriously like a child's top.

Then it stopped and just as suddenly she was released from the stony grip. She sucked in a noisy gulp of air, her hand pressed against her bruised chest. She twirled slowly on trembling legs and then lurched forward. Antoni caught her by the hand before she fell. Zorah cried out as a needle of pain stabbed her wrist. His body bent over her, Zorah struggled, feeling smothered by his presence, the flap of his cape enveloping her for a moment.

She panicked at Antoni's icy-cold touch, his hand still gripped around her wrist.

"Let go of me," she cried in a shrill voice. "Don't touch me."

He set her down on her chair and backed away, slowly and deliberately. Zorah saw her own frightened reflection mirrored in the blackness of his eyes. The coldness lingered on her skin like a draft continuing to seep unchecked through the room. She became aware of a stinging pain and she stared confused at a thin bloody slash on her wrist. She looked up again at Antoni, stunned at the redness of his lips.

"Forgive me, madam," he said in a controlled voice. "In my effort to assist you, I seem to have scratched you. Are you all right?" He reached up to stroke his beard.

"Yes," she answered, concealing the fear that continued to grip her. "It's nothing."

"Nothing!" Silwa exploded. "It looked like you were choking. What happened?"

Zorah straightened up slowly, smoothing her skirts in an effort to hide her shaking hands. She glanced at Silwa again and pursed her lips angrily. "I said it was nothing. Sometimes I am reminded of the debacle of Fire Circle." She touched her throat and saw him edge away. "The memory is not pleasant."

Silwa accepted her explanation with a heavy silence. Oh, yes, Zorah thought with growing impatience, that is something you will not discuss, isn't it, Silwa? The mess you made of Firefaire with your love of battle. Zorah sagged, suddenly exhausted. She needed to be alone, away from their prying eyes. Away, too, from their carnivorous ambition.

Zorah made to leave, one hand lingering on the gaming table to give her support. Silwa, in a show of concern, handed his papers to Antoni and lent her his arm for support. The scratchy wool of his uniform and the faint odor of his sweat repulsed her. She wriggled away from him, one hand clutched awkwardly over her wrist.

"I told you, Silwa, I'm fine," she said coolly. "I shall call you when I require your services."

His jaw tightened with the insult, but he held himself firm. He stepped back, graciously giving her room to pass with her maid. She left the room hurriedly, leaving behind the faint metallic reek of copper.

"Raving bitch," Silwa said savagely. He turned to Antoni, who was staring after the Queen, an unreadable expression on his face. His eyes remained hooded. He drew a deep, uneven breath and Silwa saw a tiny spasm ripple the muscle along his cheek. "Antoni?" he asked softly, and the advisor drew his gaze away from the retreating figure of the Queen with effort. "What's this?" Silwa said lightly. "Lusting after the Queen?"

Something snapped in Antoni's face and he blinked as if waking from a stupor. Turning smoothly to Silwa, he smiled. "She seemed almost mortal."

"You can say that after Fire Circle?" Silwa sounded shocked. "The woman's a demon." Since Fire Circle Silwa had studiously avoided Zorah when he could, her frozen beauty more daunting than ever. His gut clamped with revulsion as he remembered how she stood up after the attack, arrows piercing her throat, blood forming a collar of red lace. Chalk white as a corpse, her damnable red hair in a gout of flames, she had mounted her horse unaided and ridden away to the Keep.

Antoni chuckled, his laughter like the rattling of the knucklebones. "Yes, there was that. But you must admit, she is interesting."

"So is this," Silwa answered, pointing to the dispatch he had placed in Antoni's hand.

Antoni read it quickly, his eyebrows rising in surprise. "So the parliament favors your request for arms. You are to have your soldiers and your supplies." He lowered the paper. "Congratulations, Silwa. Do you intend to inform the Queen?"

Silwa stroked his beard. "Not yet. I want the plans set so far in motion that the Queen will not be able to contradict what is done."

"Do you still mean to rout them at Sadar?"

"The last battle will take place there, yes. But the first skirmishes have already begun," he said with a satisfied grin. "At least twenty farms have been laid to waste, and several villages known to sympathize with the New Moon have fallen beneath the eager swords of Silean militia. We'll cut out their legs before we cut off their heads at Sadar."

"What happens to the Oran survivors of these forays?"

"There are no survivors," Silwa answered matter-of-factly. "The orders are to take no prisoners and to spare no lives."

"Surely you don't mean to kill them all," Antoni asked with mild concern. "Who will farm the estates? Sileans need the labor force."

Silwa laughed and shook his head. "You're a cruel bastard, aren't you, Antoni? You don't care that we slaughter them like the sheep they are. You're only worried about your estates, and will you have enough laborers to bring in your harvests."

Antoni smiled, not offended by Silwa's accusations. "A good husbandman knows enough to save the best in his herd before he brings the others under the knife. I am only asking if you are a good husbandman, or will you slaughter the best in our flock?''

"When the battle at Sadar is finished, Oran peasants will be firmly tethered again. Not to the Queen's yoke, but to the Sileans'. There will be no more Firefaire, no hiring fairs. Contracts will be permanent and servitude hereditary.''

"And the Fire Queen?'' Antoni asked. "How will you convince her of such a plan.''

"I'll worry about that later. When I have my victory at Sadar.''

"Have you found the child with red hair?'' Antoni asked suddenly.

Silwa scowled, distracted by the question. "Yes and no. Rubio sent word she was lost in the marshes. Quicksand.''

"A pity,'' Antoni said. "We might have had some use for her. Against the Queen,'' he added quickly.

"No.'' Silwa shook his head. "Just as well she's dead, eh? We've enough trouble with our own raver. They should all hang, as far as I'm concerned.''

"Perhaps that would be best,'' Antoni murmured. "When do you plan your attack?''

Silwa smiled, the gleam in his eyes quickened. "Before the end of summer. We will march when the crops are high.''

"You'll cause a panic among the farmers.''

"That's my intention. They will beg us for protection.''

"And you will give it for a price.''

Silwa nodded. "War is a profitable business. Even a small one like this.''

Antoni held up one warning finger. "The Oran peasants may seem as sheep to you, but they may be more trouble than you know. For one thing, there is always the element of magic. Don't underestimate it.''

Silwa stared, fascinated by the long tapered nail of Antoni's finger, filed, he thought, to the likeness of a cat's claw. "Children,'' he answered contemptuously, looking up at his advisor. "Hardly a formidable opponent. And as for magic, except for the Queen herself I have yet to see anything that exceeds the simple trickery of traveling magicians. Sticks into flowers, hoops into snakes is a small weapon to use against the Silean army. No, Antoni, we will scatter them at Sadar.''

Silwa retrieved his dispatches, and standing for a brief moment before the window, he looked down on the city of Beldan.

The sun had nearly slipped beneath the horizon and was casting its last desperate rays over the city. The gray faces of the buildings glowed bright red, glass windows sparkling like mirrors reflecting the red orb of the sun. Out on the water he saw the ships, gliding into the harbor, their black hulls cleaving the blue-gray water stippled with orange sunlight. He turned away, content for the first time since he had become Regent to the Queen. When the black ships came from Silea carrying his soldiers, he would march through Oran like an ax until the whole country and not just this city would be his to command.

"Oy, you carry the basket." Slipper shoved the willow basket into Shefek's good arm.

Shefek shoved it back, refusing. "Absolutely not. I will not take on the appearance of an Oran housemaid. The shopping is your duty, my lad."

"Yeah, but it's your food we're getting. And why should I look the perfect fool for it?"

Shefek eyed Slipper up and down with a small smile. "The boot fits well in any case."

"Now, look here, Shefek, I don't like your insult." Slipper flushed angrily and, distracted, tripped over a loose cobblestone. The basket jostled out of his arms. He fumbled awkwardly for it, his body jerking forward as his hands bounced the basket into the air to keep it from dropping and scattering the food.

"Now there," Shefek murmured, neatly catching the basket before it fell. He thrust Slipper's arm through the handle, bent it at the elbow, and firmly pressed Slipper's hand against the boy's chest. "Be a good lad and carry the frigging basket."

"Z'blood," groaned Slipper. "It just ain't manly."

"Ah, so that's the source of your worry. Let me set your mind at ease, Slipper my lad, no one will confuse you with a man. Not yet, anyway. Give that velvet's nap on your cheek another good year or two." Shefek chuckled and stroked the ruff of his silver-gray beard.

"What do you know about being a man," Slipper hissed indignantly. "You're a frigging bird."

"Careful lad," Shefek warned lightly. "There's no need to let your childish temper betray us."

Slipper cast quick glances to the street, suddenly ashamed and scared at his own stupidity. They trudged down what was left of Baker's Street, the once prosperous baking houses now mostly closed and reduced to rubble. Few of the great ovens remained standing and those that had been destroyed had difficulty finding the labor or the money to replace the blasted ovens. Then, too, grain was now scarce and over the last weeks bread had become heavier and strangely dry as bakers substituted other substances not as palatable or digestible as grain. Plaster, wood shavings, and even, it was rumored, sand from the harbor. Two Silean Guards strolled on the opposite side of the street but Slipper saw their attention was drawn to the pronounced gait of the Oran maid in front of them. The Guards were nudging each other and leering at the woman, who walked balancing a heavy tray of folded laundry on her head. With her head erect and her neck stretched upward, her hips rolled, swaying from side to side. She had lifted her arms up to the tray, her hands holding it firmly in place. A Guard advanced and grabbed the woman's buttocks with one hand while the other reached around to squeeze her breasts. Slipper flinched as the woman shouted oaths at the Guard, trying to avoid the groping hands and at the same time not topple the newly cleaned laundry in the dirty streets.

"Now, there is a good example of truly unmanly behavior," Shefek said, nodding. The laundry had spilled, and as the woman reached in angry frustration to retrieve it, the second Guard slapped her hard on the buttocks. An Oran tradesman standing in the shelter of his shop slipped inside so as not to witness the scene.

Slipper turned away, embarrassed. His guts churned, tightening with an unexpected sensation of pleasure. He exhaled softly to himself. He knew it wasn't right to go on at a woman like that. But still, the feelings it aroused, they weren't entirely wrong neither. And those feelings, Z' blood, he sighed to himself, they were there all the time now. But Kai, she didn't seem to notice.

Shefek guffawed and Slipper glanced up, surprised, as he took the basket from him.

"I've misjudged you, my lad." The yellow eyes twinkled merrily at him. "Maybe you're older than I thought. Tell me how long have you been with Mistress Kai?"

"Awhile," Slipper replied, confused and mistrustful at Shefek's change of heart.

"Think of her as a mother, do you?"

"Bugger yourself," Slipper growled.

"I'll take that as no," Shefek answered. "Let me ask this in

a different fashion. Does she think of you as one of her fledg-
lings?''

Slipper was silent, his lips pressed together in an angry scowl.

"Ah. That could be awkward,'' Shefek continued pleasantly.
"How to change her mind, then?''

"Ah, leave off, Shefek,'' Slipper exploded. "I'll handle my
own affairs. I don't need advice from you.''

"Actually, I was rather thinking you needed it from another
woman.''

"What do you mean?''

Shefek paused a moment, as if searching for a delicate way
of asking a question. "Tell me then, have you ever—'' His hands
made a little gesture; the extended finger of one hand secured
tightly in the fist of the other.

"No,'' Slipper said quickly, his face coloring bright red and
his large ears turning pink as the petals of a flower beneath the
brim of his black hat. "But I've seen it often enough, down in
the Pleasure district. Busy whores ain't choosy where they do
their work. Oh, yeah, I know where everything goes. I ain't
stupid.''

"Not stupid. Just inexperienced, where your own self is concerned.''

"Yeah, well.'' Slipper shrugged. "That ain't all there is to
being a man now, is it?'' He wanted to believe his words, but
he couldn't help thinking that he'd believe them more if he could
just have the chance to experience sex. When he thought of the
whores, he thought of their nearly naked breasts, the damp flesh
of their thighs, and their hands that fluttered expertly over the
bodies of their customers. Slipper squirmed uncomfortably,
shoving his hands into his pockets. But it wasn't the same when
he thought of Kai. She wasn't exactly pretty, her shoulders kind
of narrow and her breasts, well, Slipper had to admit after
months of secretly watching the way they moved beneath the
thin fabric of her dress, they were small and hard. Not like the
whores'. But none of that really mattered to him when she looked
at him out of those dark and fearless eyes. He thought he could
drown in those eyes. And there was something about her hands,
long and tapered, like talons one moment and then, in another,
cupped around a mug of tea as soft and elegant as any Silean
woman's. She was smart, and she wouldn't let anyone frigging
back her into a corner. Not the whores that pushed her to join
them, not the Sileans, and not even the other Flocks. Slipper

respected that in her. Loved it, in fact. But maybe that was it then, he thought, kicking at a stone. Maybe she didn't respect him, never saw him as someone she could love as a man. "Frigging shit," he grumbled.

"First things first, Slipper, my lad. Let's solve one of your dilemmas before attacking the second," Shefek said.

"What are you on about?"

"That place will do," Shefek answered, placing a firm hand on his shoulder and steering him across the street to an inn. "There's a nice group over there. I saw them just yesterday, hanging out the windows, preening. One or two might do for you."

"Shefek," Slipper protested, his stomach tightening again, his guts giving a little rumble of excitement. "Shefek, you're frigging crazy. I ain't got money for that sort of thing. And how would I explain it to Kai?" His voice had risen with nervousness until he barely squeaked the words out.

"A contradiction, my lad," Shefek said, pausing at the door of the inn. "You say you've no money, but already you are thinking about how to hide from Kai the fact that you spent money to purchase some pleasure with a whore. It's yes you've said to the idea. Now go in with conviction."

"Shefek," Slipper groaned.

"I'll give you the coins."

"What do I say?"

"Get in. A man always knows the right words when this sort of thing comes along. In any case, a good whore doesn't need to be encouraged in helping you to spend your money."

Slipper pushed open the door to the inn and entered cautiously. Behind, Shefek gave a little push to hurry him along.

"Easy now. Don't lose your nerve, Slipper," Shefek encouraged as a woman, seeing them enter, rose out of a chair and crossed over to greet them. "Nice enough," he murmured. The woman gave a lopsided smile, the creases deepening around the edges of tired eyes. Her skin sagged at the jowls slightly, but she carried her back erect, her chin lifted proudly.

"Oy, dearies. Come in, come in."

Slipper licked his lips, feeling clumsy and stupid. The woman came closer and one hand reached out to tug at the lacings of his vest. She cocked an eyebrow at Slipper's tense face and then glanced at Shefek. He nodded and jerked his head toward Slipper.

The whore laughed and Slipper saw that she'd none of her back teeth left. She pressed close to him and he felt the swell of her breasts against his chest and the long hard muscle of one of her thighs wedging its way between his legs. She moved her leg, rubbing it back and forth until the warm pressure of it gave Slipper an erection. She chuckled softly under her breath.

"It'll go quick at that, love. Nice and quick. Let's see yer money first."

"Shefek," Slipper whispered, holding out his hand, impatiently waiting for the feel of coins. But Shefek gave him nothing. Slipper tore his eyes away from the whore's steady gaze and turned angrily to Shefek.

"Z'blood, Shefek, give me the money," he fairly barked, then stopped, confused, not seeing Shefek behind him. He looked over the tables and saw him slumped against the wall near the door they had entered. "Shefek," he yelled, ignoring the whore and grabbing the vagger before he toppled to the packed dirt floor.

Shefek felt heavy as he sagged in Slipper's arm. The fetid reek of his injured arm grew strong, tearing Slipper's eyes and making him cough with the unexpectedness of the stench. "Z'blood, Shefek, what's wrong?" He lifted the shaggy head and swore as he saw the brown eyes flattened into golden disks. He heard the low rumblings in Shefek's throat, knew the Kirian shrieks would follow. Feathers lay plastered against Shefek's chest, and at the end of the injured arm the hand was already transforming, fanning out into brown and gray feathers.

"Not here!" Slipper whispered in fierce panic. "Z'blood, not here!" He tried to lift Shefek, to force him to stand. He had to get him out of the inn before anybody saw him transform into that frigging bird.

"Oy, what's with the old bugger, then?" the whore asked, coming to peer over Slipper's shoulder. "Come on, dearie, grab the coins and let's have a tumble then. I know you're ready for it."

"Get off," Slipper shouted angrily at her. "Get away from me." He covered Shefek from the whore's sight, struggling anew to lift the prostrate figure. The noise in Shefek's throat was growing louder. Slipper could feel the rippling of magic as Shefek was swallowed by change. "Not here, you frigging bird," he pleaded quietly. But Shefek didn't appear to hear him. Brown and gray feathers were drifting into the air, and the close atmosphere of the inn was permeated with the sudden rotting stink of Shefek's wound.

"Z'blood, the old man's shit himself," the whore screamed, one hand covering her face, the other waving the air around. "Get him out of here. Go on then, afore I call a Guard. Zorah's tits!" She continued swearing and kicking Slipper to urge him to hurry. "What a stink. Don't come back here, you little prick. Get a corpse at Scroggles. Someone that don't mind the smell of yer old man there."

Swearing violent curses under his breath, Slipper carried the heavy and awkward Shefek out into the street. Behind him he could hear the whore still calling out insults. At least he hasn't transformed entirely, Slipper thought, both relieved and terrified that at any moment the old man's face would change into the shrieking head of the Kirian.

"Oy, Shefek, give us a hand here, for pity's sake!" Slipper begged, his arms aching as Shefek's weight grew harder to carry. Shefek's human hand clutched him tightly around the shoulder, trying to lift himself higher. Words were garbled in his throat and his eyes continued to glitter brightly like two gold coins. One leg dragged and Slipper, casting a quick glance downward, saw the tarsus of a bird and the polished talons. "Ah, frigging shit. We've got to get to a tunnel."

Slipper checked the street, grateful it was quiet in the late afternoon. By the start of next watch the streets would be crowded as people wandered the Pleasure district to drink, gamble, and, Slipper thought dismally, seek other pastimes. He was fairly certain that the whore hadn't seen much, though she might wonder about the frigging feathers Shefek had managed to molt. Now if they could just get to a tunnel, Slipper figured he could get them both back to the Bird before anyone noticed Shefek.

There, just up the street, he saw it. An old entrance to the tunnels, one rarely used by the Waterlings because it opened out to the street, like a mouth carved in the wall of a building. Slipper crossed to it quickly and ducked his head inside the dark opening. Stairs even, he thought appreciatively. He checked over his shoulder, and seeing no one taking much notice of him, he started down the stairs, dragging Shefek after him.

"Where have you two been?" Kai stared at Slipper as he came through the door of the Grinning Bird, his hat in his hand. His face was pale, but tense with apprehension. Behind him Shefek entered, his skin almost gray with fatigue and his eyes a milky brown. Shefek slumped into the nearest chair and rested his head on his hands. "You smell like the tunnels, Slipper," Kai said, and caught him by the arm.

Slipper shrugged away from her grasp, unwilling to meet those eyes just yet.

"What happened?"

"Nothing," Slipper answered, sitting down. The shop was empty and only the urns hissed with steam.

"Nothing?" Kai's voice rose dangerously. "You come back here late, looking like death, and you tell me nothing? And where's the food, then?" Her hands balled into fists. "Tell me what's going on. Where's the food?"

"Frigging shit, Kai, give us a chance, will you?" Slipper snarled. "Back off and bring us some tea. I ain't your frigging servant and I ain't got to tell you everything I do."

Kai stood fuming silently for a moment. Slipper kept his eyes firmly on the table. He knew if he looked at her, he wouldn't be able to escape the shame and frustration he now felt. He had wanted very much to go with that whore. He had wanted to fuck someone he didn't owe anything but a coin to just so that when it was done, he could go off, content, knowing he had done it. And he could have faced Kai feeling sure of himself, and maybe he might even have known better how to get her to see that side of him that was now a man. But not now. Shit, not now. If he told her, she'd only see him for a fool and a failure. How could he tell her?

"The fault is mine," Shefek muttered from between his laced fingers.

"What happened, then?" said Kai, returning with the cups. She set one down in front of Shefek, tea spilling into the saucer. She set the second cup down more carefully in front of Slipper, holding the edge of the saucer until he looked up at her.

In spite of his resolve not to, Slipper colored beneath Kai's intense stare. But her face had softened, the usual hard point of her chin lowered in an attitude of thoughtful listening. Slipper exhaled and brought the hot tea to his lips.

"I wanted to see someone—" Shefek began.

"Who?"

"It doesn't matter. In any event, something happened on the street. I was stricken."

"He kept changing back and forth into a Kirian," Slipper

added. "I had to get home by the tunnels so no one would see us."

"I don't understand," Kai said, frowning. Nervously she twisted her black hair into a knot at her neck. Slipper watched the habitual gesture, studying the way the black strands twisted around her hands. The more anxious she was, the tighter Kai twisted the hair. He knew from experience that the knot wouldn't stay but would uncurl down her back again.

"Somewhere in Oran power has been used. Called forth with such strength that it disturbed the flow. I am an aged Kirian, tied to the old stream of power. Thought I am weakened by the Queen's appetite for power, I am a part of the power she commands. But this was something different."

"How could it be different?"

"An onion has many skins. Each layer separate and distinct but attached by a single root. So with Oran magic. I am a part of the old skin, as is Zorah. Zorah has attempted to destroy each new layer of skin lest it remove her."

"Jobber?" asked Slipper, suddenly straightening in his chair. "You think it might have been Jobber doing magic somewhere?"

"Perhaps. Damn this wound. If only it would heal, I could be gone from here to find her."

"Why don't you go?" Kai asked in a tight voice.

"I can't fly like this."

"Then walk. Or ride."

"Why do you want to get rid of me?" Shefek asked, his eyes narrowing.

Kai's hand reached for her hair again and began twisting the knot. "It ain't you, Shefek. We're all to be out on our arses soon. Got another of those papers today," she said to Slipper. "From the Guards. Coming tomorrow, they said, to settle up. I don't know what to do."

"Let's see it," said Shefek, rousing a little in his chair. "Slipper lad, give us a bottle of brandy, will you? I can't read on a dry throat."

"No luck, Shefek. The bottle was in the basket that got left in the Raven."

"What were you doing at the Raven?" Kai's eyes darted up to Slipper, accusing. She handed the paper to Shefek, who busied himself with its contents.

"Nothing," Slipper muttered as he went to get more tea. "Frigging nothing."

"Hah, the thieving bastards," Shefek shouted to the paper.

"What's it say?" Kai asked worriedly.

"Don't tell me you can't read?" Shefek asked, astonished. "How did you ever hope to keep the shop open?"

"I did all right on the street. I figured this couldn't be much harder neither," Kai retorted, her back stiffening defensively.

"And you've done all right," replied Shefek, easing away from Kai's angry face.

"No, I ain't. I've just mumbled along, ain't I? And now it's finished."

"Not yet," said Shefek. "All it says here is the Sileans are imposing a new tax. Orans must now pay to be protected from the attacks by the New Moon."

"Frigging sods," Slipper swore.

"But cunning sods. They want a tax from you, my raven, to the sum of six gold Queens annually and a two-copper piece per pound of tea."

"Robbery!"

"They say it's to guard the cleanliness of the well water used in making your tea."

"Everyone knows the butcherboys piss in Oran wells when they think no one's looking," Kai blasted angrily.

"And even when people are looking," Slipper amended. "Though who's to stop them?"

Kai made a snipping motion with two fingers. "Cut it off I would if I caught them at it."

"Yes, well, that's a brave deed done, but first to the business at hand." Shefek spoke in a calming voice, his eyes twinkling with malicious humor.

"Ah, we're buggered anyway," Kai said. "I don't have that kind of money."

Shefek sucked his lower lip for a moment and then gave a low-throated sigh. "I might," he murmured at last. He glanced up at Kai. "You've another bottle of brandy, my raven. Hidden somewhere, if I know you. Give it to me."

"Why?"

"I'm thirsty. Also I am a Kirian. And Kirians can do all nature of shape-changing tricks. Given enough brandy."

"Forgery?" Kai said, a smile splitting her face, the light gleaming in her eyes.

"Let them see what they want," Shefek answered with a little shrug. "Now bring that bottle. And a handful of buttons."

"Buttons?" Kai repeated tentatively.

"Or anything small and round. Though buttons are usually the easiest to fob off as gold coins."

"Will it really work?"

"Long enough to keep the Bird out of trouble."

Kai gave a little scream of delight and leaped up from the table, rushing for the bedroom. "I just remembered there's a button basket in Zeenia's things. I used to think she was crazy for collecting them. Ah, one thing more," she said, stopping in the doorway.

"Yes," Shefek answered, his eyebrows raised in a mild surprise. He was preening his beard, smoothing the glossy hairs down.

"Teach me and Slipper to read. I want to read the words on paper."

"All right. Anything. Just get me that bottle and be a quick one."

"Promise?"

"Yes, yes, now fetch that bottle." Shefek waved his hand impatiently.

Kai flashed a broad grin before disappearing into the bedroom again.

Slipper sat down next to Shefek, pushing back the brim of his lighterman's hat. He gave Shefek a searching stare. "You really think this is a good idea?"

"Everyone should know how to read."

"Not that. I mean giving them buttons and making them think they got Queens. Could be trouble in it."

"Nonsense," Shefek replied confidently. "It'll work. All my ideas work."

"Not all of them," Slipper said, pulling the brim of his hat down again to hide his disappointment. He slowly started cracking his knuckles, one finger at a time, imagining how it might have been, how he might have come home from the whore a changed man. Abruptly he stood and stared out the window. Twilight was fading quickly. Soon it would be dark. Slipper yanked on the shop door of the Grinning Bird. "Tell Kai I'm gone for a while. I'll be back later." And before Shefek could answer, he left, slamming the door behind him.

* * *

Antoni sat slumped in the heavy wooden chair, his chin resting on a bridge made by his folded hands. He sighed with a low moan that was almost a growl and picked up his head to stare at the room. Two candles on the huge table that served as his desk illuminated the room with a flickering yellow light. Shadows cast from objects on the shelves danced with jerky movements, their shapes mysterious and distorted. The room held the faint odor of juniper spirits coming from the jars of preserved specimens that lined the lower shelves of the small study. Hanging from hooks were dried plants and two ancient skeletons. Antoni glowered at the stark skull of the smaller skeleton, unlaced his fingers, and stood. He pulled down two crumbling books and a sheaf of paper.

He sat down again, placing the books on the table before him. He drew a single candlestick closer, the better to read the fading print. The wick sputtered and spat before returning to a slow even flickering of light. The books were small and plain, their leather bindings stained with tallow grease and patches of powdery green mold. Antoni treated the books with a careful reverence, for he alone among his Silean compatriots knew the true value of these two ancient Oran books.

He opened one, the spine resisting and cracking slightly with the movement. More than two hundred years old, it had been published by the Council of Acquired Knowledge. The council had flourished in Oran long before the Burning. One of the houses of learning and scholarship, it attracted Orans interested in the pursuit of knowledge. Ghazalis had presided over the composition of the texts, ensuring that discourse on all subjects was presented in a language rich in poetry. Oran history, the uses of magic, the functioning of the natural world, math, and literature were commingled in a single volume. There were architectural drawings, some of them barely more than fantastical sketches for structures only dreamed about and recorded in the hopes that a future generation might decipher the logic in the elegant lines. On another page was a comparative record of harvests, the results of new seeds introduced into Oran's then-fertile soil.

The second book was of equal value to Antoni, for it was of a more personal historical nature. Like a diary it recorded a family history, leading back five generations, before ending with the destruction at the Burning. In this volume was stored advice on magic, written specifically for those possessed of the water element. The margins of the book were decorated with drawings of fish and water plants. There was even a short history of the Namire, explaining their transformation from human beings into creatures of the sea. Antoni drew a finger over the drawing of a Namire woman, her wide-set eyes staring back at him from the dusty pages. Along her neck was the faint etching of gills.

These two books meant much more to Antoni than a collection of Oran histories and arcane writings of a now vanished world. They were his heritage and his only teachers. They had been in his family's possession for two hundred years, since the first Sileans arrived in Oran at the invitation of the Fire Queen Zorah. Antoni's ancestor, Florian Re Desturo, had come as an officer with the assault on Oran. One of the women Florian had raped as an act of war had been wealthy and influential enough to send the child that issued from that encounter to Silea, to the protection of his Silean father. The child had been born a water element, inherited from his Oran mother. Rather than permit him to be murdered in the persecution of children with power that followed the Burning, she sent him by ship to Florian, who had returned to reclaim his Silean inheritance. She neatly tucked into the baby's blankets two books that she hoped, in time, he would use to learn the ways of his talents and something of his mother's Oran history. Though Florian had married on his return, his wife had failed to produce an heir. Thus when the bastard son arrived from Oran, Florian didn't hesitate to claim the child as his own. That the baby possessed magical power was never revealed and the books were stowed away in trunks.

With an irritated nod of his head, Antoni recalled the first time he knew he possessed magical power. He had been playing with his brothers along the edge of a river. He was small, much smaller and younger than they, but they hadn't hesitated to use him as their captured prisoner in their game of war. They had tied him up, hands behind his back, shrieking war cries and threats. Then they dunked him headfirst into the river. The swift-running water was icy cold and he thrashed his shoulders, terrified. They pulled him out and he cried and begged them to release him. But they were too caught up in their play. His oldest brother, Pelas, held the ends of his bonds and dragged him deeper into the stream. Standing on a wet rock, Pelas proclaimed death for the prisoners who would not talk and dunked the young Antoni again into the rushing water. But Antoni's furious kicking off-balanced the older boy and he slipped off the rock into the water.

Antoni was set adrift and began floating downstream. His body rolled and bobbed and his face was turned down beneath the surface of the water. He held his breath, his cheeks full of air. He could hear the rushing water and the panicked beating of his heart growing louder as his supply of air dwindled. A thin stream of bubbles escaped the corners of his mouth. He knew he could hold his breath no longer. He released the air in his cheeks and kicked out in one final desperate attempt to turn himself on his back. It was to no avail, and as he sucked in cold water, he shuddered deeply and surrendered himself to the river.

Yet nothing happened. He continued to float downstream, twirling like a leaf caught in the current. He opened his eyes and saw the wavering light dappling the muddy bottom of the river. He opened his mouth in surprise and the water sluiced in and out through his mouth and nose, cold but harmless. The water cradled him as he floated, staring wide-eyed at the passing weeds and rocks of the riverbed.

Lost in the dreamlike wonderment of the river, he hardly noticed when the grappling hook reached out and snagged him by his tied hands. Just before eager hands turned him over, Antoni remembered to shut his eyes and appear nearly drowned.

Silea was not a place that tolerated strangeness. In his short life Antoni had seen more than one witch burned at the stake. It was difficult to understand sometimes what made them witches. But the clerics knew and they were quick to point out that odd behavior went hand in hand with evil.

His rescuers handled him roughly and Antoni had to steel himself from crying out as he was scraped and bumped against the stones of the shore. From their voices, they thought him dead. Yet once on the shore, they tried to see if life remained in him. Someone straddled his chest, pumping water from his body until he thought he would squeal with pain.

At last he fluttered his eyes and blinked into the ring of faces hovering over him.

It had been hard not to laugh at their shocked expressions, and only the fear of betraying himself to them prevented it. He shivered with cold and they hastened to pour brandy down his throat. As he coughed some more, this time from the scald of the liquor, his father's men declared it a miracle that the boy had survived.

He was brought home wrapped in blankets and the story of his rescue was recounted for his father. Antoni had felt a vague unease watching his father's face shift and change like a cloud-filled sky. The man stared at him with apprehension, and when he embraced his son, Antoni felt the stiffness in his arms. They never spoke of his rescue from the river again.

When Antoni was twenty, he signed on with a regiment bound for Oran. The night before he left, his father gave him the musty Oran books without a word of explanation. Whether he knew the secret that Antoni had kept hidden for many years, his father never admitted. It was only after Antoni had been in Oran for two years, learning the language, that he was able to decipher the inscription written by mother to son as she prepared to send him across the sea to Silea.

A grim bit of irony this, Antoni mused to himself at his desk, his eyes glancing at the words on the page. He wore the gray and black uniform of the Silean Guard, denying his Oran blood and toiling to bring others to their deaths for sharing the same heritage of magic. Antoni was careful to avoid the Readers, though he knew they wouldn't waste their time reading a member of the Silean Guard. In private, he collected books and artifacts of Oran's past, trying to acquaint himself with as much knowledge about his power as was available. He wanted to learn how to protect himself against the prying eyes of the Readers and, if possible, how to use his power to realize his own ambitions.

He turned a yellowed page, the vellum stiff between his fingers.

"The gifting of magic requires the exchange of sensibilities. . . ." the passage began, and went on to describe the method by which the former Queens had succeeded in gifting portions of their limitless power to the common populace. They had raised a population of goodywives, healers, and farmers, earth elements who prospered from knowledge of the earth and plants; smiths and metalworkers who could speak to the fire, islanders turned more into fish than folk, and the Ghazali, who used the air to carry the messages of peace. Small magics put to modest use. How he hated Orans for their stupid commonness and for their lack of ambition. In that Antoni was proud to be Silean.

And yet, he had asked himself, what might he do with his power? How to exercise it to his own advantage?

The answer had been surprisingly simple and came, strangely enough, from the Queen herself. He had asked how the Readers had acquired their unique skill, eager to discern some potential weakness in their talent. She had given an explanation similar to the one contained in his book. "But supposing, madam, they become a threat, trying perhaps to manipulate their magic power into other magics?" he had asked casually.

"As I have given, so I can take back," she had replied.

His head had suddenly buzzed like an angry bee at the possibilities raised in her reply. "But why not then remove the power from all these troublesome children that you have us kill?"

Zorah had shrugged. "Their power is too general, too thinned with blood. It would be like eating bread crumb by crumb. The Reader skill is a single quality that I can remove at will."

"Like fleas from a dog," he had answered. She had frowned, irritated by his words, and then left.

But she had given him an idea. The Fire Queen herself could not be bothered to reabsorb the little magics that surfaced in the Oran populace, but perhaps he could. He formed his own plan, his own singular use for his talent. He became the Upright Man— or so they called him on the streets.

It was easy enough. It gave him entrance to Beldan's white underbelly, where children were lost and discarded. No one noticed the disappearance of a street child. As the Upright Man he cultivated the Flocks of thieves, gaining power over them with bits of money and food and the promise of more wealth. And they, in turn, squealed on themselves, turning in the odd child who carried the old power in his veins.

The first time he tried it, he was shocked by how easy it was. Struggling children offered little resistance. Water mingled with blood in their veins. All that was needed was a small cut, across the wrist. Putting his lips to the cut, he drank, calling the water in their blood to him, taking the elemental power that graced their blood. Antoni had grown used to the warm salt taste of Oran blood. Like a potent liquor it seared his throat and settled into a burning pool in his belly. He had learned to accept the vomiting and seizures that followed the drinking of blood. It was worth it. Always, it was worth it. Over the years he had acquired a rich sampling of Oran magic.

All but a fire element. Antoni pushed away the book in irritation and stood angrily. He paced around the study, picking up objects and setting them down again as he thought. He could suck every child in this country dry of magic and it still wouldn't be enough to satiate him. He knew now that what he wanted, what he had always wanted from the first time he arrived in Oran and set eyes on the Fire Queen, was to possess her. He wanted the Queen's magic, to drink long and hard at the endless well of her power. But until he was stronger himself, he could not challenge her. He had to wait. Still he had to wait.

Antoni had hoped to claim the red-haired girl, and he swore now, realizing how easily she had slipped through his fingers. He touched the small scar on his cheek, remembering only the vague image of the shrieking girl attacking him, now that she knew Antoni and the Upright Man were one and the same. She knew he was the one who preyed on the Flocks. Could she finger him? Antoni shook his head. No. Who would believe the word of a gutter brat against his own? His shield would hold against the scrutiny of the Readers.

Antoni let his hand rest on a skull and was comforted by the tingle of magic that he felt residing in the bleached bone. Namire bones, the dealer had told him conspiratorially. Antoni had thought the man a cheat until he touched a finger to the skull and felt the tingle of magic calling to his own water element. Now it throbbed pleasantly under his hand, but beyond that he could not share its magic. Only through the living could Antoni take power.

Why not the Kirian? Antoni asked himself, suddenly smiling. If he could not have the red-haired girl, surely the Kirian would provide him with an abundant supply of magic? An old Oran race, the blood still pure and undiluted by common stock. Add to that the Queen's fear of the Kirian. There was more to that than she was willing to express, Antoni thought. Might she be vulnerable, almost mortal before the Kirian? Yes, Antoni decided, rubbing a small circle on the surface of the skull. The Upright Man would appear again on Beldan's streets. He'd find the Kirian for himself and take him down. And then he would see. Perhaps this final repast would give him the courage, the edge of power to confront the Fire Queen.

Zorah sat alone before her mirror. Slowly she drew her hand away from her wrist. Blood smeared across her palm and she saw now that the thin gash on her wrist still bled. It should have healed by now.

She looked up at the mirror, staring at her face for signs of age. The face that looked back was frightened. Beneath her eyes a faint purple smudge showed the strain. A small line creased the skin from the edge of her nostrils to the outer corners of her mouth.

She opened her senses to the whirlpool of magic around her. As always, she heard the long wailing of winds, the howling of Chaos that all but deafened her. She cocked her head to one side, her lips parting in expectation. There it was again. The voice of the flute floating as before over the strident roar of Chaos. A voice that was plucked and strung like a frail bridge above the seething whirlpool.

Zorah lowered her eyes to her wrist. The bleeding had finally stopped and a small brown scab was forming. She had been careless. Thinking them easy enough to manipulate. Thinking she beat Huld at this game without a careful plan of her own. The fire girl had found her companions, two of them at least. Zorah had thought it enough to send her the emotions of hate at the sight of the earth element. Zorah's hate for Huld. She had even been delighted when she had felt the vague stirrings of envy that emanated from Huld herself, carried through the earth girl. They had communicated that much to each other through the medium of the girls. Zorah had been content to think they would never form an alliance, their mistrust and hostility enough to prevent their threads from twining into a new knot.

But she had misjudged them, had been too hasty in her celebration. Something had happened, and despite the swift current of mistrust, they had formed a tentative alliance. They had worked magic, calling on their elements with a unity of spirit and thought. No! Zorah swore to herself. No, it would not do to have them cleave together. She had to find a way to make the hatred rise to the surface, to cut the threads that even now she felt engaging, before they themselves became too aware of the knot.

Zorah leaned down and reached for a sword wrapped in a length of blue silk. Carefully she unwound it, freeing it from the fabric. She pulled the sword from the dull black scabbard and inspected the blade. She smiled at the pattern of red and gold waves on the blade's edge. Perfect after two centuries. Through the leather-covered handle she could feel the steady throb of power; the Fire Sword, funneling the power of Oran through its thin gleaming shaft. The sword was her soul, its fierce brightness the gleam of her heart. Time had stopped for Zorah, but it bled into her sword. As long as the sword remained intact, time would never touch her. Only another sword like it, wielded with the same skill that she herself possessed, could destroy it. There were no other Fire Swords left in Oran. She had confiscated them all and had forbidden the Guilds to practice the craft.

Zorah frowned, realizing the possible danger. Only the Kirian could have trained a novice to manipulate the sword's power. She had seen to it that the Kirian were sacrificed first in the Burning. And yet, one had survived. One was here in Beldan, searching, no doubt, for the red-haired girl. A Fire Sword may have survived as well. But where? At Sadar perhaps, awaiting her arrival?

Zorah shook her head and laughed out loud, the happy sound incongruous with her dark thoughts. Let them give the red-haired girl the sword. The Kirian would never find her in time to train her. And such a sword in the hands of a novice would serve as Zorah's own weapon against Huld. From the comfort of Beldan's Keep, Zorah would guide the novice's heart and hand. The red-haired girl would be the weapon to sever the threads of the knot. Zorah laughed again and raised her own sword in a defiant salute.

Chapter Ten

Alwir sat down on a large slab of granite, rolled over to his back, and stared up at the fading blue sky. The muscles of his aching calves and thighs quivered with fatigue. He drew a deep, slow breath, trying to satisfy his lungs' demand for more air. He closed his eyes, his face hot and sticky with sweat, dust, and grit.

"Now what?" said Faul, panting as she reached him.

Alwir opened an eye to her. She was standing bent at the waist, leaning over one leg raised on the boulder as she caught her breath. She looked pale, her skin grayish except where two rosy streaks flushed across her cheekbone.

"Now we wait," he answered, and shut his eyes again.

"Wait?" asked Faul.

"Wait," he replied. "They will come to meet us here."

"How do they know we're here?"

Alwir sat up, hunch-shouldered. "Once we crossed into Avadares forest they were alerted."

"By whom? We've seen no one," Faul said irritably. She looked around at the sparse forest. A fallen tumble of smooth rocks dominated the landscape, turning it gray and pale pink against the light blue sky. Tiny shards of mica embedded in the granite winked in the shifting sunlight. The trees were few and far apart. Stunted and crippled pines clung to the granite walls, gnarled roots traveling over the surface of the rocks like veins. Here and there bloomed solitary stands of violet lupines, and tucked in the cracks of the rocks were yellow eveningstars and wild flax.

"That may be. But they know."

"Alwir, who's 'they'?" Lirrel asked, hunkering down in a cleft between two rounded boulders. She plucked a stalk of wintergrass and began chewing the base.

"I'd rather not say. I don't know how much information is mine to share." Alwir lay down again on his back, his long arms trailing over the sides of the boulder.

"Can they also tell we're hungry?" Wyer asked, and his stomach growled noisily as if to add its voice.

"Shut that beast up," snapped Jobber, "or I'll not get any peace from my own." She sat on another boulder and crossed her arms tightly over her stomach. Wind shifted the red hair around her face. "Right now, I'd pay a gold piece for a savory from Mother Anders's stall over in Market Square." She closed her eyes, almost tasting the hot dripping fat on her tongue.

"I know that place," said Wyer, his voice echoing a similar yearning. "I'd rather have a full stand of ribs—"

"And fried leeks, boiled carrots, and—"

"Oh, shut up," said Faul. "You're only making it worse."

"And a bottle of Oran brandy," finished Jobber defiantly, watching with satisfaction as the look of longing came into Faul's sour face.

"There's the goats," ventured Dagar, leaning on his staff.

"Bit tough, ain't they?" Jobber asked, wrinkling her nose.

"Gamy, too, but not bad with garlic," answered Wyer.

"I don't mean for you to eat them," exclaimed Dagar. Jobber looked at him, puzzled. His black hair was sticking straight up in front again, stiff with sweat, but otherwise his wiry body showed no signs of strain from the long hike. He was a herdboy, used to the long solitary climbs into the mountains. At his side a skinny kid with a bony head and yellow eyes nibbled the edges of his jacket.

"What do you mean, then?" she asked.

"Milk. Goats' milk," he answered, gently batting the young goat away.

"Milk! Never touch the stuff," Jobber said, grimacing.

"Give me a chance to rest and I'll try and bring down a few

birds," Eneas said, sitting down on a patch of wintergrass. He pulled his long yellow hair back and started braiding it to keep it clear of his hot face.

"With what?' Faul asked sarcastically. "Your hands?"

"No," Eneas replied with a small smile. "Oran slingshot," and he retrieved a pale strip from one pocket. "I'm a pretty fair shot with it, too."

"What's it made of?" Jobber asked.

"Pig's bladder."

Jobber wrinkled her nose. "Spare me," she said, rolling her eyes.

"Beldanites"—Eneas shrugged—"don't mind your meat long as it comes all neat and looking like a sausage." He picked out a small rock from the ground and tucked it into the halfway point of the strip. "Gets a good stretch to it." Holding the two ends with the stone neatly held in the middle, he swung it over his head. "And when you let go, it'll cast the rock hard enough to knock a bird out of the air." He released the slingshot and the rock launched in the air, hitting the side of a snarled pine with a loud crack. The tree shook, the dry needles rustling in protest.

"Gonna take a lot of sparrows to fill this hollow," Jobber said, patting her empty stomach.

"Well, there are wild greens," put in Shedwyn, holding a withered bunch of green stalks that ended in cream-colored tubers. "I collected these farther back. It's not much but they're safe to eat."

Jobber and Wyer looked at the stalks skeptically before taking one. They smelled like carrots to Jobber, except that their roots were white. Soil clung to a multitude of fine root hairs. Jobber nibbled the tip of one experimentally and quickly spat out the pulp.

"Z'blood, it's enough to make me puke." Angrily she nudged a dozing Alwir awake with her foot. "Oy, how long before they get here? Am I gonna be grazing for my supper like one of Dagar's frigging goats?"

"I don't know," Alwir answered simply.

"Frigging shit, Alwir," Jobber burst out, annoyed at the man's calm. "Don't you get hungry? This whole trip up here you've hardly touched food the few times we've managed to get it."

"I'm used to being hungry. It's a companion for me," he said, and sat up again.

Looking at his thin face, the long straight nose and the high ridge of his cheekbones, it was easy to be believe him.

Jobber scowled, still irritated by Alwir's calm. "Tell the truth, Alwir, and no speeches neither. How come you're here? You ain't got a dell to worry on like Eneas here, so how come you ain't home with all them others, resting your backside against a soft cushion and ordering your servants to bring you a leg of mutton?"

Wyer stifled a groan at the mention of mutton and even Shedwyn licked her lips without realizing it.

Alwir stared at his hands, tsking at his ruined fingernails and the yellowed pads of calluses on the once soft hands. "When I was a boy, I had an Oran nursemaid. That's not unusual, I guess. Most Readers hire Oran women. It's the only way we learn anything of Oran, I suppose. She had a daughter, Fouan, a few years older than myself. I was quite taken with her, and as we were playmates, I came to know her well." Alwir looked up from his hands and smiled thinly. "When Fouan went before Fire Circle to be Named, she was Read and found to have power."

"How come you didn't know that?" Jobber asked.

"I think I did, deep down, though I never Read her myself. It didn't seem important at the time."

"She was hanged, then?" Shedwyn said, tucking the folds of her skirt between her legs as she sat, straight-legged, back leaning against a small knotted pine. Eneas moved to sit close beside her, his shoulder resting against hers.

"Mmm," answered Alwir, staring distractedly down the steep embankment of granite and scree they had just climbed. His expression shifted as the old grief stirred. He ran his hand through the light beard as if to brush away the traces of sadness. "Soon after was my initiation into the Reader's trade. I wanted nothing to do with it. I grieved over Fouan's death, and felt responsible. But I belonged to a Reader family, and to the Fire Queen, and I knew I couldn't refuse my duty, even if it rubbed against my sense of decency."

"How well I know," Faul added in a sudden bitter voice.

"So what did you do?" Jobber asked.

"You starved yourself," Lirrel answered, and then glanced up apologetically for having taken the words from Alwir's thoughts.

He smiled at her and shrugged. "Exactly. I had no control over anything else in my life except that. I don't think I wanted to kill myself so much as I wanted to scare them into leaving me alone. My father was furious at first, dragging me to the table and forcing me to eat. I'd cut the meat into smaller and smaller pieces, trying to make it disappear. When I had no choice but to eat, I drank herbal teas late at night and vomited up what I had swallowed.''

"Z'blood. That's disgusting," said Jobber. "When I think of all the times I would have cut off my arm—well, a finger maybe— to have a bite to eat, and here you were throwing it all up. No sense in that!''

"I suppose you're right," Alwir conceded with a wistful grin. "The desire to starve was my own conceit, though it did nearly kill me soon after. Once I had made a conquest of hunger, I found it hard to know when to stop. To eat at all was to turn my back on Fouan's memory and accept my life as a Reader. I couldn't do that. At fifteen I was tall enough, but frail and thin. When the wind blew, my knees knocked together, clacking like a bonebag. My parents sent me to the country, hoping I would either be healed or die quietly out of sight of the court.''

"And out of the Queen's sight, too, no doubt," murmured Faul.

"But how did you join the New Moon?" asked Jobber. "You still haven't told me that.''

"I was sent to our estates, which lay about a three-day ride from here. Once I was in the country and freed from the obligations of a Reader, it was easier to eat food again, though there were still times when I couldn't sit at a meal without feeling shame over Fouan's death. My uncle took me hunting one day and I became separated from the hunting party during a heavy rainstorm. I didn't know the area well, and after two days of riding through these woods, I found myself here.''

"Here?" repeated Jobber.

"This very spot. By that old tree over there, the one with the twisted face in the burl. See it?" he asked, pointing. Jobber peered over her shoulder and marked the tree, an ancient pine, its coiled branches holding a few sparse handfuls of brittle needles.

"Yeah, I see it," she said, turning back.

Alwir shrugged. "That was all. They came and found me here. Shared their food . . .''

"So there's hope for a meal?" Wyer said.

Alwir laughed. "Yes. Most who come here are hungry. This isn't a place one travels to for pleasure."

"And then?" Jobber prodded him with her foot again.

"And then we talked."

"Just talked?"

"Hmm. For about five days. I traveled with them through these woods, seeing my country as I had never done before. I liked with they said; they gave me a sense of pride in being Oran. And I knew I had been right, that my father's world, the world of the Fire Queen, the Sileans, and the Readers, was corrupt. They returned me to the edge of my family's estates; in fact, in all that time we had been perilously close to it. It was hard to believe that none of my father's men had been able to find me again after our separation. But I think that has to do with the power of the place."

"Sadar," interrupted Lirrel. "Site of Queen Huld's last battle. And before that an old place of power."

"And the old power still holds," Alwir added. "Sileans come here, but quickly get lost, and most often find themselves back on Silean estates with no clear knowledge of how they returned. These woods are the only safe haven the New Moon has."

"Though once away from here, you are vulnerable to the superiority of Silean troops again," amended Faul, a finger tapping the hilt of her sword.

"True. But there is much that can be done from here to strengthen our position."

"Such as?" Faul asked.

"We can live here. For a time anyway."

"Live on what?" asked Faul skeptically, waving a hand to the rock and scrub of the mountainside. "I doubt there's much game."

"We can farm. Behind the Keep of Sadar there are narrow strips of fertile land terraced into the mountainside."

Faul narrowed her eyes angrily. "I'm a fighter, Alwir. I don't plant seeds into the ground."

"Only dead men, I'll wager," said a deep voice.

Faul stood quickly, whirling around, her hand pulling the sword free. Jobber scrambled to her feet, trying to find a steady footing on the rocks. Two men were standing quietly, regarding them with amusement. They made for a strange, mismatched pair; one was heavyset, with broad, square shoulders set on a thick trunk. His features looked as if they had been carved from wood, the nose sharply angled and his chin too prominent. He carried a staff of smooth, nobbed wood, and over his shoulders hung a brace of rabbits, freshly killed and gutted. The other man was small and finely built, his expression animated as his gaze darted over them. A smile crooked the edges of his mouth, exposing white teeth. His shirt was rolled back above his elbow, displaying the compact muscles of his forearms. He carried a longbow in one hand and Jobber could make out the white fletch of arrows in the quiver over his shoulder.

Alwir had turned all the way around to face them, smiling hugely. "Treys!" he called to the taller man. And to the other, "Zein!"

"So you've survived Fire Circle, Alwir! Good for you," the smaller man, Zein, answered.

Still crouched between two rocks, Lirrel snapped up at the sound of his voice. She stood quickly and hoisted herself on the rock. Standing on the boulder, hands clenched in fists, she stared with disbelief at the smaller man. He looked at her, curious, and then the corners of his smile faltered as he recognized her.

"Lirrel," he said, half a question, half a whisper of amazement.

She didn't answer, but Jobber saw her fists tighten.

"Do you know him?" Jobber asked.

Lirrel nodded. On her face was a snarl of emotions; anger flashed in her eyes, but her lips parted with relief.

"Na ahlan," she said to the man, in Ghazali.

"Beran," Zein answered.

"It's been a long time," Lirrel said softly, speaking again in Oran to keep the anger from her voice.

"Too long," he replied, hearing it nonetheless. "I have missed you."

Lirrel looked away suddenly and closed her eyes. "I had not thought to find you here, Father, among the New Moon and armed like a soldier."

"Your father!" Jobber blurted out loudly.

"Be quiet, Jobber," Faul said.

"Be quiet?" Jobber snapped. Then turning to Lirrel: "What's the matter? Why do you look so miserable?"

Lirrel turned back, opened her mouth to speak, and then closed it again without saying a word.

"Shut up, Jobber," Faul warned again.

"I don't have to shut up if I don't want to," she shouted.

Lirrel was hurt and Jobber had no intention of ignoring it. "What's the matter?" she asked again, this time staring belligerently at the man. "What'd you do to her?" Dagar moved close behind her, his goats bounding away from the rocks with a clatter of bells.

"I left our tent six years ago," he said.

"No word!" Lirrel cried out to the trees. "No single word of farewell to me at all."

"I couldn't," he told her.

"Why?" She whirled around, the tears flowing freely. "Why couldn't you?"

"I would never have been able to leave, seeing you unhappy. And I had to leave."

Lirrel was silent a moment, the tangled knot of her emotions stretching her mouth in tight frown.

"I needed you, Father," she said. "But you abandoned me."

Zein let out a rueful sigh, his glance straying to the crippled trees and the gray stone. His shoulders folded as her accusation struck him. "Oran needed me more," he answered.

"I thought it was my fault you left, something that I had done wrong to make you leave."

"I was *ghazat*," he answered.

"So Ama told me. But now that I see you here armed among the New Moon, I am wondering if you are a pilgrim or a hunted man?"

"Both," he said.

"Can a Ghazali be both, Father? When has a pilgrim carried a weapon?"

"When he must defend all that he loves in the world, not for himself but for his children," he answered, facing her squarely.

"I have seen the results of that defense, Father. There is a village that exists no longer. They are all dead, save one."

Zein's voice faltered as he answered her charge. "I can never explain my actions and still remain honorable in your eyes. I was once a true Ghazali and I believed in the way of peace. But since then, I have had to kill so many times in battle that I can no longer claim myself Ghazali." Sorrow washed his face. "Once we were close, Lirrel—"

"I believed you," Lirrel said. "I believed what you said about the Ghazali ways of peace. And now I find you and know that you lied to me. That you did not feel those things you made me feel!"

"Lirrel," he begged. "Look to yourself. See how you have changed from the child I knew. Already I can see that hardship has changed you. You have begun to face the violence of our world, of our times. Yet you are gifted with the old power. You can play the music that restores peace, that brings harmony to the chaos we create. Would you have had me rob you of that? Hardened your heart with despair so that you could not hear the music of peace?"

"I thought you left because I was not good enough to please you," Lirrel said, wiping away the tears that stained her face.

Zein shook his head wearily. "Come," he said to the others, "come. You are all in need of rest and food. We'll camp here tonight."

Treys nodded and headed farther up the slope, angling to the right, where a small crook of trees made a ledge in the rocks. He unslung his pack and, taking out a small knife, began to skin the rabbits.

"This way," Zein said, pointing straight up the slope. "There's a cave father up that will give us shelter for the night."

They followed him, clambering up the steep sides until they reached the lip of the cave. There was a ledge wide enough for a fire in the mouth of the cave, and the cave itself was deep enough to accommodate all of them under its roof. Zein went deep into the cave and brought forward an armload of dry wood stored in the back. Alwir and Wyer stumbled in the dark cave until they found the woodpile and each gathered another armload. Wyer's foot nudged a bag of stored grain. Peering through the dark, he was able to make out the dried fruits hanging in wreaths above the sacs. Also there were water skins, and when he touched one, its sides were cool and wet.

Faul sat down on an old sheepskin, the extra padding of fleece a relief from the hard ground. She leaned back against the wall of the cave, closed her eyes, and rested. She had known caves like this before, when she was a child smuggling with her parents. Only they had been carved out of the coastal rocks and always had sandy floors and smelled sharply of salt and dried fish. Still, she thought as she inhaled the musty odor of the forest, it carried a certain familiarity, and she smiled in spite of her weariness.

Jobber approached Zein as he stacked wood for a fire. She stopped short, suddenly fascinated by the faint markings tattooed on his skin. In the fading afternoon light she could make out lines of pale brown that curved in whorls around his cheeks and his chin like the circular grain of knotted wood.

"Those marks on your face," she asked abruptly, "where did you get them? Most vaggers I've seen before have a different kind of tattoo."

Zein lifted his hand to his cheek in surprise and then lowered it slowly. "Have you seen them elsewhere?" he asked.

Jobber's mouth clamped shut.

Treys reappeared behind Shedwyn, the rabbits skinned and spitted. As he stood beside Shedwyn's shoulder Jobber blinked, startled by their similarity, the same wide-legged stance, squared off shoulders; even the tilt of the head was the same. Their features shared the same rugged quality except that it seemed as if another hand had intervened to smooth the hard edges of Shedwyn's face and give them more grace. This close, Jobber now saw the marks on Treys's face clearly, and like Zein's they circled his cheeks and chin in a familiar pattern.

"Z'blood," Jobber whispered. "Just like Growler."

"Sit down," Zein said quietly. "There's a story I must tell."

"Stories are for children," Jobber said angrily. "I want the answer to my question."

"I will give you much more than that," Zein said. "Please, sit."

Jobber sat down uneasily, Lirrel joining her. Dagar sat on the other side of Lirrel and rested one hand companionably on her shoulder. She glanced at him, surprised at his touch. And then she accepted it, leaning slightly toward him in silent thanks. Shedwyn and Eneas sat together, a short distance away from the others. Shedwyn was tense and edgy and Eneas folded his arms across his chest to give her room. Alwir waited by the mouth of the cave, should Treys need any help, his long rangy form propped against the stone wall for support. Wyer settled himself near Faul, giving her a sidelong glance of concern. Faul merely shrugged and closed her eyes as she leaned her head back against the wall of the cave.

Zein finished stacking the wood for a fire, and before he could apply his flint to the tinder, Jobber reached out in a sudden gesture of impatience and ignited the wood with a touch of her hand. Zein leaned back on his heels, watching the fire crackle, neither surprised nor impressed; he calmly took the rabbits from Treys and set them at an angle over the fire so they would cook without burning.

Zein looked up at them. "For all of Oran history until now the Queens' quarter knot was whole. The knot was infinite, with no beginning and no end. And within the cradle of the knot, Oran was balanced."

"Forget the poetry," Jobber said brusquely. "Just tell me what I want to know."

"*Ahal*," Zein answered. "I've waited two hundred years to tell this story. It seems a shame to rush it now."

"Two hundred years?" Lirrel said, confused. "What are you saying, Father?"

"Now you would have me tell the end of the story, not the beginning." Zein shrugged.

"Z'blood, get on with it," Jobber said.

"I'll try," replied Zein tersely. "The last Queens' quarter knot of Oran was destroyed by the Fire Queen Zorah."

"That's not the way I learned it," interrupted Eneas. "Most say it was the Earth Queen Huld. Because she was jealous of Zorah's beauty."

"I know the story the Fire Queen tells now." Zein continued speaking. "But it's not the truth. Zorah destroyed the Queens' quarter knot because it was the only way to stop time."

"Why'd she want to do a thing like that?" Jobber asked.

"Because she is beautiful. And because she doesn't want to die."

"Just that?" asked Shedwyn.

Zein nodded. "Just that."

"That don't make any sense," Jobber insisted. "Nobody really wants to die, but it don't make us crazy."

"Because we learn to accept it eventually. We have no choice. In the end death comes to us as it does to all things. But the Fire Queen Zorah is not like most people. She loves herself too well to let age or death rob her of her youth and beauty. She has stolen the power from the Queens' quarter knot to change the course of time. At first Huld knew only of Zorah's fears, of her desire to remain young. But as Zorah's obsession grew, Huld became worried she might do something foolish. Huld tried to convince Laile and Fenni, her sisters, that Zorah's fears were dangerous, to herself and to the knot.

"They didn't believe her," Lirrel said, suddenly seeing an image of the Queens, standing and smiling in the sun on the steps of the old Keep. Where had she plucked the image from?

she thought uneasily, glancing around and out at the shadowy trees beyond the cave.

"No," Zein said, "they were not convinced. Fenni and Laile believed they could settle Zorah's fears by shielding her from death. They protected her, treated her as a fragile child."

"And it didn't work?" asked Jobber.

"When you are afraid of a thing, will hiding from it protect you from its power to terrorize you?" Zein responded sharply.

"Nah." Jobber shook her head. "Makes it worse."

"Only Huld saw the terror gnawing at Zorah's heart, turning it into madness; it was Huld who nursed Zorah through the fevers and the nightmares. Thus she was suspicious when, in the spring of that year, Zorah changed. Changed utterly. Zorah went to the Kirian and began to practice the way of the Fire Sword. She was no longer timid and frightened, but grew bold and fierce. She trained long and hard with the Kirian, winning their trust and respect. Even they were fooled into thinking she had gained control of her emotions. Laile and Finne believed she had outgrown her fears."

"And Huld?" Shedwyn asked, wrapping her arms around her knees for warmth. An early-evening wind drew a chill down from the rocks.

"Huld saw the fear still hidden in Zorah's eyes. She mistrusted Zorah's sudden fierceness. And she worried at Zorah's new obsession with the Fire Sword. Outwardly Zorah appeared sure and steady, but all that had changed was the manner in which she ran from her fear and madness. Tired of being the victim, Zorah chose to be the master. She would not wait for death to claim her, rather she would turn the blade and become death itself."

Zein stopped, staring into the fire. He seemed exhausted, his skin sallow and his shoulders hunched tight across the neck. "Huld knew the fear remained despite what Zorah did to hide it. She caught glimpses of it in the sudden frantic strokes of the sword and she heard it late at night in Zorah's muffled screams. Huld went again to her sisters, fearful where Zorah's obsession would lead the knot. Again, Laile and Finne did not agree with her and accused Huld of being jealous of Zorah.

"In the summer of that year, Zorah invited the Sileans to Oran—for the purpose of trade, she told the others. They arrived in the fall, twelve black ships of Silean troops heavily armed, not for trade but for a battle. When Finne confronted Zorah, demanding an explanation, Zorah killed her with the Fire Sword. She had planned it thus all along.

"I was with Huld when Finne was murdered. I heard the screams as Zorah's death stroke cleaved flesh from bone and spirit from body. As Finne lay dying, Zorah tuned the Fire Sword to Finne's escaping power and drained it into her sword. Then Zorah attacked Laile and stole Laile's power, again using the Fire Sword. The sword sucked in their power, drawing a whirlpool of Oran magic around Zorah. In the streets of Beldan, at the command of Zorah herself, the Silean armies began a brutal campaign against the Oran people."

"And what of Huld?" asked Jobber. "Why didn't she stop Zorah?"

"She tried, but there was only so much she could do without endangering all of Oran. The Queens' quarter knot is the center of Oran's world, like a table balanced on four legs. When Zorah killed Finne and then Laile, our world began to shake, the table wobbling on two delicately balanced legs, spinning around in the current created by Zorah's whirlpool. If Huld died or killed Zorah, Oran would be smashed apart in the rushing flow of power. Already the effects could be felt throughout Oran; there were earthquakes, the islands were flooded under huge waves, and everywhere one looked there was fire. We fell beneath the Silean armies on the one hand, and we died, betrayed by our own queen, on the other."

"What did you do? What did Huld do?" Shedwyn asked, hugging her knees tighter.

Zein shrugged, and in the firelight his face grew haggard. "What could we do? We fled with Huld to Sadar. Those of us that still lived." Zein spread his hands and stared at them intensely. "In order to stop the flow of time Zorah needed the combined power of all her sisters. She needed to create the whirlpool with herself, untouched, in the middle. She believed the Fire Sword would draw off the chaotic effects of the rushing power and leave herself immortal, and Oran more or less whole. The Sileans would be there to secure peace among the Oran people."

"For a price," said Jobber sarcastically.

"Exactly."

"But I don't understand," Lirrel said, scratching her cheek. "Time has stopped for Zorah. So what then did Huld achieve?"

"Time hasn't stopped entirely. It only passes so slowly that

Zorah scarcely notices it. In two hundred years she has lived but
a day or two. During the final siege of Sadar, Huld was growing
weaker. The whirlpool of magic began draining power away
from her as well. Zorah didn't even need the Fire Sword to kill
Huld. The current would do that by itself. Huld's only chance
lay in slowing down the current of Zorah's great whirlpool and
cheating time. So she abandoned human shape and human time
and changed herself, and those of us who wished to continue
serving her.''

"Changed you into what?" Jobber asked nervously.

"Avadares pines.''

"Nah,'' scoffed Jobber, incredulous.

Zein ignored her and continued. "Some of these Avadares
pines have been here since the first days of Oran. They are ancient, and for them the passing of time is slow. With Huld as a
pine, Zorah couldn't sense her presence, and the flow of magic
from Huld into the whirlpool became slow enough to stop the
continual trembling of our earth. The passage of time and the
flow of magic into the void slowed to the rhythm of the Avadares
pines. Power continues to bleed from Huld into Zorah's great
void, but only in the smallest stream.''

"Are all of these trees . . . ?'' Shedwyn started but didn't
finish her question, suddenly feeling the eyes of the forest on
her.

Zein shook his head. "No. Except for Huld, there are only a
handful left who chose to remain as sentry trees.''

"Is that how you knew when we entered the forest?'' Faul
asked.

"Exactly,'' Alwir answered, and gave the meat another turn.

"And that's where you got them marks on your face?'' Jobber
asked. "From being a frigging tree for so many years?''

"Yes,'' he answered her, brushing his cheek with the back of
his hand. "Those of us who have been trees still carry the marks
of our tree. The other vaggers adopted the practice of tattooing
so that our oddity would not be so noticeable. Their marks are
similar enough to the casual eye, but they are not the same. Only
one intimately familiar with these marks would have known
that.'' Zein held Jobber's gaze steady. "I know where you have
seen these marks before,'' he said softly.

"Yeah?'' Jobber snapped belligerently. "Where?''

"He was your father,'' Zein answered.

Jobber's face froze in an expression of shock, which was

washed away by a wave of erupting fury. "That ain't true! That frigging ain't true," she shouted at Zein. She stood, fists clenched and ready to fight. "Growler picked me off the street and taught me how to fight, but we weren't blood," she yelled.

"There were four of us that Huld entrusted with the task," Zein said as if Jobber's outburst were no more than the stirring of leaves in the wind. "Twenty years ago, by the reckoning of men—time's different when you live as a tree—Huld decided she needed to act. There is a limit to her strength, and her power to slow the void is waning. The only way to stop Oran before it falls into Zorah's void is to have a new knot, one that will rebuild our center and hold the threads of the world together again. But Zorah had murdered so many Oran children, Huld was afraid there were none left who might have enough power to form a new knot. In desperation Huld managed to steal the different gifts of power from Zorah's whirlpool. It was at a cost to her, and to Oran. Huld can no longer protect Oran against the droughts, the blights of crops or the rumblings of the earth. She changed us back from pines to humans and gifted each of us with the potential for power. We carried magic, drawn from the source of the old knot, without Zorah's knowledge. It was magic we were to pass to a new generation of Queens. And so four of us left Avadares and sought out mates brave enough to birth new Queens. Each child would carry the signature of a Queen. Lirrel is my daughter, and you can see in the purity of her eyes the mark of the Air Queen. And you, with your hair of fire, are Growler's daughter." Zein finished speaking and Jobber sat down again. Her head slumped over her drawn-up knees.

"And there's me," said Shedwyn. Undoing the buttons of her dress, she exposed the skin between her breasts and a narrow patch of her stomach. On the light brown skin were faint tracings of lines, curing in a circular pattern on the rise of her belly and branching out across the tops of her breasts. She rebuttoned her dress and looked at Zein. "My father, too, carried the vaggers marks on his face. And though I have never been tatooed, the lines have appeared here on my body."

Treys turned somber eyes to her. In the firelight the brown-skinned face glowed like polished wood. "I knew your face the moment I saw you. Your father was my brother. I need not ask the news of him. For if he is not with you, it can only be that he is dead."

"He died protecting my mother and me," Shedwyn said softly.

"And then my mother died not long after him. I had not thought to ever find family again." She gave a sad smile to Treys.

"If my air element is so important, why did you leave me?" Lirrel asked Zein suddenly.

"By staying together, I endangered your life and those of our tent."

"I don't understand," Lirrel said, shaking her head.

"Cast a single pebble into a pool, it makes a small splash. Cast two and it becomes noticeable," he answered, raising his eyes to meet hers. "Huld's power clings to us like the red clay. I traveled unmolested for many years with your mother and the tent. But after you were born it was very difficult. A Reader discovered me soon after your birth. We fled. Twice we were stopped and twice more we escaped. As you grew older, I knew that we wouldn't be as lucky a third time. So I left the tent and came here to carry on the task of fighting Zorah. I could only hope that you would be safe among the Ghazali and that we would someday find each other again."

"But why aren't we under Zorah's influence?" Lirrel asked. "Why don't we feel the current of Zorah's magic?"

"Your power comes from the same source, but you have your own identity; just as a child shares its parents' features but claims its own will. In times past, the transformation of power from one knot to another would have been scarcely noticeable. The Oran people possessed small quantities of magic, and in times of change it was the combined power of the people that held Oran's cradle steady. But no longer. Zorah has murdered so many with power that there are few enough to bear the strain."

"Why didn't you bring us here, then? To Avadares. Wouldn't it have been safer?" Lirrel asked.

Zein shook his head again sadly. "No. Once you were together in one place, Zorah would have sensed too soon your power moving against the current. Separately you are not as strong, and therefore do not stir on Zorah's senses in the same way. But as you grow together, you will all become formidable. An even bigger splash in the pool. We could not risk Zorah discovering you too soon. We had to wait until we could ready the Oran people to fight the Sileans. And we had to wait until you were all old enough to form a new Queens' quarter knot."

Jobber picked her head up from her knees. "I didn't know my mother. Didn't have no family to speak of, except for Growler, and he never told me the truth about it. Why's that, then, eh?"

"He must have known he'd have to leave you as my father had to leave me," Lirrel answered, as if explaining it to herself as much as to Jobber. "He needed you to be strong, and rely on yourself. To tell you the truth might have weakened you."

"Maybe," Jobber conceded. "But if he'd told me, he might also be here alive instead of dead. I might have been more careful. I might not have done what I did. It was all my fault, you see." Jobber was speaking faster, the words coming in a jerky staccato as she struggled to get them out.

Lirrel laid a hand on Jobber's arm. "No," she said, "I don't believe that."

Jobber shook her head miserably. "We were in Market Square, me practicing the snitch while Growler looked on. I made a mistake. He yelled at me and I lost my temper. Right there in Market Square. Started stalls afire, hats, capes, anything I looked at. At first it was fun to see all them wealthy bastards jumping up like fleas, slapping at their smoking pockets. Fun, that was, until some Reader with a burning backside got a good look at us and started the alarm."

Jobber hissed angrily. "The butcherboys came after us. Growler shoved me one way, and he went another. I thought it was all a lark until I found him later, out behind the tanneries. There wasn't much left that wasn't broken or bleeding. But he was a tough bastard. They'd done him sore but he'd still managed his escape." She pursed her lips and then set them in a sullen scowl. "My own father." She shook her head. "My own father."

For a moment no one spoke. Smoke rose from the rabbits, the flesh turning a crackling brown. Then she jerked her head up and pushed back her hair.

"Well, it's done now, ain't it? Over a long time ago," she said harshly. "Least he didn't die alone. Scaffered more than a few of the butcherboys before he went." She sniffed hard and then coughed to clear the thickness from her throat.

Around the fire, bodies shifted wearily, feet scrapping over the stone. Alwir scratched his beard and Wyer exhaled a ragged sigh. Zein stole a glance at Lirrel and found her staring back at him. He thought he saw the tracings of a sad smile at the corner of her mouth.

"You're forgetting something, ain't you?" Jobber said suddenly.

"The fourth," answered Lirrel. "Where is the fourth girl?"

Treys shook his head. "We don't know. Moire was the last of us to leave Avadares. We haven't seen or heard of her since. We only know that when the child is ready to join us, she will be sent here."

"Or we will find each other," suggested Lirrel. "I knew where to find Jobber, just as I knew where to find Shedwyn."

"Yes," answered Zein earnestly. "Do you sense her, the fourth girl?"

Lirrel pursed her lips. "No. Not at all."

"Then we can only wait."

"What if something goes wrong?" asked Jobber. "I mean supposing there isn't a fourth? Supposing this other one got herself killed before she could birth the fourth? It seems to me this whole plan of yours leaves a frigging lot to chance. Supposing a Reader or Zorah got ahold of her or the child? What then, eh?"

Zein answered her, his expression somber. "Then we are lost. There will be no other chances but this. Huld no longer has the strength to give to a new knot. She has been losing power steadily and more rapidly in the last ten seasons. It's become harder and harder to maintain balance in Oran."

Faces grew pensive in the firelight and the silence heavier.

Zein forced a smile and spoke encouragingly. "*Ahal*, we've not lost yet. Even a slim hope is better than none. In the meantime there is much we can do. So let us eat." He took the cooked rabbits off the spit and began cutting the meat. He handed a haunch to Jobber, who looked at it glumly.

"I ain't hungry anymore," she said, shaking her head.

She got up and stretched, her muscles cramped, nervous tension still threading through her legs. She suddenly wanted to be alone. Away from Lirrel and Shedwyn, away from all of them. Lirrel reached out to stop her, but Zein held her back with a gentle shake of his head. Let her go, his eyes said.

Jobber walked down the escarpment a short way, her feet slipping unsteadily on the small stones. She found a flat boulder and sat on it. Dusk had fallen and only a pale pink stripe at the edge of the far horizon marked the end of a day. Around her the wind rustled the dry leaves of the pines and whispered through the clefts of the rocks. One of Dagar's goats leaped over the rocks and came up to her, bleating insistently, its eyes rolling stupidly in its wedged-shaped head.

"Go on, get out of here, beastie," she snapped, shooing it

away with her hand. It tottered off, flicking its tail indignantly at such treatment.

Alone again Jobber stared out at the black curled shapes of the pine trees. It was hard to imagine anyone as quick as Growler being a tree. But then, she remembered, there were times when he had sat perfectly still for what seemed like hours. Thinking, he told her once when she asked what he was doing. And then, tweaking her nose, he'd said how she ought to try it sometime. On the boulder Jobber let her shoulders droop and her hands relax in her lap as Growler's had done. Around her the wind died down, and the air grew still. She inhaled deeply, her nostrils flared, and smelled the faint clean fragrance of pine. As she exhaled slowly a sense of calm settled on her, gentle and caressing. She began to strip away all the carefully constructed layers of noise and movement designed to keep the painful memories hidden. And as the last fell away Jobber confronted both the intense joy of Growler's love and the wrenching hurt of his death. Like a Silean blade, sharpened on both sides, the memories cut deep.

"Frigging shit," she swore softly to the darkening sky, and felt the tears that trickled warmly down her cheeks.

Chapter Eleven

Zein roused them early in the morning, the sun's rays driving narrow shafts of bright gold light through the low-lying clouds. Mountain mist formed a damp blanket, hiding the view of the western plains below. Jobber jerked awake and then yawned widely, her jaw cracking lightly. She stood slowly, her back stiff from yet another night on the cold ground. She groaned at the ache in her neck, and the twin knots of cramped muscles just beneath her shoulder blades. Next to her Lirrel sat up, sleepy eyed, and rubbed her arms. A pine twig stuck in her hair. She blew on her hands to warm them up in the chilly morning.

"I need to sit in the sun," Lirrel said softly to Jobber. "I'll wait outside with Dagar and the goats." She rose quietly and slipped into the growing sunshine.

"Z'blood, ain't enough trash here to wrap up in," Jobber grumbled. "No wonder she got cold."

Treys gave a short laugh. "Get used to it, you will. We leave nothing behind to mark our passing. It's safer, though it makes for cold food and hard ground."

"What do you do in the winter?" asked Faul, rubbing hands over her face. Her eyes were puffy, and when she sniffled, her nose sounded stuffed.

"Go into the caves, for the most part. Some of them have

deep enough caverns and air holes that let us keep a fire without getting smoked out.''

"Like bears," Faul replied. "Sleeping through the winter."

"Ah no, not sleeping." Zein smiled at her as he doused the remnants of the fire and scattered the ashes.

"What then? Surely you don't train in these cramped quarters?" Faul looked up at the low-vaulted ceiling of the cave.

"There's much to be done. Supplies need to be acquired—"

"Stolen, you mean," said Faul dryly.

Zein inclined his head in agreement. "Returned to those who produced them."

"Now that's a vagger argument if ever I heard one." Faul slapped dirt from her thighs and looked over at Wyer and Alwir. "I can't tell you the number of times as Knackerman I caught a vagger, his hands neatly tipping into another's pocket for coins . . .'' Faul laughed at the memory and shook her gray hair free of bits of leaves and twigs. Then she assumed a hunched position, pretending to clutch a wooden staff. '' 'Gracious woman, don't mind these few small coins. I've only taken them for a religious tax. To keep the soul and spirit alive, you see,' mumble mumble something about the greatness of this knot and that Oran hero.''

"And you, Faul," Treys called to her as he packed the stores up neatly and stowed them way, "did you not always give in and let them keep the coins?"

"Bah," Faul replied, and shrugged.

"You did," Treys continued, "because you knew they was right."

"I knew they'd starve without a decent meal and I'd have the wretched task of picking up the corpses and sending them down to Scroggles," Faul snapped back.

"Well, at least we won't be troubling the Firstwatch with that anymore," Zein said. He gathered his quiver and arrows, slinging them over his shoulder.

"Any why's that?" Faul asked.

"Steal a mint house?" Jobber teased.

Zein nodded. "Almost as good. We've learned the art of clip and sweat."

"Naffy that," Jobber cried in approval. "And a good job of it, too, as long as you got a good smith."

"I don't understand," Eneas said. He tugged on his boots and stood up, giving a confused look first to Shedwyn, who shook her head, not understanding either, then to Jobber. "What's clip and sweat?"

"A lovely bit of cheat." Jobber pushed back her red hair and her face glowed like a child's. "Ain't you never seen a gold or silver coin with a bite out of it? Or maybe wondered why one coin felt lighter than another. Well?" She looked expectantly at Eneas.

Eneas frowned, still not understanding her. "So? What of it?"

"Z'blood, you're thick as a plate, ain't you?"

"I'm not familiar with thievery, that's all."

"You're a Silean, ain't you? Thought it came with the blood."

"Shut up," Shedwyn said sharply. "Shut your trap." She had been combing out her braid and now she stopped, her face darkening at Jobber's rudeness. "You Beldan cock, you think you know everything, don't you?"

"Damn more than you frigging dirt twirlers," Jobber snapped. There was a reek of copper in the close air of the cave.

"It's enough," Wyer said quickly, and stepped quickly between the two women, his broad back cutting off Jobber's view of Shedwyn. Jobber blinked and then turned away, her expression puzzled. She edged away from Wyer, avoiding looking at Shedwyn. As she did, she caught Zein's eye, probing her face for an explanation.

"I'm outside if any needs me," she said stiffly, and left the cave.

Wyer answered Eneas, his voice low and calm, as if to deny the tension. "Clip is when a bit of metal is cut off the edge of a coin. We collect enough of the bits, melt them together, and give them a new stamp. Sweating is about the same. A single coin is heated and a layer shaved off the top just so. The new layer is cooled and stamped. You can make a string of coins go a lot farther that way."

"And," added Alwir with a wry smile, "there's something satisfying about watching a Silean reach into his pocket and pull out a coin with the Queen's face on one side and the New Moon on the other. It's great to see the look of utter surprise when they discover we're in their pockets as well."

"Don't the Guilds take offense?" asked Eneas, clearly impressed with the boldness and sophistication of the forgery.

"No." Alwir laughed. "Many of the Guildmasters are our best minters."

"Clever, very clever indeed," Eneas murmured, though his eyes had strayed to Shedwyn. She was finishing braiding her hair. He could tell by the sharp jerks of her hands as she twisted the hair that she was angry. She finished and roughly flung the single braid over her shoulder. He saw now that she was talking to herself, her lips moving quietly over the words.

He approached her and touched her lightly on the shoulder. She jumped and spun around. Seeing it was only him, Shedwyn closed her eyes and exhaled noisily.

"Jobber?" Eneas asked softly.

"Aye, who else?"

"But why, Shedwyn? I thought at Cairns that there was a peace between you?"

"So did I," Shedwyn said wistfully. "But I suppose not, after all. I find it hard to like her, the things she says, the sound of her voice, or the stink of her hair. Huld's peace, times are I just want to slap her hard across the face. And she'd like to do the same to me. I'm telling you I've seen it in her face." She looked up at Eneas, worried creases on her forehead. "I know it's dangerous, so I don't hit her. But I can't stop my mouth from saying the hard words."

Eneas put his arm around her shoulder. "She's a Beldanite. That's enough to set anyone's teeth grinding. Even yours." He kissed her on the nose, and when he saw her smile, he kissed her mouth. Shedwyn responded, lingering in Eneas's embrace. He pulled away from her slowly and gazed at her, feeling the charged air between them. "Shedwyn, maybe tonight—"

"Hey, you two!" Jobber shouted into the cave. "Give o'er with the petting and get a move on. Zein says we can't wait no more."

Eneas growled and saw Shedwyn's smile widen. "Your teeth too, dear heart," she said softly. "I can hear them grinding even now." Then she laughed and took Eneas by the hand, going out of the cave to join the others. "Maybe you're right, Eneas," she said hopefully. "Maybe that's all it is."

It was late afternoon when Zein and Treys led them into camp. They had seen no warning of it as they came over a ridge, humpbacked with loose gray stones. A single sentry tree greeted them, its wide branches spread almost to the ground, the dry needles long and sharp like thorns. Around the base of the tree bloomed a profusion of wild flax, the delicate blossoms a shimmering blue. Petals fluttered to the ground each time the wind gusted. Zein stopped at the tree and waited silently. Behind him the others straggled to catch up, half-relieved that Zein had stopped his continuous climbing and half-curious at the desolate sight of the old tree.

In the lumpy burl of the stunted trunk a small face gradually appeared, pushed out through the surface of the coarse bark. The eyes were closed, whorls of dark brown circling the lids. Small fragments of bark peeled away, leaving the cheeks smooth and rounded. The mouth opened, emitting a scratchy sigh and revealing a row of teeth the color of dried amber.

"The water runs deep over the stones," whispered the tree.

"And so we still live," answered Zein with a nod of his head.

The tree sighed again and the needles trembled in the slight breeze. "Then I shall return to sleep. Enter Zein, there is a welcome for you." The face receded into the tree, a fresh scar of scoured bark the only mark left remaining of the features.

"Zorah's tits," whispered Jobber as they walked passed the ancient tree. "Did you see that, Faul?"

"Yes," Faul answered quickly. "And I think it would be wise of you to change your form of expression while you're here."

"What do you mean?" Jobber asked.

"This is Avadares, Jobber. Huld's county," Lirrel answered, coming close to Jobber's elbow. "Zorah's name, even spoken of as you do, may not be the best idea."

"Aw shit—"

"That'll do." Faul laughed. "Oran peasants think a great deal of shit."

"Humph," Jobber snorted at the narrow path. "Pig shit, cow shit, chicken shit—"

"You've got the idea," Faul replied dryly.

"Somehow it don't have the same crack."

"What about duck shit?" offered Lirrel.

Jobber stared at her incredulously. "Duck shit?" she repeated sarcastically. "Don't even try, Lirrel. It ain't in your nature to be coarse."

"Leave it to a master wordsmith, like Jobber here," Faul teased.

"You ain't half-bad yerself, Faul. I still remember a few choice phrases you shouted at me when I puked on your uniform."

"If only I hadn't been wearing it at the time, Jobber. We all could have been spared the indignity of my temper."

Jobber glanced over at Faul, worried at the cool tone of her voice, and then relaxed as she saw Faul's lopsided smile and the gray-blue eyes, soft as the flax.

"We're here!" Zein called over his shoulder, and waved them to hurry. Jobber and Lirrel urged their legs to move faster, ignoring the small sharp stones that had found their way inside their boots and were now pricking their soles. Next to them Faul lengthened her stride, the black sword held firmly in one hand.

The path curved down a ravine into a hollow dotted with birch and pine trees and ringed on three sides by huge boulders. Bushes and low-lying shrubs gave the rocky ground a dense cover of bright green. Tents of brown-colored cloth rose out of the ground like squatting hens. Several small fires released wisps of fine gray smoke. There was the faint scent of burning wood and smoked meat. A girl stood staring at their approach, pins in her mouth as she hung laundry on a rope strung between two branches. From behind trees, and filtering through the bushes, people came into the clearing to greet them. As they entered the camp, Jobber heard the sound of an infant squawling.

In moments they were surrounded, their senses overwhelmed by the sudden fecund reek of humanity and the loud voices of the camp. Oran women with bare feet and babies perched on their hips thumped them hard on shoulders and pushed slabs of new bread into their hands. An old woman gave Faul a toothless smile while her hands never stopped plying the linen piled high on a distaff tucked into her armpit. Skinny children with runny eyes and knobby knees shouted gleefully at them. Flies buzzed around them. One child tugged at Faul's sword and she jerked it away furiously.

"Z'blood!" Faul exploded angrily.

"No, no Faul!" Jobber corrected with a grim smile, batting away an eager child that hugged her around the legs. "Thank Huld, remember?"

"Whore's shit to you, Jobber."

"That's one I forgot."

"I think it's rather nice to welcomed," Lirrel said, her voice muffled as a woman in heavy blue skirts and a dirty white blouse kissed her soundly on the cheeks.

"Where are the fighters?" Faul asked, her voice growing tight with anger. "This can't be the New Moon."

"Over there, Faul, look," Lirrel answered, and pointed to a group of men and women gathered around Zein and Treys. All of them carried weapons of some sort, and though the group seemed despairingly small, Faul gave a whistle of relief. Brusquely, she cut away from the crowd of women and children and headed for Zein.

Jobber looked over the throng of people that had turned out to greet them. Wyer was embracing another man, his face sooty like a smith's. He wore the leather apron of a farrier. Alwir, too, it seemed, had found old friends; a number of young women clustered around him, flashing bright smiles and gently patting him on the back and shoulders. Lirrel had wandered off with Dagar, the goats bleating welcome to the few animals in camp. A dog barked noisily until Dagar shushed it with a bit of his bread. Then Jobber saw Shedwyn and Eneas standing amidst a group of older peasant women. They hugged Shedwyn like a long-lost daughter, petted her cheeks, and handed her their babies. Eneas looked shy and uncomfortable as the women pulled at his vest. Shedwyn laughed, her wide cheekbones lifted with her happy smile and her brown skin flushed. She jiggled babies in her arms before returning them, sometimes crying, sometimes cooing to their mothers. A thin woman with a pockmarked face gave Shedwyn a black shawl, placing it reverently around her shoulders.

"Well, at least she's right at home," Jobber mumbled, feeling a twinge of loneliness.

"Oy, Jobbernowl! You're a long way from Beldan."

Jobber spun around, startled, her heart leaping with expectation at the familiar accent. A young woman approached, her hips thrust forward as she walked with a measured Beldan gait. Blond hair fluffed around her head like a huge dandelion about to seed. And though she wore a plain brown dress, bright blue ribbons tied at either shoulder gave her a distinctly Beldan air in the rugged camp. A hand pushed away the wild hair and Jobber saw the clear blue eyes that twinkled back.

"Finch!" Jobber darted forward. "Finch, is that you?"

"In the flesh."

"Now ain't that lovely!" Jobber replied, her voice thickening with unexpected happiness at finding an old companion from the Beldan streets.

"So I've been told. And never were truer words spoken. Look who else is here," Finch said, pointing to a thick stand of gacklebushes. Two more were coming, and almost before she could see them, Jobber heard childish voices arguing.

"I knew she was coming—"

"Before dark. I told you!"

"I told you!"

"Did not."

"Did."

"Who cares, she's—"

"Here, ain't she!"

Jobber glanced at Finch, who was laughing quietly. "Still at it, those two?"

"Yeah. Never one starts but the other finishes the thought. You know how it is with twins. Sometimes I wonder if one doesn't piss for the other."

"Trap!" Jobber called as a small face appeared above the bushes, white hair stark against the dark green of the leaves. The face crinkled with a smile and Trap plunged through the bushes into the clearing.

"Still wearing that lighterman's coat, I see," Jobber said. "Hasn't grown any smaller on her neither."

"Maybe just a bit," Finch replied.

A second figure poked through the thick undergrowth and Jobber saw Mole, his thin frail body barely covered by a shirt and trousers. His feet were crusty with yellow calluses. His normally pale skin had darkened to a light brown and his white hair was cut very short to his scalp. He raised a hand in greeting.

Jobber touched her head and looked at Finch. "What happened to his hair?"

Finch shrugged. "Lice. We all get them one time or another up here."

"Oy, Jobber. We knew you was coming!" Mole called out, still extricating himself from the bushes.

"Z'blood." Jobber sighed, her throat squeezing and her heart pounding. "It ain't half-naffy to find you all here. But how? How?" She asked turning to Finch. "Beldan is a long ways away for you as well."

"It wasn't too bad. We traveled with a vagger woman. Right banger with that staff of hers, too. Despite what I once thought, I learned that butcherboys got brains after watching her open a few of their noggins like eggs." Finch gave a delicate shudder.

"Oy, Jobber," Trap called, a little breathless from running. She slowed down, waiting for Mole to join her. Jobber saw them glance at each other and then at her, their expressions growing serious.

"You lied to us, Jobber," Mole started to say.

"You ain't a boy," Trap finished.

"And yer hair—"

"Fire element, ain't you?"

"How come you never—"

"Joined with Kai and the Waterlings like us?"

Jobber ran her hands through her hair. Not that again. Even Finch looked at her, curious, and maybe with a hint of suspicion.

"How come, Jobber? Not even Kai knew your lay until the night we fled Beldan. She told us about you. How you could hide your aura with a vagger trick?" Finch scratched at a scab on her forearm, not looking directly at Jobber.

"It's a long story," Jobber said wearily. "And it seems so long ago."

"There's nothing but time here," Finch replied. "No pockets to snitch, no neat little purse to prig."

"I'm thirsty."

"Go on, Finch—" Mole started to say, nudging Finch in the side with a sharp elbow.

"Get her the bottle of brandy we got stored for her," Trap finished, and beamed with pleasure at Jobber.

"You knew I was coming, did you?" Jobber started to smile again at the thought of a drink of brandy.

"Known if for a while," Mole answered lightly. He lifted his face to the stirring winds, his pale blue eyes a reflection of the afternoon sky. "Smelled you in the air, two days ago."

Jobber held her nose and pretended to gag. "Sounds pretty narky to me. Ah well, let's have a look at this bottle." Laughing, she shoved her hands deep into her trouser pockets. Matching Finch's slow and even strides, with Mole and Trap following behind, Jobber strolled across camp as if down a paved Beldan street.

"Faul Verran, I would present you to Masters Go Shing and Veira Rune. You no doubt have heard of them before?" Zein asked Faul, his eyebrows raised in polite question.

Faul scowled as she looked at the pair of vaggers standing before her. Their faces meant nothing to her, and their seeming age and small stature didn't impress her. In fact nothing in this frigging camp impressed her. It all smelled like poverty. Haggard farm women, dirty underfed children, soured meat, and misery. What was she doing here?

"I have had the pleasure of seeing you work, Firstwatch Faul, and was impressed with your style." The older man spoke to her, smiling. He'd few teeth left, but his small black eyes commanded attention.

"You saw me? Where?"

"In Beldan once. Many years ago."

Faul found herself nagged by the man's name. Go, she repeated to herself. Go Shing, hearing something very familiar in the almost musical sound of the name. It came to her and she paled.

"Go Shing!" she blurted out in shocked amazement.

The old man chuckled and, half-embarrassed and half-pleased, turned to Veira Rune. "So they do remember me in the world."

"You founded the Swallow school." Faul was speaking rapidly as she remembered her training under the Firstwatch Serena. "Those techniques are so difficult. Sharp and light as the swallow, changing sword position from high to low in quick succession." Faul smiled. "Brilliant. And almost impossible to beat."

Go beamed and then sucked on his few lower teeth. "You flatter me too much."

"But that was more than two hundred years ago—" Faul started, now seeing the faint tattoos that circled his face.

"You see the answer already in my face," Go replied. "I have been one of Huld's sentry trees."

"Will you teach me?" Faul asked.

"I no longer use the sword. Two hundred years of being a tree have changed me. I no longer feel one with the steel, but prefer the sentience of wood. It is the staff now that I carry."

Faul tried to hide her disappointment, but Go saw it anyway.

"If you like, perhaps I can give you my thoughts on your own peculiar style, Faul Verran."

Faul smiled. "I would like that. I would like that very much."

"You will, of course, help us to train the others?" Veira Rune now spoke up and for the first time Faul noticed the woman carried a quiver of arrows and a longbow. Like Go, she had tattoos on her face. Two long braids wrapped around her head, framing the wide forehead and intelligent eyes. She carried her back erect, though her trousered legs appeared slightly bowed. She wore small leather gloves that covered the fingers only to the first knuckle. Her nails were short and blunt. Faul sniffed and realized Veira carried the odor of horses.

"You mean to train these people?" Faul's question indicated her disapproval of the idea.

"Some of them, yes. But most of the New Moon fighters are scattered throughout the mountains in separate camps. You'll meet them later."

Faul sighed with relief. "I thought . . ."

"This is a base camp for the children with power fleeing the Readers. They must learn enough to protect themselves, should it come to that. But none of them will be going to fight at Sadar."

"I see," Faul answered slowly, not certain how Jobber or Shedwyn was going to like the idea of being left behind. And oddly, Faul found herself not certain how she liked the idea of leaving Jobber. She had grown used to her over the last months. Irritating as Jobber was, Faul would miss her.

"It won't be for awhile," Zein said softly and then winced apologetically. "I 'heard' your thoughts. In this camp there are few secrets to be had. Too many air elements."

Veira laughed and raised her longbow meaningfully. "At least among air elements our arrows always find their mark."

Faul's eyes widened and the words of an old song sprang to her lips, the sad tune graceful even in Faul's unmusical voice. "Her steed did tremble battle weary, but she rode on, quick and steady, And Veira's arrows found their mark, and in many a Silean breasts were buried." Faul stopped, seeing the pleased expression light up the woman's face.

Veira turned triumphantly to Go. "There now, it seems I'm not entirely forgotten either."

"My mother used to sing that," Faul said in amazement. "I'm afraid I don't remember the rest. Only that verse."

"Don't worry," Go chuckled. "Veira knows it."

"Old man," Veira warned, one finger wagging at Go. "I ought to—"

She stopped as the sound of arguing reached them. They turned, concerned eyes following the noise, searching the camp for the source.

"Tcha!" Zein cursed softly as he spotted Eneas and Shedwyn surrounded by a group an angry laborers. "I should have known there'd be trouble. Come on." He pulled at Faul's sleeve.

"I know who you are!" a man in a dirty brown smock was

shouting. "I've toiled your lands before. Gotten the boot of your overseer in my back. Frigging Silean bastard come here to spy."

"Enough, Farnon," Zein said quietly but firmly.

"You've been duped!" Farnon yelled, turning to face Zein. The big slab face was ruddy with anger. His eyes flashed dangerously. Around him a group of laborers grumbled.

"You're wrong about Eneas," Zein said.

"He's a Silean lord," Farnon hissed the words.

"He's *ghazat*. A fugitive, like the rest of us."

"No! Not like the rest of us," another man said. He was a tall farmer with a long horse face and a scar over one eye. He carried a sickle strapped to his belt. "Look to his face. He's never had a day of labor in his life. How can you trust him?"

"Will you trust me then?" Shedwyn spoke up, thrusting herself between Eneas and the angry clutch of men.

Farnon sneered. "Hiding behind the skirts of a girl."

"Not any girl," Treys said, raising his voice over the jeers of the crowd. "But the child of Huld."

A hush settled on the men, some regarding Shedwyn with curious eyes, other looking to Farnon to see what he would say next.

"A girl nonetheless," Farnon said bitterly, "and easily enough deceived by the likes of a fair-headed man." He took a step closer to Shedwyn, his lips twisted into a unpleasant smile. "What did he promise you then, girl, a place in the big house? Silk and lace, eh?"

Eneas roughly pushed Shedwyn out of the way and lunged for Farnon. He threw his fist, launching it into Farnon's squared jaw. Farnon's head snapped back and he grunted in surprise. Eneas didn't wait but punched again, driving his other fist toward his staggering opponent.

Farnon bellowed, spitting blood, and ducked his head. Eneas's punch went wide and Farnon tackled him, his head driving into Eneas's midsection.

"Frigging bastard," he roared as Eneas went down. Farnon scrambled on top of Eneas's chest and slammed a rock-hard fist across his exposed face. Blood erupted from his nose, splattering his cheeks and hair. Eneas thrashed and bucked, trying to overturn Farnon's heavy weight.

"Stop it," Zein shouted. He reached down and, with the back of his fist, rapped Farnon hard across the temples with his knuckles. "I said stop it!"

As Farnon shook his head, dazed by Zein's blow, Eneas succeeded in pushing him off his chest. Hands reached down to pull him up and separate him from Farnon.

Alwir grabbed Farnon by the front of his smock and glared into the florid face. "You know me, Farnon."

"Aye," Farnon replied, still hostile. "And a fair speech it was you made at Fire Circle."

"Then listen to me. I trust Eneas."

"Huld's peace," Farnon swore savagely. "Why is he in Avadares? He has no people here."

"I've come to avenge the deaths of those in Cairns," Eneas said between gasps.

"Who died?" a woman called out from beyond the circle of men. "Who has died at Cairns?" she cried shrilly.

"Everyone, except the goatherd Dagar," Eneas answered. "Cairns no longer exists."

The woman stumbled to her knees, cries of grief pouring out of her. She bent over to the ground and with desperate movements dug her hands into the rocky soil until they started to bleed. The tall farmer with the scar lifted her by her flailing arms and carried her to a tent. Farnon stood surrounded by his men, his ruddy face stark and pale. He wiped at the small trickle of blood at the corner of his mouth.

"So, it has begun," he said. "As you predicted, Zein. The villages would be the first to die."

"I wish it could have been otherwise," Zein answered.

Farnon nodded and lifted his craggy head to Eneas, studying the young man with hatred. "Remember this, Silean, I've got my eye on you. One false step, and I'll kill you."

Shedwyn handed Eneas a cloth and he took it without looking at her. His eyes held Farnon's gaze, refusing to be intimidated. And not until Farnon had turned his back and left with his men did Eneas touch the cloth to his bloody nose.

In the yellow glow of the campfire, Dagar looked skeptically at his bowl of food. He didn't recognize what it was supposed to be. A strange sort of stew had been ladled out of a communal pot and served with a slab of brown bread. He sniffed it. It smelled like meat, but the texture was sticky and lumpy, like porridge. He lifted his spoon and made a face as the stew slid slowly off the end of the spoon and landed with a dull plop back in his bowl.

Dagar sighed and set the bowl down. He took the bread and thought longingly of the warm, greasy taste of the rabbit meat they had eaten the night before.

"Do you not want to eat?" Zein came beside him and squatted on his haunches. He held a bowl in his hand, a spoon halfway to his lips.

"Excuse me, sir—"

"Zein. Just call me Zein."

"All right," Dagar said, and then cast a guilty glance at his bowl. "What is it? What am I eating?"

Zein laughed, his dark eyes almost lost in the long folds of his eyelids. "Avadares soup. Mostly a mixture of nettles, grain, and the barest hint of meat possible. It's not much, true. But it will serve you well."

"So you say," Dagar replied, and for the sake of appearing grateful picked up his bowl as if to eat.

"Tell me this," Zein asked, his voice serious. "How is it you have not the bitterness or the hatred of the others? You have lost your village, you have had to bury your family. But I don't 'hear' the same rage in you. Why?"

Dagar shrugged and lowered his eyes. He felt the sudden catch in his throat as the muscles of his chest and neck squeezed. "It's there."

"And yet it doesn't control you?"

"Maybe it does." Dagar drew out a slow breath, waiting for the muscles to relax again. "Maybe it makes me run the other way, though. I don't want to be like them. Do such a terrible thing to another person. Lirrel showed me how to look away." He paused, finding it difficult to explain the feelings that still warred within him. He hated the Sileans, broke out in a cold fury when he recalled the mutilated faces of his family and friends. But hate like that was a hole into which one fell and never climbed out of again. A darkness out of which there could be no light. And when Dagar felt the suffocation of his hate and his fear, he imagined the salt-white butterflies freed over the stones of Cairns and his heart softened, released from the grip of rage.

"How did Lirrel do it?" Zein demanded. In the firelight Dagar was surprised by Zein's drawn features, the eyes searching intently as if to find an answer to some private pain.

"Ask her yourself," Dagar said, withdrawing from the intense stare.

Zein sighed, and his eyelids drooped wearily. "I don't think my daughter likes me."

"She's hurt, that's all. You disappointed her. She'll change. Not as much as you'd like. But enough to matter."

Zein smiled to Dagar. "For a goatherd you understand a good deal."

"Goats are easy. People harder. But not by much." Dagar shrugged and scratched his cheek. "They all want to be cared for." A goat came close to him and he gave the inquisitive creature his bowl of Avadares soup. The goat sniffed delicately and then turned away, refusing to touch it. "But neither of us likes this stew. Maybe I ought to give you a hand at the food." Dagar looked up hopefully. "I'm not bad at foraging. Got to when you live off the mountains. What do you say then?" he asked.

"I'd be grateful for anything," Zein said easily. "Even I am growing weary of this fare. One thing more, Dagar . . ."

Dagar looked up, wary of the pleading in Zein's voice.

"Will you talk to Lirrel for me? She will trust you."

"Why?"

"Because there are no swords rattling in your head. She will hear you clearly. Tell her that I have always loved her. Will you do that for me?"

"Aye," Dagar said quietly. "Aye, Zein, I will."

"*Ahal*," Zein answered, and prepared to leave. Over his shoulder he called out, "Tomorrow. We begin the training tomorrow."

Dagar watched him, walking steadily through the camp, stopping here and there to give a word to someone who was hunkered down before a fire or just a reassuring touch on the shoulder. Every face smiled in response, grateful for his words. Like a good goatherd, Dagar thought, knowing his herd.

Dagar decided to look for Lirrel, wanting very much to see her, and not just for Zein. He loved the pearl glow of her eyes and the soft blackness of her hair. She was the same height as himself and he liked to stand near her and gaze directly into her face. On her skin she carried the scent of wood perfume which even the dusty fragrance of Avadares pine had not obliterated.

He found her sitting by herself, her legs straight out before her, a little stick in her hand as she tapped the ground rhythmically. She was humming, her eyes shut tight as she listened to the tune she was composing. Dagar paused, uncertain whether or not to disturb her. Just as he thought to leave, she opened her eyes and smiled at him.

"Ahal, Dagar. Come and sit. I know you want to."

"And so I do. I won't deny it." Dagar said, hiding his shyness behind candor.

Lirrel laughed softly, the little stick still tapping out a beat. "Do you play the flute?" she asked.

"Aye. Most herdboys do. Keeps the hours from being too lonely."

"Do you have it on you?"

Dagar nodded and from his shirt pocket retrieved a set of herd pipes, six short reeds that had been twined together with string.

"Play it for me," Lirrel said, and inclined her head to listen.

Dagar inhaled sharply and then blew air across the tops of the pipes. The sound was unexpectedly sweet and hollow. He played a tune he had himself composed, one that always reminded him of spring in Avadares when the hawks circled in the warm air and the young goats bleated for joy at the new grass. He could feel the little trickle of sweat start at his temple as he played, nervously at first and then with growing confidence. When he finished playing, he smiled, pleased with his own effort. Then he looked up at Lirrel, startled to see the tears on her face.

"That bad, am I?" he asked, trying not to sound hurt.

"That good," Lirrel answered, and sniffed noisily. "I'm sorry. Too many things have reminded me of the past. Your flute pulled them out of me like threads breaking on a warp."

"I'm sorry."

"No." Lirrel laughed in spite of her tears and wiped her eyes with the corner of her head scarf. "Sometimes it's good to cry."

"Lirrel," Dagar started, thinking this was a good place to begin, "Zein has spoken to me."

"*Ahal*, I know."

"Will you not forgive him?"

She shook her head. "My forgiveness means nothing. It is not me he has betrayed; it is all the Ghazali. Zein has abandoned the way of the peacekeeper."

Dagar leaned close to Lirrel, gazed intently into the twin moons of her eyes. Firelight flickered there, as did his own reflection. He wanted to see beyond the whiteness, to see into her heart. She had seen his pain once and now he wanted to know the extent of her own. "I lost my family. There weren't no time for forgiveness. Or kind words. Everything ripped away." Lirrel's expression faltered, the calm reserve bending to the sound of his voice. "Aye, you know how I feel. A wound that can't never heal," Dagar said softly. This close to her, he wanted to kiss her, taste the woody perfume on her lips. "Even you have a measure of sorrow. Even you must learn to loosen it to someone. Can't carry it all yourself. Tell me."

Lirrel began to draw circles in the dirt with the little stick.

"It's hard to speak of it without getting angry, without feeling hurt."

"Even a peacekeeper has got to feel anger sometime."

"*Ahal*. Just so. When I was a child," Lirrel began softly, "Zein was a hero to me. I thought him perfect, handsome, and a proud Ghazali, believing in the old ways of the peacekeepers, even as we were reduced to performing at inns and country houses. I strove to be a peacekeeper like him, to please him and gain his respect. Even my flute that I practiced was an effort to show him that I, too, could follow the old ways." She lifted the stick from the dirt and tapped it on the ground. "He left our tent one night. He gave no word of farewell, no word to me." She shook her head. "I thought it was my fault," she said in a small voice. "I thought I had displeased him. I blamed myself. And for months I grieved his absence as one grieves the dead."

"When did you stop grieving?" Dagar asked. Two of his goats had found him and were settled by his feet, their spindly legs tucked beneath them and their warm bodies leaning companionably against his legs. He reached down and scratched one on the head.

"My aunt Aini saw the way I was, and she helped me. I was apprenticed to Zahavra's tent. They were great dancers and I learned to play many of the old and now forbidden tunes. I practiced and studied very hard. It was the music finally that roused me from my self-loathing and gave me back a sense of harmony and balance as a Ghazali. It became a source of strength. When my time was over, Aini gave me the bone flute I now carry. It was made from the arm of my grandmother and it is a great honor to have it. It was a gift that proved to me that I was worthy once more. And though it has never replaced the love I had for Zein, it eased the sorrow of his parting."

"And now?" Dagar said, glancing over at Lirrel.

She dropped the stick and clasped her arms around her chest.

"Finding him again has not given me the joy I had hoped for so long ago. How could he do this?" Lirrel cried out bitterly. "How could he betray his own people so? To take up arms?" Anger surged in her face. She slapped a hand to her chest. "I, *I* struggled to be perfect like him. But he deceived me. It is worse than being abandoned."

"Lirrel, it's not—" Dagar started to say as he took her by the arm to comfort her. But she refused his comfort and stood angrily. The goats scrambled to their feet, frightened by Lirrel's brusqueness.

"You asked to hear it. You wanted to hear me speak the words of my pain. And so I did," she said harshly. "Now leave me alone."

She stormed away, her black skirts flapping against her legs. Twigs and leaves crackled under her feet. Dagar watched her and swore at himself and then at Zein. But there was nothing more to be done tonight. Tomorrow, he told himself with a heavy sigh. Tomorrow he would find her and apologize. And the subject of Zein would be hers alone. He lifted his flute to lips and began to play to ease the wrenching of his throat. But with each breath he inhaled, he could still smell the faint odor of Lirrel's wood perfume.

Shedwyn lay curled in a blanket on the ground as she stared up at the sliver of a moon, caught between the leaves of a birch tree. The air was moistened by the evening dew. Around her she could hear the quiet muffled sounds of the camp settling down for the night, though someone was playing an Oran lute. Shedwyn smiled, guessing it to be Alwir. Someone had produced the small stringed instrument and Alwir's face had lit up at the sight. Although it was horribly out of tune, he had worked the better part of the evening, retieing broken strings and tuning it. The instrument had a thin, twangy sound, but beneath Alwir's skilled fingers the notes had come alive. He had played dance tunes, and the camp's small children twirled in delight. Then he had accompanied the older men and women as they sang songs of bravery, broken vows, and the long dying of Oran. Now they had gone to their beds, and Shedwyn realized as she heard the distant notes that Alwir was playing for himself alone.

Lying beside her, Eneas cleared his throat and swallowed thickly. Shedwyn lifted up on one elbow and looked at him. He was lying on his back, his once long straight nose now swollen and bumpy. Zein had tried to set it but she knew it would always be crooked.

"Hurt much, does it?" she asked.

"No," Eneas answered and turned to face her. "I'm just glad I didn't get killed." He smiled and gave a dry laugh.

"Huld's peace. I couldn't believe it when you went after him like that."

"Had to."

"To prove yourself?"

Eneas shook his head slowly and carefully. "I couldn't stand the way he was insulting you."

Shedwyn snuggled closer to him and reached an arm across his chest. "It was fairly done, dear heart."

"Though I'll never be pretty again," he said, gingerly touching his nose.

"It ain't your nose I love most, you know." She slipped her fingers under Eneas's shirt and felt the goose bumps on his skin prickling her fingertips. She gently stroked his chest, the flat of her palm coming to rest on his nipple. It made a hard, neat seed in the center of her palm.

"What part do you love?" Eneas asked, rolling on his side and drawing Shedwyn closer to his body. She kissed his neck, tasting the dust of Oran's red soil where it mingled with the dried salt of his sweat.

"Well, I need to know all the rest of you to say for certain," Shedwyn answered softly, sliding her hand lower down his trunk and letting rest just above the waist of his trousers. His skin felt cool to the touch. She heard him murmur in reply as he rested his face in her hair, kissing her temples. She felt his body strain as he pressed his hips against her hand. Her heart began to beat faster, driving like the rhythm of Alwir's dance tunes. Blood rose to her cheeks, making her warm and breathless. She fumbled with the ties of Eneas's trousers, tugging them loose. Impatiently she slipped her hand deep between his thighs, feeling the soft tangle of hair and the sudden warmth of his flesh. She gasped in surprise, delighted by the silky hardness of his skin as she gently stroked him. He groaned in her ear, and she felt his hands tighten around her back, his fingers digging into the muscles of her shoulders.

There had never been time for this at the estates. Always they'd had to keep one eye out lest they be discovered. They had kissed, but their embraces had been quick and furtive. But not now, Shedwyn thought, her breath growing shallow, her limbs easing gracefully, indulgently into the contours of Eneas's arms. And not here. Avadares was where she belonged. She could sense every rock and tree, the gnarled roots like veins traveling over the mottled granite. She could feel the subtle shifts of soil and minerals as water slowly passed through the underground caverns, pushing the stones to the surface. And, Shedwyn believed, she could almost sense the presence of Huld, her blood like the thick, slow-moving pitch bubbling through the trees. Eneas rolled her on her back, and she sighed as his weight pressed down on her. Above her the leaves of the birch shivered as the wind shook them.

Eneas unbuttoned her bodice, lying his cheek against her breasts. Without hurry, his hand traveled the length of her thigh, raising her skirts as it moved upward. He circled her nipples with small kisses, moving from one breast to the other, his hair draping her shoulders. The night air was cool, and beneath Eneas's warm, teasing kisses Shedwyn's nipples hardened with excitement. His hand reached her inner thigh and she arched her back, lifting her hips. She shuddered as his fingers probed, curiously at first, and then rested between the swollen folds.

Shedwyn placed her hands on either side of Eneas's head and gently brought his face to hers. Moonlight shone on the long flat plane of his cheeks. He smiled at her. She kissed him, her tongue raised to the roof of his mouth. His lips were soft compared with the hard flexing of his shoulders and back. He raised himself over her, his weight on hands. She lifted and parted her knees wider to settle his body deeper between her thighs. With her hands at the small of his back, she guided him, receiving his first thrust with a sharp cry of pleasure.

He rocked her back and forth with the easy motion of his hips. Shedwyn felt her body respond, muscles squeezing in tight circle that expanded from her center, radiating up into her chest, driving the air from her in short furious gasps. She locked her legs around his waist, digging the hard calluses of her heels into his back.

Everything seemed to join itself to her, not just the length of Eneas's body, but the ground on which she lay, the stones scattered to one side by their movements, even the fluttering leaves of the birch. Shedwyn opened herself to Eneas and at the same to Avadares. Her mind reeled with the rich confusion of sensations; she heard the beating hearts of the sentry trees and they in turned recognized her, saluting her with the dry shake of their branches. The great stones ground together; shining fragments of mica cheered away as Eneas's hipbones dug into her pelvis. The dew lay on the bushes in wet drops no sweeter to Shedwyn than the salty sweat that beaded Eneas's skin. She felt the earth shift beneath her, as if sharing the gathering tension of her body. She arched her back, letting the rising threat of the rumbling earth carry her. Avadares trembled, the humpbacked ridges of the mountains sending stones cascading down their sides. Shedwyn gripped Eneas more tightly, her body taut and compressed as she waited for the final release. The stones of Avadares sang to her, their voices booming in her ears.

"NO!" Eneas shouted above her, his rasping voice like a slap across her face. "No," he groaned, and abruptly rolled off her, his body wrenched from her. Shedwyn gasped at the sharp coldness and sudden silence of the mountains. All she heard was the furious pounding of her heart and her racing pulse that refused to slow.

"Eneas, what is it?" Shedwyn said, turning to touch him. He lay staring angrily into the sky, the rapid rise and fall of his chest in contrast to the hard line of his profile. "Eneas?" she called again. "Please, what is it? What's wrong?"

He jerked his head toward her and she stifled the cry as she saw the angry face. "Nothing," he said.

"Nothing?" Shedwyn said quickly, confusion growing with her frustration. "Why did you stop?"

"I needed air."

Shewdyn swallowed, her throat dry and constricted. Then she settled herself on her back, the stones pricking her beneath the thin blanket. "Will you not finish what we started?" she asked, trying to keep her voice steady.

"If you wish," Eneas answered, his tone distant and cool. He pulled her to him again, but this time his embrace was tentative and awkward.

What have I done? Shedwyn asked herself as Eneas went through the motions of love like a man engaged in an unpleasant task. He finished quickly, the stifled groans sounding to her ear as if he resented making even this admission of pleasure in her.

What have I done? she asked herself again as he rolled off her and curled into sleep, his back to her.

Shedwyn bit her lip to stop the tears that brimmed in her eyes. She edged her body close to him and draped her arm over his side. She hugged him close, grateful that he did not refuse. With her face pressed against his damp shirt, she cried, her body shaking with muffled sobs as she clung tightly to Eneas.

Chapter Twelve

Gonmer stood angrily at attention, her arms pulled behind her back, her legs planted a shoulder's width apart. The sunlight spilled in from the window, shining brightly in her face and making her feel hot and stuffy in the black uniform of the First-watch. Behind her, Lais fidgeted and Gonmer grew more ir-ritated as the page shifted from one foot to another. She had to resist the urge to turn around and tell her page to stand still.

In front of her, and well shielded from the light, Advisor to the Regent Antoni Re Desturo studied a sheaf of papers, his black eyes piercing the scribbled words on each page. Hardly an advisor anymore, Gonmer thought irritably, wanting to scratch the sweat that itched her nose. More like a Regent now that Silwa had scampered off with his troops on a campaign to Sadar. The Silean army had arrived in the black ships not three weeks ago, as much a surprise to the Fire Queen as they had been to Gonmer. But the Fire Queen had not seemed to care much that a Silean army now roamed the streets, preparing for battle. In a strange way, Gonmer thought, she had seemed almost amused and had removed herself from further involvement in the affairs of Beldan. Silwa and Antoni, it appeared, were allowed to do as they pleased.

Gonmer felt the stirrings of a headache. The presence of the

Silean army in Beldan had been one more assault on the suffering city. The summer had been hot and dry, food scarce and the water neither clean nor plentiful. There had been foot riots, and even the most common among Beldan's women, armed with little more than their fury and desperation, had risen against the Silean Guard. Many had died. Many more continued to die from the lack of food. But the rioting continued. The newly arrived Silean army was like salt in the city's wounds, taking food and supplies as they pleased for their campaign against the New Moon. For them it was no different then the hunt, a sport from which to derive some little bit of glory. Gonmer frowned disgustedly. The Silean army by their blunt and often brutal actions had done much to turn the ordinary Beldanite into a loyal supporter of the New Moon. Acts of defiance were growing more numerous, and for that reason the scaffolds had remained in Fire Circle and Beldanites were hanged daily for treasonous offenses against the Sileans.

Gonmer cast another glance at Antoni. There had been no sense in some of those hangings. She had argued against them. But Silwa and then Antoni insisted upon it, claiming it was the only way to teach Beldan and all Orans a simple lesson in logic. Reprisal, they had said. Every act of sedition must have its reprisal. A man insults the Guard, or a child paints a new moon on a wall, and two or more will be hanged for the crime. Gonmer had seen the crowds gather at the scaffolds, seen the rage shudder through them as the traps were dropped and bodies jerked at the end of their ropes. And when it was done, and they moved silently away, she saw the looks of contempt they gave her.

Gonmer exhaled softly but Antoni raised his head to the sound. He sat in the shaded corner of the room, his face all but obscured by the dark shadows.

"Not in a hurry, are you?" he asked.

"No, Advisor," she replied in a tight-lipped voice.

"Good," he said evenly, returning his eyes to the papers. "Because you have handed me a puzzle here and I will not be hurried to solve it. When did you notice the bags of buttons among the collections?" he asked.

Gonmer was silent, thinking back to the first time she had noticed the counterfeit coins. "Ten days ago, I think—"

"You think? You don't know?" Antoni asked scornfully.

Gonmer swallowed her anger, though the blood left her cheeks and her hands grew cold. "Ten days ago," she said firmly. "I was checking a second time the list of names against the amounts collected. There had been no shortage the first time I examined the bags. Then I found this bag and, when I checked again, discovered the collection was short. There are two more bags like this, filled with buttons not coins."

"Any chance someone helped themselves to the contents of this purse?"

Gonmer straightened her back. "Do you accuse me?"

"You would scarcely come to me with this if you were helping yourself to the coins, Firstwatch. Perhaps your page—"

"My page does not perform her tasks alone yet. She attends me at all times. And besides," Gonmer finished, biting down on the words, "I trust her, completely."

"Indeed, how fortunate for you," Antoni answered. He steepled his fingers together and leaned back in his chair. He placed the long white nails of his forefingers against his lips as he sat, thinking. "Could the tradespeople be deceiving you at collection time?"

"That would be difficult. The Guards are required to count out the coins and enter the amount into the ledger before leaving the shops. Unless, of course, it is the Guards who are making the switch?" Gonmer suggested.

"You are there, are you not, Firstwatch?"

"Yes."

"And have you seen anything that would lead you to believe the Guards are engaged in thievery?"

Gonmer thought hard, wishing she could find some small fragment of evidence to incriminate the Guards. But there was none, and she knew it. It was why she had brought the problem to Antoni in the first place. Someone was playing fast with the Guard and with herself. If they were successful, Gonmer believed there would be a good deal of it later on. It had to be stopped now.

"Well?" Antoni asked impatiently.

"No, nothing."

"What about the shopkeepers?" Lais said softly from behind Gonmer. Gonmer turned toward her, annoyed but curious.

"What about them?" Antoni asked.

"Well, I was thinking, the way that Kirian could change his shape right enough. Maybe he can the shape of other things? Like buttons into coins."

"Long enough to be counted and brought back to the keep," Gonmer added, nodding her head in agreement.

"Yes, yes," Antoni repeated, rising from the table. "Not a bad idea. The Kirian may be paying for his lodgings by such a device. Is there any on this tax roll you would most suspect?"

Gonmer snorted. "Almost all of them. This tax roll covers the Pleasure district and a good part of the Guilds. Any one of those artisans and shopkeepers could be your man."

"Well, then, there's an easy enough answer to that." Antoni smiled unpleasantly. "Arrest them."

"All of them?"

"Just one or two from each shop. But do it quietly. I want people from this list to simply disappear. We don't want to give any warning to our real traitor. So use stealth, and leave no witnesses."

Gonmer's headache began to throb in earnest and in her throat she felt a burning thirst. She wanted a tankard to wash down the sour taste. Like Faul, she recalled with a new understanding. Gonmer saw again the tall woman hunkered down in a chair, the short black hair hiding much of her face as she drank tankard after tankard, never satisfied.

"And one thing more," Antoni said, his fingers resting on the table, the long nails poking dents into the pile of papers.

"Yes?" Gonmer said, uneasily staring back at the sight of his eyes. A stray shaft of sunlight lent the black pupils a hard glint of red.

"I want a room in the prison where I may question them privately. Arrange it."

Gonmer bowed her head and then left quickly, fairly pushing Lais through the wooden doors in her haste. Out of there. She wanted out of there. The whole thing stank like shit in her nostrils and lined her mouth with the taste of bile. A drink was needed. Maybe several. Later, afterward, she would confront the task of making a list of innocent men and women who would disappear forever from the streets of Beldan.

Sweat trickled down the sides of Dagar's head. The air was humid. Sunlight filtered softly through the heavy green foliage of the woods. Sucking in the hot moist air, Dagar felt like a fish swimming in a green pond. Blood pulsed madly beneath his cheeks, and his heart boomed in his chest. He swallowed, trying to catch an extra breath before the command came to strike again. He blinked rapidly as one salty drop fell from his eyebrow and stung his eye.

"Again!" Jobber commanded, fists raised in a guard. "Again and again until you have it right!"

Dagar raised his fists, trying to copy Jobber's movements. His arms trembled, the muscles tired and overstretched. His fingers refused to tighten in a solid fist.

"Strike first to the face, block, and then forward with the counter," Jobber was saying, her hands following with lightning speed to the words.

Dagar stole a glance down the line of students, wondering if anyone else was feeling as clumsy as himself. The clearing had room for a about twelve students to train at one time. Like Dagar, they were all young, mostly around their Naming age, though unlike Dagar, many of them had the old power. Jobber shouted the order to move and Dagar responded without thinking, pitching his body forward and making an attempt to punch the air. Then he shifted forward and punched on the other side. Around him he could sense other students moving with the same plodding steps, arms drooping as they tried to hold a guard. They were tired. Too tired. He stared angrily at Jobber, whose white face surrounded by the corona of red hair was intent on striking at an imaginary opponent. She looked furious, and somehow Dagar guessed her rage wasn't meant for the attacker but at them, for being too slow or too addlepated to do things the way she wanted. She pushed too hard, Dagar thought. And then when they got tired, she yelled too much.

Dagar stole another glance toward the camp beyond the perimeters of the training field. He could just make out a second group of students learning to wield the staff. He couldn't actually see Go, who was instructing, only the top of his staff as it appeared slashing upward over Shedwyn's shoulders, and he heard the crack as the wood of their staffs clashed together. In spite of his fatigue Dagar smiled to himself. Go and Shedwyn made a fine pair. There was tall Shedwyn with her big breasts and wide hips, the sort of girl any man in his village would have wanted to marry and give ten children. And then there was Go, small and wizened like a fall apple left on the tree until spring. But for all his smallness and his age, Go was quick and fast and he could manipulate the long staff with a lethal effort. Dagar had worked once with him, and come away with purple bruises on his shins, ankles, and forearms. Had Go not pulled the attacks, Dagar's bruises would have been breaks.

Jobber was yelling at them again to drive harder. "More spirit!" she shouted. Dagar hardly heard her. It was the same thing she had been saying for most of the morning. Maybe, he thought sourly, she hoped it would stick better if she screamed it at them.

As he moved forward with the next attack, Dagar caught sight of Lirrel walking through the trees. She was wearing a black Ghazali dress, a placket of red embroidery down the front. She wore her hair loose, and when she passed though a patch of bright sunlight, it shone with the rusty tint of henna. She reminded Dagar of the redwing birds that once passed through Cairns in the spring on their way to the western marshes. He sighed and wiped away the sweat on his forehead with the back of his hand. He wished he could be with her, walking beside her in the forest. Since that night two months ago he had not mentioned Zein to her. And she in turn had apologized one day for having been so rude to him. The time together now was spent in sharing music and talk. Dagar turned his head to follow Lirrel's form as it disappeared deeper into the woods. He'd rather now be listening to the music of Lirrel's voice than the shrill cawing of Jobber's instruction.

"Umph!" The air whooshed from him in a sudden shock of pain. He curled over his stomach and stared bewildered into Jobber's angry face. She had kicked him hard in the stomach, and he had been so busy watching Lirrel, he hadn't seen it coming.

"Don't fall asleep," Jobber snarled.

Dagar straightened up slowly, trying to ignore the queasy pain in his belly and his own choppy breathing.

"Whose side are you on?" he asked angrily.

"Yours, idiot. If you ain't aware of what's going on all the time, you're going to get your gut run through by a Silean sword next time."

"Maybe that's better than having to learn how to fight from you," Dagar answered hotly.

"Now look," Jobber said, red hair crackling. "I never asked for this task. If it was up to me, you could just all go out with a handful of rocks and throw 'em at each other. Do a lot more good than trying to teach a bunch of left-footed, thickheaded, short-armed—"

"Problems?" asked Zein, suddenly appearing at Jobber's back.

"Them," Jobber said, staring disgustedly at her students.

"Her," replied Dagar, jerking his head in Jobber's direction.

Zein's face remained pleasant even though the other students clustered angrily behind Dagar's back. "*Ahal*," he said softly, his eyes straying to the dense foliage as he appeared to think. Jobber watched him, a scowl on her face. Then Zein smiled and inhaled a quick, short breath. Taking a step back, he motioned Jobber to assume a formal, preparatory stance.

"Sometimes it's helpful for your students to see the attack in order to understand it," Zein said lightly. Without looking at Dagar, he spoke: "Please pay attention to the movement of the hips; they must move as one with the arms in order to achieve speed and power."

Dagar watched moodily. He'd seen this demonstration before and it hadn't helped. Jobber had used him in fact as the hapless attacker and he'd wound up on the ground before he knew it.

Jobber feigned the attack. Like an arrow, Zein's fist shot toward her face, clipped her hard on the chin, snapping her head back. Zein blocked her feeble attack, knocking her arm to the side, exposing her midriff, and then slammed the counterpunch home to her stomach. Jobber grunted hard, eyes rolling at the suddenness of the strike, and even Dagar winced in sympathy.

"Tighten down," Zein murmured to Jobber, whose face had lost its arrogance and another shade of color. She wiped her mouth and Dagar saw the small cut that opened on her lower lip. But her eyes never left Zein, and Dagar watched in amazement as Jobber contained her temper and held her stance. And he wondered at that. It was easy for Jobber to get angry, shout obscenities, and bray like a cow pricked by a gadfly. But here, punched twice, she had silenced her tongue and channeled her temper into something more controlled and more powerful.

"Again," Zein said to Jobber. This time Jobber made no pretense of cutting short her attack. She exploded in Zein's face, moving with astonishing speed and cold fury. Dagar flinched, half expecting to see Zein sprawled flat across the training ground.

Instead Zein stopped her attack with the same technique, a swift jab to her face while blocking the attacking arm and landing a counterpunch to her stomach. With a final flourish, he hooked an ankle around her leg and swept her to the ground. As she fell, he followed the sweep with a strike that stopped short of the back of her neck. Then he stepped back.

Slowly Jobber pushed herself up from the ground, bits of leaves and twigs clinging to her hair. Dagar was certain her temper would get the better of her now. He cast a nervous glance at Zein. Zein continued to smile untroubled and helped Jobber up by pulling on the collar of her shirt.

Once standing, Jobber assumed her stance again, her eyes glittering like polished jade and her cheeks flushed red. Dagar was surprised, for she seemed neither humiliated nor outraged by her total defeat at Zein's hands. Instead she glowed with excitement, her hair shimmering brightly, as if this attack had urged her to redouble her efforts. Dagar stared, fascinated, and an edge of respect for her crept into his thoughts as she remained stalwart. He tried to imagine himself displaying as much dignity as Jobber now showed, and unconsciously he straightened his shoulders and stood more erect.

Zein was still instructing. "When training, always attack as if you mean it. And when you work with each other, 'touch,' " he said, holding up one fist and repeatedly hammering it into Jobber's stomach. "Partners, tighten your belly muscles"—he gestured with his chin toward Jobber—"like Jobber here. Harder and harder." He kept the punch swinging and Jobber's eyes fixed forward, the short exhaled grunts the only indication that she acknowledged the blows.

Zein stopped punching and Dagar stole a glance at Jobber, saw her lids half close, and heard the long-drawn-out sigh.

"Try it again," Zein said to the students, and sauntered neatly away, his attention drawn elsewhere.

Jobber turned to the students, and they backed away. Dagar expected her to begin yelling at them once more. Instead, she spoke calmly, saying very little, repeating one or two fine points regarding this particular attack. Only the bright glimmer of yellow flames in her green eyes betrayed the passion beneath her controlled exterior. As Dagar took his place in line again he realized she had no need to say anything. Zein had shown both of them their mistake, demonstrated the need for spirit and commitment in every attack. It was the training that mattered, that taught the self to find strength and courage and forget both foolish pride and fatigue as they fought. Watching Jobber erupt with each attack as if it were her last, Dagar understood the heart and soul of the fighter's way; it was to empty oneself completely into each attack and then do it again in the next attack, and the next, until the movement became as familiar as lifting a spoon to the lips.

Shedwyn stared down at her big feet, leaning heavily on the staff. She felt light-headed, blinking away the shining yellow stars that appeared to gather around her toes. She shut her eyes and the stars remained, glowing brighter behind the blackness of her closed lids. The afternoon heat swirled thickly, smelling warmly of pitch and her own sweat. Flies buzzed in her ear and one landed on her arm, attracted by the moisture on her skin.

"Z'blood," she exhaled, feeling her breath hot on her hands where they clutched the smooth staff. "I'll never be able to do it," she said, struck by discouragement. "I move like an ox, the left hand can't follow what the right hand is doing, and I have feet—" She stopped and opened her eyes, trying to find the appropriate word to describe her feet. She flexed her toes, the hard calluses of her big toe resembling the yellow skin of an onion.

"They're good feet," Go scolded her. "If they were smaller, you'd fall over."

"Why can't all of me be smaller? Then I'd be able to move faster," she moaned. "Like Jobber."

"Jealous?" the older man asked. He looked at her with his bird-bright eyes and Shedwyn fidgeted under the keen stare.

"No," she answered quickly, and then frowned. "Aye," she sighed with a wistful scowl. "She makes it look so easy. Like water."

"Like fire," he corrected. "That's her element. It's not yours."

"How should I fight, then?"

"Watch your uncle."

Shedwyn shook her head glumly. "How can that help?"

"We are different," Go said, and Shedwyn, looking down at the man shaped like a bundle of gnarled sticks, laughed. Go held up his hand, smiling back at her laughter. "Very different. I am like the pulled branch that springs back and snaps in your face. It's how I hold the staff, how it flows from my body. But Treys is like the tree, rooted to the spot, the staff shifting in an impenetrable arc around him. Study him, learn what you are by watching another shaped like you. Treys is over in the birch grove. Go now and see what you can learn from him."

Shedwyn settled the staff on her shoulder and set out through the camp to find Treys. She caught sight of him in a tiny clearing set back among a copse of white birch. For a moment it looked to her as if he were fighting the trees, his staff rising and falling as he faced each of them in the circle. She came closer, noting how he held his own stance as if firmly planted. Both hands gripped tightly around the middle of the staff. He sculled the air, the blunted ends rising and falling. The staff slashed through the frail leaves on the low-lying branches, sending the torn leaves fluttering in all different directions. *Crack!* One end of the staff fell across the neck of a tree. Treys stepped back smoothly, changing the direction of the staff and driving it downward on the shin of the tree.

He started to change direction again, aiming the tip of the staff for the throat of the third tree, when he saw her watching and stopped.

"How's the training going?" he asked, brushing off the bits of shredded leaves from his shoulders.

"Well enough," she answered. She felt shy in his presence, the desire to accept him as kin at odds with the fact that he was still a stranger to her.

He nodded, a pleasant smile on his broad face. "Would you care to work with me?" he offered.

Shedwyn shrugged, trying to hide her insecurity. "Aye," she answered, wishing she could refuse, and approached the clearing.

"Come," he said, "meet my opponents!" and he pointed to the ring of white birch. On each tree was a carved face, some with rolling eyes, bulging noses, others with fat jowls and tongues protruding between frowning lips.

"Were these real people?" Shedwyn asked, staring uncertainly at the comical faces.

"Oh, no." Treys laughed. "Only real in my imagination, and to my staff. They are a very obliging enemy since no matter how hard I hit them, they refuse to fall down."

Shedwyn laughed nervously and brought her staff down, resting it awkwardly in her hand. She looked at him, suddenly aware he was studying her.

"Come, show me what Go has been teaching you," he said gently, and moved to the edge of the circle of trees.

Shedwyn took a deep breath and brought the staff up to her side in a ready position. She almost started and then stopped when she realized that her sweating hands were too slippery to hold the staff firmly. She started again, swinging the staff forward in an overhand downward stroke. She tried to shift her feet as Go had done, a sharp tiny step, and swung the staff to the side, blocking an attack. Her step was too slow, and she finished the blow unsteadily. If only he wasn't watching, she thought nervously to herself. She ran through a series of attacks and counters, each time trying to duplicate the quick, snapping strikes that Go taught her. Twice her grip slipped and she nearly lost her hold on the staff. Once she landed a blow against the neck of a tree, but because she hesitated at the last moment, the staff bounced off the wood.

Then she stopped and groaned to herself. Grimacing with disgust at her own performance, Shedwyn stood staring accusingly at her feet, her hips, and her breasts. She could pick tobacco, harvest a field of hay, ret linen, and churn butter. But this, this required grace and she had none.

"It's a good beginning," Treys said.

Shedwyn shot him a withering glance.

"All right, you're terrible," he amended, and Shedwyn let the staff droop at her side. "You're too stiff and you hold the staff as if it were a snake."

"Nice words, those."

"Now don't get angry. I would have spared you the truth, but you'd not have it."

Shedwyn sighed and shrugged. "I suppose I did ask for it."

"Now I will ask you for the truth," Treys said, and came to stand in front of her. "Why do you hate yourself so?"

"Myself?"

"Hmm," he answered, nodding.

She shifted under his gaze and tried to look away. Was she so transparent?

Treys answered her thought. "Fighting shows the best and the worst in ourselves. It's revealed on the face and in the movements. And all I can see is that you are at war with yourself."

"Nothing on me makes sense," Shedwyn said brusquely. "I've always been too big, my back too broad to keep covered, and my feet . . ." She stared savagely at the tops of her feet, stained green from the grass. "Frigging lugs." Then she looked at Treys and saw the start of a sympathetic smile. "You don't understand," she said.

"Ah, but I do. I remember well the feeling. On me nothing

seemed to grow at the same time. One season it was my arms; the next my legs had to hurry and catch the rest of me. Worst was my hands, big and flat like spades. I never felt right in my body until I was well into being a man.'' He laughed suddenly and Shedwyn heard an echo of harshness in the sound. "And when I was finally a man, I was turned into a tree.''

"You have skill with the staff. Why don't I?'' she asked.

"You can. You will. It's all a matter of finding your center and allowing the staff to move as if it were part of your arms. Don't make it separate from yourself.''

Shedwyn shook her head. "You make it sound easy.''

Treys put his staff down gently on the ground and took her by the shoulders. "No, not easy. But not impossible either,'' he said adamantly. Standing this close, Shedwyn searched Trey's face for signs of her father and found them in the almond shape of his eyes and the high forehead. "Be proud of what you are, Shedwyn,'' he said firmly. "I am. You are a strong sapling, with a back like the oak, but supple like the birch. All things will come to you if you are but patient and trust in yourself.''

Shedwyn averted her eyes, a new sadness crowding her mind. For the last two months Eneas had scarcely acknowledged her. It wasn't that he was mean or cold, merely distant. He hardly touched her, and when he did kiss her, she felt as if a sword lay between them like a barrier she could not cross. He wouldn't talk to her about it, denied, in fact, that anything was amiss. But recently she had seen him smiling and laughing with another Oran woman, a recent arrival fleeing from one of the outlying villages.

"What is it?'' Treys asked her, drawing her face closer to his own.

"Eneas,'' she said softly.

"Might have known,'' he answered with a nod of his head. "Lovers' spat?''

Shedwyn shook her head quickly, her brow wrinkled. "He won't talk about it. All I know is, one moment he was loving me, the next''—he shrugged, the fingers of her hands spread wide—"the next he was turning over and sleeping as if to avoid me.'' She looked at Treys in confusion. "I don't what I did.'' She hesitated, finding it strange to be talking to Treys of this and yet realizing that maybe only another man could explain what Eneas was thinking. "I thought maybe he was angry because he realized he wasn't my first," she said, getting the words out in a hurry.

Trey's eyebrows lifted with mild surprise. He gave a small smile that creased his cheeks. "And your first, now, did he have the same reaction as Eneas?"

Shedwyn shook her head, coloring slightly. "No. It wasn't the same with him. I was younger then. And not much in love, I suppose. Just curious. I think we both sort of held our breath and rushed through it." She laughed at the memory. "It was over quick, and it was relieved we were, rather than pleasured."

Treys gave a loud sympathetic laugh. "At least some things haven't changed." And then his face grew more serious. "But it wasn't the same with Eneas, eh? No, 'course not. This one you love."

"Aye, and I thought he loved me. Now I don't know. Maybe he finds me ugly." Shedwyn touched her chest. "Maybe these marks here have turned him away."

Treys reached down and retrieved his staff from the ground. He stared at it thoughtfully and then looked at Shedwyn. "Maybe he's scared."

"Of what?"

"Of you, I expect." He straightened. "Shedwyn, you aren't an ordinary Oran farm girl. You are special, and what's more, you're powerful in a way Eneas might find worrisome. For all his being here, he's still Silean-born and he's more used to women he can control, women that will look up to him for protection, rather than a woman that can shake the rocks of Avadares with a mere thought."

Shedwyn listened to Treys, heard, even as he spoke, the sound of the earth as it rumbled that night she and Eneas had made love. Had Eneas heard it, too, she wondered suddenly, had she frightened him away? "I am still human for all that," she said fiercely. "And I need him."

"Aye," Treys replied. "And with luck, Eneas will come to know that. But you can't push him there. He must find his own way to you."

"What do I do until then?"

"Accept what you are. Be strong in that knowledge."

Shedwyn looked down again at the length of her body. When would it not feel so awkward to her? When would she not feel despair at the sight of her own feet?

"If only that strength came in a different package," she said glumly.

Treys hit her lightly on the shoulder. "Enough of the self-misery. It doesn't set well on those fine-looking shoulders of yours. Come on, let me help you to see more clearly. Take up your staff and we'll train together."

"All right," Shedwyn agreed, raising her staff again, grateful to have her attention drawn elsewhere.

"First the feet."

"Aw, no," Shedwyn groaned. "Can't we start somewhere else?"

"Do you plant a tree by its branches or by the roots?"

"Do you mean to bury them?" she answered, looking down at her wriggling toes and then up at Treys. "That wouldn't be so bad."

"Until you started sprouting extra toes," he retorted. "Come on. No more delays. Our companions are waiting," he said, gesturing to the ring of carved faces on the trees.

"It's easy to see what they think of my feet," Shedwyn muttered, looking at one face with a thick brow overhanging a wild-eyed stare.

"Then we'll thrash them soundly for their ignorance," said Treys, and held his staff up high in the air.

Shedwyn sighed and tucked her staff under her arm. All right then, she told herself, she was resigned to wait until Eneas came to his senses. And in the meantime she'd accept Treys's opinion of herself. It was at least a crow's sight better than the one she had carried most of her life.

Chapter Thirteen

It was early in the morning, the night's torches still burning outside the shop, when Shefek and Slipper left the Grinning Bird and headed to the dockside markets to buy the day's catch. Kai remained in the shop, grumbling softly as she used a damp cloth to clean the belly of the tea urn. It was sticky with fingerprints from a group of cutters that had come in late at night and used it to warm their cold hands. She couldn't blame them; after all they were only children, and despite the heat of the summer, their hands were always stiff and aching from tying and cutting knotted rugs. Between the six of them, they'd had just enough coppers to purchase three cups of tea and two sticky buns. They had passed the cups around, and while waiting a turn at the mug, they had warmed themselves around the tea urns.

"Always taking care of someone," Kai muttered angrily. She stopped rubbing the brass urn to stare at her distorted reflection. Her narrow face seemed longer still, the sweep of black hair pulled into a skinny braid. She frowned, and in her reflection, the corners of her mouth stretched down almost past her small chin. "Scrawny dell, ain't you?" she whispered to the scowling face.

"Oy, 'nother cup, will you?" a voice called to her.

Kai cast a glance over her shoulder to the man sitting near the windows. He'd come in not an hour ago, still reeking of ale from a night's drinking. A journeyman weaver by the worn look of his leather boots and the blue neck scarf tied proudly at his throat. His jacket was worn at the elbows and there were bulges in the pockets where small shuttles and bobbins had stretched the wool. He read from a sheet of paper, the tiny black letters like a pattern of checks in fabric. He sniffed angrily, not at her, Kai realized, but at something written on the paper. "Bastards," he hissed, and he shook the paper, the words rippling with the movement.

Kai filled a new mug and took it to him, even as he continued to swear at the paper. "Bad news?" she said lightly, trying to cover her curiosity.

"Frigging Sileans, have a look at that then," the weaver replied, shoving the paper in her face.

Kai screwed up her eyes the better to follow the small print. She read slowly, taking care not to let her lips move with the words. Shefek had done well teaching her to read, and she had been an apt student, but she felt shy reading in front of others. Some of the words she didn't know, but there was one word that couldn't escape her attention and that was "taxes." Another round of taxes. She swore noisily, wondering how long Shefek could keep up the button game.

"Z'blood, there'll be a brangle over this," the journeyman said to his teacup. He rose quickly, stuffing the paper into one of the tattered pockets. He turned to Kai briefly, his haggard face lit with two reddened eyes. "Mark it well, the trades won't take the tax lying down." Then he left, the tattlebells over the door jangling loudly as he slammed the door.

"Seems to be everyone's story these days, don't it?" Kai said miserably. "Ain't much to do on it, neither." She wiped the journeyman's table and shook her head, thinking of all the promises she had made that were still unfulfilled: Form an army of Waterlings to fight the Upright Man and all the other Silean bastards. Join the New Moon. All the promises Kai had made to the dying Zeenia and had not kept. But how was she supposed to do that all alone? Except for Shefek, no vaggers came to the Grinning Bird. Kai didn't know who among the Guildsmen were members of the New Moon—so who could she trust? And as for the Waterlings, she sighed more deeply still, those that mattered had fled the city and she didn't know where they were, and the others, like Stickit and Terridown, had joined the whores on

Blessing Street, sick and tired of the shacks at the Ribbons. She had done nothing, it seemed, except learn how to read. Kai pursed her lips angrily. Maybe that, too, was just conceit, giving herself airs she didn't need.

The tattlebells rang merrily and a child slipped into the shop.

"Oy, Kai. Not half so hot in here as over to Scroggles." The boy gave a wide grin, the teeth startlingly white in a face smudged with black soot. Two blue eyes, red-rimmed with irritation, peered out from beneath the hacked-off brim of a lighterman's hat.

"Oy Neive, come in. It's going to be hotter still," Kai replied, thinking of new round of taxes and the lethal expression on the journeyman's face. Oh yes, there'd be more for Scroggles in a day or two. There was always work to be done at the public crematorium, and since the massacre at Fire Circle, the pyres had never lessened and the pall of black, greasy smoke clung to the neighborhood.

Kai smiled at Neive, a boy not much older than ten. He made his living as an ashboy, shoveling buckets of ash from the funeral pyres and sweeping away the remnants of bones. He was paid very little but was allowed to pick through the pockets of the dead before they were committed to flames, for whatever trinkets remained. And afterward, he sifted through the ash and rubble, looking for the odd coin and bit of jewelry that might have escaped his attention and survived the fire. Neive sat at a table, resting his chin on his hands. The sleeves of his black coat were frayed. His wrists were red and dotted with small burn scars.

"What will you have?" Kai asked good-naturedly.

"What can I get for this?" Neive produced a small gold ring set with a tiny garnet.

Kai took it and held it up to the light. "Pretty that. A lovers' ring. Where'd you find it?"

"Off a dell. They fished her out of the Hamader last night." Neive leaned forward, his young face taking on a confidential look. "Been stabbed, she had. If it was the same dart as give her the ring, well, he couldn't have loved her so much, now could he?"

"How do you know she was scaffered by her own man?" Kai asked with a bemused smile.

"Didn't take nothing off her, did he? I mean the ring there. Who else goes to the trouble of scaffering a dell but not taking the goods? Nah, I've seen it before, I tell you." Neive leaned back in his chair and sniffed, his nose running as usual. He wiped the soot from the corner of his eyes.

"I suppose you have," Kai answered almost sadly. "You always go through their pockets?"

Neive nodded matter-of-factly. "Got to eat, you know, and truth is, the lightermen aren't paying me as well as they used to."

Kai glanced at the dirty fingerprints that streaked the surface of the table. She imagined them raking through the pockets of the dead woman, then slipping off the tiny ring while leaving a sooty residue on the lifeless white hand. She tossed Neive back the ring and he caught it neatly.

"On the Bird today. Keep it for next time. What'll you take?"

Neive's mouth gaped and then quickly shut as he wasted no time in deciding. A free meal didn't come along often.

"A couple of them sticky buns, tea, and you got any of those meat pies?"

"Yeah to all of it," Kai said, and turned to get the food. As she did, she happened to glance out the window and see the tall slim figure of the Knackerman on the other side of the street. Kai paused to watch the woman and the page and two Guards that flanked her. She didn't like the look of it. The Knackerman was walking toward the Bird, her eyes fixed straight ahead, on the door. Behind her, the page and the two Guards scanned the street.

"Whore's shit," Kai swore, her street instincts screaming a warning.

"What?" Neive asked, twisting his head around to follow where Kai was staring.

"The Knackerman's coming. Guards as well. Go on," she snapped to Neive. "Get in the back and mind you don't make a sound."

"I ain't done nothing," he protested.

"I don't think that'll matter. They've drawn their swords. Go on now. Get in the back and hide yourself well."

Neive waited another instant, but at the sound of their boots on the steps of the Grinning Bird, he bolted to the back, ducking down in a small cabinet beneath the old marble sinks. Kai saw him tuck in his legs and pull the cloth curtain.

"Don't make a sound," she hissed urgently. At least Shefek and Slipper were gone. She might manage this one on her own. She reached for a cloth and began cleaning the urns. The tattlebells over the front door jangled, announcing the arrival of the Knackerman in the shop. Kai heard the Knackerman swear, annoyed by the alarm of the bells.

"Firstwatch," Kai said evenly, turning about to face the woman. She dropped the dirty cloth and tucked a clean cloth into the folds of her apron strings. "Get you tea, madam? Or some new buns?" She heard her own voice sounding forced and thin in the crackling tension of the shop. Next to Gonmer stood her page, with a pinched face. She sneered at Kai's words. One Guard checked the window by the door and then nodded to Gonmer. He bolted the door.

"Do we look like we are here for tea?" Firstwatch Gonmer asked irritably. The second Guard was poking around the corners of the room, lifting the lids off of the great tea barrels and driving the point of his sword through sacks of flour.

"Oy now, no need for that," Kai said angrily as the Guard upended a barrel of salted fish. The hard flat rectangles skittered across the floor and were crushed under the Guards' heels. "What's all this for?" she snapped at the Firstwatch.

"Shut up," ordered the page, and roughly pushed Kai back away from the Firstwatch. "You'll answer only when spoken to."

"That's enough, Lais," Gonmer said. "Join the others searching."

"Searching for what?" Kai demanded. Her palms were sweating and she wiped them on the clean cloth at her apron.

"Buttons," the Firstwatch answered slowly, a humorless smile on her thin lips.

"Buttons?" Kai fairly screeched the word as the Guard and the page continued to ransack the shop, spilling the contents of canisters and barrels. Her heart drummed and she silently cursed Shefek for his cleverness. Why had she ever agreed to his plan? A crash sounded in the kitchens as crockery and platters were smashed on the tiled floors. Cupboards and drawers were being flung open and their contents emptied. Kai hoped Neive had enough sense to keep quiet and not move from his hiding place.

Kai's hands curled into fists in the folds of her skirts and she gritted her teeth. Stay calm, she told herself. They ain't got nothing on you. They can't hurt you

"Oy, Firstwatch, have a look at this!" Lais called from the bedroom. She reappeared carrying in her hand two pale brown feathers banded with gray. She stared meaningfully at Kai and then at the Firstwatch. "They're from him, all right. I'd remember the color anywhere."

Gonmer drew her sword free from her scabbard and held the point pressed against Kai's throat. Kai swallowed slowly, feeling the muscles contract away from the steel. "Where did you get these?" Gonmer asked in a cold voice.

"From a cockerel I killed. I'm saving the feathers for a pillow."

Gonmer shook her head. "There are no cocks in Beldan of this color. None in Oran, I'd wager. Try again."

"I found 'em."

"Where?"

"The street."

"Which street?"

Kai shrugged, the movement scraping her throat against the point of the sword. "How should I know?"

"Let's hope you will remember," Gonmer replied, with a resigned voice. She lowered her sword and replaced it with a quiet hiss. "Bring her," she ordered.

A Guard jerked Kai's arms behind her, tying her wrists together with a leather thong. He pulled the thong tight and Kai cried out as it sliced into her skin. The Guard pushed against the small of her back, and she stumbled forward.

"Where are you taking me?" Kai asked loudly, desperately hoping that Neive under the counter would hear and pass the word onto Slipper.

"To prison."

"But why? I ain't done nothing."

"You can tell that to the Advisor Antoni himself," Gonmer answered without turning around. "After, of course, you tell him where you got those feathers." She jerked opened the door, scowling again at the noisy bells. She checked the street once more before exiting. Then ducking her head back inside the shop, she stared hard at Kai. "Come quietly now. Any trouble, and I'll kill you where you stand."

Kai nodded, hardly hearing the threat. A cold nauseating fear was driving through in her veins. The Upright Man. They were taking her to stand before the Upright Man. Would he know her? Remember her from that night in the alley when they had fought? She walked dizzily, her breathing becoming shallow as her heart pounded wildly. Her stomach tightened around a hard lump of terror as the Guard pushed her through the door of the Grinning

Bird and out into the quiet street. Kai looked up at the sky, as
if in this last moment to memorize the pale blue color, speckled
with small clouds. She felt the sun on her cheeks as it lifted over
the tops of the weather-beaten buildings. But even the golden
glow of sunlight could not warm the sudden chill on her skin.

"Go on now, be honest with me, Finch," Jobber was insisting. "Do you think I'm a raving bitch?"

Finch laughed and shook her head of dandelion hair. It fluffed
over her face, covering her blue eyes. She brushed it back and
briefly Jobber saw her pallid face before the curtain of hair fell
down again in her eyes. "You do scream a lot," she answered.
"And you get plenty tweaked when things aren't to your liking."

"Frigging shit," Jobber moaned, hearing her worst fears con-
firmed. She stared morosely over a falling sweep of mountainside. She and Finch shared the duty of lookout. Their hiding
spot was an ancient aerie carved over time in a natural hollow
in the rock face. It was still cluttered with tiny bones and chaff
from its long-departed owners. The first time they settled there,
Jobber joked that if she got hungry, she wouldn't have far to go
to find something to chew on. The aerie was an ideal place from
which to look down the mountain and spy on the thin switchback
trail that led through the forest and up the steep rocky slopes of
Avadares. For more than a month they had been coming to this
post, resting with their backs against the sun-warmed stone.
Waiting and watching, they found plenty of time for talk.

Piqued, Jobber looked over at her companion, who was absorbed in picking a scab off her forearm. Under the fluff of hair
Finch's face looked much younger than Jobber knew her to be.
But that had been Finch's stock and trade on the street, a face
like a lost waif that turned the harder hearts to soft pity. After
two months of sharing this post Jobber still wasn't sure how old
Finch was. But then she didn't really mind not knowing either.
It was habit on the street never to tell everything, always holding
back. Even from friends.

"Now look, Jobber, don't get your trousers twisted," Finch
complained as Jobber continued to sulk. "I only told you the
truth. But I'll tell you the rest of it if you've a mind to listen."

"What?" Jobber asked.

"Maybe you are a raver, but you're also good at what you do.
Ain't no one except the vaggers that are anywhere near as deadly

in a brangle. And most of them got weapons. You just got those clubbers.''

''So what? I'm a bully now instead of a raver. I can beat up everyone smaller than me. That's not what I want.''

''Then what do you want?''

''To be liked.''

''For what?''

''For being a decent sort of dell. Straight-fingered.''

''You are a decent sort of dell,'' Finch insisted.

''Ravers and bullies don't make decent dells,'' Jobber argued.

''Jobber, if you was a real raver, you wouldn't give chinkers what folks thought of you. Point is you scream at them 'cause you care about them. 'Cause you think if you scream louder, they'll work harder and not get scaffered at the first brangle. Am I right?'' Finch's blue eyes peered up at Jobber from beneath the yellow fringe of hair.

''Yeah, I guess,'' Jobber admitted.

''Then your problem ain't that you're a raver. Problem is you don't know how to teach what you know. Sometimes folks will give more if you give them a better reason for doing it.''

''Such as?''

Finch hunched her small shoulders, her fingers spread wide. ''Respect them. Praise don't hurt either. How'd you learn? Can't think it was someone standing over you screaming.'' She smiled. ''You're too proud for that. Nah, someone released your spirit, they didn't crush it.''

Jobber squinted at the blue sky, a lone hawk circling lazily in the warm updrafts. Watching the splayed tail feathers and tipped wings, she thought back to her own training with Growler. Finch was right. Jobber could remember Growler saying to her, ''Bitter, bitter, sweet.'' That was the way to learn, that was the way to teach. Push hard, push hard, and then praise. She'd only done the bitter and forgotten the sweet.

''I'm right, ain't I?'' Finch nudged Jobber out of her memories.

Jobber turned to her and smiled, thinking how it drove her nearly mad that half the people of the camp seemed to be able to tell you what you were thinking. It was bad enough to have Lirrel always snagging her thoughts. But Finch too? ''What's your element anyway?'' Jobber asked, abruptly changing the subject.

''Guess,'' Finch replied.

Jobber was about to say air. But then she hesitated as the answer seemed too obvious. Finch grinned with delight.

"Come on, what is it?"

"Air," Jobber said, knowing as she said it from the triumphant look on Finch's face that she was wrong.

Finch laughed out loud. "Earth!"

"Never," Jobber scoffed.

"True. I can sense metals. Always knew whose pockets had coppers and whose pockets had sillers and Queens. Came in handy it did."

"I'll wager it did," Jobber said more softly, staring at Finch. It was hard for her to believe that she was an earth element. Finch was so different from the other earth elements in camp. They were mostly farmers' children, like that Arnard Brestin, from whose parents they had taken the big gray horse that night on the run. It seemed to Jobber they all had faces like clods of dirt, their eyes big and stupid like the faces of their animals. She shook her head, disgusted with herself. Nah, that wasn't fair. The real reason she didn't feel comfortable around them was because they reminded her of Shedwyn. And Shedwyn always annoyed her, though why that was, she couldn't say.

Jobber cracked her knuckles one by one, the dry sound of the bones reminding her of something else.

"Eeech, do you have to do that?" Finch squealed. "How I hate the sound."

Jobber laid her hands quietly in her lap, her face troubled. "Do you ever dream, Finch?"

Finch shook her head. "Never. Too dangerous on the street, ain't it?"

"Yeah. That's right. I never dreamed neither till I come to this place. Now I can't seem to stop."

"Must be 'cause you feel safe. Sleeping deeper."

"Nah, that ain't it. These are bad dreams. Dreams about dead people climbing out of the ground and grabbing me by the ankle. Old bones dancing round. And—and a woman made of stone, looking on at me. Gloating like." Jobber didn't want to admit that the woman in the dream had reminded her of Shedwyn.

"Z'blood," Finch said, and gave a delicate shudder. "Must be the food, then."

Jobber gave a hollow laugh, trying to shrug off the eerie tension of her dreams. "Yeah, you're probably right on that score.

Leastways it's improved since they let Dagar do the cooking.
Don't think I could eat much more of that Avadares stew.''

"Oy Jobber, look,'' Finch called, pointing a finger to place
farther down the mountainside. There was a small party of people using the switchback trail. Jobber could just make out the
figure of a man leading a team of reluctant horses along the
narrow trail. On the buckboard of a small covered wagon sat
two women dressed all in black. Trailing behind the wagon, on
which was painted a huge blue eye, followed a small herd of
goats nipped into line by two ragged black and white dogs.

"Don't look all that dangerous, do they?'' Finch said.

"Nor hunted either,'' Jobber added as she watched another
man appear from behind the wagon juggling a handful of balls.
"Oy, I know who they are,'' Jobber said her face growing more
cheerful. "Ghazalis.''

"But what are they doing here?'' Finch asked. "I didn't figure
them for this fighting stuff. What do they want with the New
Moon?''

"Run and fetch Lirrel. She'll know what they're about.''

Finch left, scrambling over the rock face. With her pale yellow
hair she looked to Jobber like a milkweed seed blown over the
gray and pink stones. Jobber continued to watch the Ghazalis as
they turned one corner and started back the other way across the
mountain trail. Lifting up from below, Jobber could hear the
mellow sound of a flute being played. She smiled at the music.
Bitter, bitter, sweet, she thought to herself, hoping that after
weary months of hard training and nightmares, there might be
time for a bit of pleasure.

Chapter Fourteen

Lirrel *waited at the end of the switchback trail where it reached* the crest of the mountain and then turned west toward the camp. At her shoulder Zein stood silently, watching the approaching wagon. Hidden by trees a short distance away were Jobber and Finch, just within earshot.

"Fairuz's tent," Lirrel remarked, noting the painted blue eye on the wagon's cuddy.

"Bear performers, aren't they?" Zein asked.

"Used to be. The Sileans charged a safety tax, and then an animal tax on the bears. Now its mostly dogs and tumbling. When I was last in Beldan there was talk of Fairuz's tent joining with Zahavra's." Lirrel smiled ruefully. "It was hoped that between dancers and dogs we might all be able to eat." She turned to Zein, her expression thoughtful. "What was it like when Ghazalis went on pilgrimage and dancers were sacred, not sideshows for inns?"

"Different," Zein answered with a slow shake of his head. "All of Oran was different, then." He cupped his hands around his mouth. *"Ahlan na sehlan,"* he called out to the man leading the horses.

"Beran," the man shouted back, and the team and wagon rolled to a stop a little ways down the trail.

Zein continued calling out to the man, who answered but did not move from his place with the wagon down the trail.

Jobber shifted her feet nervously. "Oy, Lirrel," she whispered after it had seemed that Zein and the man had had more than enough time to introduce themselves. "What's going on?"

"We're exchanging greetings."

"You're what?"

"Exchanging greetings. It takes a while," Lirrel said, concentrating on the replies of the man below.

Jobber rolled her eyes.

"I think it's naffy," Finch said. "Better than 'get your frigging arse off my stoop,' " she added in a perfect basso imitation of a Beldan tradesman.

"At last," Jobber breathed, seeing the man approach with his team and wagon. When he reached Zein, he took him by the arms and both men kissed on the cheeks. The women dismounted from the buckboard and embraced Lirrel. Then Lirrel kissed the older woman's hand.

"Friendly types once they get together, ain't they?" Finch said.

Lirrel beckoned Jobber and Finch to join them. Slowly the two left their hiding place and ambled down the mountainside.

"Just so long as they don't try that friendly stuff with me," Jobber said under her breath to Finch.

"I dunno," replied Finch, one eye squinting at the Ghazalis. "Make it easy to nip a purse. Those women have a fair bit of the yellowman on them. Oh, yes," she said, rubbing her hands. "I can feel it!"

"I wouldn't if I was you. Lirrel's gonna know it," Jobber warned. " 'Sides, it ain't exactly right. They could be on our side."

Finch sighed and shoved her hands in her pockets. "Suppose you're right. Feels like I'm getting out of practice, though."

The Ghazalis were bent in discussion when Jobber and Finch reached the wagon. Lirrel's face had darkened as she listened to the low voices and the quickly spoken Ghazali words. Lirrel glanced up and Jobber saw that the pearl-white eyes were clouded with pain.

"Head back to camp and tell the others to prepare food," Zein ordered. "And tell Treys and Veira to call a meeting. The news isn't good."

Jobber hesitated, waiting to ask Lirrel what was happening,

but Zein barked at them to get going. Jobber jumped at the harsh
tone of his voice and turned on her heel. Her heart sank as she
ran, ducking tree branches and feeling the long grass whip across
her ankles. It wasn't hard to guess the news, wasn't hard to
imagine the worst. She had seen Cairns, and since then the
butcherboys had had two more months to wreak their havoc
on the Oran people. It had only been a question of how much time
the New Moon had before they must begin their assault against
the Sileans. But thinking of their numbers and their inexperi-
ence, Jobber couldn't help concluding that the time had come
too soon.

    That night most of the camp gathered at the central fire; only
a few of the older boys remained at the night-watch duty. At the
head of the fire the Ghazalis sat on small red rugs, the knotted
fringes a dirty brown. The gold bangles on Fairuz's arm sparkled
brightly as she lifted her hand to adjust her head scarf. At her
side Zein sat, cross-legged, one hand with splayed fingers resting on the ground. He leaned forward to view the assembly, his
dark eyes passing slowly over them as he noted who was present.
Lirrel was at his side, her head bent downward and the little
mirrors of her head scarf winking in the light. In her lap she
clutched her flute. Next to her Dagar sat, carefully retieing the
twine cords of his reed flute. A goat peered curiously over his
shoulder for an instant and then disappeared into the shadows,
its neck bell giving a gentle clank to mark its passing. Farmers
and laborers sat clustered close together, shoulders rubbing as
long-handled pipes were shared between them. Farnon sharpened his sickle, the whetstone dragging across the blade with a
slow grinding screel. Though they waited patiently, the women's
hands remained in constant motion, working as they knitted,
spun yarn, or rolled bandages in preparation for the months to
come.
    Only Shedwyn sat idle, her legs outstretched before her, the
soles of her feet taking the warmth of the fire. Eneas was next
to her, his knees pulled up to his chest, his arms wrapped his
arms around his legs as his fingers wove nervously together.
Jobber sat between Finch on the one side and Mole and Trap on
the other. Trap huddled into her black coat, and she and Mole
exchanged worried glances, as if experiencing the tension in the
gathering. Wyer stood behind them, his back leaning against a
tree. His arms were crossed over his broad chest and his ex-

pression in the shifting firelight seemed solid as iron. Next to him Alwir squatted on his haunches, his long arms and hands dangling over his knees. On the other side of the circle, the vaggers sat, cross-legged, staffs resting on their shoulders. Firelight shadows flickered on the whorled patterns of their stern faces. Faul sat next to Go and Veira, her legs tucked under her knees, the black scabbard of her sword lying close to her side. And wedged here and there between the adults were the children of the camp, some of them standing, some sitting cross-legged or leaning tiredly against each other. They fidgeted, shifting their feet, scratching their heads, anxiously watching the adults and then the Ghazali. Their eyes were keen; they were excited to be included in such an important meeting, but impatient for it to begin.

Cloaked in the darkness, Fairuz began to speak, and though the fire was large and the summer night warm, an uneasy fear settled a chill on the assembled camp. Fairuz's gravelly voice and the occasional whisper of wind through the dry pines was the only sound heard over the crackling of the fire.

"Ten from our tent. Another eight from Mahaina's tent. *Ahal*, I tell you the Ghazali are being slaughtered everywhere." Fairuz paused, her black eyes dazed with fatigue and horror. "We were three wagons at the start. A Silean troop stooped us on the road, demanding we pay them for the use of the road. It was no small sum either. We argued, claiming our right under Oran law to travel the roads untaxed." She stopped speaking, drawing the black shawl closer around her head. Her face almost disappeared inside the shroud of black wool. She took a long-stemmed pipe and filled it with coarse brown tobacco. Zein gave her a light from a stalk of wintergrass. Fairuz's hand trembled as she held the pipe. She sucked in deeply, holding the smoke in her lungs, steadying herself before she continued.

"They took the men and they took the boys. They lined them up against the wagons. 'You, you, and you'—they pointed and took some of them away. We waited. All day we waited for our men to return. For our children to return." Fairuz stopped speaking again and sucked on the pipe, the embers in the bowl burning a bright orange. Smoke trickled from her mouth and wreathed her face in its milky cloud. "The Sileans came to us in the evening. They said you have paid the tax, now go. Where are our men? we demanded. They laughed, and said they were dead. That is how the tax was paid. With Ghazali lives."

"They didn't even let us take our dead," Idris said. He was the man Jobber had watched leading the team of horses. In the firelight his black hair glistened, falling over his forehead. Jobber could just see the tail end of a jagged scar that went from his cheekbone and disappeared into his scalp. Bear performers, Lirrel had said. That scar seemed to Jobber the essence of the Ghazali—embracing savagery and eventually taming it, even at a cost to themselves. She cast her glance to Zein and saw his hard-set face. Well, there's one who thinks the cost too dear, Jobber thought. Next to him, Lirrel's bowed face was hidden by a drape of hair. But Jobber knew Lirrel, and saw her anguish in the tight hunch of her shoulders, her hands gripped around the flute on her lap.

"There is more," Bibi, the younger Ghazali woman, continued. "Much more."

"We know the Sileans are attacking Oran villages," Zein said. "Some survivors have managed to find their way here. Though there are very few of them."

"We can do little to protect the villages," Treys said. "We don't have the numbers yet."

Bibi nodded, and her scarf slipped off her head to reveal tiny glistening black braids, each finished off with a blue bead. "The Sileans are quick to take advantage of that. They have been given the orders from the Queen to confiscate any lands held by Oran farmers suspected of giving aid to the New Moon. Before long you will not need to defend the villages. They will be gone completely. Turned into Silean estates."

"And the Oran farmers?" asked a boy from the far side of the campfire. Jobber peered into the shadows to see who spoke. It was Arnard Brestin, his frightened heart-shaped face reminding Jobber of his mother.

"Most of them dead," Idris answered. "The Sileans have no need for prisoners."

"And there's an increase in the taxes, no doubt to pay for the attacks against the Oran people, all in the name of defending them against the New Moon," Fairuz said. "Since last month there's a bread tax in Beldan, and already there have been food riots."

"Successful?" asked Jobber, eager for news of Beldan.

Fairuz shrugged. "The women of Beldan are fiercer than most. But even they cannot win against the butcherboys."

"That's always been the problem," Alwir said, running his

hand through his hair. "We're not unified. Ghazalis, farmers, Beldanites. We fight in small skirmishes, always, always out-numbered and outskilled by the Silean armies."

"And there is something else that keeps Orans apart from each other," Tafar, the juggler, spoke up. "The Queen has de-clared an award of land if Orans will come forward willingly and expose those born with the old power. I've heard it said in one village an Oran farmer, afraid of losing what he had, bribed the village Reader and turned in his neighbor's children, though all of them were without power. The Reader and the farmer split the neighbor's holdings between them."

"Oran against Oran. That's the worst," said Shedwyn, shak-ing her head. Beside her Eneas stared intently into the fire. He slipped his arm over her shoulder, but whether to give comfort or seek it, Jobber couldn't tell.

"And there's another piece of news," Fairuz said grimly. "As we were leaving Beldan, we saw Silean warships in the harbor. We watched the ships unload, man after man, their swords shin-ing like a cat's claws. They were preparing to march when we fled, fearing more violence in Beldan."

"March where?" Shedwyn asked.

"Where else," muttered Alwir. "Sadar. They are coming to Sadar. Silwa knows that Sadar is to be our stronghold. He thinks to meet us there early."

"Then we will meet him him on the road," Zein said matter-of-factly.

"You underestimate Silean affection for war," Faul said dryly.

"And you underestimate our strength, Faul," Zein replied.

"A bit hard to believe, ain't it?" Jobber spoke up. "I mean, look around. Not much in the way of a real threat, are we?"

Zein smiled. "You are not all there is to the New Moon. There are other camps scattered through Avadares." Jobber's eyebrows furrowed skeptically. Zein chuckled. "There are even some camps hidden right under their noses, on the Silean estates in the western plains. It won't be easy, but not impossible to consider either."

"But there is still the problem of facing the Silean armies at Sadar," Faul countered.

"We will not show them our face," said Go softly. He shifted his staff from one shoulder to another as he turned to speak to Faul. "Sadar is a crumbling fortress, just sitting on the edge of the mountain. Below is the plain. Those Sileans that make it that far will have to camp on the plains as the only river that still carries water flows at the base of the mountain. Very little else exists on the plains anymore, and the Sileans will have a long way to go to fetch wood and other supplies. As long as they remain at Sadar, they are cut off from the estates.''

"And where will we be?" Faul asked, frowning.

"In the ruins."

"Without water and wood and supplies?"

"Not quite. There is an underground stream well hidden," Go answered, "and there are supplies cached throughout Sadar. We have spent ten years making Sadar appear the ruin it is, while using it to hide our few riches."

"And at night, when the Sileans sleep, we can pick them off a handful at a time," Veira said. She smoothed the fletch of a new arrow, lying in her lap. At her knee rested a small ball of string and a little knife.

"And during the day, we shall disappear in the mountains behind Sadar," Go finished with a small smile.

"Get in. Strike quickly. And then get out," Faul said, understanding at last. "What do you guess are the chances of our success?" she asked.

"We hope for the best," Zein answered simply.

Lirrel gave a short joyless laugh. "The best, Father? To hope that you will kill as many as you can?" She lifted her face to him, anger flashing like steel in her eyes. "It's wrong, morally wrong. The Ghazali are peacekeepers."

Irritation flattened Zein's features into a hard mask. "If we do not fight now, there will be no Ghazali left in Oran. No one to speak for peace."

"If Ghazalis fight, there are no peacekeepers. We can die as we have chosen to live, or we can kill our own faith by embracing the Sileans' love of war," Lirrel answered sharply.

"You don't understand," Zein said, meeting her gaze. "You weren't at the Burning. You never saw how many died. Once I was a peacekeeper, but the Sileans and the Fire Queen have robbed me of that faith. Now I must do whatever I can so that Ghazali like you can survive to be true peacekeepers once more."

"Does the pure grow from the corrupt?" Lirrel demanded.

"The pond lily is white and pure when it blooms," Zein answered her evenly. "It grows by searching up through the murky water for the light while remaining rooted in the decaying, black

mud. You will not lose your purity, Lirrel, because I have sacrificed mine.''

Lirrel was quiet, though her hands clutched the shaft of her
flute more tightly. Her knuckles were white and bloodless. A
cough stirred the camp as people waited, either embarrassed or
intrigued by the argument between Zein and Lirrel. Abruptly
Lirrel picked up her flute and placed it to her lips. She started
to play and Zein edged away from her as if afraid of the music.

The flames of the campfire sparked higher into the air, stirred
by the wind born in the shaft of Lirrel's flute. The melody was
rasping and tuneless, the musical notes seeming to dissolve into
the sounds of rushing water. Lirrel's breath came in snatches,
breaking into the tumbling notes like stones cast in a stream.
Sweat beaded her forehead and her fingers stabbed at the note
holes, forcing the music from the throat of the flute. And then
abruptly she slowed her playing, and from the flute's mouth
drifted sad musical passages. Fragments of the forlorn tune lingered in the air as if captured in the dry leaves of the pines
overhead.

Then Lirrel stopped playing and, setting down the flute, stared
blankly into the fire. Around her the Ghazalis waited, expectant.
Mole leaned his thin chest forward, his head cocked to one side
to hear Lirrel. His shorn yellow hair shone like a cap of old gold
in the firelight and his child's face was scoured with lines of
worry.

"There are Sileans. Many of them spread across the plain,"
Lirrel whispered hoarsely to the hushed camp. Her silvery eyes
drew streaks of gray across the iris like trails of smoke. "Sadar." She sighed and the smoke-colored eyes changed to brilliant green. "They have come to Sadar."

"Z'blood," swore Finch silently, and put a hand on Jobber's
shoulder. "I ain't never seen anything like that before," she
said.

Lirrel moaned. Across her eyes the light glowed orange.

"Fire?" asked Zein.

Lirrel nodded. "On the plains. Burning."

"Is it our future or the past you see?" he asked sharply.

Lirrel turned to him with her glassy eyes whirling orange and
gray, streaked with green. "So many dying. Old and new." Her
hands shook as she lifted her flute again to her lips. Eyes
squeezed shut, she played. The sound gathered in notes, drawing

its breath from the hushed mouths of the camp. And as Lirrel played, the strands of music were woven into a lament.

When she stopped playing, her eyes were silver again and she sighed deeply as she set the flute down.

Zein stood briskly and turned to Treys. "We break camp to-night. If we travel early tomorrow, we will reach Sadar at evening. It's time to join with the others."

Jobber stood up and started dusting the dirt off her trousers. "I'm ready," she said.

"No," Zein said. "None of the children, and especially none of the three of you, are to come."

"Hold on," Jobber started to complain.

"I said no and that is a command," Zein answered firmly.

"You're gonna need everyone you can get. What was the point of us doing all that training if you were planning on leaving us here when the fighting starts?" Jobber asked angrily.

"The three of you are too precious to lose. You are our last hope for a new Queens' quarter knot. If one of you dies, then we have no reason to fight at all."

"Then what about the rest of us?" Finch said. "We ain't that important."

"But we think you are," Zein said, a smile easing the tension of his face. "There are so few of you left. The old Queen's quarter knot took strength in the sharing of power. People like yourself, Finch, were the mortar that held the bricks. The new knot will need you. You'll all be safe here. Regardless of what happens at Sadar." He turned to Fairuz. "Your tent is welcome to shelter here." The old woman nodded and sucked deeply on her pipe.

"Oh, naffy, and then what do we do if you don't come back?" Jobber asked.

"Wait for the fourth queen."

"Z'blood. Of all the frigging stupid plans."

"Don't be so eager to die, Jobber," Faul said. "The time will come soon enough."

Jobber swore and kicked a stone far into the bushes. It hit one of Dagar's goats, who rushed terrified from the bushes, her neck bell clanging in alarm.

The camp broke apart quickly, the adult members packing up their belongings, hoisting their store of weapons: swords, long-bows, pikes, and scythes. Shedwyn helped to measure out the supplies of food to be carried by each person. And as they came to collect their rations, she stared a long time into their faces, wanting to remember all of them. Veira Rune gave her a wide smile as she accepted her share of the supplies, and Shedwyn noticed that many of the arrows in her quiver were new, the fletches a beautiful gold and green. Shedwyn held the bags open for Egan, his wife Sarena, and their son Ourst, all of them laborers. Farnon came up to help them, his slab face ruddy in the firelight, his eyes bright. He shared a joke about the weather and Shedwyn laughed to ease the tension. In the last two months she had come to know Farnon better. She had learned that beneath his gruff and sometimes violent outrages there existed a true passion for the land and for the cause of all Orans. And in that she had formed a friendship with him, though he never stopped chiding her for her love of Eneas.

"Will you do me a favor, Farnon?" Shedwyn asked the burly man, laying a hand on his forearm.

"Perhaps. What is it?"

"Eneas. Will you look after him for me?"

"Oh, aye," Farnon answered curtly. "I intend to keep my eye on that one."

"He's a good man," Shedwyn insisted. "Haven't you learned that?"

"Battle shapes a man's purpose. Whether he's good or not remains to be proved." Then Farnon softened his tone and, chucking Shedwyn under the chin, looked into her eyes. "If only I was a younger man . . ." He chuckled to himself and released her. "For you, Shedwyn, I'll keep an eye on the lad."

"Huld's peace, Farnon," she offered as he left, called away by another laborer.

Shedwyn returned to her own tasks. She rolled blankets for Gavin, Owe, and Fion, miners from the north, their backs stooped from years of working in the low ceiling shafts, the skin of their hands hard as turtle horn. She packed torn strips of linen for bandages and gave them to Go. He no longer smiled and it disturbed Shedwyn to see his usually affable face so reserved. Alwir took his rations and Shedwyn saw the tail of a battle flute sticking out of his vest pocket. The metal shaft was painted a crimson red. Alwir nervously chewed the edges of his mustache, his face distracted. Impulsively, Shedwyn embraced him, pulling his lanky frame close to her chest. Her arms felt the twin ridge of muscles that lined his spine and she pressed her hands flat against the thin plain of his shoulders. He embraced her back, wrapping his arms around her waist and lifting her slightly off her heels. In the crook of his neck, Shedwyn grimaced, wishing it was Eneas that held her so closely.

"Huld's peace to you, Shedwyn," Alwir whispered.

"And to you, Alwir."

He pulled away from her almost reluctantly and she wondered as he gazed at her whether he meant to kiss her as well. But if he wanted to, he didn't, dodging shyly away from her as someone else approached behind her. Shedwyn spun on her heel and found Eneas at her shoulder.

"Walk with me, Shedwyn," Eneas said softly.

"There is much to be done," she replied, not willing to relinquish her hurt pride.

Eneas took her hand and brought the fingers to his lips. "I'm a fool, Shedwyn."

"Aye, you are."

He scowled at her fingertips and then forced a half smile.

"You have a right to be angry with me. I can't deny you that. But I want you to know the reason. To know my thoughts before I am to leave here."

Shedwyn felt her anger dissolve and swore at herself for being weak. Eneas had tied his blond hair back with a leather cord in the style of a Silean soldier. But Shedwyn saw in his face the changes that the summer had brought. He had lost the arrogant stance of a Silean gentryman, bowlegged from horseback while others walked. His black boots were badly scuffed and the smock he now wore had once belonged to an Oran farmer. Even the hand that held hers was rough and callused. "All right," she agreed, nodding. "I will walk with you."

He gave a relieved smile and, taking her by the arm, led her through the woods, away from the hustle of the camp.

They climbed a small rise of rocky stones that lifted out of the dense underbrush and stands of trees. On the nearly barren slope of the hill, they could see the sprinkling of stars in the night sky and the quarter moon that painted stones a pewter gray. Wild flax tucked in the crevices of stones bobbed on their long stems as the wind blew. Shedwyn heard the calling of night doves in a nearby pine.

Eneas sat down on a flat stone, his long legs stretched out before him. He tossed a few stones down the hillside. In the faint light of the moon Shedwyn could hardly see his features. But perhaps, she thought, he had meant it that way.

"That night, when we lay together," Eneas said, "I realized something."

"What?" Shedwyn asked.

"Huld's child, Treys called you. And so you are."

"Eneas—" Shedwyn started quickly. "It doesn't matter—"

Eneas stopped her. "Yes, it does matter. It mattered to me that night because I hadn't known what that meant. Shedwyn" he peered at her in the dark—"when I entered you, it was like laying siege to the whole frigging Avadares." He laughed and shook his head. Shedwyn heard the bewilderment in his voice. "Most men worry on being the first. Well, Silean men anyway," he quickly amended.

"Did it bother you that you weren't?" Shedwyn asked softly.

"I didn't have time to worry on that. Even as I held you in my arms, it felt like you were growing larger, and I was disappearing beneath an avalanche of stones. Everything about you changed."

"I was still myself, Eneas," Shedwyn said, laying a hand over his.

Eneas shook his head and taking her hand, drew her close to his side. "No. Avadares has changed you. And that night you were changing even as I tried to match you, stroke for stroke."

"What happened?"

"I got scared."

"Scared? Of what?"

"Of you."

Shedwyn nodded unhappily. Treys was right. "Are you still?" she asked quietly.

He placed an arm around her shoulders. "I'd be a fool if I wasn't, but a greater fool still if I let it keep me from loving you."

"I'm like any other woman, Eneas," she said. "I have my pride. And I can't escape being jealous."

"Ah," Eneas said, giving her arm a squeeze. "You mean Arian?"

"The woman with the black hair and the tiny waist and feet?"

Eneas nodded. "Shedwyn, listen to me," he said, holding her squarely by the shoulders. "I needed time to think, and discover my place here. It was you who warned me that I would have to do just that. I needed to be less Silean and more Oran before I could face you again. Magic isn't something Silean men ever know; we're taught to despise it, fear it. I had to forget that part in me, and to get used to the notion of magic. I never courted Arian, Shedwyn, but I never turned down the chance to talk to her, to learn about Oran women—''

''That's a tale if ever I heard one,'' Shedwyn snapped

''But the truth. You're the only one I ever wanted.''

''Easy to say now that you are leaving.''

''There is still this night.''

Shedwyn felt Eneas's hand leave her waist and stroke upward, coming to rest on the side of her breast. She flushed, her breath catching as his thumb slid over the fullness of her breast, teasing the nipple.

''Eneas,'' she said, stopping his hand and gently pushing it away. ''You hurt me that night with your coldness. How can I be sure that it won't happen again?''

''It won't.''

''You made me feel ugly,'' she argued. ''And Arian with her little feet—''

''Can't even match the beauty in your back teeth.''

''Huld's peace,'' Shedwyn snorted, but let Eneas draw her closer to his chest, his arms circling her.

''Give us another chance, Shedwyn. Give me another chance.''

He pulled her down to the ground, stretching out beside her. She felt the damp patch of wild flax flattened beneath her, cushioning her back from the small stones. Shedwyn sighed, letting Eneas run his hands over the side of her body, and feeling the warmth of his thighs against hers.

''Promise it will be fairly done, Eneas. That you won't shut me out again.''

''I promise; but only if you promise not to send a storm of rocks down on camp.''

Shedwyn laughed a deep-throated laugh as she settled herself in the shelter of his arms. Eneas was tugging the buttons of her bodice free with his teeth, his hands reaching under her skirts to fondle her buttocks. ''I promise to contain my lustful ravings to yourself alone,'' she said, and opened the ties of his trousers.

From between the moist cleft of her naked breasts, Eneas groaned happily. ''You'll have me crawling to Sadar, too weak for now't else.''

''Aye, now't else,'' Shedwyn proclaimed, smiling as Eneas

rolled her on her back. She wrapped her legs tightly around his waist, feeling the smooth skin of his hips against her inner thighs and the soft nap of his hair on her belly. "Oh, aye," she repeated with a sharp gasp, clasping him tightly as he lodged himself deeply within her.

No, it would not be like the last time, Shedwyn told herself, rising to meet Eneas's eager thrusts. For this time it was not the trees with their veined roots that she sensed, but the blood that pounded in the veins of Eneas's limbs. The pungent scent of pines and red soil was mingled with the salty sweat and lavender of Eneas's skin. And it was not the stones of Avadares that she heard, rumbling loudly as they threatened to erupt, but Eneas's voice calling out her name over the rocky hillside.

Jobber wandered aimlessly through camp. She knew she should have been helping to pack supplies, but it irritated her to watch the same tearful farewells played out all over the camp. She had seen Eneas and Shedwyn disappear a while ago and figured they were making their own good-byes. For some reason it raised her hackles. Right now she wanted a bit of peace and quiet, away from everyone.

Jobber cut through a path in the underbrush and found herself in one of the outer training circles. Two torches had been set up to allow the vaggers to train at night. Faul was in the center of the circle, practicing. Jobber leaned against a tree to watch her.

Faul was wearing a sleeveless shirt and sweat sheened on the muscular arms. Her profile in the torchlight was hard and angular. She raised the sword in a two-handed grip, high over her head, and brought it down quickly, stopping it with a sharp exhalation when it reached chest height. Over and over she executed the same movement, and Jobber found the rhythmical rise and fall of the blade hypnotic. A red ribbon of light shimmered along the edge of the blade, leaving a faint arc of light in the air to mark its downward passage.

"You're ready," Jobber said loudly.

Faul turned her head slowly, as if withdrawing from a trance. Sweat darkened the gray hair at her temples. "I'm not happy about leaving you here," she said softly.

"Don't get sentimental," Jobber warned, not wanting to hear some elaborate farewell. Especially not from Faul. Faul who was almost like Growler.

Faul shrugged. "I've left you two bottles of brandy. They're hidden in the bushes near the washing stone by the stream. Help yourself."

"Trust you to keep a couple of bottles hidden."

Faul smiled. "Old habits, Jobber."

"Yeah, I suppose. Well, look, I'll wait till you get back," Jobber insisted. "Then I'll drink you under the bushes."

Faul's gray eyes sparkled with little flames from the torchlight. "Like the last time?"

"I've grown up since then," Jobber retorted. "You won't find it so easy next time."

"Next time," Faul repeated. She returned her attention to the sword in her hand and prepared to continue her practice.

"Oy, give us a look at that," Jobber said quickly.

Faul hesitated, not comfortable with committing the sword into Jobber's hand.

"Show me how you do that," Jobber asked, feigning interest in the sword. In fact she had no interest in the sword. She disliked weapons, finding them awkward to hold. She preferred her hands and her feet, rather than trusting in a length of steel that could be dropped at the crucial moment. But Jobber wasn't ready to let Faul go; she wanted to hold her attention for a few moments longer before they parted.

"Don't cut your feet off, Jobber," Faul warned.

"Different sort of blade, ain't it?" Jobber held the sword upright and inspected it carefully. The steel edge undulated with alternating red and gold waves. The smooth leather of the grip was dry, even though Faul's hand had been sweating.

"It's one of the finest swords I've ever used," Faul answered. "They don't make them like this anymore."

Jobber raised the sword in a two-handed grip as she had seen Faul do earlier. She lowered it slowly, tightening her fists around the handle. Again she raised it and felt a sudden stirring of heat, as if a liquid fire coursed through the shaft of the sword. She lowered the sword, this time certain of the fiery blood pulsing in the red wave pattern. The sword was alive, its breathing sounding to her like the exhalations of giant bellows. In her grasp, the handle warmed and then became hot. It throbbed pleasantly, the heat rising from the handle and reaching up the length of her arms. Jobber stared transfixed at the sword and then gasped as she felt the excited rush of heat surge across her chest and caress her neck and face. Her heart pounded, and her cheeks flushed with color. Her hair bristled, gathering the sparks of yellow fire like gems. Deep within her core, the fire element stirred, waves of heat rippling like clear molten metal.

"Z'blood," she whispered at the sword. A strange longing overtook her as she recognized something deeply familiar in the touch of the sword. Her hand felt warm, her skin beginning to shine with a radiant heat.

"Give me the sword, Jobber."

Faul's voice came faintly to Jobber, nearly lost in the crackling of fire and the roar of the bellows.

"Give me the sword!" Faul yelled, and grabbed it away from Jobber. "Frigging shit! It's hot," she shrieked, dropping the sword on the ground almost instantly. Wisps of black smoke curled into the air as the sword scorched the grass.

"I'm sorry," Jobber said weakly, backing away from the sword and from Faul's furious face. "I don't know what happened."

Faul used the hem of her vest to pick the sword up, gingerly testing the heat of the blade with a fingertip. Then she sighed gratefully. The sword had cooled again.

"You could have ruined it like that," she grumbled. "Softened the edge so that it would have been no good to me."

"Look, I said I was sorry," Jobber snapped. Yellow sparks crackled in her hair, lighting up her frightened face. The air reeked of copper.

Jobber and Faul faced each other, confused and uncertain what to say next. Faul broke the silence.

"There's no harm done. But I have to go now. Treys and Veira wanted to talk to me before tomorrow morning."

"Yeah sure," Jobber replied, averting her eyes and staring off into the woods. "Take care of yourself." She began walking quickly back to the tents and noise of camp.

"You too," Faul called.

Alone in the woods, Jobber stared at her hands, terrified. When Faul had grabbed the sword, its parting had caused Jobber searing pain. Jobber thought the skin had been ripped from her palm, as if the sword were a part of her body, a shining limb of fire and light. But in the gray light of the moon, she saw only the pale skin of her palm smudged with dirt. The pain lingered in her memory and in her unsettled heart. Jobber swallowed hard and rubbed her empty hands against her trousers, hoping the coarse fabric would remove the feel of the sword.

* * *

Zein moved steadily through camp, searching for Lirrel. She had left quickly after they broke up, refusing to talk to him. He ground his teeth in determination. Though she might not wish to see him, he would not leave this time without a word of farewell. Perhaps if he had not done so the first time, she would have been more forgiving to him now.

Zein spotted Lirrel at last, sitting with Bibi, her back resting against the wagon wheel. Dagar was nearby, and though he appeared to be busy, comforting a crying child, Zein marked well the way his eyes watched Lirrel. Zein caught his glance and Dagar smiled encouragingly at him.

Zein squatted down before Lirrel and stared into her face. The rounded cheeks of the child he once knew were thinner now, more womanly, as the bones became pronounced. In the soft glow of her eyes, misted with tears, he saw the sorrow that he caused her.

"I did not want to leave without saying my farewell to you, daughter."

Lirrel nodded, her teeth raking her lower lip.

Zein brushed back a lock of black hair, gently settling it behind her ear. "Will you forgive me?"

The moonlit eyes studied him. "I must learn how," she answered. She reached for him, putting her arms around his neck. "Though I cannot accept what you do, I do love you, Father," she whispered.

He held her tightly and then released her. He touched the moon-shaped earrings that dangled from her earlobes. "It is enough."

Zein stood and settled the quiver of arrows more squarely on his shoulders. Dagar came to him, ready to speak, but Zein stopped him with an upraised hand.

"There is no need for you to ask, Dagar," he said with a light smile. "I have already heard the direction of your heart. You are on the way to becoming a Ghazali and I would be the last to take you from the path of a peacekeeper. You do not have to come with us to Sadar."

"Thank you, Zein," Dagar replied simply. "I think—" He stopped and then said more firmly, "I *know* that my place is here and not on the battlefield. It is not fear that keeps me away."

"I understand. No one will speak against you," Zein finished. "You will have your own trials to meet."

"Soh hail na Oran," Dagar said in Ghazali.

"Oran's peace to you," replied Zein, trying not wince at the flatness of Dagar's accent. It would improve, Zein told himself as he started off in search of Go and the other vaggers. It would improve, like everything else in Oran. Hard work and struggle would bring them at last to a new peace.

Chapter Fifteen

Kai huddled against the wall of her cell and stared glumly into the dark, cavernous ceiling. She didn't know how long she had been sitting in the near dark, but it had been long enough to numb the the initial terror of her arrest. On her shoulder blades, Kai recognized the feel of the corrugated ridges of the cell's stone wall. It was like the hollowed-out walls of the tunnels where she and the Waterlings had once hid. Like the tunnels, the prison cells beneath the Keep must have had their origins in the days when Beldan was mined for basalt. The mining was stopped after the Burning, but the honeycomb of tunnels and caverns had been put to other uses. Kai hugged her arms over her chest, breathing in deeply the odor of the damp stone, wishing she was hiding in the protective dark of the tunnels and not here, waiting her turn before the Upright Man.

She was not alone in her prison cell. She guessed there were at least twenty others, though the darkness of the cell made it impossible to be certain. Some languished alone in the shadows like herself while others gathered in small clusters around candle stubs. Over the weak flutter of candlelight, she saw the haggard faces of her cellmates, floating like masks suspended in the dark. Occasionally she caught the angry murmur of their whispered conversations. She was surprised that she recognized a few of the faces, most of them Guildsmen and journeymen, their colored neck scarves identifying their individual trades. As she peered into the dark corners of the cell, Kai also saw prisoners stretched out on straw pallets and heard the muffled groans and wet coughs of people dying. It occurred to her as she studied her cellmates that there were no street snitches, no whores, and no burlymen, here. Only Beldan's artisans, journeymen, and a few shopkeepers. She snorted in the dark. How long had she been trying to gather enough courage to meet with these people? To find among them supporters for the New Moon? Kai shook her head, her scalp scraping along the cell wall. She had been too shy, too nervous to approach them. She couldn't stop thinking of herself as a snitch and a Waterling, and these people, though they were Oran the same as herself, were of a higher class. "And now when it does no frigging good, here we all are," she muttered to herself. "Too late. You let it go too late."

"Oy there," a man called her, the stub of the candle in his hand. "Can I sit?"

Kai glanced up at him uncertainly. His face was rounded, the dark eyes bulging slightly. He rubbed his free hand along his cheek, as if unused to the stubble of a beard. In the dim candlelight it was impossible to tell the color of his scarf, but his clothes carried a faint smell of linseed.

"Ain't much else to do in here," she answered, suddenly glad for the chance to speak to someone.

"Can you tell me what time of it day was when the Guard picked you up?"

"Morning," Kai said, frowning.

"That makes three days for me, then," he said, and then looked up into the shadowy recesses of the cell. "I wonder what my wife is thinking now." He turned to look back at Kai. "They came in the morning as I was opening the shop. I'm a woodwright. There was only me, even the 'prentice was in his bed, the lazy sod. Ah well"—the man sighed—"spared him this, I suppose." And then the smile disappeared, and his eyes became distracted by the small flickering of his candle. "I just wish my wife knew."

"The name is Kai," Kai said, trying to draw the man's eyes back into her, to keep him talking in the darkness.

"Gener. Gener Donan," he answered, and the smile returned to his face.

"Butcherboys tell you why they arrested you?" Kai asked, twisting her black hair into a knot at the nape of her neck.

"They yammered something about buttons. And the taxes. Z'blood, always the frigging taxes. They'd squeeze the blood from iron if they could."

"How long do you figure they'll hold us?"

Gener shrugged. "Till they get what they want, I expect."

Kai rubbed her shoulders, the stone wall seeping cold into her back.

Then Gener spoke to her, lowering his voice so that only she might hear. "The word is also they're looking for New Moon. Myself, I've never gone in with that lot. Not to say I mind them, I just never joined with them. But there's others here that have, and those lying next to the wall, well, they got the truth beat out of them right enough." Gener wiped his mouth with the back of his hand. "Makes you sick, it does. The advisor himself does all the questioning and there's no shortage to the hurt he'll do. Even to the women." Abruptly he seized Kai by the wrist. "Look, if you know something, now's the time to think well on how much it means to you to keep silent. Might be worth your life and maybe some others' if you speak up. So you don't wind up like those buggers there, headed for Scroggles with most of their skin peeled away."

Kai jerked her wrist free and drew away in alarm. The man was a squeal. She could feel it in her bones. Maybe he'd been into the Upright Man already, maybe this was the bargain he'd made. Scare them. Get them to squeal on themselves, and maybe he'd be let free. Kai eyed him with disgust. This careful little artisan had probably never brangled with the Guards before in his life and now he was running scared. She lifted her chin. "I don't know anything. Nothing at all," From the corner of her eye she noticed that others were watching her, appraising her conversation with Gener.

"That's too bad for you," Gener was saying softly, and when Kai turned to look at him, she was suddenly repulsed by his pudgy face and the lips that seemed too wide.

"Get away from me," Kai hissed. "Go on." She flung an angry arm at him, striking him on the shoulder.

He drew away from her, his bulging eyes straining between pink lids. "You'll find out. You'll find out," he snarled at her.

Left alone again, Kai felt the terror return to her limbs. Nothing, she swore vehemently to herself. They'd get nothing from her. She'd burn in the smoke of Scroggles before she'd give away Slipper and Shefek. But despite her resolve, she began to shake with the cold and her teeth chattering violently.''

The heavy tramp of boots and the hard rattle of keys sounded outside the bars of the cell. Kai looked up and saw a man hiding papers under the stones just before the candles were snuffed. In the total darkness, the stamping of the boots seemed louder and more threatening. Torchlight appeared outside the bars and Kai averted her eyes from the sudden brightness. Four Guards approached, their hulking forms black in the corona of torchlight. Keys jangled in the lock, and the cell door was thrown open. A body was shoved inside, groaning as it rolled heavily to one side. Two of the Guards entered the cell quickly and raised their torches high over the heads of their captives.

For a brief instant Kai saw the body of a crumpled man lying on the ground. He was covered with blood. His face was crisscrossed with many small slashes and his skull had been shaved of hair. He wore no shirt and his back was a latticework of raised welts. The torchlight moved, returned him to the shadows as it passed over other prisoners, their faces suddenly appearing in the light like startled animals, frightened yet defiant. The Guards were looking for someone. Someone in particular, Kai thought nervously as she watched them search, pushing and kicking out of the way those whose turn had not yet arrived.

Kai lowered her eyes as a Guard angled toward her. She heard the scrunch of his boots and saw the circle of light bloom on the ground near her feet.

"Oy, you!" the Guard commanded.

Kai looked up.

"You the one from the teahouse?"

Kai nodded silently, not trusting herself to speak a reply.

"Get up."

She hesitated, feeling the watching eyes of everyone in the cell. The man on the floor groaned and then retched noisily as he curled his body into a knot.

"I said get up!" the Guard repeated, dragging her by the arm to stand.

"Let go, you frigging bastard," Kai blurted out, finding the courage to speak in her growing rage.

The Guard jerked his hand back to slap her but the second Guard prevented it.

"That ain't your job and you know the advisor doesn't like it when we do his work. Just bring the little bitch. He'll fix her soon."

Kai was wedged between the two Guards, one shoving her forward to the door of the cell. As she was led down the corridor, past the cell, she caught a glimpse of Gener's face staring at her from between the bars.

It seemed to Kai they walked through a maze of passageways, twisting and turning endlessly through the stone corridors. Worse than the tunnels, she thought, trying at first to mark her way and then becoming confused and lost. Something wet seeped through the thin soles of her shoes and the rank odor of stagnant water filled her nostrils. Other stenches made her gag. They passed prison cells, much like the one she had been in, filled with people, their faces pressed against the bars. She saw the mutilated corpses, piled alongside the bars, waiting to be removed. And even down here in the thick night of the prison she heard the dull buzzing of flies.

They halted before a low door, the frame carved out of the rock. The Guard turned the key and opened the door, stepped to one side to allow Kai to enter. Light from the room flooded the corridor with a golden glow. Kai blinked at the bright light, a hand shielding her eyes. A Guard shoved her into the room and slammed the door shut behind her.

"Well, well, is this our shopkeeper?" a man's voice asked. Kai's blood chilled as she recognized the Upright Man's voice.

"Not much to look at, is she?" another voice said, and Kai raised her eyes to see the Reader that sat next to Antoni, a large wooden table in front of them. The Reader was young, certainly not much older than herself, and she thought for a moment she recognized his features. His face was thin, a sparse beard of light brown hair covered his chin. His eyes were a blue gray, almost the color of the silver Reader's emblem on his chest.

"Never underestimate Oran scum, Re Aston," Antoni said slowly with a thin-lipped smile.

The name jogged Kai's memory. Alwir Re Aston, sentenced to hang at Fire Circle. But he had escaped with the others during the massacre. His brother, Kai guessed; this one had to be his brother.

"I know my trade, Advisor," the young man answered, affronted by Antoni's words.

"Hold up your hand," Antoni commanded, and Kai flinched at the coldness of his voice.

She held it up so that he could see the mark tattooed in the fleshy pad between the thumb and index finger. Those that passed before the Readers' prying eyes received the mark as proof of their purity from the taint of Oran magic. No Oran could be hired for labor without it.

"Named, it would seem," Re Aston said, sounding disappointed.

"Read her."

"Sir?" Re Aston asked, frowning.

"I told you before, never underestimate Oran scum. That, Re Aston, is why we are here. We have seen that buttons can be made to look like gold. That tattoo may be just as easily another trick."

Re Aston unfocused his gaze, the blue color of his eyes whirling like a milky agate. Kai knew he would see nothing from her. Like all Readers she cast no colored aura, no crown of light to betray her talent. The wolf well suited among the sheep, her mother had once called Readers. Even still, Kai found it daunting to stand beneath the penetrating stare of the Reader. And what about you, Upright Man? she seethed. What would happen if the Reader turned his gaze on you? Would he see the mosaic of light that I did that night? No, she reminded herself angrily. He knows how to shield it and shield it well. Too precious a stolen gift to let slip.

"Nothing." Re Aston blinked rapidly and turned his head slowly to face Antoni. "Nothing to her at all."

"I don't know as I'd go that far," Antoni replied, standing behind the table. "I'd say there's quite a bit to this little rag." He leaned forward, resting his weight on his fingertips. The rounded edges of his polished nails scraped along the surface of the table. "Strip," he ordered.

Startled by the unexpected command, Kai shrank back. She clutched the worn fabric of her bodice and felt the hammering of her heart beneath her fist.

"I said strip," Antoni ordered, and motioned to another Guard standing by the wall. The Guard jerked her arms away from her bodice and ripped it open with a savage tug. The buttons torn off, clattering on the ground as they rolled away. Kai struggled furiously with the Guard, holding together the torn bodice. The Guard slapped her hard across the face, and as her head reeled, her arms were flung to the side. The Guard jerked the dress down off her shoulders and then her waist, letting the skirts fall to a limp bundle of cloth around her ankles. The shoulder seams of her old shift he cut with a knife and, with a final tug, drew it, too, down past her waist. Lifting each foot, he took off her shoes and threw them into the corner, where they joined a pile of other stolen shoes.

Kai shivered, hugging her thin arms across her naked chest. Her cheeks flared bright red with humiliation. Frantically, she tried to reach down to take back her dress, but the Guard stopped her, pulling his sword and edging her back with its point. He then picked up the garments and flung them to another corner of the room. Kai saw where they landed, and then looked down to her own bare feet and long spindly legs. She closed her eyes, feeling the stares of the Upright Man and the Reader on her naked body. Then, slowly and deliberately, she forced her arms to her side, raised her head, and stared back at them with as much dignity as she could find.

"Yes," Antoni said with a sardonic smile. "A good bit to this rag. Even stripped she has the audacity to give airs."

Antoni crossed from behind the table, walking slowly toward her. Kai tried to match the steady glare from his eyes. She faltered, seeing the pinpoints of red in his black pupils. Would he recognize her? Remember her from the night in the alley when they fought?

"You keep bad company, pretty-pretty." Antoni sneered as he pointed to the old scar that snaked over Kai's hip and ran a jagged line down her flank. "And this one?" He pointed to the second scar that ran from her collarbone to the rounded curve of her shoulder. He came closer and Kai could smell the cloying sweet incense that perfumed his clothing. "An interesting scar this," he murmured to her, his eyes watching her closely. "Stitched I'd say, and not too many months ago." He touched the scar and dug one of his nails into it. The wound had healed but was still sore and Kai's shoulder buckled under the pressure of his nail. "Where did you get this wound?" Antoni asked, pressing more deeply until a small line of blood appeared beneath the edge of his nail.

Kai gasped at the pain that lanced through her shoulder. "Fire Circle," she stammered, the words spitting out of her. "I got it at Fire Circle!"

Antoni stopped and withdrew his hand from the scar. He

reached into his pocket and withdrew a linen handkerchief and wiped away the tiny smear of blood under his nail. "You're lying."

"No, I ain't! One of them Sileans got me."

Antoni shook his head and looked at her with mock disappointment. "Lying. I always know by the way you Oran's stink when you are hiding the truth. I want the truth now."

He walked backed to the table and picked up two brown and gray feathers. "You know what these are?" he asked without looking at her.

"Cock feathers," Kai answered, rubbing the ache in her injured shoulders. Her bladder suddenly felt full, insisting that she empty it.

Antoni shook his head and tsked softly. "Again."

"Cock feathers," Kai repeated.

"Too much spirit," Antoni said to Re Aston. "These Orans need to be broken into honesty." Then over his shoulder he called to Guard. "Shave her," he barked.

Kai crouched defensively as the Guard brushed past her and opened the door. He called out and two more Guards entered the room, one carrying two strands of braided leather, the other a short knife and razor.

"No!" Kai screamed, and tried to wrestle away from them. "No!" she continued to scream as one Guard jerked her arms behind her and tied her wrists tightly together. She kicked out with her feet and the Guard bound them together at the ankle. Her head thrashed back and forth as she refused to let the Guard with the knife approach. Growling obscenities at her, the Guard grabbed her around the neck and wedged her neck in the bent crook of his arm. He squeezed tightly until she started to choke. Then he released his grip slightly. Kai struggled again, and once more he tightened his grip on her until she heard the roaring in her ears as her body clamored for more air. The Guard released her just before she lost consciousness. And as she struggled to suck in air through her bruised throat, she felt the tug on the back of her head and then the sawing motion as the knife hacked away her hair. Staring down at the ground, her body bent by the Guard's strong hold around her neck, Kai watched as locks of black hair fell silently to the floor.

Her eyes lifted and in panic she saw the Upright Man's lips part in a cold smile. It wasn't going to be easy, this. Hold on to your anger, Kai told herself, hold on to your anger or he'll break you like day-old bread.

Two Guards marched on either side of Kai, each gripping an arm to keep her moving. Her feet dragged uselessly, and if not for the Guards she would have fallen. She was exhausted from terror and the pain. She blinked slowly, her eyelids swollen. The torchlight flickered like distant stars out in the night sky. The water was cold beneath her feet, and the small stones when her feet brushed over them felt like daggers in the fresh wounds. They had beat the soles of her feet with a rod. In her arms she clutched her clothes, though it hardly seemed to matter to her anymore that she was naked. Kai moaned softly, mildly surprised by the whistling sound that accompanied her breathing. Her ribs ached from where they had kicked her, and even the shallow rise and fall of her breathing caused her pain.

The Guards stopped and withdrew their support. Kai wavered, her knees buckling, and clutched her clothes tighter. She swallowed, her throat thick with the pulpy taste of blood. Her leathery tongue seemed to stick to the roof of her mouth.

The keys jangled in the lock, and the door to the cell was opened.

"In here and be quick," the Guard said to her as he shoved her forward into the cell.

Kai stumbled, crying out as the Guard's hand found the welts that crisscrossed her back. As her weight settled on her feet, shooting pain from her beaten soles caused her to stagger and then fall. The cold floor of the prison cell seemed to rise to greet her and her bones rattled at the final insult of impact. She wanted to vomit and leaned forward over her knees, her stomach heaving. There was nothing, only the small quantity of blood that she had swallowed. Kai remained hunched forward, her chest resting on her knees, and wondered if she would ever rise again. Tears formed in her eyes—tears of relief that the torture for now was over, and tears of rage knowing that it would begin again. The Upright Man had told her he wasn't finished with her. Not until she told him what he wanted to know.

In the dark cell Kai gave a small, joyless smile. She hadn't told the frigging bastard anything. Nothing at all. And then she started to cry, as the pain in her body overwhelmed her.

Through the tears she saw a tiny circle of light as someone set a candle down to look at her.

"Z'blood, the bastards," a man swore.

"She's nothing but a girl and look what they've done to her," another voice whispered.

"Here now," the man said, and Kai felt herself being gently raised by the shoulders.

She looked up into the worried faces, confused as to why they should care what happened to her.

"Here's some water," a woman said, holding up a little cup. She held it for Kai, letting her take small sips. Then she dipped the hem of her skirt into it and wiped Kai's face.

"I told them nothing," Kai said at last, shocked at the croaking sound of her voice. The woman wiping her face was crying softly, tears leaving dirty tracks down her face.

"Hush now," the woman said, and taking the blue weaver's scarf from her neck, she went to tie it on Kai's shaven head. Kai stopped her, the effort of lifting her arm causing her fresh waves of pain.

"Nah. Leave it."

"You must know something if they kept you more alive than dead. Most in here have not been so lucky," the man said quietly.

Kai squinted at him, seeing now the red scarf of an iron worker. He had a squared-off face, a black row of eyebrows meeting across his forehead. A new growth of beard darkened his cheeks but couldn't hide the twin creases in his cheeks.

"How long can you keep it to yourself?" the man asked her, his stare suddenly intense.

"Not long," Kai said, and met his gaze.

The man laced his fingers together and then unknit them nervously as Kai watched him. The muscles of his forearms bunched and he ground his teeth. Then he swore and wiped his face with his hand, scraping his fingers through the rough patch of beard.

"I can't do it," he said, and Kai nodded, understanding him.

"I don't want to die," Kai hissed. "Not scaffered like some animal by the butcherboys, and not by the New Moon to protect themselves neither."

"What else is there?" the man asked curtly. "They will have you singing their tune. And how many of our people will die because of it, eh?"

"I ain't going to sing their tune," Kai said between gritted teeth, "because I don't plan on hanging round here."

The man stared at her, perplexed, and then burst out with a coarse laugh. "Think you can escape?"

Kai nodded, a small smile pulling the corners of her mouth. While the Guards beat her, while she lay with her cheek pressed against the stone floor of the room, she had concentrated on the feel of the stone. It was like the tunnels and it carried the odor of dampness. Kai thought of Slipper finding his way through the night corridors by the smell of the water and the silent messages the water whispered to him alone.

"And how do you plan that, my girl? Even if you could get out of this room, there's nothing but passages and tunnels. Not to mention Guards." The man spoke sarcastically, but his face was tense, as if he dared her to prove him wrong.

"I know someone who could find their way. Even in the dark."

"From inside?" The man edged closer, taking a quick glance over his shoulder.

"Outside."

"Outside!" the man exclaimed, and the look of disbelief returned. "How do you plan to tell them where you are?"

"I need some paper and a pen—I know you've got some—" Kai said quickly before the man could deny having any. "I saw you hide it."

"You can read and write. A girl like you?"

Kai nodded slowly. "Yeah," she croaked, "even a dell like me."

The man hesitated.

"Give them to her, Farier," the woman said.

"No, Mirin. It's all I have to keep me sane down here."

"Give them to her, Farier," the woman insisted.

"All right," Farier snapped. "All right, I will. But how do you plan to get the message out?"

"A corpse. On its way to Scroggles." Kai struggled to speak clearly. Her head throbbed and every part of her body ached from bruises. She moved her head and the welts on her back ignited with pain. "I know someone, there. He'll see the note. He'll know where to take it."

Kai watched the pair from beneath half-closed lids. Farier and Mirin exchanged worried glances, each trying to decide. At last Mirin turned to Kai.

"There's a woman, died last night. You can get your message out with her. But say nothing to anyone else."

"Gener's a squealer," Kai replied, and Mirin clucked her tongue in agreement.

"We don't know who else in here might be."

"One more thing," Kai said, shifting her weight on the hard ground, trying to find a way to sit that didn't cause her pain. "Give me the dead women's clothes. And put mine on her."

"Except for your shaven head, you don't look at all alike," Mirin said softly.

"Then fix it. The Guards won't look too close at a dead woman if her face is done in."

In the candlelight Mirin's skin faded a waxy color, the flesh sagging beneath her eyes. She sighed heavily. "My sister," she murmured to the stone floor.

"Eh?" Kai asked, not quite hearing the whispered words.

"My sister," Mirin said more firmly. "The dead woman was my sister."

She got up abruptly and went to the pallets of straw. Kai watched her lift the body from the straw, the limbs already stiff. With desperate motions, she freed the clothing from the awkward torso and wrenched the skirts off. When she came back to Kai, her face was drawn. "Here," she said as she handed Kai the bodice, soiled with blood, and then the skirts, which smelled of feces and urine.

Slowly Kai handed her own clothes to Mirin. There were no buttons left to the bodice, but at least the garments were clean. there was not even blood, and the urine that had pressed so painfully in Kai's bladder had been evacuated over the polished boots of the Guards.

Kai dressed in the dead woman's clothes, her stomach gripping with revulsion at the stench. She took a shallow breath to steady her pulse and wiped a hand over her mouth. She looked at her hand and saw the little razor cuts on the palm and up the side of her forearm. The Upright Man had made those strokes, enjoying the pain it brought to her.

Farier brought her a tiny strip of paper that he unfolded, square by square. He gave her a narrow stylus with a sharpened point. There was no ink.

Kai jabbed the point into one of the cuts, wincing with the needle-sharp pain, and carefully drew a sketch of the Grinning Bird with the bloody ink.

Neive would know that it came from her. He would recognize the clothes and he would go through the pockets of the corpse.

He would find this note. Kai's mind imagined it, held on to the fragile thread of hope it represented. Underneath the portrait of the bird, she drew a fish. All the Flocks carried a symbol with which they marked their territory, scratching it into the brick and plaster of Beldan's buildings. Neive couldn't read, but he'd know the mark and he'd know the message was meant for Slipper. Then Kai wrote: "Under Keep. Tunnels. Find me. K." The letters scrawled on the papers were hardly legible. But it would be enough, Kai told herself. Slipper would come. All she had to do was wait for him and stay alive.

She got up slowly, the new skirts too long for her, the bodice gaping at the neck. The fabric prickled the raw flesh on her back. She limped over to Farier, who was bending over the corpse of Mirin's sister. She handed him the folded message.

"Put this in the skirt pocket. He'll find it there."

Farier did so quickly, and Kai noticed his breathing was harsh and labored. She glanced down at the body and bitter-tasting bile rose in her throat. The face was almost gone, battered and crushed by the rock Farier held in his trembling hand. Only the delicate fragments of bone and a few teeth indicated the humanity of the corpse's face. Seeing the faceless woman dressed in her clothing was more than Kai could bear. She turned away, retching, as the bile scorched her throat. And in between the violent spasms of her injured guts, Kai sobbed, clinging desperately to her quickly dissolving hope.

Chapter Sixteen

"**A**h, that's good," Silwa said, *gasping slightly as the liquid* burned in his throat. He took another sip and his eyes closed, squeezed shut by the pleasant sting.

"Incredible," said the officer, sitting across the makeshift table and setting down his own glass. "Incredible that such a dull people can make such a potent drink. What do they call it again?"

"Mother's Tears," Silwa replied with a smile at his empty glass.

The officer laughed, and in the glow of the camp lantern his youthful face flushed a ruddy color and his eyes gleamed. The black hair tied back into a single braid was coming undone at the temples, a few strands hanging unevenly across his forehead. He undid another button on his uniform, opening the constricting collar of his wool jacket. "Named, no doubt, because too much of this and the old man can't raise his stuff."

"On the contrary," Silwa said. "After a glass of this you'll fuck anything in a skirt."

"Judging by what I've seen of the women here, I'll need it."

"You were well entertained last night," Silwa argued.

"The novelty of Oran women wears off quickly, unlike their smell."

"Reies," Silwa replied with mild annoyance, "I told you to wait until we're done with this campaign at Avadares. Then, when we return to the Silean estates, I can assure you the Silean gentry will be waiting, spreading their daughters' legs for you as a gesture of gratitude."

"And no doubt to freshen up the bloodlines," Reies grunted into his glass before taking another swallow of the the liquor. "From what I've seen of them they're all starting to look too much alike."

"Maintaining purity is hard in this place," Silwa said sharply. "There can be no mixing of Oran and Silean blood. It's too dangerous."

"For who?" Reies asked gruffly. "Wouldn't it be a boon to have a bit of the evil magic in battle, eh?"

"You've enough of the demon in you already." Silwa laughed lightly and poured his young officer another small glass of Mother's Tears.

Reies belched loudly, his chin tucked into his neck. He rocked back on his chair. "This is hardly much of a campaign, Silwa. A few villages putting up a pathetic struggle. I had looked for something a little more interesting."

Silwa frowned in agreement. "I, too, had anticipated more from the Orans."

"Difficult to believe that these New Moon have much to offer us in the way of a real challenge."

"We've not reached Sadar yet. There is an army waiting for us there."

"How long before we arrive?" Reies's chair rocked back a little too far and he nearly toppled over. He managed to stop himself by clutching wildly at the edge of the table. The lantern wobbled and the light wavered over the walls of the tent.

Silwa eyed the young man with distaste. A man that couldn't hold his liquor, or keep his prick down, wasn't his idea of a reliable officer.

"We should be there in two, maybe three days."

"What are you planning once we get there?"

Silwa shook his head. "There have only been two other rebellions since the Sileans first came to Oran. One was in Beldan, not long after the Burning. It was led by the Guildmasters and employed the strong arm of the city's street mob."

Reies gave a contemptuous laugh. "How long before the Guildmasters lost control of their troops?"

"Exactly. They weren't organized and the objectives were less than clear. Though they did a fair damage through sheer zeal."

"And the second rebellion?" Reies fumbled in the pocket of his uniform jacket and tugged loose a pipe. He sucked on it, scowling at the bitter taste. He then took out a small knife and began to clean the bowl of dirty black ash.

"The second was more interesting," Silwa replied, taking out his own pipe. The bowl was mellow brown, polished to a satiny sheen. He packed it and, drawing out a light from the lantern, lit the tobacco with a stem of wintergrass. "Islanders staged a revolt, sabotaging the trading vessels that came from Silea. Bloodier and more costly than the first, but it, too, ended quickly. I don't expect this to be any different." He exhaled a milky cloud of smoke and watched as it circled overhead.

"Do you really believe these people have magic power?" Reies asked. He touched his forehead and then his chin with the tip of his thumb to ward away evil.

Silwa smiled at the gesture. How long had it been since he had done that himself? Not since the first time he slept with Zorah. "The Fire Queen certainly. As for the rest, I think these peasants are only possessed of a talent for being overworked and underfed."

"Then why does the Queen need us?"

"She's a woman. What does she know of politics? Of government and trade?"

"Then why do we need her?" Reies asked, leaning back in his chair, the pipe stuck in the corner of his mouth. He stretched out his long legs and his knee bumped against the edge of the camp table, spilling a small pool of Mother's Tears.

"She's like this liquor," Silwa answered, pouring himself another swallow before his nearly drunk companion tipped over the entire bottle. "By Silean law, this liquor is considered dangerous and illegal. Like magic. But we close our eyes to its existence when it is in our interest to do so. As long as the Oran people have this drink to numb their senses and a Queen who appears to champion them, we shall have fewer problems dominating the Oran populace."

"But the magic power? Are you not worried she will turn against us?"

Silwa shook his head. "No. Advisor Antoni Re Desturo believes her power is waning, or growing less reliable at least. She will need us more, not less, in the future."

Silwa placed his glass on the table and knocked out the dying ashes from his pipe. He stood and refastened the top two bottons of his uniform, smoothing down the jacket. Then he buckled on his sword and glanced down at his officer. "I'm going on a final round of the camp. Care to join me?"

Reies stood, weaving slightly on his feet. "Is that a command, Regent Silwa?"

"Have you something more interesting to do?" Silwa asked.

The young man looked flustered and then shrugged. "I wanted to review the documents you had on Sadar."

Silwa nodded, only half-convinced of Reies's sincerity. "Very well, tomorrow then."

Silwa left the spacious tent and stepped into the night air. It was warm, the wind dry and mild. When he looked out at the camp, he could see the glow of firelight spread throughout the field and hear the pleasant hum of men conversing. He breathed in the familiar smell of camp: human sweat and horses, the smoke of cooking fires mingled with the sizzling of salt pork, the sweet odor of oil rubbed into leather saddles and black boots. A page carrying a lantern hurried to his side, preparing to light his way. Silwa started for the perimeter of the camp and then remembered he had forgotten to tell Reies where the documents on Sadar were stored. He turned on his heel and then stopped, the page nearly bumping into him from behind. Reies's page was standing at the entrance of the tent, and next to him was a young Oran girl, her head downcast and her hands clasping her skirts. Silwa waited in the shadows and watched until Reies's page gave the girl a little shove and she entered the tent.

"Frigging bastard," Silwa swore irritably. Two months out of Silea and all he can think of is plowing his way through the local drudges. Given the officer's youth and the amount of Mother's Tears he'd consumed, Silwa decided Reies wasn't likely to get much sleep. And neither was he if he returned to his own quarters next to the main tent. Better to camp among the pages' tents tonight rather than have to listen to the girl's howls. He turned smartly, his heels clicking together. He stormed off toward the first sentry post, his page nearly running to keep pace.

Zorah sat in her bed and rested her chin against her drawn-up knees. She had awoken from a dream with a sense of urgency. Her eyes stared wildly in the darkened room and sweat beaded her forehead.

How long had it been since she had dreamed like this? Dreams that took her even while she was awake? Not since Pinon's death. Her mother, Pinon, had been a Fire Queen like Zorah, but with short coppery hair and a quick temper. They had been traveling up Dalarna Mountain, seeking the site of Myre's Cave, where the Kirian dwelled. Pinon had hoped to secure a Kirian to instruct Zorah in the ways of the Fire Sword. It was spring and the mud oozed rust-black, the wagon lurching from side to side as it sank unevenly in the soft soil. They became stuck on a rise, the horse straining to pull forward, the wheel digging deeper in the mire. Impatient with the delay, Pinon lost her temper. She leaped from the wagon and began to push it with the servants. She threw her weight behind the rear wheel, willing the wagon out of the mud. And then Zorah heard that awful cracking sound. The axle snapped like a branch and the horse lost its footing. The wagon jerked backward, unbalancing Pinon, and as she fell it drove her under the backward-rolling wheel.

In her bed Zorah clutched her knees tighter, her throat constricted. She could see Pinon's white face, hear again the terrified screams as her body was crushed. And in the malleable corners of her child's heart, Zorah had blamed herself for Pinon's gruesome death. She had remained in the wagon, her weight adding to it, as the wheel ground the flailing woman into the soil like an unwilling seed. It had been because of Zorah that they were even in the mountains. It was her fault, she told herself in the weeks that followed. And it was her punishment to be afflicted with the plague of dreams that came filled with images of Pinon's dying. But after a while Zorah realized with a new sense of private shame that the nightmares were not so much relieving the horror of Pinon's death as foreshadowing the terror of her own death, waiting for her in the future.

Zorah jerked herself savagely out of bed. She stood shaking, staring defiantly around the candlelit room, the little flames flickering shadows on the wall. No, she thought savagely, she'd not give the dreams their power. She undressed, throwing off the linen nightgown. It swirled to the floor as she reached for her clothes. She dressed quickly, roughly pulling on the training garments.

After they buried Pinon, the servants had sent Zorah to Beldan, not knowing what else to do with her. They had hoped perhaps that in the company of the other Queens, older by a few years, she would forget the pain of her mother's death. Zorah

smiled grimly as she tied the laces to her vest. She could remember quite clearly her first days in Beldan, the city new to
her, as Pinon had insisted she be raised in the north among the
old Farriers Guilds. She had gotten lost, and attracted by the
black belch of smoke, she had stumbled into the courtyard of
Scroggles, the public crematorium. She saw the stiff and bloated
forms of the dead laid out in neat rows, waiting their turns in
the huge communal pyres. The sight at once repulsed and mes-
merized her, drawing her closer, unable to look away. She stared
into the face of an elderly man, his grizzled cheeks sunken, his
toothless mouth gaping in a permanent lopsided grin. A hornet
buzzed in and out. Next to him was a child, a black bruise
spread over the side of her face. The mother had tied a garland
of everlasting flowers around the child's neck, and the dry, pale
petals rustled in the hot wind. Farther down a lighterman drew
a coarse shroud over the body of a young woman. For a brief
instant it had seemed as if the eyes of the corpse winked. But
as Zorah reached out to stop the man, she saw that it was only
coins laid over the hollowed sockets. The lighterman had picked
them up and pocketed the two silver coins before he finished
sewing the shroud over her face.

After that, the dreams became worse. No longer confined to
the images of Pinon's death, they multiplied into a thousand
grotesque visions of death, nurtured by the secret visits to Scroggles. And each time Zorah looked upon the faces ravaged by
death, she refused to accept the thought of herself grown ugly
like the corpses of Scroggles. She denied that her beautiful face
would be corrupted by such an evil, that her nearly perfect limbs
would contort into such rude postures. And slowly it became an
obsession to find the means to hold back forever the hideous
grasp of death.

In her chambers Zorah straightened her shoulders and pushed
back a heavy lock of coppery hair. She reached for her Fire
Sword, lying close to the bed. She held it close to her cheek and
relaxed at the steady hum of power vibrating through the steel.
She breathed a deep sigh and brought the sword down before the
light of her hearth fire. Slowly she slid the sword from its scabbard. Flames sparkled around the guard, and a shimmering orange and red light pulsed along the edge of the blade.

And then it struck her, the reason for her waking. She laughed,
a hard, brittle sound in the peaceful room. It was not the dreams
that had awakened her but the warring cry of a Fire Sword. She

had been jerked out of sleep by its shrill voice, like a claxon calling her to arms. A Fire Sword. Not hers, but a another sword, somewhere in Oran.

She turned her gaze from the sword to the fire. "So, my little street thief," she whispered to the flames, "you have found your sword. Touched it and felt the stirring of its power." Zorah resheathed her weapon, her head cocked to the changes in the howling of the magic storm around her. Opening her mind to the flow of magic, she could sense clearly the moment when Faul's sword had lain in Jobber's hand. She smiled with understanding, aware of Jobber's confusion at the unexpected union between fire and steel. She could hear the beautiful but strident voice of the sword, roused to life by the element in Jobber's blood. And then Zorah frowned, realizing that the union had been brief, and the sword was no longer in Jobber's possession.

"No matter," she said. "I have you both, fire thief and Fire Sword. It won't be difficult to convince one to come to the other."

Zorah started walking to the training grounds, and Guards snapped to attention as she passed, her hair billowing in a gout of coppery flame. It was too difficult, she thought, to bring the sword to Jobber. The sword was held by someone who was deaf to the real power invested in the blade. It was better, she decided, to bring Jobber to the sword. To Sadar. Zorah's heeled boots clicked smartly on the stones as she smiled at the poetic irony of her plan. She would use Jobber and the Fire Sword against Huld and all her pathetic band of traitors.

Zorah reached the training ground, empty now as the Guards did sentry duty elsewhere. She stepped into the circle of light cast by the torches and drew in a deep, calming breath. She released her sword, saluted the circle, and began to practice her strokes.

Zorah moved restlessly out of the wedges of shadow and into the pale gold circles of light, followed by the whispered strokes of the Fire Sword. She practiced an Oran sword style, with its own specialized footwork, as different from the rugged straight-armed style of the Silean two-edged blade as the scythe is to the plow. Shifting her weight forward, she swung the blade upward, "honoring the sun." The tip of the blade sparkled red gold as it pierced a circle of light. Zorah pivoted on the balls of her feet, knees flexed, and drove the blade downward, a two-handed grasp called "cutting the straw." As she wheeled around again the sword left a thin gleaming trail of light in its wake. She grunted lightly with short exhalations at the termination point of each technique, then inhaled a quick breath through her nose before moving into the next attack position.

Beneath the fine mask of sweat on her face, Zorah felt a growing measure of calm. The dreams were vanquished on the training ground. They were shredded into fragments by the graceful motion of the blade, cutting, slashing, driving its steel-edged sharpness through the core of her fear. The frayed ends of her concentration knitted to the task at hand. There was no idle moment, no chance that the nightmares could slip in and take her. As long as she kept moving. As long as she followed the bright arc of the sword.

Zorah felt herself becoming one with the Fire Sword. Each thrust seemed increasingly effortless, as if the Fire Sword were an extension of her hand, her arm and shoulder. She felt the stroke first in the hollow of her belly, saw the blade extend itself from her arm, uncurling like the limb of a waking cat.

But the peace Zorah sought ebbed away and the movements of the sword wove a latticework of unease around her. She grew increasingly aware of her isolation in the void of the storm. She was alone, cut off from the living and dying world of Oran. In the rarefied air of the void there could be no time, but neither could there be the pure release of magical power. It was a price Zorah had once accepted, never to feel again the fullness of the Fire Sword, splendid in its destructive power. Zorah had experienced the shock of Jobber's hand on the Fire Sword, remembered in that shared moment the extreme pleasure and pain of the fire. But the touch was secondhand, its vitality diluted by distance. Even still, the moment bubbled angrily in Zorah's heart, envy agitating the sparks that erupted in her hair.

Standing in the dimly lit training circle, Zorah recalled with bittersweet anguish the power of the Fire Sword. Fire and steel entwined like a pair of mating snakes, the explosion of heat as molten blood poured from the core of her being and outward along the shining red-gold blade. A sword that cut through stone, that radiated a heat so fierce that anything caught within its blistering rage blackened into wisps of smoke. Anything except Zorah, the source of its fire.

Zorah clamped her jaws tight, hearing again the exalted cries torn from her lips as the surging flames engulfed her, wrapped her in a lustrous veil of blue-white heat. Like sex. Zorah smiled painfully at the black leather handle gripped tightly in her fist. "No, better," she said, and the muscles of her guts contracted and her neck was flushed with a sudden heat. Firefaire was a weak imitation of the real power of the sword. A balm for her heart's desire. It was never the same, and the Great Bonfire in which she purged Oran of bad luck never burned hot enough to soothe the ache in her veins.

Trapped in the net of emotions, Zorah wondered if she dare use the Fire Sword to call her power once more. If she did, she would destroy everything, herself included. Time would escape if the Fire Sword were called to release rather than absorb power. Was it worth it? Had she bartered her immortality for too great a price? Zorah shook her head, watching the blossoms of fire cascade from her angry hair. "Ah, for that one moment—" she sighed—that one inexorable moment of pleasure when power would explode like a crushed star, and she would feel again the magma of fire raging in her blood. Her breath was shallow, her skin prickled as the cool night air blew against her warmed skin. How long had it been since she had felt truly alive? Zorah grasped the handle, squeezed it with fear and anticipation.

"Madam?" a voice called. Zorah struggled to compose herself again. With slow, deliberate movements, she returned her sword to the safety of its scabbard. The moment of indecision was gone, but not so the frustration.

"Yes?" she snapped, turning angrily. The torchlight caught the hard yellow gleam in her green eyes.

"Forgive me for intruding, madam." Antoni stepped from the edges of the training ground into a circle of light. He was dressed casually, though Zorah's quick eye determined that it was calculated, intended to please her. His soft white shirt was open at the neck, his trousers were tight, revealing the length of a well-muscled thigh, and his black boots gleamed in the light. He wore his hair tied back tonight, and as he faced her, Zorah noticed the clean line of his jaw beneath the closely cropped beard. He was handsome in his own ruthless way, she thought, surprised by her interest. He approached her, his gaze holding hers.

She shook her hair, the last few sparks falling like tossed flowers. "You're not intruding. I'm finished," she answered, aware that her voice had softened.

Antoni smiled at the tone.

Zorah glanced at him from half-closed eyes. Why had she been frightened of him before? she chided herself. He was easy enough to understand. Since Silwa's departure, it had seemed to her that Antoni had changed. His manner had grown more familiar, almost more intimate. He was trying to seduce her, she thought, annoyed and amused at the same time. Any other time she might brushed off this advance. But something of the restless frustration remained, tapping insistently in her veins, scratching the surface of her skin. Antoni's presence invited distraction and that made it agreeable. She tried to imagine what it would be like to couple with him. His legs between her thighs. That face looking down at her. How different would he be from all the other Silean lovers she had taken? After two hundred partners Zorah experienced only a sense of dislocation with each coupling, as if she watched herself and the man performing. She judged them by their ardor, their endurance, and sometimes their creativity, though there was little enough left that surprised her.

"The hour is late to be training."

"I don't need an advisor."

"Something else, perhaps?"

Zorah smiled and exhaled softly. "What did you have in mind?"

He stepped closer and she could smell the peppery odor of his skin, feel his eyes on her body. He reached out to touch her, and the smile hardened on her lips as she forced herself not to flinch. His touch leaped at her senses, cowed her desire beneath a sudden curtain of fear. On his fingertips was a cold dampness, like the touch of slick clay. Like the rising dead of her nightmares, his hand was wet and dank despite the heat of his body. She shivered and Antoni moved closer, as if thinking her moved by pleasure. She stared into his eager eyes, and backed away brusquely.

Standing alone, she grasped the hilt of her sword. "Why didn't you join Silwa at Sadar?" she asked, an edge to her voice.

"He didn't need me," Antoni replied, his expression wary at her sudden coldness.

"Well, I don't need you either," Zorah said sharply, and pushed past him.

Even as she left the training ground she could feel the steady burn of his gaze on her back, hear the hunger in his thoughts like a dog baying at the moon. Why had she allowed herself, even for a moment, to be swayed by the man? she asked herself angrily. Why had she allowed him the opportunity to touch her? She grimaced with disgust. "No more," she said out loud. She would concentrate on the task at hand. Bringing Jobber to Sadar. Bringing Jobber to the Fire Sword. And in that union she would find the release denied to her. She would experience again the purging roar of fire. Zorah took a deep breath and imagined she tasted the bitter ash of the Burning and the sharp perfume of blazing steel.

Neive turned down Twopenny Street, jumping over the rubble that lay in little heaps on the broken cobblestones of the street. He patted his pocket, once more reassuring himself that the scrap of paper was there. He took a ragged breath, trying to force down the memory of the woman's body that had come that morning to Scroggles. It wasn't the lack of face that caused his heart to leap. It was her dress, Kai's black dress, that he recognized the moment the corpse was hauled off the prison cart and dumped onto the muddy flagstones of Scroggles's courtyard.

He had remained hidden for a long time in the cupboard of the Grinning Bird. Hidden in fear of the Firstwatch and the Guards that tore apart the tea shop. He didn't want them to take Kai, but even less did he want them to find him. He was an earth element. No one knew that yet but him. He had learned of his element when he discovered that by sifting through the ashes of the dead, he could hear the parting words of the corpse, ghostly voices issued with breaths of smoke. What was once human had become an element of earth, flesh into carbon ash, bone into white powdery calcium, all traces of humanity returned to the soil again. It wasn't just the odd coin Neive searched for in the ashes of the dead, but for the sound of their ghostly farewells. He was the last person to whom they spoke before they were returned again to the Oran soil.

When the Guards had left with Kai, Neive ran rabbit-scared through the streets until he came to Scroggles. Few would care to look for him here, among the piled corpses. He knew he ought to tell Slipper and the other man, Shefek. Knew he owed Kai that much. But fear prevented him from returning. The Guards might come again, and the second time he might not be so lucky. Neive pulled the lighterman's hat down over his forehead and kept his head bent to work, sweeping and sifting the ashes. He hoped he could forget the debt, could free himself from its obligation.

And then this morning, the Guards had brought the woman. He had seen the black dress from across the courtyard. Two bare feet, swollen and blackened with wounds, lying turned out from beneath the hem of the skirts. Neive had approached slowly, cautiously, the corpse seeming to accuse him the closer he came.

He stopped short, staring down, shocked and confused by the battered face.

"Frigging bastards," grumbled the master lighterman as he went to fetch a shroud. "Kicked her frigging face in, the shitting whores. But not until they tortured her, the poor wretch."

Neive bent on his knees to inspect the body. His eyes saw the bodice that refused to close over the swell of a woman's breast. He stared at the hands, wide at the palm, the thumbs padded with hard calluses. Kai's dress, but not Kai's body, he realized with a small groan of relief. Gingerly he slipped his hands in the pockets of the skirt. The first one contained only the dried flakes of black tea. But out of the second pocket Neive pulled a folded paper, his eyes widening at the drawing of the Bird and, beneath it, the symbol of the fish.

He stood abruptly, staring over his shoulder. The lighterman was absorbed in talking to a companion, their heads shaking angrily as they conversed. Neive didn't wait any longer. He took to his heels, running hard even though the cobblestones hurt his feet through the thin soles of his boots. The note was from Kai. He knew it. And this corpse was a warning to him of what was waiting for her. Being scared of the Guard would not be reason enough to prevent him from delivering this last message. And so he ran, dodging the Guard as he went through the city streets, even though most of them scarcely paid him a second glance.

On Twopenny Street, Neive slowed his step. The Grinning Bird looked dark and closed. Where were Slipper and the vagger? He decided against going to the door of the shop, aware now that a Guard strolled down the other side of the street, perhaps innocently enough, but perhaps not. Neive walked past the shop, quickly glanced up at the stoop, and kept on going. It didn't feel right to him. He opened his senses and heard the muttered warnings of the stones through the soles of his feet. The strolling Guard had stopped and leaned against a burned-out building, slowly breaking open a loaf of bread. Neive saw the eyes that watched the doorway to the Grinning Bird as he ate the chunks of brown bread. Now Neive was sure the shop was being watched.

That could only mean that Slipper was still free. But where? Neive kept walking, nervously fingering the scrap of paper in his pocket. He reached the corner, undecided what to do next. From the alley doorway of a small herbal shop a hand shot out and grabbed him roughly by the lapels of his jacket. Before he'd time to yelp in surprise, he was pulled down two steps into the darkened doorway and a hand was clapped over his mouth.

"Don't say a frigging thing," Slipper hissed in his ear.

Neive shook his head beneath the clammy hand.

"What are you doing here?" Slipper asked. "I saw you go by the shop. Saw you take another look. You're up to something."

"I don't see how he can answer you, Slipper, if you insist on keeping your hand over his mouth," Shefek said softly.

"Yeah, but I don't want him squealing to the street the second I let go of him, neither," Slipper protested.

Neive gurgled in his throat to get Slipper's attention and pointed to his pocket. He went to retrieve the paper, but Slipper stopped him with a growl.

"I'll get it," Slipper snarled, and reached carefully into the pocket.

"If he had a weapon in there, it would hardly be enough to do you much harm," Shefek said.

"Ain't never met up with an oyster knife, have you, Shefek? Well, Kai and me did once. Right little pisser he was, too. We tried to help him and he cut us both badly, Kai across the hip there and me on the arm. Frigging bastard stole from us and capered away. Nah. I don't trust anyone," he said flatly.

"Given my present condition, I am not in a position to argue with that wisdom," Shefek replied with a sharp laugh. "So what does he have then?"

With one hand clamped tight around Neive's face, Slipper pulled out the note and peered at it in the dark.

"Paper," he answered, sounding disappointed. "Wait a minute. The sign of the Waterlings, that fish there." His voice rose in excitement. "Only Kai could have sent this." He turned back to Neive, who was waiting impatiently to be freed. "Kai send you?"

Neive nodded. In a manner of speaking, Neive reasoned, she had. Slipper freed him and patted him apologetically on the shoulder.

"I'm sorry. Things is a bit touchy now. I come back to the shop, find Kai gone, the place upside down—"

"The butcherboys took her!" Neive blurted out. Slipper's face froze. "I was there when it happened. Kai hid me so I wouldn't get caught."

"If the butcherboys got her, how'd you get this, then?" Slipper asked, his eyes narrowing. His hand moved from Neive's shoulder to his chest, his fingers curling tightly around the collar of the old jacket.

"On a corpse."

Slipper's hand jerked convulsively, lifting Neive off his feet by the jacket collar. "Whose corpse!" he snarled.

"Not Kai's. Z'blood, put me down, you banger. All I did was to come here to help you and get this message to you. I don't want no trouble with the butcherboys. But I owed one to Kai. So read your own frigging message and let me go!" Neive was sweating, his heart pounding with fear and anger.

"Put him down," Shefek said, "but don't let him go. Not yet." He put a restraining hand on Neive's shoulder and edged closer.

Neive stared at Shefek, startled by the eerie glow of his eyes in the dark. They reminded him of the feral cats that roamed the alleyways, their golden eyes round with malice. He had always thought Shefek was just a vagger. But now he trembled at the dry voice and the sweet rotting stench of the arm on his shoulder. A small white feather drifted between them.

"Tell us again," Shefek said, irritably waving away the feather.

Neive drew in a deep breath and explained to them how he had seen the Guard arrest Kai yesterday and how today the corpse had come to Scroggles, wearing Kai's clothes, a scrap of paper in the pocket. And that was all he had to do with it.

"Good lad," Shefek said calmly, and patted him firmly on the shoulder. Neive watched in puzzled amazement as more white feathers drifted in the air. Z'blood, he's killed a cock, he thought, and he's carrying it under his robes. That's got to be what stinks so bad, he told himself.

Slipper turned the paper over and held it up to the slim rays of light that slanted into the hollow cavern of the dark doorway. "Z'blood," he swore harshly, and Neive saw his shoulders sag.

"What is it?" Shefek asked, concerned.

"Read it yourself," Slipper said, and handed the paper to

Shefek. The Kirian took it and glanced quickly at the paper. Neive saw the old face harden with anger, and the eyes glowed a sulfur color.

"Can you do this?" Shefek asked. "Use the tunnels to find her?"

Slipper was quiet, one hand in a fist, the knuckles rapping against the door frame.

"Frigging right I will," he answered softly.

"And what then?" Shefek probed. "How do you intend to get her out?"

"I'll figure it when I get there."

"Not good enough," Shefek argued. "You can't fight the Guard alone."

Slipper turned on his heel, bristling with rage. "Then you will come with me. You're a—"

"Shut up, Slipper," Shefek warned, glancing quickly at Neive.

Neive scrunched himself closer against the shadows, not wanting to be seen, not wanting the responsibility of knowing their secrets.

"Well, will you come, Shefek?" Slipper asked, his trembling voice barely concealing his rage.

It was Shefek's turn to pause. Then he shook his head. "I cannot enter the tunnels."

"Why not?"

"The Kir—" He stopped himself, flustered. "I will not be imprisoned in the tunnels."

"You're afraid," Slipper accused. "You're afraid of the tunnels, ain't you?"

"No!" Shefek barked defensively. "No. It is just that in tunnels I cannot be what I am. There is no room for flight."

Neive didn't understand Shefek, but he saw clearly that Slipper did and something hard in Slipper's expression softened with comprehension.

"Shefek, I know the tunnels. I can find the way."

"How?" Shefek asked coldly.

"The water." Slipper removed the lighterman's hat from his head and crushed it in his hand. Slipper looked up at Shefek, determination shaping his features. "I'm going for Kai," he explained quietly. "I need your help. But whether I get it or not, I'll go." His eyes widened, his mouth stubborn in the squared chin. "I am a man, Shefek," he said earnestly. "There is more to being a man than fucking whores. I've had my share of that this last month. It's has done little to change me. But knowing Kai has. To her, I owe my life. And I won't leave her now.''

"So, my young hawk." Shefek chuckled, stroking his silvery beard. "You would shame me into an act of honor."

"Is such a thing possible?" Slipper asked.

"The Kirians created honor as a thing of beauty. But it was humans who taught us shame so that we might struggle to attain it." Shefek sighed and rubbed both hands wearily though his beard. Then he turned to Neive. "And you, little carrion rat. You will join us."

"Me?" Neive squeaked in reply. "Oh, no, I ain't good at that."

"Sorry, Neive, but I can't let you go," Slipper answered with a sad shake of his head. "I don't mean to say I don't trust you. But, well, it means too much now to let you go off on your own again. Just as soon as we find Kai and get out of the prisons, we'll let you go."

"You're frigging daft!" Neive started to shout and Shefek's hand shot out and slapped over his mouth. Neive gagged at the stench of the hand and more feathers blustered in the air, landing on his head and nose.

"Sorry, little rat. But you'll have to come quietly," Shefek murmured in Neive's ear.

Slipper shoved open the door behind them with his shoulder and Neive saw the mossy steps that led downward from the level of the street. The cold, fresh smell of seawater rushed out of the open door.

"Down to the tunnels, then," Slipper said as he started down the steps.

Neive felt Shefek hesitate.

Slipper's head reappeared from a lower stair, an impatient scowl on his face. "Are you coming?" he demanded.

As if preparing himself for a painful blow, Shefek inhaled quickly and held his breath. Then he pushed Neive before him through the doorway and down the narrow stone steps.

The darkness folded over them. Neive could hear Shefek muttering soft words near his ear, and he realized as they descended deeper into the confines of the tunnels that the old man's words were meant to push back the edge of terror. He listened to them, and felt a calming influence in the rhythmical cadence. He was so intent on Shefek's low chant that he hardly noticed when

Shefek released him, allowing him to follow Slipper in the tunnels on his own. But by then, even if he had wanted to escape, Neive could make no sense of where he was. He walked blindly, one hand out, grabbing at the hem of Slipper's jacket, while behind, Shefek continued his murmured chant, a bare foot occasionally catching on Neive's heel.

Chapter Seventeen

Faul's heartbeat quickened as she peered from the bushes at the Silean sentries gathered nervously around their fire. They wore their swords now; their hands fiddled with the wrappings and cords on the hilts. Nearby an extra stand of pikes was stacked, each leaning against the other, their polished blades gleaming with oil. Faul gave a thin smile. Since the last two nights they had doubled the guard. And well they should, though little good would it do them. In two nights twenty New Moon fighters had managed to take at least a hundred Sileans. And during the days archers had taken another hundred more. Be certain of your target, Zein had ordered them. Don't waste the arrows being clever. One good shot, then go. That was the strategy. Get in, get out.

Watching the ponderously slow progress the Silean troops made toward Sadar during the day, Faul could appreciate the New Moon's fluidity, their small groups scattered along the road, inflicting damage like tiny swarms of gnats attacking the flank of a huge bull. Already she could see morale had weakened some. Officers were snapping orders, expressions grim beneath their helmets, and the infantry looked tense, alert for the arrow that might chose its mark among any one of them as they marched to Sadar.

But deep down Faul didn't believe the New Moon could do enough, fast enough. There had to be at least two thousand Sileans, and of the New Moon, less than six hundred by her estimate. Not very good odds. And not enough time to pare them down, she thought worriedly. They'd do something soon, she guessed, something decisive, something that might force the New Moon into the open. They'd have to, or else Silwa would lose the confidence of his troops. His paid troops anyways. She knew Silwa could count on the hard core determination of the Silean militia. Those were homeboys, conscripted from the Silean estates in Oran. They didn't fight for a soldiers' pay, but to keep firm in their grasp the land their father's had already stolen from the Oran people. She had seen at Cairns how the threat of losing their land, their way of life as privileged nobles had deepened their hatred toward the New Moon.

Faul shifted on the balls of her feet, keeping her muscles poised but relaxed. She waited for Zein's signal, the soft call of an owl. The Sileans were but a day from Sadar, billeted in the tumbledown foothills of Avadares. The forest was thicker here, providing the New Moon with additional coverage and the Sileans with the harder task of having to guard a camp spread out beneath the trees, separated by bushes and outcroppings of rocks, heaped together like barriers. These ten men, who sat staring nervously at their fire, casting glances into the night shadows, were more alone than they might have imagined, Faul thought, already planning in her head the order in which she would dispatch them. Throughout the camp, in at least ten other places, other fighters would be sizing up their own quarry.

As she waited Faul felt her senses sharpen, honed to every movement of the forest, every scent carried in the breeze. A stone poked the soft leather of her boot and she moved her foot quietly. An insect buzzed irritably in her ear and she brushed it away gently. She knew her own scent blended with the forest, the acrid smell of her sweat muted by the subtler fragrance of pine and the musty odor of soil. Her clothes were dark; they'd not see her until she wanted them to. She could move as quietly in the woods as Go or Zein, her footfall hushed beneath the dried leaves. Whether that was of her own doing, or something of the old power that Huld's forest lent to the New Moon, Faul was never quite certain. But living in the forest had opened her senses, making her aware of things that didn't belong there. Her nostrils flared at the pungent smell of the Guards' fear in their sweated uniforms, the prickling odor of illicit liquor hidden beneath their jackets, liquor passed around at night when they thought themselves away from the watchful eye of their commanders. Faul could even smell the Oran peasants, dragged on the campaign as servants, cooks, and unwilling whores. They carried a rich, feculent smell from the farms and livestock, which clashed with the harsh metallic stink of steel.

Faul picked up her chin, listening intently as the rustle of leaves brought the hunting cry of an owl. It was time.

She slipped through the trees, carefully threading her way through the bushes without a sound. She stopped just outside the perimeter of their campfire, still hidden in the shadow. She frowned quickly and drew out two stones from her pocket. The circle of men was spread a little wide. She wanted them closer together, preferably in a string, one lined up behind the other.

She pitched a stone four feet to the right. The man closest to her leaped up, reaching for his sword as his eyes searched the bushes. He made a move forward but a second man stood behind him and held him back.

"Wait," he hissed.

Faul cast another stone and a third man stood, joining behind the back of the first two. Better yet, thought Faul as she saw them line up like a row of tenpins about to be bowled at. Automatically the others closed ranks, huddled expectantly. Faul released her blade, just an inch from its scabbard. The first man drew his sword and edged forward, peering into the bush next to Faul.

That's right, Faul thought with a quick inhalation.

"Anything?" the man behind him asked.

"No," he answered.

"Oy, it's probably nothing," said another farther back. Faul could hear the tension in his voice, feel his jangled nerves in the vibrations of the air.

The first man still waited for something more. Faul watched the drop of sweat that trickled down one side of his head and heard him swallow dryly. Then she saw the moment she had waited for, the suddenly easing of his stance as he relaxed his shoulders.

"Yeah, maybe—" he started to say, turning to the others.

Faul's sword slashed through the air, the deadly arc of the blade swift as a streak of lightning. She cut across his back, the sword drawing through the man at the waist like Farnon's sickle through a sheaf of wheat. She stepped forward, following the swing of her blade, and turned it with a snap of her wrists into a short upstroke across the neck of the man behind him. She caught the final fleeting look of shocked horror on the man's face before the blade separated the head from the body. Shifting forward again, she slashed downward through the third man's shoulder as he struggled to draw his own blade.

Then she turned and faced the remaining seven, who clamored backward out of the way of the falling bodies and released their own swords. She moved swiftly, her blade flashing across and down, across and down, carving a benediction on two more, who barely cried out as they fell beneath her weapon.

"Oy, Guards!" one shouted, and Faul lunged forward, drawing her sword upward in a two-handed grasp that opened the man's back along the spine.

"Z'blood," she swore, hearing distantly the cawing of a Silean alarm. The camp was roused. She had to get away quickly. She swung the sword to the side, slashing at the man who closed into her left. She missed him, but as he reached for a pike, she snapped her sword upward and caught him under the arm. He fell hard and she had to tug her blade free from his unwilling body before she could turn and run. As she reached the dark shadows of the bushes she paused long enough to wipe her sword before returning it to its scabbard.

Behind her the Silean troops were shouting curses, and officers barked orders to pursue the fleeing rebels. Faul heard the groaning cracks of broken branches as the Sileans plunged into the woods after her. She smelled pitch and smoke and knew they carried torches, afraid to venture far into the dark woods without light. She ducked her head and ran into the deeper shadows of the trees. Then she stopped as she made out the kneeling figure of another fighter. By his knee he held a bow, and on his back a quiver of arrows. She passed him, but he gave her no notice, his concentration fixed on the approaching sounds of the Sileans and the flickering of their torchlight. Faul crouched behind him, out of the way, and caught her breath.

She looked up suddenly, hearing the Sileans close by. The archer in front of her stood slowly, raising his bow, an arrow nocked and ready. The light flashed for a moment and Faul saw the furious face of a Guard beneath the torch. She heard the twang and felt the snap in the air as the arrow left the bow and buried itself in the Guard's chest. The light faltered and the torch was dropped. Around her in the woods Faul heard the angry hum of arrows and the Sileans roaring in their pain and fury.

"Fall back, fall back," one cried. "Douse the torch, you shitheads, before they take us all."

The forest went dark again, though Faul continued to hear the groaning of men dying and the crackling of torn branches as the living fled from the woods, back to the relative safety of the camps.

The archer shouldered his bow. In the dim light of the night sky Faul saw that it was Zein.

"*Aha,*" he said with quiet finality.

"Get in, get out," Faul repeated, and then fell in behind him as he jogged through the woods to the caves higher up the mountains.

Jobber was jerked violently awake and bolted upright. Something was wrong. Her gaze darted around the sleeping camp as she tried to locate the source of her unease. Images grabbed at her mind with the lingering residue of a dream. She opened and closed her fists, feeling something missing in her grasp.

"Z'blood," she swore softly, and rose, furious. Near her Finch groaned in her sleep and curled into a tight ball. Jobber edged away from her and moved quickly into the woods. She felt an urgency to get away from them, to hide her thoughts from them. From Lirrel. Jobber cloaked herself in a shield, something she had not done since leaving Beldan. The shield around her aura felt thick and impenetrable, hiding not only the shimmering light of her aura, but her thoughts as well.

Jobber began to run, climbing up over the rocky slopes of the hillside. At the crest of a ridge, she forced herself to stop. Bent double at the waist, she panted hard, confused at the urgency of her flight. What was she doing? What was she running from? She stared up at the clear sky, the moon shining brightly upon her.

And then the vision exploded in her head. "Frigging shit," she moaned as a horse veered down on her and a man with a sword lashed out. There was a searing pain as she felt herself falling, saw her arms covered with the shadow of blood in the moonlight. The stones dug in her sides as she rolled to the ground, gravel cutting open her cheek with gashes. She cried out in terror and the firehair crackled and sizzled.

She lay on her back, gasping, waiting for the horse to trample her. But the vision was gone, and above her Jobber saw only the night sky and the distant sparkle of stars. She held up her hand, and beneath the fine speckles of dirt, the skin gleamed white in the moonlight. There was no blood. No wound. But the pain remained in her hand. Jobber closed her fist and suddenly understood. She knew what was missing, she knew what caused her hand to ache now.

"Faul's sword," she said to the stars, and then shook her head. "No, my sword!" she amended. And as if the stars rewarded her for correctly answering, Jobber felt a warmth seep through her body, gentle and caressing. On the breeze she smelled the fragrance of rose water mingled with the familiar taint of copper.

Jobber rose, calmly. She didn't hurry, but neither was she willing to waste another moment basking in the sudden pleasing warmth. She drew the protective shield tighter around her thoughts, glancing over her shoulder to see if she was followed. There was no one. Not even the sentry trees raised their branches to her in salute as she passed them, walking steadily over the ridge of the mountainside.

Jobber was going to Sadar. She was going to get her sword. And even though she heard the small voice of protest in the corner of her mind, she ignored it as unimportant. The nightmares would stop for her when she retrieved her sword. And for the moment, nothing else mattered.

"Do you really think your friends are going to come?" Farier asked Kai again.

Kai nodded, the pain rippling up her spine as she did. "Yes. I've told you that before, Farier." She glared at him over the dying flame. There was one candle left between them, the wick nearly gone.

"Leave her alone, Farier," Mirin answered curtly. "Do you have to take away her hope?"

"Why do you have so much faith in this Slipper?" Farier persisted.

"I know him," Kai answered him. "He's a good man." She fell silent, wrapping the skirts tighter around her chilled flanks. Her fingers felt stiff, the joints aching. Slipper, she thought, loneliness carving a hole in her resolve. She could see him, his lighterman's hat pulled over one brow, his chin cocked forward. He'd slouched to one side, leaning against the doorway, pulling the strings of her apron as she'd passed by, her arms loaded with the tea trays. "Get away with you," she had snapped at him as if he'd been a child. But he wasn't a child anymore, and only now was she coming to realize it. Loyal, resourceful, that was Slipper. And Kai depended as wholly on him now as he had once long ago on her. She refused to lose faith in him. He would come for her. Kai shifted her thoughts, not wanting to edge too close to despair. "I'll make you a deal, Farier," she said in a hoarse whisper.

"A deal?" Farier asked with a hint of sarcasm in his voice as his eyes wandered to the roof of the cell.

"When we get out—"

"If we get out—"

"When we get out of here," Kai repeated more firmly, "you will join forces with me and let me share in the leadership of Beldan's New Moon."

Farier gave a low whistle. "Say we do get out of here, why should I?"

Kai smiled and in the candlelight the black eyes sparkled. "Because you will need a good hiding place. And I know the best. Underground. And second, because I know the Flocks and I can bring to you an army of the unseen. Snitches and pickpockets. And last, because I am a Reader, and I will bring children to the New Moon. Oran children, with the old power. And though they are children, most are street-smart and quick."

"A Reader?"

If it hadn't hurt so much, Kai would have grinned at the look of astonishment of Farier's face. He rocked back on his heels, regarding her in silence.

"Well?" she asked. "Is it a deal then?"

"Yes," he replied, nodding his head more vigorously. "Yes."

Kai spat into her palm and held out a hand. Farier winced at it, but gamely spat into his own palm and sealed his hand to hers. Good, thought Kai, even the highbrow Oran Guildsman knows when it's best to make an alliance with gutter trash.

"A leader, remember," Kai added. "I'll take no second best from the Guilds."

Farier smiled. "Mistress Kai," he said in a humbled voice, "get us out of here and I will personally see to it that you become master of your own Guild."

"What sort of Guild?"

"The Guild of Surprises."

Kai smiled again, even though it hurt. "I like that." She chuckled, then closed her eyes, hungry and weary, pain a constant companion. She could tell the razor cuts on her arm were getting infected, for the flesh was tender and at times the skin burned. Kai leaned carefully against the wall of the cell, trying to find a place where her back did not hurt. She reached up a hand and felt the narrow trickle of water that seeped through an opening in the stone wall. She let the cold water dribble over her fingers, remembering how Slipper would touch the water and know where he was. She whispered softly to Slipper, praying that the words she spoke would be carried away by the trickling water to where he would find them. The water would lead him here to her. And as she closed her eyes and began to doze, she thought only of Slipper's arm through hers and the sun warming their backs as they sat on the docks and watched the ships enter the harbor.

Chapter Eighteen

Shedwyn was awakened by Lirrel roughly shaking her about the shoulders. She blinked at the gray light of the dawn sky, confused and annoyed. She was tired, every joint in her body stiff and slow to respond to her waking.

"She's gone! Get up!" Lirrel was shouting.

"What are you saying?" Shedwyn asked, sitting up with effort. Her mouth tasted gritty, as if she had eaten sand. She rubbed her face and the skin felt cold.

"Jobber's gone. She must have left in the night." Lirrel was tugging frantically on Shedwyn's arm to make her stand more quickly.

"So what?" Shedwyn muttered. "Good riddance, I say."

"What's the matter with you?" Lirrel snapped. "Don't you understand the danger?"

"No," Shedwyn replied thickly, though it seemed somewhere in the back of her head that a warning sounded. But it was muffled by layers of thoughts weighing heavily on her mind. Shedwyn looked up at the peak of Avadares, captivated by the pink glow of the stone in the sunrise. Shards of mica glittered like bits of silver in the gray.

"I didn't hear her leave," Lirrel was saying, her hands held over her ears. Her face was drawn and sallow with worry. "I didn't 'hear' her. Not since we first met has Jobber been out of my head, and yet she manages to flee from me in the middle of the night and I don't hear her. Something is wrong. Very, very wrong.''

The camp, roused by Lirrel's cries, had woken and gathered uneasily about her. Finch shoved back her tousled yellow hair and bit her lip.

"Think she's drunk somewhere? I know Faul left a bottle or two behind.''

"No!" exclaimed Mole, before Lirrel could answer.

"She ain't here," Trap finished with a shake of her head. "I don't hear her neither.''

"Then where is she?" Dagar asked, looking at Lirrel. The goats huddled close to his thighs, bleating noisily. They bumped their hard heads against his hand, looking for a handout or a pat.

Shedwyn kept her eyes on the sunlight spreading over the face of Avadares. She saw for the first time the single ancient tree that clung to the high ridge behind camp. Its branches spread gracefully to the ground, its trunk twisted by the wind. She inhaled slowly and the taste of resin clung to the roof of her mouth. As the sunlight bathed the tree in its golden light she saw the branches lift, greeting the rising day. And from the fork in the main branch, a face cast its shadow.

"I know where she is," Shedwyn said without taking her eyes from the shifting tree.

"Where?" Lirrel demanded, and then jerked her head around to follow the line of Shedwyn's stare. She gasped, seeing the pine tree, the carved head raised above the shoulders of wood. Around the head was a wreath of mistletoe; the clinging ivy draped down the back in the fashion of hair. The tree shuddered and dry needles sprinkled to the ground.

Shedwyn smiled and nodded her head in recognition.

"Where is she?" Dagar asked impatiently.

"Sadar," Shedwyn replied. "She has gone to Sadar.''

"But why didn't Lirrel know?" Mole spoke up. "Why didn't we hear it?''

"Someone is shielding her," Shedwyn said.

"Zorah!" Lirrel blurted. "Zorah has her.''

"The nightmares she was having," Finch said, a hand slapping her forehead. "They weren't hers at all but Zorah's!''

"What do you think she means to do?" Dagar asked.

Shedwyn turned sharply and addressed them, her voice cold and stern. "Pack. We leave at once for Sadar."

No one moved, stunned by Shedwyn's unfamiliar tone.

"I said move! The stupid child will get us all killed unless we stop her first."

"But the others," Lirrel argued, "they told us to wait here."

"Damn her! She's dangerous, don't you see that? She wants us all dead. For the last time I order you to move," Shedwyn shouted to them, and around the camp the stones of Avadares rumbled. Little clods of dirt exploded angrily. A girl began to cry for her mother, terrified of the quaking ground. Shedwyn turned away roughly, striding through camp, shaking late sleepers awake and barking out orders.

The children obeyed her grudgingly, fright and anger in their faces. In her own heart she felt the coldness of granite, hammering against her brittle bone. Her gentle smile was gone; there was nothing supple about her and she avoided touching her own flesh, afraid of discovering it had become stone. She couldn't explain to them, not even to Lirrel, the terrible rage she felt, the desire to crush the life out of Jobber. Two hundred years of resentment now formed a bitter gall in her throat, a taste only death could cleanse. Shedwyn glanced up one final time at the ancient pine. The branches swept against the stones, and the head bowed as if in farewell. She suppressed the sudden cry that rose to her lips. Her eyes burned and she wanted to weep, but she no longer knew why.

By midday, they had left the camp of Avadares, the children forming straggling lines. The older ones, like Arnard and Dagar, kept watch on the perimeters of the group, urging them to quiet when their cries and protestations grew too loud for safety. Lirrel followed close beside Dagar, finding comfort in the easy way he moved through the thick underbrush and in the words of encouragement he whispered to the smaller children struggling to keep up.

"Lirrel," Dagar asked, tugging his hair in a gesture of concern, "why are we doing this?"

"We have no choice but to follow," Lirrel answered.

"You are Ghazali. Do you mean to fight?"

"No. But there is more going on here than I understand," Lirrel said softly. "We must stay together and follow Shedwyn."

"Are you sure it's Shedwyn?" Dagar said pointedly.

Lirrel clasped him by the arm and he stumbled, clinging to her in order not to fall.

"The old Queens are strong, Dagar," she said. "They think to live again, and I don't know if we can stop them."

"Huld's peace," Dagar said, without thinking.

"If only that were true," Lirrel answered him.

She clung to Dagar as they pushed their way through the woods. Ahead of her Lirrel could see Shedwyn, taller than the rest. She walked in the shadows and it seemed to Lirrel that she was draped in a black cloak. When she turned to look behind, forest light dappled her face, and she appeared no longer flesh and blood, but mottled like the granite stones of Avadares.

Kai crouched closer to the cell wall at the sound of the approaching Guards. The stamping of their boots made her flinch and she clung to the remnants of her courage. The torches appeared outside the cell bars and showed her the four Guards standing there. Once more the key jangled in the lock, the cell gate screeched open.

Who would it be this time? she asked herself. Every time the Guards came now, it was not to bring food, but to drag another one of their number away. Gener was gone. Another woman, a linen weaver, was gone. They waited in silent dread as two Guards circled the cell, searching for the next prisoner.

"Oy you!" the Guard shouted to Farier.

No! Kai screamed to herself. No, please don't take him. But she bit her tongue and kept herself quietly huddled in the corner.

Farier stood, and though he didn't turn to look at her, Kai saw the wistful smile on his lips that bade her farewell.

And then a sharp cracking sound startled the Guard next to Farier. He turned, hearing the heavy thud of a man falling against the bars, and at the same time the light wavered as a torch was dropped.

Kai straightened her body quickly, grunting at the pain as she peered passed the Guard. The second Guard outside the cell was struggling with someone, and as Kai watched openmouthed, two hands appeared, clamped themselves around his face, and snapped the neck with a savage twist. As the Guard slumped forward Kai caught the bright yellow glow of Shefek's eyes. And just at his shoulder was Slipper, desperately peering into the cell.

Farier moved quickly, striking the Guard before him hard across the face with a rock in his hand. The last Guard in the cell dropped his torch and pulled his sword free.

"Kai, are you in there?" Slipper called, grabbing the keys from the dead Guard and hurrying to open the cell gate.

"Yes! Yes!" she shouted back, rising to her feet.

"Get him!" Farier shouted to the other prisoners in the cell, motioning to the remaining Guard.

The Guard didn't wait, and even as they jumped, he forgot his sword and lifted the alarm whistle to his lips. Farier fell on him, but not before the Guard succeeded in blowing two shrill blasts. Farier pounded him on the face with his rock, smashing the whistle into his mouth. After the scuffle, the cell was strangely hushed. Farier glanced up, his face intent.

"Frigging shit," he swore as they heard the distant stamping of boots. "If you know the way," he said to Slipper, "get us out now. The Guard will be on our throats in a few moments."

"Where's Kai?" Slipper demanded as he unwound a long length of rope from his waist.

"Here. I need help," Kai called.

"Go on," Slipper said to Farier, "all of you take a hold of the rope there. Neive, you start. I'll follow. Take them back to the tunnel below Market Square. You remember?"

"Yeah! I remember," Neive shouted.

"You mean we're to follow this child?" Farier asked angrily. The sound of the boots was growing louder, echoing in the corridors. Other prisoners had heard the alarm whistle, and throughout the honeycomb of prisons screams and cries echoed.

"He's an earth element. The stone guides him. Now go on. It's your only chance out of here." Slipper turned away from him, pushed aside the fleeing prisoners, searching in the dark corners for Kai.

"Kai!" Slipper called again.

"Here!" she answered, trying not to sob with relief.

He came quickly to her, but seeing his horrified expression, Kai hid her face. Until that moment she had forgotten what she looked like. She felt his hands on her shoulders, and gently he pulled her toward the shelter of his arm. One hand lifted her chin and met her eyes.

"What have they done to you?" he said, his voice choked.

"Slipper, Kai, you've no time," Shefek called from the gate.

"Can you walk?" Slipper asked, holding her steady around the waist.

"I can try."

"Can you run?" he asked, moving her quickly to the gate and out into the corridor. They could see the light of torches stretching forward on the walls of the corridors.

"I'll have to, won't I?" Kai answered. She forced her legs to move, groaning as pain lanced her body with every step. Slipper held her tighter around her waist and her bruised ribs stung.

Guards burst into view, their swords drawn and ready for the attack. Kai screamed, and in the same moment Shefek stepped smoothly between her and the Guards. She felt the brush of his vagger's robes against her legs and caught the stench of his wounded arm.

"Get out of my way," he said to them over his shoulder.

Kai and Slipper withdrew farther down the corridor and watched as Shefek met the Guards.

The first Guard attacked, slashing his sword over Shefek's head. Shefek's arms snapped up in a cross-handed block, catching the sword arm at the wrist, driving the blade upward. Before the surprised Guard could change direction, Shefek clasped a hand around his wrist, jerking it down, while his other hand slammed into the Guard's face, breaking the nose. Shefek stepped back and, holding the Guard's flailing sword arm with two hands, drove his knee into the elbow, smashing it. The Guard's fist opened, and the sword was released. Swiftly Shefek leaned down and retrieved the sword.

Now armed, Shefek shoved the injured Guard aside, and in quick succession slashed the arms of two more advancing behind him. Blood splattered over his white beard and the vagger robes. The Guards pressed, looked for an opening in his defenses, but Shefek closed the gap in the corridor with the rapid back-and-forth swinging of his sword. Even still, Kai saw it coming, knew the moment when there were too many Guards.

So did Shefek, for though the space was confined, he drew back from the onslaught. Lifting his face to the low ceiling, he shrieked a Kirian's cry of rage. The sound exploded in the corridor and the Guards halted. They covered their ears, deafened by the booming cry.

And as he continued to screech, Shefek transformed. The arched wings were crushed against the low ceilings, the pinion feathers bent against the ground. But his neck snaked forward with lighting speed and the iron beak tore open the chest of a Guard. The Guards stumbled back, terrified by the Kirian's attack. A few struggled bravely to fight him, but he crushed them in his talons. And as the remaining Guard turned to flee, Shefek screeched in rage after them, clapping his beak against the stone walls. The loud rattle vibrated dangerously in the corridors, and small cracks appeared in the ceiling.

"Shefek," Kai gasped, afraid his rage would cause the walls to close in on them. "Shefek, it's enough."

Awkwardly the Kirian turned, his huge body jammed between the walls. And in the bright gold eye a tear formed.

"Shefek, you must change," Slipper pleaded. "I can't get you out of here fast enough if you're like that!"

The Kirian's feathers rustled with annoyance and Kai hid her face from the stench on the breeze. When she looked back, she saw that Shefek was changing, transforming again to human shape. It took time, and Kai saw that Shefek, too, was not well, his injury worse than before. His human frame seemed smaller and more frail. When he was done, he staggered forward to them. His skin was pale in the dim light, and his white beard sparse, barely concealing his rounded chin. His eyes were sunk in his head, deep-set wrinkles folding around the lids.

"Z'blood," Kai said, "you look awful."

"We make a fine pair then, my raven," he answered hoarsely. Then he patted his nose. "Too big this time?"

"Let's go, while we have the chance," Slipper said tersely.

Slipper and Shefek put Kai between them, each supporting her with an arm. Half dragging and sometimes lifting, they led her through the tunnels.

They walked, and sometimes when the path turned downward, they ran. When the pain became too great, Kai made them stop and rest. With her back against the chiseled wall of the tunnel, she would listen, but there was no sound, just the silent darkness. Only the changing odors of the tunnels, sometimes musty like the dirt and other times carrying the tangy scent of salt water, marked the distance they traveled.

"How did you find me?" she asked, to keep her mind from giving in to the howling of pain in her body and the terror of the total darkness.

Slipper grunted his reply. "Neive helped us." They were descending a steep incline, his feet scraping sideways along the rough uneven path. "I kept following the water only to discover that the water went where I could not."

"And in a spontaneous moment of honesty, or perhaps because he didn't wish to spend the remainder of his days in the tunnels, Neive confessed to being an earth element," Shefek said archly, but Kai could tell by the strain in his voice that he, too, was unnerved by the darkness of the tunnels.

"Ah, it's better than that," Slipper argued. "Once he knew he was among others like himself, he was glad of the company. He makes a good Waterling, Kai; you'll know that when you see him."

Kai snorted. "In the old days I would have read him straight off, first day he'd acome into the shop. Since the Bird, I've lost the habit."

"Anyways, once he figured out what I was doing, he tried using his element to guide us through the rock. And it worked. Then between us, what I knew from the water and what he learned from the stone, we found you. But Kai," Slipper said softly, "even if Neive hadn't been there, I'd have kept looking for you until I found you. You know that, don't you?"

"Yeah," Kai answered simply.

"Oran help us," Shefek groaned. "Is that a light ahead?"

"Yeah," Slipper answered, and Kai could almost hear him smiling. "Market Square. Main tunnel."

"Is there a way out for me?" Shefek asked, and his voice held the tremor of desperation.

"Yeah, not too far away. But are you sure it's safe?"

"I don't care. I can't stay here anymore."

Shefek stopped talking as they entered the large cavern of the main tunnel. After the darkness of the tunnels, it was like entering into a sunlit room. Neive had started a fire, and around the edges of the cavern, groups of people turned anxious faces toward them.

"You made it!" Farier cried, bounding across the cavern to meet them. "I wasn't sure you had survived. We heard the screams, but we didn't dare stop."

"I did like you asked, Slipper," Neive said proudly as he poked at the fire with an old chair leg. "Brought 'em all here and didn't lose a one of them."

"You did a good job, too," Slipper answered. "Weren't scared?"

"Not too much."

"How about you?" Kai asked Farier. "Were you and your people scared in the dark?

Farier nodded his head. "Terrified. I hate the dark," he confessed, and looking up at the high ceiling, he shuddered. "But I hate the Sileans more."

"Then our agreement?"

"It holds," Farier said firmly.

"What agreement?" Slipper asked, frowning.

Kai turned to him and smiled. "This is the home of the New Moon now. Beldan's army of snitches, vaggers, Waterlings, and Guildsmen. All together. What do you think, Slipper?"

Slipper grinned, his teeth fanning out from edge to edge across his long face. "Yeah. It's not bad, Kai. Not bad at all." He looked at Farier and then pointed to a number of barrels stacked against the walls. "There's some dried fruits in there, that is if the rats ain't got to them first. And there's some blankets over there."

"Maps?" Farier said quickly, his glance straying to the ceiling again. "Can you give us maps of the tunnel?"

"Yeah. Later. Take care of your people first. I got other things to do right now."

Farier withdrew with a sympathetic nod, but not without first touching Kai lightly on the shoulder. It was a gesture of respect, and in the gratitude on his face, she also saw quiet astonishment.

Kai shivered as a cold draft sucked through the tunnel. Slipper stripped off his jacket and draped it around her shoulders. She leaned into him, exhausted. He set her down gently and went to fetch a cup of water from a barrel that collected the drops from small trickles running down the cavern wall. He gave it to her and she pursed her lips at the familiar sour taste of rust.

He laughed at her expression and then his face became somber. "Z'blood Kai," he whispered as he brushed away the dirt on her cheek. "I was afraid I'd lost you for good."

Kai brought her hand to her face, feeling the sting of tears. "I must look awful. No hair, beat up and brangled. Stinking like someone else's shit." Kai choked back the sobs but her shoulders heaved uncontrollably. Slipper drew her close to his chest and held her carefully so as not to press against the welts on her back.

"Don't matter to me, Kai, you know that."

"Slipper," Kai said between stifled sobs. "I was afraid I'd lost you, too." She looked up at him and he beamed at her.

Shefek's gravelly voice interrupted them. "Well, my raven and hawk united." He squatted down on his haunches, one hand resting on the ground for balance, the other, his injured arm, resting limply across his thigh. Little white feathers floated around him. "As it should be," he murmured. "But it should also be that I am once more on my way."

"Where?" Kai asked, struggling to stand up. She grimaced with pain and Shefek restrained her.

"North. To Sadar. I was a fool to wait this long. My arm will not heal enough for me to fly this time." He slapped his thigh. "Shank's mare, it must be."

"But why Sadar?"

"Jobber is there. I know it now. Felt the change in the currents of air just before we came underground." Sefek's expression was distant, his eyes fixed on another place. "I've got to get there and soon."

"Or else?"

Shefek shook his head, brushing away the feather that clung to his lips. "Damn feathers," he muttered.

"Or else what?" Kai insisted.

"That remains to be seen. There are a number of possibilities. Not all of them include me. But I believe I am needed all the same. So I am leaving."

"Now?"

"Now," he answered firmly. "Will you show me the way out of here?" he asked Slipper.

Slipper shook his head. "I'm needed here, with Kai. Neive, think you can find the way to Grapler's Bridge?"

"In the Pleasure district?" Neive answered, scratching his head.

"That's it."

"Yeah. Easy enough."

"Take Shefek, he's leaving."

Neive nodded and stood.

Shefek chuckled and then glanced at Slipper. "Spoken like an officer in the New Moon, Slipper." The light sparkled in the twin disks of his eyes. "Grapler's Bridge. Isn't that where we met?"

"So it is," Slipper said with a lopsided grin. "So it is."

"Oran's peace be with you both," Shefek said as he stood, his knees creaking. He frowned at them and gave them a little slap.

"Good-bye, Shefek," Kai said softly. "Take care of yourself."

"We'll meet again."

"Do you say that with a Kirian's sight?"

Shefek paused, considering. A hand stroked the silver whiskers, brushing away the remaining stains of blood. "I will return to Beldan. And with luck, so will the New Moon of Sadar."

"Then tell Jobber, when you see her, that we'll be ready and waiting when she comes back," Kai replied.

"So I will, so I will," Shefek said softly.

He left with Neive, casting one final glance over his shoulder before he disappeared down the tunnels. His eyes were round, glowing disks, reflecting the firelight of the cavern. Then they winked shut, and all that remained was a downy, white feather, drifting slowly as it was caught in the rising updraft of warm air.

Chapter Nineteen

Silwa stood on the plains of Sadar in the early dawn and shook his head. A dry, hot wind blew across the barren plain of gray, compacted soil, scattered with loose gravel. The plain lay like a shallow dish surrounded by tall spires of pink and gray granite that formed a wall of stone. At the base of the peaks were slag heaps of slate-gray shale, their jagged edges sharp and brittle. His maps had shown a river cascading between two of the peaks behind Sadar. All there was now was a dry gorge splitting the rock face of the mountain. Nothing grew on the plain, not even the tough stalks of mountain grass whose roots could dig deep and crack the granite in search of water.

What a wretched place, Silwa thought. Hardly the sort of place he'd have chosen to make a final stand. At least the remains of Sadar were interesting. The ancient stone Keep perched on the precipice of one tall spire, its craggy face staring down morosely at the plain. The sides of the mountain were scarred with the trails of steps and pathways that once marked the many entrances up the steep side slopes to the Keep. The rain and wind had done their work, hammering away at the stone walls until much of the Keep appeared as a careless tumble of rock. Only two square towers remained intact, bridged by a walkway and para-pet that rose over a main gate. Farther up, behind Sadar, Silwa could see the ridged fields sliced into the side of the mountain, held by terraces of stone.

"Reies," Silwa barked, tapping his thigh in thought.

"Sir?"

"What do you make of it?"

"I don't think they're here," Reies answered, squinting as he followed Silwa's moody stare up the slopes of Sadar.

"Oh, they're here, all right. The bastards are hiding. Like vermin."

"But sir, the scouts we sent out said there was no sign of them."

Silwa turned, his face full of disgust. "The two scouts that returned, Reies. And what of the three scouts that did not return?"

Reies didn't answer, rather shifted his feet and adjusted the weight of his sword on his belt.

Silwa turned back to stare at the Keep. "They're not stupid, Reies. Remember that. They chose this place wisely. How much water do we have?"

Reies thought a moment before answering. "Enough for two nights. Three with rationing, then we'll have to fall back."

"Two nights," Silwa repeated, growing irritated. "Our disadvantage, then. I'll wager your inheritance they've water somewhere hidden in the Keep. An underground spring perhaps. But we have only two days in which to make a decisive attack." Silwa was quiet, considering his situation. The troops would hold for another day or two, if they had something to fight. The night raids and the surprise attacks by archers had unnerved most of the Silean soldiers newly arrived to Oran. They were used to open battles, squads of men lined up across the fields advancing upon a visible enemy, not a silent enemy that attacked at night. Rumors of Oran magic were spreading and he had seen the warding-off gesture, thumb to forehead and chin, repeated often throughout the camp. The local Silean militia had done well, though. One of them had even managed to kill his night attacker. Silwa had found it distasteful that the guard mutilated the body of the New Moon fighter afterward, but he said nothing about it, knowing it was an effective way to draw off fear in the camp. The New Moon were mortals, given to bleeding and dying the same as any.

Silwa pursed his lips. War was a gamble with nerves and emotions; play your men like a tune filled with hate, blood lust, overwhelm them with the power of their weapons and the thrill of battle. When placed into battle by an officer's skilled hand, each man became a god dispensing death, and each man became supremely selfish, clamoring to save his own miserable skin. What emotions did the New Moon have? he wondered. The same perhaps, but tethered to others; righteousness and heroic sentimentality. Silwa smiled. Was that enough to change peasants into soldiers? Or would they panic like scattered sheep when confronted with real weapons?

"Oy, Reies, have the Orans in camp bound and brought here immediately," Silwa ordered smartly.

"All of them?" came the confused question.

"All," Silwa snapped. "And be quick."

Reies saluted and turned on his heel. At the edge of camp, amidst the fluttering of Silean pennants, Reies bawled out Silwa's order. Troops in black and gray uniforms dispersed to round up every page, herdboy, and serving woman, every Oran peasant they'd conscripted along the march to Sadar. The sounds of the women's terrified wailing rose up to the spires of Avadares.

"What do you think?" Faul asked Zein, leaning her chin against the wall of Sadar's walkway.

"I had hoped we could take out more," Zein answered. His brown tattooed cheek was covering with a light dusting of gray powder from the stones.

"Do you think they've figured we're here?" Treys asked.

"Silwa's no fool," Faul said. At that they heard the wailing of women from the camp. "Z'Blood," she swore as the shrill noise reached them. She squinted hard to see better across the plain to the encampment of Sileans below. "What's he doing?"

"Jabbing spears into a haystack, waiting for us to jump out," Zein answered.

"Sounds more like he's jabbing peasants," Faul retorted.

Zein looked out over the parapets, feeling his belly grip with anger. The screaming continued, and every cry scraped razor sharp across his face.

"Look," Treys cried out, and pointed to the mounted soldiers, riding slowly toward the middle of the plain. Behind them, struggling to keep up and not fall, were ten Oran peasants, bound together by the wrists. The riders stopped a short distance from camp and untied the ropes that dragged the peasants. Their horses wheeled around quickly and they began to gallop back.

The peasants, still bound by the wrists but freed from the Silean Guard, stared with frightened confused faces at each other. Without a word they began to run toward the Keep, pulling those that ran too slowly.

"Oh, no," Zein whispered, suddenly seeing the line of Silean crossbowmen standing at the edge of the camp. The crossbowmen knelt, one foot to the stirrup of their crossbows as they pulled the cord back, secured it, and loaded a bolt. "No!" Zein cried, knowing it was useless, as he saw them take aim and fire the bolts at the backs of the fleeing peasants. The force of the bolts pitched them violently forward, slamming and rolling them against the hard stony soil. One boy had escaped the barrage of arrows and was struggling to free his wrist from the bounds that shackled him to the others lying dead or dying on the plain. Frantically he scratched at the heavy ropes, his eyes glancing up in terror as he watched the crossbowmen reload. He pulled at the rope, yanked it, trying desperately to free his hands, all the while screaming at the dead to release him. Zein hardly felt the hard stone scrape against his ribs as he pressed himself fiercely against the walls. He heard the sharp bark of an order, and then the angry twang of the fired bolts silenced the boy's pleas.

Zein turned away and saw Treys at his shoulder, murmuring words softly, his face etched with sorrow. A prayer, Zein thought, and turned back angrily to stare at the dead, studded with the pointed black fletches of the Silean bolts. They needed more than prayers.

Two more horseman appeared, and behind them another line of Oran peasants shuffled and scraped, trying to keep up. Once again, the horses wheeled and turned back to the camp. This time, the freed peasants didn't hesitate. Holding on to each other, they ran, zigzagging across the plains, trying to outdistance the bolts. And again, the Silean crossbowmen reloaded their weapons and fired the steel-tipped bolts into the backs of the peasants.

"Zein!" Treys said sharply. "We have to do something!"

"We can't," Zein answered. He gripped the stone tightly and his knuckles turned white with fury.

"We have no choice," Treys argued. "How can we stand here and watch our own people killed?"

"It's what the Sileans want! Don't you see? Silwa is trying to force us into an open war. He wants us to show ourselves. We can't win against them like that."

"Zein, we will lose if we do nothing," Treys spoke slowly. "This battle at Sadar was to prove to the Oran people that the time was right to force the Sileans from our land. That we of the New Moon would fight for them. Instead, our people will think that we betrayed them, fled, and left them victim to the Sileans." He leaned heavily on his staff, tearing his gaze away from the corpses on the plain. "We must fight for them. We must," he insisted. "Look, our people are ready. Just say the word."

Zein turned around and saw the New Moon's army gathered at the lower courtyard. They looked up at him, waiting. Weapons shifted from hand to hand as a restlessness stirred across them, like wind over water. He recognized most of those with the brown tattoos that marked their faces. They were the remnants of Huld's army. They had been here before. But this time there was no Queen Huld to shield them from the worst of the battle. Zein's gaze wandered over the others gathered in the courtyard; Farnon and his laborers waited, their shouldered pikes and scythes sharpened; Veira was surrounded by her archers, the green and gold fletches like leaves among the longbows; the iron-hard expressions of the northern miners, ferriers, and plow makers; and next to them a solid knot of Oran women, scarves tied tight around their heads, their hands holding the curved sickles. Zein wavered, knowing the certainty of their failure if they fought the Sileans on their own terms. And yet as he heard again the screams of the fleeing peasants and the harsh snap of bolts splitting the wind, he knew that they wouldn't turn away. A stalling tactic then. One that might allow some of his people to escape into the mountains before it was through.

"Raise the standard," he ordered. They would show themselves then to the Sileans. A man lunged up the narrow stairs, running to the outer edge of the eastern tower. It was Eneas, his blond hair whipping in the wind and the Oran smock gusting like a sail around his body. He reached the flagpoles and Zein heard the scratchy creak of rusted pulleys as the flag of the New Moon lifted into the sky. Against the pale blue of the dawn sky, the broad square of black cloth unfurled in the wind, and on its face a rising new moon glowed with gold threads.

Zein clambered down the eroded stone stairs to the central courtyard. Standing on the rim of a cracked and dry fountain, he called out orders to those gathered. "We will divide our forces—"

"That's murder," someone shouted from the crowd. "We're too few as it is."

Zein squinted to see who spoke and recognized Veira, Huld's markings on her face a dark brown against her amber-colored cheeks.

"I agree that it is not the best of situations, Veira. But I think it the better position to appear as if we are stronger by threatening the Sileans from different points. Make them divide their forces, tempt them to defend their flanks as well as the front line. In that we have the advantage. They don't know the mountains. We do. I want a front line of archers to take out as many of the Sileans as we can. Distract them for a while. The rest are to divide into smaller units and begin driving against their flanks. Force them to divide their officers and their troops."

"You'll need someone to defend your back," Treys said. "One unit will remain here for that purpose."

"Agreed," replied Zein. "Go, take two of the units along the north ridge, and Veira, can you and the horses give them some trouble along the southern face?"

"Yes," she answered briskly, picking out those who would go with her.

Zein nodded. "All of you, be prepared to withdraw quickly if needed. Inflict what damage you can, but when it goes hard against you, get out."

Zein stopped speaking, mentally counting the arches of the longbows and the full quivers slung high over their shoulders. How many of them were left? Not as many as he would have liked, but still enough to inflict losses on the Silean army. The Silean crossbow was powerful, but slow and hard to load. Its bolt, though deadly, had a short range. One good Oran archer, with a full quiver of arrows and a longbow, could outshoot the Sileans in distance and speed. And they could do it standing or riding a horse.

Suddenly they heard the blaring horns of the Silean cavalry and the faint barking of orders being issued. Zein stared out at the upturned faces of the New Moon army. Again, he was called to battle. But not like last time when he went unwillingly, forced by Zorah's armies into acts of killing. He had few Ghazali scruples left to hinder him now. This was a battle that he would welcome.

Faul watched Zein as he spoke, her hand tapping impatiently against the hilt of her sword.

"The Sileans have forced our hand," Zein was saying, "pressed us into a battle not of our own design." Then he smiled, his teeth flashing white against the dark skin, and he raised his fist. "We shall show them that the Oran people are not without courage."

"Or frigging foolhardiness," Faul murmured softly. She looked over at Alwir and Wyer, their faces flushed, hands clasped around their weapons. She snorted. They'd go out naked for the New Moon, she thought. And what are your reasons for being here, Faul Verran? she chided herself. About to end your pissing life against Silean steel? Love for the rebellion? She shook her head. That gave her credit for more goodness than she had. Revenge for the slaughter of innocent peasants at Cairns? Not a bad reason, she thought, feeling the lurch in her stomach as she recalled the stench of the dead. Or was it duty? Faul weighed this sudden thought, seeing for a moment the elegant cold face of the Queen, followed by the furious dirt-smudged countenance of Jobber. She winced at their glaring differences and at the same time the stark realization of their similarities. Once a Firstwatch, always a Firstwatch, she thought. The Fire Queen Zorah no longer wanted Faul's services. But Jobber did, and it was for Jobber alone, for the promise that stinking gutter brat held for the future of Oran, that Faul knew she would join Treys and defend Sadar.

"Well, this is it at last," Faul said to Alwir, whose narrow face was concentrating on stringing his bow.

He looked up and gave her a quick smile. "I'm ready."

"Why are the young always so quick to embrace death?" Faul asked with a wry smile.

"Jobber once accused me of running away from a battle I initiated. She was right. I've been waiting for this moment—"

"To redeem yourself?"

"Yes."

"How is it Jobber got us both here, while she's back at camp drinking down my brandy?" Faul asked.

Alwir was about to defend Jobber when he saw the amused expression on Faul's face. "Better than having her here, giving us her opinions on everything."

"Bitching and cursing—"

"And probably getting herself killed," Alwir said.

"Defending us," Faul finished with a slow shake of her head.

"Maybe it is better to think of her getting drunk on my brandy, and then sleeping it off under some bush." Faul squeezed Alwir's shoulder lightly. "Fire's luck today," she murmured, and went to join Treys on the parapets.

The New Moon army scurried through the courtyard, gathering weapons and saddling their scrubby horses. Veira led her units through the crumbling archways and through the back gates of the Keep. From there they would follow the herd paths, along the upper rim of the dried riverbed to the southern face of the mountains. Go embraced Zein, holding him for a long moment before he released him. Then he left, taking his troops with him through the underground passageways beneath Sadar. The passageways would eventually open out into the caves that pocked the face of the northern ridge.

The remaining archers took up their stations along the parapets of the Keep and across the main gate. In the courtyard below, Treys and Faul waited with the rest of the unit, pikes and spears flashing in the morning sun. At a nod from Zein, Alwir pulled the red tin battle flute from his pocket and began to play. A shrill tune spilled over the sides of the Keep and swept across the plain to the Silean camp.

Silwa heard the music and smiled. A challenge at last. He stepped out of the shade of his tent and saw the flag flying over the tower. And he hadn't even had to kill that many, he thought mildly. He grunted. Sentimental shitheads. He'd send them to their graves today, grind the seditious bastards into the stones. And return home a new hero.

"Reies!" he bellowed, and hurried to his horse. A page waited to help him up into the saddle. "Prepare the troops to advance. There's a flat ridge at the top of the slope to the main gate. We should be able to use the battering ram against the gate. And bring up the mantelets. I want as many men against the wall as possible. Attilio!" Silwa called to a second officer.

"Sir!" Attilio answered, already mounted on his horse. Silwa smiled at the man, the polished silver buttons of his uniform sparkling brightly in the rising dawn. But not as bright as his teeth, Silwa thought. Eager bastard. He was one of the Silean militia, whose father owed a broad estate in the western plains. "Take the Silean militia and guard our flanks. I don't much like the looks of these mountains. Too many places for them to hide."

Attilio jerked the reins of his horse and galloped through the camp, calling out to the Silean militia. Within moments they were mounted, their horses kicking up a curtain of gray dust as they spread out to either side of the plain.

Silwa watched them ride away with satisfaction. It was his game now. From astride his charger, he gave the command to move and the Silean army lurched forward, spreading out across the plain of Sadar like an unfurled bolt of black and gray cloth. They trampled over the bodies of the Oran peasants as they marched forward, sights fixed on the rising gates of Sadar. Silwa rode behind the rows of crossbowmen and foot soldiers, watching the parapets of Sadar. He saw the New Moon army step forward, their bows held up over the walls, quietly waiting the approach of the Sileans. He was almost disappointed when he saw how few of them there were.

"Wait, wait," Zein ordered, watching the Sileans approach. He had already noted the flanks of Silean militia, their faces turned toward the southern and northern ridge. Grimly he hoped that Go and Veira would remember to pull back if they started taking too many casualties.

Zein tightened his hold on the bow, the string laid back to his ear. He judged the moment the Silean crossbowmen were in range of the Oran longbow, but still short of their own range. The morning sun peeked out from behind the mountains, rising over Sadar and shining brightly into the faces of the advancing Sileans. In that blinding moment Zein shouted "NOW!" From the parapets came the snapping and whirling of Oran arrows. The first line of crossbowmen fell beneath a hail of arrows. But Zein and the rest didn't stop firing. They continued to ply their bows, arms flexed to retrieve a new arrow, fire, and then retrieve another. Only in the relentless snow of arrows could they hope to outmatch the slower skills of the crossbowmen. Zein heard the cries of men dying, the stinging whir of arrows, and the roaring of Silean officers. He felt the cold thrill of a clean kill, the arrows finding their mark. And beneath that, he felt burning shame as he abandoned forever the Ghazali way.

Alwir heard the sudden thunder of voices and turned to see Veira's unit tearing down the shale face of the southern mountains, firing their arrows from the backs of their ponies. The Silean militia surged forward to meet them accompanied by the screeching of clashing swords and the high-pitched whinnying of terrified horses.

Thunk! A Silean's bolt sped past Alwir's ear and buried itself in the archer next to him. The man spun like an autumn leaf in the air and fell over the sides of the parapets. Alwir laid another arrow against his cheek and searched for his own target among the advancing crossbowmen.

"Move that ram up here, damn you!" Silwa cried, galloping his horse to the middle of his troops. "Get it up to that gate and be quick." The ground rumbled with the heavy wheels of the ram, soldiers grunting as they strained to push it up the slopes. "Bring up the mantelets," he called to another unit that struggled behind the cumbersome weight of the wooden shields. Sheltered behind the wooden wall, other soldiers carried the ladders they would use to scale the walls once the mantelets were in position. Silwa rode back and forth across the lines, encouraging his men, shouting orders to close the ranks and keep the lines together. As the Silean armies rose up over the slopes of Sadar, Silwa glanced back once, cursing when he saw how many of the gray and black uniforms littered the field behind them.

Zein ducked and shouted down to Treys. "They've succeeded in bringing the ram over the ridge. We'll try to keep them off the wall, but you'll have to handle to gate."

Treys raised his fist in answer and his unit moved forward into position. Over the main gate was a smaller walkway enabling a handful of fighters to perch almost directly over the attacking Sileans. As the Sileans wheeled the battering ram forward, its metal point driving against the doors, archers fired arrows at the soldiers. Those that fell, killed or wounded, were immediately replaced by others behind them. With every thrust, the ram sent shock waves through the ancient Keep, booming like the doleful knell of a bell.

Zein cast a worried glance at the southern ridge. He could see Veira's people pinned down, wedged between boulders, trying to pick off the Silean militia as they scrambled up after them. They had lost a lot of their horses and Zein wished Veira would hurry and get her people out of there before it was too late. To the north Zein saw Go, leading a small wedge-shaped charge. They had waited until the Sileans were nearly on them and then burst from the mouth of a cave. Zein could just make out the flashing of Go's long-handled pike as he swung the weapon, running on foot through the mounted soldiers, killing horses and men alike. From the shelter of two other caves, archers continued to fire arrows, forcing the Sileans to slip and fragment as they tried to avoid the attack.

Another shock wave from the ram caused the Keep to shudder and Zein heard the splintering of wood. He looked down and saw the long gash cutting through the wood of the gates. The mantelets had reached the walls and now along the walls of the parapets the Sileans were raising ladders to scale the sides of Sadar. Damn, Zein thought as he fitted an arrow and shot a man off a ladder. Two more and then another followed behind him, swarming the walls. Damn, Zein swore again as he shot another. Then he stopped thinking as the Sileans poured over the top of Sadar, their swords drawn.

Eneas raised a sword defensively as the head of a Silean soldier appeared over the sides of the parapet. The soldier wasn't much older himself, his eyes staring wildly as he shouted and swung his sword. With a two-handed grip Eneas brought his blade down in a blazing arc across the man's face, stepping back with horrified satisfaction as the blade cleaved the features in two and blood sprayed over his hands and chest. He wanted to vomit, but another soldier drew his attention and in panic he swung his sword upward, his teeth gritting against the shock of the crashing blades and the shrill screech of the metal. With his back forced against the stones of Sadar's Keep, Eneas fought. And as each slashing stroke excised his Silean identity, he replaced it with the newfound fury of an Oran, struggling to survive. Not for Shedwyn and not even for Cairns did he fight at last, but for himself and what he wished to become.

Farnon spared a glance and saw Eneas, cornered against the parapet as a Silean soldier swung back and forth, gouging an opening in the youth's defenses. Farnon sprinted up the stairs, knocking Sileans over the sides with his long-handled pike as he cleared a path to Eneas. He swung sideways, cutting the backs of a Silean's legs. As the man buckled, screaming in his agony, Farnon stabbed him deeply with the pike. The bloodied man fell across Eneas, who thrust him away with desperate fury. Close to the edge of the parapet, Eneas stumbled and started to fall. Farnon caught him with one large outstretched hand and dragged him back. Eneas was saying something, his lips beginning to move, when Farnon was jolted from behind. He howled in rage, his back arched sharply, and he released his hold on Eneas. Farnon toppled forward into Eneas's arms, gazing down in surprise at the point of the Silean bolt that was exiting from his chest. The steel tip sprouted between his ribs amid a stain of blood. Farnon closed his eyes, aware only that Eneas laid him down gently. The gravel pressed into his cheek and he opened his eyes a final time, to glimpse the seams of gray stones etched with a spreading pool of his blood. As he heard the breath leave him, the air rattling through the remnants of his shattered chest, he felt a tremor shudder through the Keep followed by the victorious shouts of the Sileans as the ram cracked and splintered the gates of Sadar. "Bastards," he muttered as he died, "they've breached the gate."

Faul gritted her teeth, waiting for the horseman to reach her. She saw his wide-open mouth surrounded by a black beard and heard his shouted curses. As he leaned his body forward, poised over the neck of his horse, sword upright and ready to swing, she stepped to the side, dragging her blade under the horse's chest. A huge gout of blood burst from the wounded beast, and it collapsed, sending the man on its back toppling forward onto her returning swing. Not for the first time Faul marveled at the sword, at its strength and the ease with which it could cut and slash as if nothing in the world, not even the stones, could stop it. Without turning, she heard another Silean closing in behind her. She passed the sword to her left hand and drove the blade backward. She felt it push against his uniform, the momentary resistance of the squared end point as it penetrated flesh, and then the whispered sigh as it slid from the body, its deadly task completed. She swung the blade forward, changed hands, and prepared for the next attack.

She glanced around quickly, taking in the smaller battles being waged around the courtyard. Treys was surrounded by four Sileans, rooted to the spot, his pike's blade sculling the air. She grunted lightly, reminded of his ring of carved trees. The Sileans were not as obliging as his trees, for they fell, hacked and wounded beneath his rapid strokes.

But it wasn't going as well with the others. Faul saw the bodies of other New Moon fighters, some covered with bolts, others dismembered, dying where they had fought. Exhaustion was creeping through her body, replacing the eager fury of early battle. How much longer? she thought, and then drove the question away as she dodged a Silean's attack.

"How much farther?" Jobber cried out to the frightened birds that scattered at her approach. It seemed as if she had been running most of the night, seeing in the distant twinkling of stars the bright gleam of light on the sword's edge. Since the morning she had felt the stirring of the Fire Sword, heard its shrill voice calling out to her.

"Frigging shit," Jobber swore, tripping over the stones. Someone was handling the sword, someone who didn't know how to use it, how to make it sing its fearful song. Fire blistered her palms with the longing to hold the sword again.

Jobber stopped abruptly in her tracks. Before her appeared the crumbling back of Sadar's Keep, lifting out of the scrubby ridge like a mountain of gray stone. Now that she was here, the sight of it raised an unexpected terror for her. It was the place of her nightmares. She hesitated, not wanting to approach closer, the fear becoming more palpable. She felt trapped, unable to move or look away. The sword was here. Here in this place. She could feel it, sense its metallic soul. She would have to enter within the dark granite walls of Sadar to take what was rightfully hers. Jobber shook her head in the wind, feeling the fiery red hair billow about her face. Blue sparks crackled angrily. On the morning breeze she heard the piercing cry of the battle flute and the answered roar of men and women joined in battle. So, she thought, Silwa was here. It had already begun.

Jobber gasped, her hand clamping around the air as she sensed the Fire Sword released once more from its scabbard. The fire touched bone and blood, passed through again to the cooling air. But it wasn't enough. The Fire Sword cried out to Jobber, and the desire to hold it again boiled in her heart.

"Go on, Jobber," she coaxed herself, feeling as though a hand pressed against the small of her back, pushing her from behind, while another drew her on. "Through the back of the Keep. No one will stop you."

She lowered her head and began to run, her arms pumping the morning air as her long legs reached out to shorten the journey.

* * *

"Shedwyn, stop!" Lirrel called.

"No, I can't," Shedwyn answered, refusing to slow her pace.

"We must, the children can't keep up."

"Go as you must," Shedwyn said without turning around. "I will see you there." And she continued on, her body set squarely on the path before her, the small stones erupting around her as she passed.

Lirrel stopped short, her chest heaving, her mouth open wide as she tried to catch her breath. Her heart slammed into her ribs as much from fear as from running.

Dagar reached her and took her by the arm.

"Shall I try and catch her?" he asked, his grave face pale in the early-morning light.

"It's no good," Lirrel said, swallowing thickly. "I must try some other way to stop this battle between them."

"Can we do anything?" Finch joined them, her hands forced against her hip. She spoke in short gasps as a stitch in her side stole away her breath with darts of pain.

Lirrel glanced up at the sky, watching the few clouds capture the pink light of the rising sun. "It is like the past has come again. Two Queens unable to speak to each other, filled with hate. And on the plains, people die." Slowly she lowered her head, then jerked it up in startled surprise. "That's it," she said softly. "The past has come again."

"What are you going to do?" Dagar asked. Children clustered around him as once the goats did. But they were silent, each trying to gain a breath, their young faces strained with exhaustion.

"A vision of the past," Lirrel said. "There on the plain."

"Yes!" said Mole, his eyes widening. The light of the morning sun colored his pale face. "With all the dead—"

"Old and new," finished Trap, pulling back her white hair to show her frightened face.

"But we lost that one," Dagar objected.

"It is meant to frighten the Sileans," Lirrel argued. "It will give the impression that there are more of the New Moon."

"But a lot more of them as well!" Dagar countered.

"Yes, but wounded and dying. How can they give commands to men who are illusions? It will confuse them and give me a chance."

"To do what?" Dagar nearly shouted.

"To stop Shedwyn and Jobber from killing each other."

"Lirrel," Mole started to say, touching Lirrel sadly on the shoulder. "There ain't none of us here—"

"Got the skill to make a vision like that," Trap finished. She drew the edges of her coat tighter together.

"I will do it. I can bring forth a vision of a battle. But you"— Lirrel pointed to all of the children—"all of you will have to hold the vision as best you can. Together it can be done."

"We'll try!" shouted a boy, and Lirrel saw that it was Arnard Brestin. He had tied a red scarf around his neck and it brightened the pallor of his sweating face.

"I'm on for it," came another cry, this one from a girl with long black braids. She was a miner's daughter, her hands stained blue from the coal.

"Count the Waterlings in," Finch said, letting go of her side and straightening her back. Mole and Trap nodded solemnly.

"We have to hurry," Lirrel urged. "There's no time to lose."

She drew a deep breath and started running again, her feet pounding over the rocky path to Sadar. Dagar jogged next to her, casting her worried glances. She turned around to encourage the others and felt her tired spirit gather new strength. Strung out behind her like a collection of motley beads, the children of Oran ran to Sadar's Keep.

Shedwyn reached the back gates of Sadar and paused long enough to rest her hand against the flanks of stone. She smiled at the familiar cold touch of the granite. She stared through the smoke of battle and found the path she wanted, up the stairs that led to the parapet. With every step she took the stones mingled with her flesh, rumbling to greet her. "Returned," they whispered in grinding voices. "She has returned to us at last."

Shedwyn wanted to stop, to take welcome from the stone. She could feel herself slowly transformed by the glittering mica and the pink-veined granite. The screams of the horses and the groans of dying men and women mattered hardly as much as the sounds of the rumbled song, this long-awaited cry of joy echoing in the Keep of Sadar. Her skin was cold to the touch, rough and hard like the granite surface. She touched her breast and it felt impenetrable to the arrows that buzzed like angry wasps. Her hair had come undone from its braid and unfurled in waves about her. Shedwyn lifted her hand to her face, surprised and yet content to see it mottled like the granite; along her wrist the gray veins lined the pink stone. And deep within her core, she sensed the solid flesh of Oran's body, her element as dense as the hard-packed soil and as brittle as the shale.

A vagger tore past her, weaponless, and then turned and cried out in astonishment. The man fell to his knees, his head bowed before her.

"Queen Huld," he shouted. "You've come at last."

"Huld?" Shedwyn answered distantly, and then remembered with a flash of fury why she was here. Not to greet again the stones of Sadar, but to find Zorah. To keep her from the sword. She reached down and brusquely lifted the man to his knees. "The girl, where is she?" she demanded, her voice booming in her ears.

"What girl?"

"Zorah!"

The vagger shook his head, confused and frightened. "We have not seen her. Has she come with Silwa?"

Impatiently Shedwyn let him go and turned away, to continue her search along the parapet. She shoved aside the bodies of fallen men, scarcely paying them a glance. Her eyes stared over the courtyard, feeling Zorah's presence, sensing the heat of fire. She stumbled over a man. As she lifted herself she saw his face. It was a farmer's face, scrubbed by the winds and sun, tanned a deep leathery brown. Even in death, the squared jaw was defiant. Shedwyn stared at him, recognition creeping slowly to her. She touched the worn smock and saw the ugly shaft of the Silean quarrel.

"Farnon," she whispered to the man. "Farnon," she repeated. The name blew across her skin like the summer wind, bringing with it a memory of the farms, the scent of hay, tobacco, and dung. Her hand trembled and on her skin the gray-mottled shades of the stone faded, replaced by the warm glow of flesh. And then it seemed the stone closed around her again and the name was thrust from her mind as the reek of copper filled her nostrils. Shedwyn stood slowly, her knees aching with cold. She saw the red flame of hair on the far parapets. A white face stared back at her from beneath the blazing crown. Ignoring the vague stirrings of doubt, she was seized by hatred.

Jobber stared wide-eyed at the battle. She had sensed the current of magic shift and flow through her, and her emotions raced violently between gloating satisfaction and terror. Her ears buzzed, and she shook her head, the red firehair crackling with her agitation. Blue and gold sparks ignited in the air, and the sharp smell of copper joined the acrid stench of smoke and battle. This was her moment. Her chance at last. Why was she holding back? With the Fire Sword, she would take them at Sadar and that would be the end of it.

No! Jobber thought suddenly confused. Take who at Sadar? Her body tingled, flushed with heat. She looked across the expanse of courtyard and saw the wintry face of Huld staring at her from the far parapet. *"Huld!"* she said savagely. Fury erupted in her heart, as if the scorching heat of her hate might erase the wintry smile on Huld's stone face. And then Jobber turned away in furious desperation.

"My sword!" she roared. "Give me my sword!" It was nearby. She could feel the pulse of liquid fire echoed in her own heart. She looked down at the courtyard below, trying to find in the multitudes of battles the one person who wrongly carried her sword, her bright shining soul. Each cut it made sang in Jobber's ears, deafened her to the cries of the battle. She ducked to avoid the swinging slash of a Silean sword, kicking out with her leg to topple him. But she had no thought of killing him, only getting him out of her way as she searched for her sword. She would have her weapon and then she would have Huld.

"Not much more," Silwa shouted to Reies. His horse pranced, avoiding the fallen bodies and responding to the excitement of the rider. Silwa was happy. The New Moon had offered a fight. Not much of one, but enough to revive the passion of war. The lust of battle. He'd had one or two good kills, and around him the shouting of men, the dust and heat rising from the battered plain, filled him with a sense of well-being. This is where he belonged. His gaze flickered up the parapets, following the ladders and lines of Sileans pouring over the top. Not much longer now, he thought triumphantly.

Then he stopped and frowned. He drew the reins tight to still his restive horse and peered at the far wall of the west tower. He watched as people scraped cautiously along the ancient wall. Too small to be adults, he thought, studying their figures, black against the bright sunlight. Children? he guessed, puzzled that the New Moon should have been so desperate as to employ children in its ranks. They appeared unarmed as twenty or so of them spread out along the tower wall, linking hands as they went. His eye followed the parapets farther down, attracted by the sudden burst of billowing red. A banner, he thought at first, and then was shocked as he realized it was a woman's hair.

"Damn!" he swore. The thief with red hair. It had to be the girl reputed to have power.

He urged his horse forward to the main gate, alarm tightening in his gut. His mind leaped to the image of Zorah, wounded with arrows as she rode away from the massacre of Fire Circle like a demon. If the New Moon counted such a one with power among their numbers . . . He cursed again and whipped the flanks of his horse, trying to get to the gates as quickly as possible. Until now the battle had been ordinary, the chain of events expected. But Silwa knew with certainly—as he recognized the firehaired girl on the parapets, and guessed the truth of the children on the tower—that if they carried the old magic, it would change all that.

"Now what?" Finch asked Lirrel, clinging tightly to her hand. They had followed Lirrel over the dried riverbed and had looked down to see Veira and her unit, half of them dead, the other half still valiantly fighting. The underground passageways had led them into one of the towers; they had climbed it unnoticed, and now stood on its high wall, the wind swirling with dust, the air resounding with the cries of battle.

Standing here, high above the plain of Sadar, Lirrel had felt herself almost swept away with anguish at the sight of so much carnage. It was harder than before to quiet the terrified weeping of the smaller children.

"All of you, let me feel your power. Share with me the wealth of your elements. Imagine it as a thread and cast it to me so that I can weave the fabric of a vision. Do you understand this?" she asked. The older ones, like Arnard, Finch, and the twins, lifted their heads proudly, refusing to be terrorized by the ugliness of war. The others struggled to bury their fear and imitate the bravery of their older companions. *"Ahal."* Lirrel nodded and smiled encouragingly when she was certain they were with her. "We begin."

Lirrel closed her eyes to the scenes of violence in the courtyard below. She was afraid to look too closely at the battle, afraid to see her father among them, either fighting or dead. She had to concentrate, to direct her sight inward and see only the past. Using their combined power, she meant to draw the nightmare of the Burning from the stone walls of Sadar's Keep.

On one side Lirrel gripped Finch's hand, its long knobby fingers curled tightly around hers. On the other side she held Arnard Brestin, the wide girth of his palm covered with the calluses of a farmer's son. She was aware of Dagar in front of her, shielding her from the battle below. Her stomach fluttered nervously and she swallowed the rising panic in her throat. Finch gave her hand a squeeze and so did Arnard, to let her know they were ready.

Along the line of children power was called forth, vibrating from one to the other like a plucked string. As each child linked the gift of power to the other, the sound deepened into a chord. Lirrel gasped at the surge of magic, many-hued and layered with the texture and personality of each child. She recognized Finch's affinity for metals, like a vintner's sensitive palate. From Arnard, Lirrel felt teeming life beneath the soil as the fragile roots of wheat barely reached beneath the surface in search of sustenance; from the miner's girl with black braids, she received the gift of water and she could sense where the dew hid among the deposits of shale, dripped beneath the surface and collected into the underground streams. Another child opened Lirrel's senses to the terraced fields, the seeds lying barren in the soil until water could bring them to life. And Lirrel smiled in spite of her fear as she felt the touch of Mole and Trap, twins even in their gift of magic, as their separate identities intertwined one with the other. Oran magic flowed from hand to hand, filling her with wonderment at the rich tapestry of power. Like the center pole of a Ghazali tent, Lirrel stood erect, gathering their power under her control and raising a cloth of magic over the Keep of Sadar.

Lirrel's eyes snapped opened, burning white, and she trembled as she felt the weave of time separate and the past spill through the torn opening. The noise of the battle intensified, and the earth thundered ominously. Thick black smoke rose in twisted columns on the plain. With the shriek of splitting wood, the gates of Sadar burst into a shield of orange flame.

Silwa's horse reared, neighing shrilly at the sight of the flames. He fought to control it but it wheeled around terrified. Silwa saw on the plain behind him an army spread out and fighting. For a confused moment he stared, stunned, at the multitude of Oran peasants battling fiercely with Sileans. Where had they come from? Beyond them twisters advanced, black smoke and fire rising in long triangular columns, their deadly points carving scars on the face of the plain. Silwa turned back to the Keep and bellowed with rage as he saw a new line of longbows firing down at them. He shouted an order to a unit of retreating Sileans, dimly aware of the changes in their uniforms. They ignored him, as if they hadn't heard, and continued careening down the slopes away from the Keep. As they dashed past him, Silwa's horse rose in terror, its front hooves landing heavily and passing through the body of an escaping soldier.

Faul swung her blade and stepped back, bewildered. Something had happened. The courtyard was filled with soldiers and peasants using weapons she had not noticed before. Fire was erupting from the cracks between the stones. Z'blood, what was going on? A band of Sileans threw themselves forward, attacking an Oran fighter. Faul rushed to assist the man. But as she swung the sword, it passed through them with a rush of air, and she jumped back, horrified that nothing she did could change the deadly outcome of their attack. Try as she might, she found no purchase among the ghosts of the Sileans, and as she watched, they hacked the man apart.

"Treys!" Faul shouted above the battle sounds. "Treys!" she cried out again, searching for him among the many small skirmishes in the courtyard. She caught sight of him, backed against a wall, his pike slashing furiously against an attacking Silean. She ran to him and killed the soldier, cursing as she did. "At least this one is real!" she shouted to Treys. "What's happening?"

Before Treys could answer, the sound of rumbling and the scraping of stone drowned out the noise of battle. The walls of Sadar began to explode and crumble, sheering away as they fell inward. Faul looked up and yelled a warning as the stones rained down to the courtyard. She heard the Silean officers shouting, calling for a retreat from the collapsing stones. Treys gripped her shoulder and Faul spun around to face him.

"Look," he cried, pointing to the parapets.

Faul followed his gaze and saw a woman standing on the parapets, broad at the shoulder and wide at the hip. Dark hair billowed behind, and as she turned to the crumbling courtyard, Faul felt the dash of cold shock, recognizing the woman's face. Shedwyn! But her skin was the mottled gray of granite, her cheeks and forehead speckled with glimmering mica.

"That's Shedwyn!" Faul yelled.

"No. It's Huld!" Treys called, his eyes transfixed on the woman. "This is a vision of last battle of the Burning."

"Look, up there on the tower!" Faul said, pointing. "It's Lirrel and the others."

"It must be Lirrel that's doing this," Treys shouted. "We must stop them. Its too dangerous!" He sprinted across the courtyard toward the door of the tower. He collided with a fleeing Silean, whose terrified expression showed clearly his surprise at touching something of substance in the courtyard of battling ghosts.

Faul started to follow Treys but stopped, seeing Silwa unhorsed, his face black with fury, slashing and hacking his way through the fleeing soldiers at the gate. It seemed to make no difference to him that he killed some, while the sword merely passed through others. Faul changed her direction and bore down on him.

On the tower Lirrel struggled to hold together the threads of power that shaped the vision. They snapped fitfully, straining against her grip like the halyards of the *Marigold* in the high winds. Lirrel clung to them, afraid to let go, afraid of the direction the threads seemed to drag her. She could sense Finch and Arnard holding tightly to her, and behind them the tugging of the others. Their resistance was the only thing that kept her from being carried away completely. Her arms ached as if wrenched from their sockets, and in her ears she heard the shrieking howls of Chaos. No, she thought desperately, they were being pulled into the Chaos. It was Zorah's raging void, drawing them in, sucking them into the currents of her whirlpool as it drained away their power. Lirrel had dug deep for enough power to create the vision, and like a young root she had tapped into the layer of Zorah's influence. As Lirrel struggled against the current of magic, she drew more and more upon the strength of Finch and Arnard, the girl with the black braids, Mole and Trap, and all the children. And with a terrible awareness, she knew she could not leave them to help Shedwyn and Jobber, that as they held her back from the edge of Zorah's whirlpool, she, too, was the thin shield that kept them from joining the raging storm of the Chaos. Jobber and Shedwyn would have to fight for themselves. What else could she do?

Lirrel raised her eyes to the sky, seeing the black columns of smoke spiraling high into the clouds. She sagged, tasting the bitterness of defeat. But at her side Finch and Arnard, thinking she wavered from fatigue, redoubled their efforts, and all along the line of children Lirrel felt the spurt of power as each reached deeper into himself. No, she thought angrily, she must not despair, she must keep trying. Huld and Zorah were like fragments in her vision, terrifying images of the past, but with a power to destroy. Shedwyn and Jobber, though caught in the web of the past, belonged to solid flesh of the present. Lirrel began to hum, the notes rising through her throat like a chorus of angry bees. It was not a song of words, or even images; it was the rattle of the heart while in flight, the threading pulse, fearful of battle, and the draining grief of death and exile. There was no hate or revenge in Lirrel's song; that belonged to the old Queens. But rather it was solace that she sang of, the peace that comes at last when pain is shared and loneliness banished.

Faul had engaged Silwa and they were struggling, swords crossed high in front of their faces as they pushed against each other. Jobber's gaze lingered on the figure of Faul and something struck at her consciousness. Loyalty, the faint memory of love. The emotions tangled together as she saw the sharp-angled figure of Faul slip, duck Silwa's attack, and retreat. Faul turned swiftly and swung the sword in a savage upstroke. The memory of Faul was shattered as a radiant flash of white light burst along the edge of the red and silver steel.

Jobber screamed, her ears deafened by the strident cry of the Fire Sword. She had found it at last! Fire bristled around her and thick black smoke veiled her eyes. She could no longer see Faul, but it didn't matter. The clear voice of the sword drew her on, guided her through the dense smoke of the courtyard.

Jobber stepped through a curtain of smoke and saw Faul stumble, wounded, blood flowing from a gash on her side. The sword clattered to the ground and Jobber felt the hardness of the stones jangle her bones when it landed. Silwa had raised his sword, prepared to deal Faul the death stroke. The Fire Sword lay at his feet, and he stepped on it in his eagerness to kill Faul.

Jobber bellowed angrily, feeling Silwa's boot as if it rested on her throat. She grabbed him from him behind, thrusting him away. He turned to strike her, but his sword met only the air as she dove for the sword lying on the ground. She rolled on her back, her eyes meeting Silwa's.

His face was white with rage, blood caked on his face. Gray

lips drew back from his teeth. He raised his sword, his body heaving as he readied himself for this final assault. He drove the sword down into Jobber's prone body. But she rose to meet him, the Fire Sword lifted from ground, and before his sword had reached her, she stabbed him first.

He cried out, hovering impaled on the bright sword. Jobber stared at him as his eyes rolled upward in shock, the whites gleaming. He smiled thinly and blood trickled from the corners of his mouth. The smile stretched into a grimace and darker blood poured over his chin and through his beard. And still she held him, forced him upright on the point of her sword. His hand fluttered briefly and then closed around the blade where it entered his body, severing his fingers as he tried almost reluctantly to remove it. Blood splattered on Jobber's face and she shrieked as if scalded. She rolled away, jerking the sword free from Silwa's body. He fell heavily onto the ground beside her.

For an instant there was silence. Jobber heard the dull hum of Lirrel's song, like a voice calling to her from the distance. She strained to hear it, but could not answer. Terror claimed her as she saw the ghostly figures of her nightmare misting into shape. Jobber clung to the sword. The rose of fire bloomed wildly in her heart, casting its searing heat through her veins. The Fire Sword in her hands responded, and along the red and silver edge of the blade, fire erupted.

Slowly Jobber rose from the stones, drawn upward by the brilliance of the sword's flame. Staring into the white flame, she felt her terror subside, calmed by its purifying beauty. The flames would free her. Cleanse her of the nightmares and of death's withering touch. She stared in wonderment at the bright blaze. Now that she was joined to the sword, the world seemed simple. She would burn away the evil of Sadar. She would destroy Huld within the circle of the sword's avenging fire.

Jobber inhaled a slow breath, basking in the heat of the sword's fire. She glowed with a deep red flame, her hair changing its color from copper to a white corona of fire surrounded by a halo of crystalline blue. The ground murmured angrily and small fissures opened between the stones. Flames escaped from between the cracks and licked at her feet.

Somewhere Jobber heard the harsh cries of Sileans and Orans fleeing from the flames that cascaded around her like the fixed points of a star. She walked slowly through the courtyard and out to the blasted plains of Sadar, transfixed by the shimmering heat of the Fire Sword. Where she walked the ground was scorched black, and behind her black smoke curled into the air. She paused at the gates and looked up to the parapets with a feral grin on her white face. Huld was still there.

The land buckled and heaved in response. Cracks opened in the walls and the walkway over the main gates of Sadar collapsed inward with a cloud of thick gray dust.

"NO!" Lirrel screamed, her song stopped as she was slammed against the stone wall by the power of the Fire Sword. Blown grit stung her face, choked her breathing as the air filled with dirt and ash. "Jobber," Lirrel cried out, "I can't reach her."

"You must," came the reply, and Lirrel recognized Finch by the rusty taste of iron. *"Again, try again."*

"We'll hold on for you," and this time it was Mole, his voice like the brush of a feather.

"We're here, Lirrel!" Lirrel heard the rest of them adding their voices in agreement.

Panic bubbled in her mind, scrabbling against the wounding heat of Jobber's rage. The burning sword enclosed Jobber in a crucible of fire, the walls too thick for Lirrel's song to penetrate. Impossible, she thought, I can't breach the fire; and she felt the steady undertow of Zorah's power grasp more tightly. But the children clung to Lirrel, refused to relinquish their power to her despair. She had no choice but to brace herself again. Lirrel braided the threads of power, wrapped them about her so that like the sail ropes drawn through the hawspipe, their power would drain out in a slow clicking measure. She must endure, she told herself as she braced herself against the onslaught of Zorah's power.

Jobber was deaf to Lirrel's song, but perhaps, she prayed, Shedwyn was not. Lirrel began to hum again, and this time she drew her music from the land. She gathered the grinding notes of the mill, softened them with the dull thrust of the plow through spring soil. She raised the pitch to the clear sweet voice of the lark, his song lifting with the mist on the fields and the lowing of cattle that settled the melody like dew on the pastures. Lirrel sang to Shedwyn, knowing she was different from the stone-hearted Huld. Lirrel sang to the warmth of Shedwyn's touch, the generosity of her spirit and flesh that yielded like the fields.

* * *

Shedwyn, standing on the parapet, was suddenly disoriented, dazed by the past that seemed so solid while the present existed only as a dream. She felt encased by stone and now it seemed to crack, a small scattering of stones eroding from her fingers. She looked up into the sky, hearing the lark's song, astonished by its sweetness amid the clashing of battle. The music welled in her until she felt the hot tears streak her face and melt away the coldness that had settled there. She turned her eyes again to the courtyard and cried out, seeing for the first time the battle at her feet.

Eneas, his blond hair rusted with blood, lay slumped against the cracked fountain. His face was hidden from her but she saw the black pool that drained from his fingers.

She screamed his name. ''Eneas!'' He didn't answer.

Shedwyn clamored down the stairs of the parapet, clinging to the walls as steps crumbled like dried salt beneath her feet. She reached the courtyard and turned around, seeing the dead and wounded, the blackened streaks along the stones that marked Jobber's passing. Out of the thickening smoke of battle, terrified faces loomed, some bleeding from wounds, others contorted as they shouted battle cries. They hovered in the mist, disappearing as she ran past. Her foot nudged something, and nearly tripping, she glanced down and saw Faul lying in a messy heap. Faul groaned and then swore as she dragged her injured body away from Shedwyn's foot.

''Forgive me,'' Shedwyn said breathlessly, her eyes frantically searching for Eneas.

She saw his legs first, the scuffed black boots covered with gravel. Her eyes followed the line of his farmer's smock, then his head curled over his chest, the blond hair matted with dirt and blood.

She ran to him and swiftly bent to touch him. She felt the faint beating of his pulse and saw the shallow rise and fall of his chest. The sleeve of his smock was torn and showed the deep slash on his arm. A second gash on his temple was crusted with black ash. Quickly she tore the hem of her dress and wrapped it around his wounded arm to stanch the bleeding.

Again, Shedwyn stopped, hearing Lirrel's song raised above the cacophony of the battle. And as if to bury the song, she heard the rumbling of Sadar like the gnashing of granite teeth. Flames sprouted in the cracks, leaping from the fissures. Shedwyn shivered as a coldness seeped in her veins again, numbing her hands.

Huld. Shedwyn recognized the presence of the Earth Queen. It was not what she expected; Huld had not the cool sap of a living tree, but the brittle hardness of the rocks, the harsh clang of the hammer against the anvil. There was no bending beneath Huld's will, no graceful arch of benevolent shade. Only the black and white of the granite and the sharp chiseled edges of her envy.

But Lirrel's song was more powerful, cracking the shell of coldness. Shedwyn felt the snap of a branch as she thrust away Huld's coldness. Lirrel's song rose in her ears, urging her to the plains of Sadar. Shedwyn stood, reluctantly moving away from Eneas. She had bandaged the worst of his wounds. It wasn't much but it would have to do for now. Jobber needed her, and if she didn't stop Jobber, Zorah would destroy them all.

Shedwyn ran through the courtyard and jumped the smoldering ruins of the gate. Then she stopped, stunned by the nightmarish vision. The plain of Sadar had been gutted by Jobber's passage. The ground heaved plumes of smoke and hissing steam rose from the deep cracks. Lines of fire burned in rippling waves like stands of wheat ripening in a setting sun. The dead of the Burning had been disinterred by the quaking ground, tossed through the widening cracks to the surface of the plain. Gray and black skeletons lay coupled, their bony limbs entwined with the newly dead of the day's battle. And in the center of the plain, glowing blue white and wreathed with petals of orange fire, Jobber waited for Shedwyn, holding the Fire Sword, the hilt resting against her breast, the blade cleaving the air above her.

Shedwyn drew a ragged breath and began to run down the slopes of the Keep.

Jobber watched her running, zigzagging through the plain, scattered with the dead and dying of battle. She studied the stony expression on Shedwyn's face and smiled with satisfaction. Let her come, she breathed, and the flames around her rippled with color. "Let Huld come to this final death," she hissed.

Shedwyn looked up and, seeing her, stopped running. She was panting, her breathing labored. She bent over at the waist as if to catch her breath. And then, without warning, she straightened, and in Jobber's veins the hate surged at the sight of the wintry smile on her face.

The brown flesh of her skin was changing, turning a motley gray as her feet, her legs, and her hips hardened to stone. She lifted one foot and it moved with a slow, heavy effort. Shedwyn looked up into Jobber's face and for a brief moment Jobber saw mute terror reflected in her eyes. Her lips formed words that refused to escape from her throat. Jobber saluted her with the Fire Sword and then held it out to the side, prepared to strike.

Shedwyn's flesh compacted into granite. But it didn't bother Jobber. Stone was no protection against the Fire Sword.

"Jobber," Shedwyn cried, her words sounding garbled and forced. "Jobber, help me!"

Jobber's green eyes flickered, and her face softened with hesitation. The sword wavered as she suddenly noticed its heavy weight.

"Huld!" Jobber cried out, almost in anguish.

"Not Huld!" Shedwyn answered. "Shedwyn."

"Shedwyn," Jobber whispered, her face puzzled. The name strangely connected to some remote part of herself. She stared at Shedwyn's form, a body carved of granite. *Huld. Playing tricks!* Her temper flared, banishing her doubt.

"Jobber, put down the sword," Shedwyn pleaded.

"I am Zorah," she snarled in reply. "And I have waited these long years for you, Huld! Now you will join the others!" She slashed the sword sideways at Shedwyn's head.

Shedwyn ducked her head and shoulders, the only part of her not yet cast in stone. The sword hissed in the air, cutting a lock of her flying hair. The tassel of hair burst into flame and vanished. Shedwyn fell slowly and heavily to her knees.

"You are Jobber, not Zorah," she screamed desperately, looking up to see Jobber raise the sword over her head. "I am Shedwyn, not Huld. Lirrel waits for us. Listen. Listen to her!"

Jobber paused again. The sword waited, trembling overhead. Shedwyn, she thought, confused by the conflicting memory. Huld was cold and hard. But not Shedwyn, her breasts and belly patterned with the circles of bark, her sweat scented like earth. Jobber saw the woman before her from two pairs of eyes and felt rise within her two emotions, one composed of fear and rage, while the other spoke of friendship and a grudging admiration.

And in a rush of notes Jobber heard Lirrel's voice, heard the chorus of children's voices joined to it as they rose above the howling of Chaos. Their presence brushed across her burning cheeks like a small breath of cool air. Jobber felt tears evaporate in wisps of steam on her cheeks. She had no fear of these, they would not abandon her to the nightmares and the terrors that haunted her. Not like Huld had done so long ago. *"Choose your own path,"* Jobber heard, and knew again Lirrel's voice. She shook herself like a dog trying to free itself of a collar.

But Zorah would not let go. She shrieked in Jobber's head, demanding vengeance. She jerked Jobber's arm up again, squeezed her hands tighter around the hilt of the Fire Sword, and tried to drive the sword down across Shedwyn's kneeling body.

"No," Jobber snarled, bristling with her own awareness. "You ain't going to use me! Damn you to the dreams! This is my life, my sword."

Shedwyn's head snapped up at the sound of Jobber's voice, the sword shaking violently overhead. Jobber's face was screwed tight with the effort, and she hissed as air was forced from her lungs.

The point of the blade turned down in small forceful jerks. Jobber growled, spitting every obscenity she could think of into the air. Every muscle strained against the current as, slowly and deliberately, she lowered the sword. The blade point touched the ground and the earth split to receive it. She leaned on the hilt and drove her weight down on it. Along the blade's edge the white flame was extinguished as the sword entered its scabbard of soil.

Jobber waited, bent over the hilt of the sword, deafened by the howling of Chaos. Her stomach heaved and hot blood flashed like lightning beneath the surface of her cheeks. Her heart slammed repeatedly against the bones of her ribs, making her gasp. She tried to quell the storm of fire, reaching deeply within herself to tame the fire rose. She folded her magic, petal by petal, drawing it tightly together. There was nowhere Zorah could enter her, and Jobber felt her driven out as the petals of power snapped shut again. She felt her muscles spasm as Zorah's presence shriveled with the gutted flames. Then, with a groan, she let go of the hilt and sat back on her heels, shaking with exhaustion.

Around them, the air grew quiet. Even Lirrel's song ceased to play in Jobber's head. The lines of fire died down, snuffed out by the breeze. Wind carried fresh, cool air that shredded the banners of smoke and cleared the plain of its black pall. But it was little better being able to see the final outcome of the battle. The broken skeletons of the Burning and the bodies of those recently killed lay scattered throughout the plain. Jobber saw the scenes of her nightmares—the charred corpses, bones scattered across the long black scars on the land. No one moved on the plains and she saw now that nothing had escaped her destructive touch. Oran and Silean alike had fallen beneath the flames. She glanced up and saw the remnants of the Keep, the gates blasted open, a tower reduced to rubble. She wiped her face with her hands, unable to bear the sight any longer.

"I did this."

"No," Shedwyn answered.

Jobber grimaced with self-loathing. Her eyes clouded over and she felt the sting of tears. "Who else?"

"Zorah," Shedwyn said. "And Huld," she added softly.

Jobber looked up, startled. Shedwyn was rubbing her hands along her upper arms as if she still felt the coldness of the stone.

"We were just pieces meant to be moved and sacrificed in a game between Queens," Shedwyn said bitterly.

"I thought Huld wanted to save Oran from Zorah."

"Huld doesn't do things out of love for Oran, any more than Zorah does," Shedwyn answered. "I know her now. She's hard like the granite she chooses. The world must be as she sees it. Everything ordered, nothing out of place. Huld never could accept Zorah's weakness, her fears. She bullied Zorah into becoming what she is."

Jobber nodded, understanding, knowing now the driving terror of the dreams and Zorah's loneliness. "Yeah. Zorah had to fight any way she could. The Fire Sword gave her that. But not Huld."

"Look, Jobber, everything is changing," Shedwyn said.

Jobber saw that the horse had vanished. Many of the blackened corpses were fading. But there were still many more of the dead that remained. Too many dead, she thought with a sharp stab in her chest. Her eyes rested on the sight of Zein's body, lying on his back, his arms stretched wide as if to receive the sky.

"Lirrel?" Jobber asked softly, knowing that she must be the one to tell Lirrel of her father's death.

"At the Keep. Come," Shedwyn said, rising stiffly to her feet and extending a hand to Jobber. "We'll go to her."

Jobber stood and then shivered with the cool breeze. She looked down at herself, realizing for the first time that her clothes had been burned away. She was naked, her red firehair covering her white shoulders and breasts.

"Frigging shit," she swore absently, too confused, too weary to know what to do.

"Here," Shedwyn answered, stripping off her ragged brown dress and pulling it over Jobber's head. Obedient as child, Jobber shoved her arms through the sleeves. The dress hung like a sack on her spare frame.

"What are you going to do?" Jobber asked, frowning at Shedwyn, who wore only a frayed petticoat that covered her from the waist to the calves. She tried not to stare at the patterns that curled up from Shedwyn's belly and extended like leaves across her full breasts.

Shedwyn knelt at the side of a fallen Silean crossbowman. She tugged his gray and black jacket free from his body and put it on. It was too tight across the shoulders and she had to hold it closed in front. Jobber touched Shedwyn on the arm, suddenly wanting to say something, needing to express her gratitude and to apologize for the long months of anger. Shedwyn smiled wearily and shook her head. Not necessary, the look said.

"You can't leave that here." Shedwyn pointed to the hilt of the Fire Sword.

"No," Jobber replied. "It's mine, ain't it?" She paused before freeing the Fire Sword from the ground. She held her breath, letting it out in a long hiss between her teeth as the sword reemerged, perfect and beautiful, the edge still glinting with razor sharpness. And though the flame was gone, Jobber sensed the steady pulse of life along the shaft. She looked at Shedwyn, lifting her chin proudly.

"Let's go," she said in a husky voice. "And from now on, Zorah and Huld be damned. We choose our own path and we make our own frigging history."

"So," Antoni said in a cold voice, "how many dead?" He was staring down at his hands, the outstretched fingers resting on the papers of his desk.

"Eight Guards killed in the struggle," came Firstwatch Gonmer's weary reply. "Another ten or so have been lost in the tunnels since the search began."

Antoni's fingers flexed into a fist and he could feel the polished nails biting angrily into his palms. "And the Kirian?" Gonmer's silence caused him to look up sharply. Her expression had hardened. "I asked about the Kirian, Firstwatch."

"There is no word. The Kirian, like the rebels, seems to have disappeared."

Antoni exploded, feeling his nerves snap with fury. "Frigging piss-ignorant woman." He stood, wanting in that moment to grab the Firstwatch by the throat.

Gonmer stepped back, her hand moving quickly to her sword, and her eyes flashed a warning of their own. Antoni heard the click of the sword guard as her thumb released the blade.

"Shut up, you arrogant bastard," Gonmer hissed. "I am not answerable to you. Only to the Queen, do you hear?"

Antoni eased himself back from the table, away from the reach of Gonmer's sword. Though he thought little of her, he knew enough to respect her temper and her sword. But the Kirian, the Kirian was gone, and the knowledge of that made the anger seethe in his heart.

"The loss of the Kirian puts us at an extreme disadvantage," he said, his jaw aching as he struggled to keep from shouting the words.

"It is not the only problem I confront, Advisor," Gonmer replied just as carefully. "The New Moon has managed a successful escape, and where they have gone in the tunnels below is a mystery. All of Beldan seems ready to burst with one riot after another, and it is my task to hold these fragments together."

"It was your queen that ordered the Kirian found, was it not?" Antoni answered.

"Indeed, but even the Queen no longer seems to care. And that has been another problem."

Antoni paused before speaking again, wondering at Gonmer's words. "I don't understand you," he said.

"You have been locked in your study too long, Advisor. I suggest you get out and see what has happened. For my part, I have a bleeding city that needs attending." And without another word she spun on her heel and left Antoni's study.

Antoni stood at his desk, a finger held to his lips as he thought. The Kirian was important enough to him. And it had been important enough to the Queen. What had changed? He straightened the papers on his desk, realizing that in these last days, when he had not been in his study, he had been on Beldan's streets as the Upright Man, trying to acquire news of the Kirian. He had avoided the state halls and corridors of the Keep, avoided the Queen. But it had seemed he had missed something important in his obsession with the Kirian. Perhaps it was time to see Zorah.

Antoni brushed back his black hair carefully and smoothed his beard. He pulled on the green cloak of his office, tying it loosely on his shoulders. As he left his study, in an unexpected moment of chilly superstition, he touched the Namire's skull for reassurance.

On the parapets of Beldan's Keep, the Fire Queen Zorah wept bitterly. She had spent two hundred years freed from the violence of the past, and in a single day it had returned. She knew she had not lost entirely. If she was weakened, so was Huld. And the young Queens still had not formed a knot. But Zorah had not won at Sadar either. Silwa was dead. The Sileans lost to the New Moon. And worse, worse yet, Zorah thought angrily, that girl Lirrel had dammed the flow of time. She had managed it only for a moment. But it had been enough.

"Madam?" Antoni Re Desturo called from behind. Zorah had heard the quiet scrunch of his boots as he approached and thought they sounded uncertain. No doubt the servants had called him, she thought angrily. They had fled from her, afraid. She had paced furiously from room to room, bellowing curses and shoving people into the walls. And she knew she had spread a sheet of fire with her burning rage as she had wandered the corridors of the Keep. But it wouldn't do for Antoni to find her here on the parapet, clutching her sword and weeping like a child.

Zorah wiped the tears off her face and collected herself before replying.

"Yes, Antoni?" she asked in a low voice.

"Are you well, madam?"

She turned around and faced him. So, she thought, appraising the startled look that crossed his face. She didn't need the glass to tell her that she was changed. That she was no longer a young woman. She touched her hand to her cheek, feeling the flesh soft and loose over the hollow of her cheekbone. She removed her hand from her cheek and saw veins that hadn't been there before snaking over the knuckles.

She brought her hand to her side and raised the Fire Sword in the other.

"Well enough." She squared her shoulders. "Well enough. Silwa is dead. His army has lost at Sadar," she said harshly.

"Look to your own neck, Antoni, for the rebellion of the New Moon has just begun, and before it is through, Oran will shed more blood than you thought possible."

She left him standing speechless on the parapet, shocked more, she knew, by the lingering image of her middle-aged face than by her proclamation of doom.

In a ditch off the main road leading from Beldan, Shefek lay on his back and pondered the stars. It was easier than trying to plumb the depths of his pain. The stars twinkled brightly, the sky was clear. But his pain continued, and his head felt muddled with the dizzy flow of magic.

"Sit up," he ordered himself. "Get moving."

Sighing, he lifted himself from the ground where he had fallen almost senseless. His last memory was of the black line of trees etched against the orange glow of the twilight. And then, without warning, the world had collapsed and tossed him like rubble to the ground.

He looked at his arms and his hands. His shoulders and arms were still covered with feathers, but his hands were the shaking bones of an old man. The feathers were no longer brown, but soft white.

"So," he said to the outstretched arm. "We have aged."

He stood with effort, slowly shaking the dust and dirt off his legs. He touched his nose, thinking it felt smaller than usual. He would fix everything, later after he'd a chance to rest somewhere away from Beldan. He gazed around at the quiet forest and the long empty stretch of Oran road and gave a wan smile. "Jobber has found her Fire Sword and the Oran world is still whole. Perhaps I am not too late after all."

And with shaky steps, Shefek climbed out of the ditch and began the long walk north. "I should be there by winter," he told the sky. And beneath the light of the quarter moon, the white feathers of his shoulders shone like the new snow.

THE BEST IN FANTASY

THE BEST IN SCIENCE FICTION

BESTSELLING BOOKS FROM TOR